GermLine

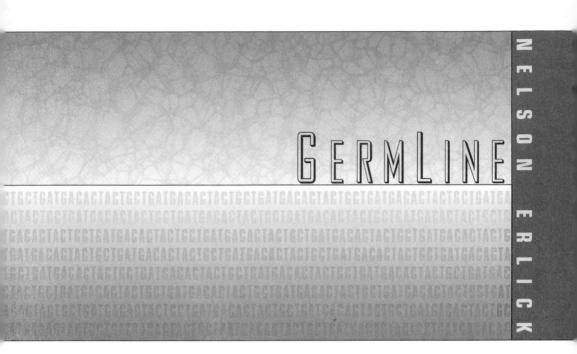

GERMLINE

NELSON ERLICK

A TOM DOHERTY ASSOCIATES BOOK

NEW YORK

GERMLINE

A Forge Book
Published by Tom Doherty Associates, LLC
175 Fifth Avenue
New York, NY 10010

www.tor.com

Forge® is a registered trademark of Tom Doherty Associates, LLC.

Library of Congress Cataloging-in-Publication Data

Erlick, Nelson.
    Germline / Nelson Erlick.—1st ed.
        p. cm.
    "A Tom Doherty Associates book."
    ISBN 0-765-30094-X (acid-free paper)
    1. Genetic engineering—Fiction. I. Title.
    PS3605.R58 G47 2003
    813'.6—dc21

                                                    2002034689

First Edition: January 2003

PRINTED IN THE UNITED STATES OF AMERICA

0 9 8 7 6 5 4 3 2 1

For Cheryl—
who always knew that I could,
and made it so

ACKNOWLEDGMENTS

My unending gratitude for *GermLine* extends in many directions:

To the physicians, scientists, ethicists, reporters, and undiscovered philosophers—sources of the hundreds of documents on which I constructed this work. If only humanity developed at a pace that rivaled its science.

To my editor, Natalia Aponte, who cultivated this work with her deft insights; to my assistant editor, Paul Stevens; to the many people in the copyediting, art, marketing, and sales departments at Tor Books; and to all Tom Doherty Associates who've supported me and worked tirelessly on my behalf.

To my agent, Susan Crawford, who happily nurtured this literary novice, who always had a word of encouragement, and who always made me feel special as she guided me through the heavily mined road to publication.

To my mother, Estelle, who made my education a priority even after my father died; to my children, Rayna and Melissa, who conscientiously respected the "Do Not Disturb" sign on my door; but most of all, to my wife, Cheryl, whose skillful editing of my barrage of drafts enabled this work to be born.

GermLine

PART ONE

THE FIRST COMPONENT—YEAR 6 OF THE PLAN

SUNDAY
The Loring Estate
Berks County, Pennsylvania   *12:48 A.M.*

Beneath the spinning laser lights, in the midst of his ballroom crammed with guests dancing to the band's charged Latin beat, E. Dixon Loring stared up at the bearer of disaster who walked along the mezzanine. The courier, in turn, located Loring, the party's host: a robust man, six feet two inches tall with perfect posture, a thick shock of black hair, and strong, wide, chiseled features. The courier's eyes never wandered from Loring. Slowly, the courier descended the grand staircase and skillfully slipped among guests meandering across the ballroom floor. As he approached Loring, he reached into his jacket pocket.

Not yet fifty, Loring had achieved success much earlier in life, and had long since perfected an aura of confidence, power. Those entering Loring's sphere felt compelled to gain a sliver of his grace. But never the courier. Loring gulped down his Dom Perignon.

The courier handed him an envelope.

"Have you seen the contents?" Loring asked.

The man's lips grew taut. "The envelope is sealed, sir."

Barely able to hear the courier's voice above the soiree's din, "Did he say anything?"

"He said that it was inadvisable to transmit the decrypted information by any means other than courier."

Loring tore open the envelope. Merlin had obviously cracked Bergmann's personal files. If those files corroborated what—

"Sir, I'm sure he didn't intend for you to read it—here," the courier said, glancing at several guests, uncomfortably close.

Loring shot a scowl at the courier, then unfolded the envelope's contents. He scanned the document, picking up key phrases:

- ". . . we are not creating replacement tissue for grafts or breast reconstructions . . ." on the middle of page one;
- ". . . organic scaffolding will be used to make towers for the suspension bridge to Hell . . ." on the bottom of the page;
- ". . . I've read their Reconstruction Treatise. It details . . ." on page two;
- ". . . the SUE must be destroyed . . ." on page four;
- ". . . everything in ReGenerix Technologies must go. The horror must be stopped now, *before* it's born . . ." on page five;
- and finishing with ". . . Claire, I've left instructions for you and the children. You'll find them in the usual place. I have loved you, always. You've known, but I'm not sure the children do. When this is all over, tell them. Maybe they'll understand. Good-bye, Claire. God forgive me."

"Bergmann's cracked," Loring muttered.

"Sir, would you like to formulate a response to—"

"How long ago did you receive this?"

The man touched a button on his watch. "Two hours and forty-two—"

Loring shoved the courier from his path, briskly weaved through his guests, and charged up the grand staircase two steps at a time. At the mezzanine level, he whipped out his wireless, punched in "#1," and held it to his ear. He strode down a deserted hall to a private elevator.

"Yes, Mr. Loring?" a voice sounded over the receiver as the elevator doors shut.

"Merlin, where are you?" Loring asked.

"Research Triangle Park, North Carolina," the voice answered. "Did you get my—"

"Where's Bergmann?"

A pause. "We don't know. He's not at his house. We're en route to the facility now. ETA is ten minutes."

"Seal off ReGenerix Technologies."

"Already done."

"We may be too late." The elevator doors opened. Loring headed for the last room on the right. "Merlin, you read Bergmann's logs hours ago. Why didn't you stop him yourself?"

"It was your decision to make, not mine," the voice whispered. "And Bergmann is a pivotal element in the Plan."

Loring burst into his library at the end of the corridor. The door locked behind him. "After all these years, don't you know that I trust—" A wailing horn sounded from his receiver. "What's going on?"

After a moment, "Security breach at ReGenerix."

"Where?"

"Bio-scaffold Room. A team is on its way."

Loring hurried to the desk at the far end of the library and booted the computer system with inlaid keyboard on his desk. "Patching in to ReGenerix closed-circuit."

"Here, too," answered the man at the other end.

He sat back and waited for the projection screen on the far wall to activate. The ReGenerix Technologies Incorporated logo, a golden bird rising above a field of grain, filled the screen. After submitting to a retinal scan and voiceprint analysis of his password, the security camera view of the Bio-scaffold Room appeared on-screen. Six machines lay in view, each containing fine strands of polylactic acid polymer that emerged from copper-colored rods and wound onto densely wrapped spools. Beneath each machine lay stacks of micron-thin porous plates. Loring panned the surveillance camera past a central workstation to the remaining scaffolding. Within the seventh machine, a man in a white coat lay on his back, eyes open, chin snuggled impossibly between shoulder blades. "Merlin, is that—"

"We'll know in a moment," the man answered.

Loring watched four guards burst into the room. Guns drawn, three of them covered the fourth, who rushed to the man caught in the machine. Loring manipulated the security menu and spoke directly to them. "This is Mr. Loring. Is that Dr. Bergmann lying there?"

All guards turned toward the security camera in the corner opposite the machines. The nearest man answered, "Uh, no, sir."

"Then who the hell is it?"

"Dr. John Neuman, a project manager."

"Dead?"

"Very, sir. His neck's crushed. Not the sort of thing that could happen by acci—"

"Any sign of Bergmann?"

The guards looked around and shrugged. "Sir, we—"

Loring heard a distant bang. The camera shook. "What was that?"

"An explosion," Merlin answered in his ear. "It's in the Archive Room."

Bergmann—it had to be! The Archive Room contained project backup data. If Bergmann engineered a catastrophic loss of the mainframe data in Command and Control, and took out Main Lab, he would eradicate the two million man-hours of research behind Project MacDuff. "Merlin, were all project files downloaded to designated backup sites, off-campus? Or are all copies still in ReGenerix's mainframe?"

"I don't know. It will take some time to check," he answered.

"Get on it!" To the security personnel staring at the camera, "Bergmann will be heading for C and C. Get a team there, now!"

The lead guard depressed his communicator. After a static-filled exchange, "There already is a team there, sir."

"Great. Have them—"

"Sir, they can't get in. The titanium doors have been sealed and pressurized."

"How long to breach it?"

The man sighed. "Twenty minutes."

"You'll have to do better than that!"

"Sir, even if we were under full-scale attack—"

"We *are* under full-scale attack! Blow them off if you have to!"

"Dixon, we've got another problem," Merlin's voice rang in his ears. "Someone's activated Protocol 1117—from inside C and C."

Loring crossed his arms. "Don't tell me. The override's been taken out."

"I'm sorry. There's nothing we can do. In ninety seconds, all Project MacDuff files will be irretrievably purged from ReGenerix's mainframe."

"Which means that we'll have to take Bergmann alive—"

"Unless we have a full backup set of project files off-site," Merlin finished. "I should know soon."

"You were right, old friend. I should have listened to you and had Bergmann removed at the first sign of trouble. You're due another big 'I told you so.' As usual."

"Do you smell something?" Loring heard one of the guards onscreen ask.

The four men in the Bio-scaffold Room lifted their heads and sniffed.

"Yeah, I do," one man answered. He crinkled his nose. "Bitter, like—"

"Nitric acid?" another finished.

Loring checked the screen. Behind the guard on the far right, at the base of one of the machine legs, was a small white disk. He zoomed in on the machine's base. As the site focused, it appeared to be two biscuits shaped like disks strapped to the machine's support struts by duct tape—with blasting caps and timers attached. "Get out of—"

The camera displayed static.

"What's happening, Merlin?" he yelled into his wireless.

"I've just entered the building. Bio-scaffold is gone. The mainframe has been purged. Bergmann is in Main Lab. And Dixon, whatever he has planned for the SUE and for himself, we will not get there in time."

Loring winced. "Without off-site copies, this will be a total loss. Six years!"

"Have faith. We are not there yet. Hold!"

"Merlin, what is it?"

No answer.

"Merlin?"

"There may yet be a chance. Dr. Bergmann in Main Lab would like to speak to you."

"Put him through!"

The screen displayed Main Lab: a sterile, white, three-hundred-foot-long chamber with a seven-story ceiling. Impregnated high in the back wall was the eighty-by-twenty-five-foot double-thick observation window from C&C. Main Lab proper, seemingly built to accommodate a battalion, was empty, except for a single, hastily constructed dais supporting a black cylinder on a bolted table. Free-standing poles, cameras, and monitors partially ringed the cylinder, all controlled from behind by a workstation. Dr. Wyndom Bergmann strode to center stage, his yellow biohazard suit muffling footsteps that echoed across the expanse. "Nice tux, Dixon. Leaving the party, or just arriving?"

"Wyndom, you said you were taking a month's vacation."

"No, *you* said I was taking a vacation." Bergmann laid his hand on the cylinder's gleaming black veneer and ran his fingers along its long axis. The SUE was precisely four feet long and utterly smooth, except for fiberoptic ports protruding from each side and flattened ends with hormonal- and nutrient-infusion pumps and excretion-sac outlets. The new modifications, specifically the infusion pumps and sonographic monitor for sequestered application or network integration, had not yet been installed. Bergmann ripped off the hood of his biohazard suit and exposed his ruddy face and thick blond hair. "You lied to me."

"I informed you, in writing, that we were pushing forward with the prototype."

"Initialize, yes, demonstrate, no! Tell me, Dixon, who did you invite to watch the beginning of the end of humanity?"

Loring pressed back into his chair and released a long sigh. "You're overwrought. I shouldn't have scheduled the demo without you. I allowed production pressures to override the human side of the equation. I know this was just once a dream in your mind. That the SUE is your handiwork."

"Classic E. Dixon Loring, charming to the end."

"I'll cancel the demo if that's what you want. But we are, after all, working for the betterment of man."

Bergmann checked on three disks planted at the base of the SUE and workstation. "I'm no longer gullible."

Loring zoomed the camera in on the disks. Each had blasting caps. "What are those?"

"RDX, the main ingredient in C4. Hexamine with nitric acid and acetone, baked with flour. Archives was first, then scaffolding. There's half a dozen planted here and in C and C."

"Wyndom, pull back from the edge. We can forget what's happened."

"Forget that I had to kill poor Neuman? Forget the four men who died when the scaffolding room went up?" Nearly in tears, "Forget the plague you plan to unleash on the world? Correction, the world you plan to create as a plague?"

"Your SUEs could save ten million ba—"

"I've seen your treatise!" Bergmann pointed at the black cylinder. "Look at the size of this place! Room enough for ten thousand Bokanovsky bottles!"

"The document was a capabilities treatise. Wyndom, don't throw your life away on a piece of fiction."

He banged on the SUE's fiberoptic port. "Without this, you can't complete your plan."

"I order—"

"You are no longer in a position to order people."

"I can take the lab by force."

"But not in time to take me alive." Bergmann turned away from the camera. He reached into a sack stashed behind the workstation, removed a biscuit, stuck a blasting cap in it, and held it out, gently. "And I cannot allow you to take me alive."

"Dixon, it's me," Merlin's voice sounded through Loring's wireless, still pressed tight against his ear.

"What have you got?"

"A complete set of project files at the San Francisco facility," Merlin declared.

Loring turned back to the screen with a subdued grin. "Wyndom, you don't want to die. Think of your family. That track-star son of yours at NC State. That brilliant daughter at NYU. And lovely, faithful Claire. What will become of them?"

"You'll never find them!"

"You're forcing me to—"

"I've destroyed all specs and data on Project MacDuff. In moments, this lab goes too. You've lost."

"Before you blow yourself and a quarter billion dollars into next week, you might want to reconsider." Loring leaned forward. "The information has already been disseminated."

Bergmann smiled. "Nice try. You never saw this coming."

"Three weeks ago, the Executive Gala. You were drunk, loud, more belligerent than usual. With that big mouth of yours you shot off 'Bokanovsky' one too many times." Loring sat back, grinning. "Wyndom, you're brilliant, but you're not the only one who reads classics."

"You're stalling!"

"Check it for yourself. All Project MacDuff files have been copied and stored safely beyond your reach."

Loring watched as Bergmann carefully placed the explosive on top of the SUE and took out a notebook computer. He punched in a series of commands. "It's true." After a long, shuddering exhale, "At least you don't have my soul."

"A soul? Life is just chemistry, which we can quantify and manipulate."

Bergmann grabbed a freestanding pole and smashed it against one of the Main Lab cameras, then against a monitor filled with Loring's smile. The monitor showered sparks, tipped, and crashed onto the floor. He spun around with the outstretched pole, striking each camera and monitor to a glittering symphony of orange-yellow sparks and glass shards.

Loring's screen went blank. Reestablishing contact with one of the security cameras in C&C, he directed the camera toward Main Lab, then zoomed in through the great window onto the lone dais with the black cylinder. "Destroying the lab accomplishes nothing. Another site will be up and running within months, probably weeks." Loring whispered, "Surrender the lab. Spare your family the grief."

Smoke filled C&C, obscuring Loring's view. The shadows of three guards appeared through the haze. They trained their automatic weapons on Bergmann, visible on the lab floor far below the window.

"Wyndom, it doesn't have to end here."

"You're right, it doesn't." Bergmann, resigned, visibly shaking, picked up the RDX-impregnated biscuit sitting atop the SUE. "But hopefully, it will." He threw the explosive at the control room. It arced, long and loping toward the glass—and fell short of the wall. It disappeared from view.

A searing blue fireball erupted. The security camera stopped transmitting.

Loring turned off the screen, strutted to one of the library shelves behind him, and picked up his favorite novel. He skimmed it absently, fluttering through its pages, and lingered on the last paragraph while he listened to Merlin confirm what he already knew. Relieved, he closed the book.

PART TWO

THE SECOND COMPONENT—YEAR 7 OF THE PLAN

SATURDAY

Between Tiburon and Belvedere, California   2:31 P.M.

Kevin Kincaid, MD, PhD, took his foot off the accelerator, rolled down the window, and motioned the line of traffic behind him to pass. Sailboats, single-masts, crimson, white, topaz, and blue, bursting with wind, skirted across the brisk bay's shimmering water in a visual symphony. Beyond the corner of Tiburon peninsula, I-580 bisected the bay. He sucked in sweet brine air.

"We lost?" a sultry, sleepy voice behind him asked.

"Nope. We're heading north on Paradise Drive and," turning his 140,000-mile minivan to the right, "now on Antilles Way. We're a mile from the marina." He shifted in the driver's seat for the third time in half a mile. He'd already slid the seat back as far as it would go, trying to find some semi-comfortable position. Nothing helped.

"When are you going to take care of your problem?" asked his wife from the backseat.

Kevin Kincaid was a huge, overpowering man of Irish descent: six feet seven inches, with thick, rust red hair, great green eyes, and freckles peppering his clean-shaven face. He could feel his wife scrutinizing his oversized belly. Too many hours spent with patients in the operating room or on the hospital floor had left him with too little time to care for himself. Between patients, he'd gobbled down anything starchy, or sweet, or that prolonged his stamina. Now, seventy-five pounds overweight, his belly hung far over his belt and chafed the steering wheel as he drove. His gray suit, the only one that fit, was frayed from being let out too many times. And with his meager stipend and two children and a wife to support, there wasn't enough money for a custom-tailored new one. But his legs remained thin and his puffy face had the still-handsome outline of a thin man trapped inside an obese body. "When I'm done the residency," he said. "Promise."

"I've heard that before," she said. "Why are we slowing down?"

Kevin gazed at his wife. "To take in the view." His photographic memory, along with his strong intellect, had helped him sail through medical school. Now, the peaceful image of his wife set against the beautiful harbor would be permanently seated in his mind—and always accessible.

Helen Kincaid, eyes closed, sat on the second-row bench between her sleeping children. Silken strands of mahogany hair cradled her face. Her delicate fingers stirred, her white gold wedding band sparkling in the afternoon sun. She opened her gray-green eyes, cocked her head, and smiled. "You're sweet." She tried to snuggle into her seat. "Kids are quiet."

Kevin glanced along the periphery of the rearview mirror. A toddler with curly brown locks slept in a child seat on one side of Helen while an infant in a seat restraint gurgled on the other side. "Looks like Jessica and Kathy are both out for the count."

"Twenty minutes of peace. If nothing else, I should thank your uncle for that."

"Helen, he is my only living relative."

"No, he's not!"

Yes, of course. Donny, Kevin thought. Without looking in the rearview mirror, he could feel her disapproval at his avoidance of his only brother.

"At least Donny's not bizarre."

"Uncle Dermot isn't bizarre. Eccentric, maybe."

"He once told me that when he stares hard at the horizon, he can see the back of his head. Kevin, don't place the future of this family in that man's hands."

"We haven't heard what he has to say."

Helen fiddled with her diamond and gold wedding ring. "I don't have to. You're finishing your residency in two weeks. You've already accepted a great offer in Philadelphia with a chance to do first-class research. Then, your uncle, who's been just across the bay all these years, who you've only seen once, who's never seen your children, out of the blue calls you with an opportunity of a lifetime. Should I be suspicious?"

A glossy wood sign ·proclaiming "North Tiburon Marina" appeared on the right. Porsches and Mercedes lined the access road and filled the yacht club parking lot. A man, with an *L*-shaped scar on his temple, lay stretched out in his BMW convertible, soaking in sun and sea. Kevin turned his ancient green minivan onto Leeway Road and chugged up a winding, eucalyptus-lined drive. Cool, pungent air mixed with brine as they passed stone-arched gates lining the road. "These places start at three mil. Uncle Dermot might know more than you think."

Helen unbuckled her seat belt, leaned forward, and placed her hand on her husband's cheek. Kevin slowed down and pulled over to the side of the road. She swiveled his face toward her. "Kevin, promise me you won't make any commitment before we've discussed it."

"Helen, I—"

"Promise me!"

As he nodded, she drew his face into hers. Her lips met his, then parted. He appraised her trim, six-month-postpartum figure, and slowly smiled.

"Don't even think it," she said, returning his smile.

He grinned. "I wasn't."

"Of course you were. Everything's still tender, hon. I'll be back to normal in a few weeks." She patted his stomach. Excess pounds built from Coke, fried foods, and Baby Ruths wiggled. "And while we're on the subject, if I can lose my belly, you can lose yours. You've got to take care of yourself, family man. Physically *and* financially."

"I promise. No commitment till we talk."

They drove to a wrought-iron entrance with a sign marked "Kincaid," then up a manicured private road to a circular driveway by a house with floor-to-ceiling glass blocks joined at odd angles. An older woman with French-braided silver hair, long earrings, and Hawaiian print dress burst out of the glass foyer and charged at the car. Before Kevin could slam on the brakes, she'd pressed her face against one of the tinted side windows and was cooing at the baby.

"Good to see you, Aunt Chandra," Kevin said after getting out.

"Let me see those little ones!" Chandra squeaked.

Kevin unloaded the portable playpen, infant seat, diaper-laden knapsack, and toy bags while Helen gently placed the infant, Kathy, in Chandra's rocking arms. Kevin hoisted toddler Jessica on his hip. As

he handed her off to Helen, he noticed a burly, solitary figure reminiscent of his long-dead father standing in the glass foyer.

"Your uncle's quite anxious to see you, Kevin," Chandra said.

"What about, Aunt Chandra?" Helen asked.

"Oh, something about 'leading the human race into the next era.' "
She looked up at Helen. "Tea?"

The man lowered his binoculars and rubbed his face, irritating the
scar on his temple. After seven hours in the BMW convertible parked
in the marina, his back throbbed. He picked up the wireless phone
and punched in a preset number. "It's Blount. Dr. Kincaid has a visitor. I checked the plate. Car's registered to his nephew, Kevin, a doctor
at UCSF, Mount Zion, 'cross the bay."

"Is he alone?" a throaty voice asked.

"Didn't see anyone else. Didn't have a good vantage, though."

The voice on the phone hesitated. "For now, do nothing."

The living room was airy: a vaulted ceiling surrounded by glass walls
overlooking a tiny English garden. Kathy gurgled happily between
Helen and Aunt Chandra's arms as Jessica pushed a toy bubble
machine across the carpet. Kevin sat stiffly on the couch and played
with a loose thread dangling from his worn jacket pocket.

"Something to drink, lad?" Dermot Kincaid, PhD, asked, the residual brogue still strong, though he'd left County Cork as a child. Six-
foot-five, thinning scalp of red hair, barrel chest and belly, the chief
scientist at PolyPepGen, Inc. had a curriculum vitae of sixteen single-
spaced pages.

"No, thank you. I'm still on call."

"Don't see each other much, do we?" Dermot stood, hands behind
his back. "You remind me of your father, God rest his soul. But you're
the spitting image of me when I was your age."

Kevin appraised Dermot's face and figure.

"Lookin' at yourself thirty years hence? Hmmh," rubbing his belly
and laughing, "maybe less. Thought's not appealing, eh?"

Jessica picked up an old toy bucket filled with K'nex plastic construction pieces. "I'm sorry, Uncle Dermot," Helen said. "She's too

young for pieces that size. She could choke on them."

Dermot bent over and traded the child a doll for the bucket. "They're not for the kids." He patted the toddler and grinned at Helen. "They're for your husband."

"Dermot, why don't you and Kevin go out to the patio and talk?" Chandra suggested.

The elder Kincaid tucked the bucket of play pieces under his arm. "I'll start the grill."

"Now, Dermot, you be careful. Last time you almost started a fire."

Kevin followed his uncle around a half-Olympic-sized indoor pool, then out to a tree-enclosed patio with an off-white chaise lounge, chairs, and table with matching umbrella. Dermot took a Dominican from a humidor on the table, ignited the propane grill, and lit his cigar on the hot rocks. After a few puffs, "What do you have lined up after your residency?"

"Something comfortable."

"Comfortable, eh? You signed papers?"

"Not till I pass the state boards."

"Good," blowing a smoke ring, "then you can work with me."

"For you?"

"No, lad. Not for me, *with* me."

"At PolyPepGen?"

"Nope."

Kevin plopped into the chaise lounge. "What'd you have in mind?"

Dermot unscrewed the top to the bucket and turned it upside down. Hundreds of plastic pieces clattered onto the glass table. Red, green, yellow, blue, purple. Half-inch rods with teeth; mini-ladders; clothespin-shaped pieces with four tendrils; half-starburst arrays with four sprouts ending in two receptors. A few pieces clanged on the brick patio. "Amino acids. Life's building blocks." Dermot picked through the pile of plastic for three small yellow, blue, and green rods. "Tiny, nonpolar amino acids like," pointing to each rod, "glycine, alanine, valine," He fished for purple and blue clothespin pieces. "Larger, charged and uncharged amino acids, like arginine, glutamine." Grabbing large yellow and green starburst arrays, "And very large amino acids, like proline, tryptophan."

Kevin repressed a smile: Uncle Dermot was an eighth-grade science teacher at heart.

"Only twenty different types of amino acids." Connecting the plastic pieces, "String a few together, you get an elementary polypeptide.

String thirty or forty, you get a full-fledged protein." He held out the plastic chain, an unstable necklace of disjointed shapes. "Fifty thousand different proteins per cell, that we know of. My boy, proteins are the foundation of life. They form nerves, bones, organs, muscles, skin, hair. Without proteins, we're just bags of water. But," twisting the plastic necklace, "amino acids in proteins don't join like a chain. They fold, bend into beautiful, magnificent shapes: four-residue beta-hairpins, helix-turn-helix, beta-alpha-beta motifs, coiled-coil motifs. Now, for small polypeptides, like proteins of forty amino acids, you can somewhat predict how it'll fold. The three-D shape it'll take."

Kevin said, "Like the Dead End Elimination algorithm for predicting protein structure that's based on a protein's minimum energy configuration."

Dermot nodded. "At least medical training hasn't completely stifled your academics, eh? But," sweeping all of the pieces on the table into Kevin's lap, "what if your protein had *thirty thousand* amino acids? What would it look like?"

"That's hard."

"Hard?" slapping his thigh. "A supercomputer using plausible rules for protein folding would require years to figure it out. Yet, the protein folds into its shape, instantly. Until we figure out how chains of amino acids fold into proteins, we'll always be a step behind Nature, looking up her ass, trying to decipher her proteins, instead of designing better ones ourselves."

"Nature's been designing proteins three billion years. We've been at it thirty. We've got a hell of a lot of catching up to do."

"Less than you might think, lad." He turned away, manipulating the plastic necklace. After a long, rich puff, "Kevin, I may not have been around, but I've been following your academic achievements since you were finger painting. You're too brilliant to be wasting your time cutting brains and spines."

"I'll also have an opportunity to do genetic research. Maybe work with vectors, very cutting-edge, maybe the key to solving genetic diseases. And remember, it's DNA that makes proteins."

"Uh-huh." Another long puff. "Even as a resident, I suppose you've had disappointments. Patients going sour. Incurable brain tumors. Spines mashed beyond repair. Must be frustrating. No matter what you do, a lot of your patients die, become vegetables, or cripples."

"I'm an MD first, a PhD second. I treat people first, study them second. I took an oath to give my patients the best I could—not a satisfaction-guaranteed warranty. Yeah, many of my patients will die or worse, no matter what I do, no matter how hard I try. I've learned to accept that. Every good doctor does. It goes with the territory."

"Doesn't have to, lad. Aren't you tired of cutting and sewing like a seamstress?"

Kevin stood. "Is that what they call brain surgeons these days?"

Dermot swiveled about and tossed the warped plastic shape into Kevin's lap. "I'm offering you the chance to design a brand-new nerve cell, one that transmits information twice as fast as existing nerves and is less prone to injury. You'll have top-notch neuroscientists, specialists in neurotransmitters and nerve synapse structures, at your call."

Kevin chuckled. "I've always enjoyed playing those computer evolution games. You know, the ones where they give you a planet or a city and let you build your own life-forms and civilizations. It's very satisfying to play God."

"This is not a game, lad. Try screwing your head into reality."

"C'mon, Uncle Dermot. Stop pulling my chain. The reality is that nobody can predict large protein structures, let alone design them!"

"It took mathematicians three hundred years to prove Fermat's Last Theorem." Rolling the cigar in his hand, "Child's play. I've developed a software package that *perfectly* simulates the environment of different cells. Considers water-attracting, hydrophilic, constraints. Water-repelling, hydrophobic. Thermodynamic. The presence of proteins and factors already existing in the cell."

"How does—"

"A physics-based computational approach, lad. Totally unique. My protein prediction software program uses multibody interactions from an expansion of the free energy based on the molecular relative weight, as determined by Z-score optimization, conformational space annealing methodology, and multiple linear regression. This allows hierarchical *ab initio* prediction of a protein's structure. Even using a Q8 refined accuracy index—the standard's only a Q3—my program's *perfect*." Approaching Kevin, "My program's magnificent, fully compatible with every major protein database on the planet. You tell it what properties you want your protein to have, and it'll design it for you." Dermot put out the cigar on the glass table. "Kevin, I'm offering you a chance to be a partner in my new firm. To lead the human race into the next era. And become rich beyond dreams of avarice."

"Let me see the program."

"It's not safe to keep it here. I have it at PolyPepGen, under lock and key."

"You're a PolyPepGen employee. Isn't the program theirs?"

"*I* developed it! But they're burying it. No publicity. No credit. *My* breakthrough is as important as Watson and Crick's discovery of DNA. What I've accomplished warrants nothing less than a Nobel prize!"

If it exists, Kevin thought. He said, "But what can you do, legally?"

Dermot shook, his face reddening. "Reverse engineering. I've made a few personal changes in the program's specs. I'm calling in an independent software design team to create a new program from the ground up. In six months, I'll have my own program, free and clear. Then, Kevin, you and I can get down to serious work."

Kevin swallowed hard. The man was a genius, but it was impossible to distinguish reality from risky extrapolation. Kevin's father had always said that his younger brother had been touched. "Maybe we can talk in a year or—" His right jacket pocket beeped. "Excuse me." He took out a wireless phone. "Dr. Kincaid speaking." He nodded. "I understand. Right." Pause. "Uh-huh. I'll be there ASAP." And hung up. "Emergency at the hospital. I have to go back into the city."

"Kevin, what I'm offering you could be the way to fix poor Donny."

He wheeled around angrily. "Don't do that! Don't you ever do that!" He headed to the door. "I should be back in time for dinner."

Before the door slammed, he heard Dermot mutter, "Boy's got his priorities screwed up."

Anthony Blount swung his binoculars from bay to hillside, and waited until the minivan disappeared before reporting in by wireless. "The nephew just left. I got a better look this time. He was alone."

The voice on the phone asked, "Any activity in the house?"

"I saw Kincaid and the nephew talking in the back. And before you ask, I don't know what they said. You know the doc's too smart to let his house be bugged. And there's too many trees. I didn't have a direct line of sight, so I couldn't use a dish. What about the nephew?"

"He is not your concern."

"And Kincaid?"

The voice hesitated before answering: "Proceed."

Kevin beeped the horn again. Half a mile from the marina, and traffic was still crawling. A thick cloud hung over the waterway—angry, black, acrid.

The emergency hadn't been. The trek back to San Francisco, a complete waste. The pain-relieving device he'd implanted into Mrs. Fitzroy's back had worked flawlessly. No infection, no cerebrospinal fluid leakage, no faulty electrodes, no broken lead wires—just normal, expected postoperative pain. A problem that could have been fixed by a simple phone call to increase the dose of her pain pills, instead of a two-and-a-half-hour trek through traffic.

The air tasted bitter, burned. His nose stung. Swirling beams of blue and red lights from police cars flashed in his eyes. The line of cars crawled forward on the slick road toward an armada of fire engines. Police waved on rubbernecked drivers. Firemen in full regalia manned the trucks and hoses. *Fire at the marina?* he wondered. He didn't see any fire there, despite the hoses trained on the yacht club. He looked in the other direction. Police cars blockaded Leeway Road. He gazed up.

The hillside was charred.

Kevin slammed on the brakes. He kicked open the car door, ran out into lumbering traffic, and charged the roadblock. Skirting around a screaming traffic cop, he headed past ash-laden trees that smelled like burned antiseptic. Fire engines, field communication units, elevating platform trucks, and rescue vehicles with weary firefighters were slowly descending the hill. He chugged past the first of the stone-arched gates. The private road beyond led through black matchsticks to rubble. Foul, choking air seared his starved lungs as he stumbled forward. The wrought-iron entrance—the sign that had marked "Kincaid"—was now black, brittle. Trees that had lined the roadway—gone. He bore down toward the circular driveway, never lifting his head from the road. Men shouted directions around him. Their words indecipherable, alien, detached. Except one, who yelled, "Bet it all started right here. Damn these propane grills!"

Kevin's head lifted against his will. Dermot's glass house looked as if it had been thrust into a blast furnace, then left to melt. Near what had been the pool lay two large black, zippered bags. Kevin put his hands to his giddy head as a man placed two tiny body bags beside the others.

PART THREE

THE FINAL COMPONENT—YEAR 17 OF THE PLAN

ACGD Commercial #1—
"Germline Gene Therapy: There but for the Grace of God"

Client:	Association to Cure Genetic Disabilities
Agency:	Hedges, Coates, and Jones
Title:	Germline Gene Therapy: There but for the Grace of God
Length:	60 seconds
Production Co.:	Ellison Michaels Productions, Inc.
Date:	November 8

The following commercial aired on all major broadcast and cable networks the evening of Sunday, January 19, and late night/early morning Monday, January 20:

[VIDEO]: *The camera zooms in on a montage of young children suffering from genetic diseases. Shots emphasize the children's disabilities, including facial and physical deformities. Montage of shots of children in hospital beds hooked up to heart monitors and ventilation machines. Final shot freeze-frames on sick child gazing forlornly at camera.*

[AUDIO]: *Off-camera voiceover (VO) of Dr. Kevin Kincaid begins halfway through opening montage.*

DR. KEVIN KINCAID (VO): There, but for the grace of God, goes my child. Cystic fibrosis, muscular dystrophy, neurofibromatosis, sickle cell disease, Tay-Sachs, retinoblastoma, fragile X syndrome, Lesch-Nyhan syndrome, Down syndrome. The list of genetic diseases that attack our children goes on and on. So many spend their lives in sickbeds. And die, so very young.

> [VIDEO]:   Dissolve to Kincaid standing Rod Serling–style in front of full-size graphic of human chromosomes with hundreds of call-outs marking genetic diseases.

KINCAID (ON CAMERA [OC]): The cells of our bodies contain DNA, the blueprint of life. DNA, written on twenty-three pairs of strands, called chromosomes. These chromosomes contain more than 30,000 genes that make us who we are. And sometimes, seal our fate. Our DNA has millions of places for tiny, fateful errors. For genetic diseases.

> [VIDEO]:   Dissolve background to graphics of genetic diseases.

KINCAID (OC): Genetic diseases that strike fear in a parent's heart. Genetic diseases that lay dormant, but haunt us in later years: Alzheimer's, Huntington's, breast cancer, ovarian cancer. There, but for the grace of God, goes you, or I.

> [VIDEO]:   Dissolve to animation of DNA entering cell.

KINCAID (VO): But for the first time in human history, we *may* be able to cure these diseases. To rid humanity of them, forever. The way is called germline gene therapy. Its promise is unlimited. And over the next few nights, I'll give you a peek at that promise.

> [VIDEO]:   Dissolve to opening montage.

KINCAID (VO): But there are those who fear this promise. Who have already banned it because of wild, unfounded misconceptions. This is not right.

> [VIDEO]:   Freeze-frame on face of child dying in hospital.

KINCAID (VO): Phone, fax, or e-mail your U.S. senators and tell them to *support* House Bill 601, to lift the ban on germline gene therapy. Tell your senators that you want to give our children a chance!

[VIDEO]: End Tag: Add supered letters to lower third of screen.
SUPPORT HOUSE BILL 601!
GIVE OUR CHILDREN A CHANCE!^{SM}
Paid for by the Association to Cure Genetic Disabilities.
Hold image for five seconds. Fade to black.

MONDAY, JANUARY 20
El Desemboque (near Isla de Tiburon)
Seri Reservation
State of Sonora, Mexico   *2:31 A.M.* (MST)

Lance Morgan had waited motionless beneath a moonless, starry sky in the cold sand for the desert to again grow silent. The footfalls and voices were gone, leaving only the distant sounds of sea lapping against beach. He'd chosen his observation site well: prone against the wayward side of the high sand dune, just below its crest, he was hidden from both the sea and the village. He poked his head slightly over the dune crest and brought his night-vision binoculars to his eyes. The binocs transformed black night into a harsh, quasi-surrealistic green. Isla de Tiburon, an isolated, restricted wildlife sanctuary, peeked over the horizon. Before it, the seemingly tranquil waters of El Infiernillo strait hid their treachery: changing currents, shifting sandbars, shark schools. Each had nearly killed him before he made the mainland. And at the shoreline was the Seri village of El Desemboque, a handful of traditional domed huts of ocotillo sticks and tarp scattered between metal-roofed concrete dwellings. He checked the estimated two miles of desert stretching between his position and the village. Nothing moved among the giant saguaro cactuses marching to the sea.

Tall, ungainly, emaciated, Lance had four days' growth on his face. Stringy blond hair fell about his shoulders. He wore a ripped flannel shirt and a belt with a big silver and turquoise buckle that held up well-worn jeans that matched the pale blue of his eyes. Shivering in the cold night air, he pulled out a pocket recorder and whispered, "Tracy, I made it off Tiburon Island. Was damn lucky. Right now, it's after two A.M. and I'm looking out over the main Seri village. You'll have to settle for audio. The camera doesn't record in pitch dark." He rubbed his frosty fingers. "I can't let the video I shot affect me. It's graphic, but it's not enough. I've got to *prove* that Tiburon is real. Show what the Collaborate's planned for us all. And I'm telling you, Sis, it's worse than Dad imagined. Much worse."

Lance clicked off the recorder and scanned the village. Two patrol boats pulled alongside a rickety dock. Twenty Seri men with long dark hair and dressed in jeans and long-sleeve shirts assembled on the beach. The boats quickly docked. Mexican soldiers disembarked, their semiautomatic rifles poised. Searchlights drenched the beach, burning out chunks of Lance's night vision. One boat lowered a black, zippered bag onto the dock. One of thirty burly soldiers hoisted it onto his shoulders. Weapons drawn, the unit advanced on the villagers.

After centuries of slaughter by Spanish conquerors, European colonists, and provisional governments, in the 1960s, the Mexican government had expatriated the entire Seri tribe, the last few hundred, from their native Tiburon. They'd moved the nation onto the desert mainland in prefabricated cement bunkers and made them totally dependent on daily deliveries of water trucks. Now they belonged to the Collaborate.

Lance refocused the binocs. A soldier gesticulated heatedly to four Seris. The marine contingent slowly swung their rifles toward the tribesmen. The Seri elders locked arms. An officer pointed to two soldiers. Both fired their rifles. Sand sputtered behind the Seris, but the tribesmen did not waver. The clipped *pop* sounds reached Lance seconds later.

The officer pointed at a Seri elder with shoulder-length hair in the middle of the human chain, then directed four rifle barrels at the tribesman. He waited, shrugged. With a flick of the officer's wrist, the elder Seri collapsed, dead before the sounds of rifles reached Lance. The Seris scattered. With their searchlights and weapons and black sack, the soldiers marched into the desert on the far side of the village.

Lance slammed his fist into the sand, then whispered into his pocket recorder, "Mexican troops just showed up at the village carrying a body bag. Killed a tribesman. I think the troopers have a specific place they want the body buried, regardless of tribal custom. Tracy, we need something to corroborate the tape. I'm going to see where the troopers bury the body." The soldiers were passing beyond view. He gathered his equipment, placed it in a knapsack, and added, "Sis, whatever you do, don't share any of this with the others!"

West River Drive
Philadelphia, Pennsylvania   *4:33 A.M.* (EST)

Drenched in sweat, steam rising from sneakers, Dr. Kevin Kincaid ran relentlessly in the early morning cold. Street lamps reflecting off the sluggish Schuylkill River eerily illuminated the runners' path on Philadelphia's West River Drive. Breath condensing into icy fog capsules, legs churning against frozen asphalt, Kevin dug deeper into himself to hasten the arrival of the second wind. The path led beneath 170-foot-high concrete supports for the twin bridges overhead, and the 100,000 cars daily traversing the river. Time to head back.

Kevin returned along the winding river path. Four miles to Boat House Row, a string of century-old rowing clubs that, outlined in soft white lights, glowed like gingerbread houses. Six miles to the hospital. A perfect running day: no ice on the ground; the air too cold for muggers. When would his second wind, and its release, come?

Though his hair was trimmed short and he'd grown a mustache, both peppered with errant gray hairs, Kevin retained the same handsome, facial features he'd had before Tiburon. But his belly, his bulk, were gone. He was very lean, thirty pounds underweight, but powerful-looking with broad shoulders and thick, muscular legs and arms. He exuded energy and vigor, but there was a worn quality just beneath the surface. And Kevin's eyes seemed darker, much darker, than during his days as a resident. Over the past ten years, running had become more than exercise that had shed his excess pounds, as Helen had wished. He used running to reinvigorate his mind—a fleeting mechanism to counter the agonizing accuracy of his photographic memory constantly replaying the day he lost his family: the reek of charred flesh, the sight of body bags, the shock and horror of realizing what had happened. Each foot strike propelling him off the ground brought him closer to that treasured moment of release when the flute that had played "Amazing Grace" at the triple funeral stopped playing in his head.

The triple funeral, three caskets: two with the horrifically charred remains of his children; the third, empty. They'd never found Helen. Most of the Marin County officials had said that while they generally recovered all of the bodies following a fire, on occasion, one might remain missing. Perhaps she was lodged under a piece of bulldozed foundation, or buried under debris, or so badly destroyed by fire that nothing remained but a few errant bones. He'd almost accepted that he would never find his wife—until he learned months later that the lead investigator of the tragedy had not only refused to close the case, but had been examining Helen's background, and even had the gall to question her friends, as if she were responsible for the fire. Ten years later, the case was still open.

Kevin passed beneath the stone arch of an old trestle crossing the river. The parkland between river and jogging path widened, exposing an antique water-pumping station. Three miles to the hospital. *Purge the body, purge the mind.* That aphorism had built his physique, increased his stamina, honed his surgical skill, and vaulted him to national prominence in genetic research.

The release came. He smiled and closed his eyes as endorphins flooded his mind with luxurious, euphoric warmth. The funeral's haunting flute fell silent.

Kevin opened his eyes. A runner had appeared forty yards down the path, heading in the same direction. Strange seeing a woman running alone, here, this time of day, of year. The runner's hair, silken, almost mahogany like Helen's, fell freely down her back and bobbed across her sleek running suit with each heel impact. He closed the gap. In the pale yellow light, her running suit looked amber. He remembered once, against his wishes, Helen had run at night. The street lamps had turned her blue suit to orange, the yellow strip running from the left calf to right shoulder, white.

The jogger ran directly beneath another street lamp. A white strip appeared on her suit.

"Helen?"

The woman turned toward him. It looked so much like Helen's face. She turned away and ran harder. He shook his head an instant—it couldn't be.

Kevin drew closer, almost bumping her. He stared at her profile as she tried to ignore him. They passed beneath a street lamp. She glanced momentarily at him. It *was* Helen's face, Helen's hair. And she had gray-green eyes—Helen's unique shade. Kevin felt his arms reach out to grab her.

She quickly pulled away, dashed across the road, ducked beneath an overpass, and disappeared.

Kevin lost his footing and tumbled into the road. Headlights bore down on him. He slipped and fell. The approaching horn blared. He rolled onto the curb just as a two-toned Chevy van swerved away. Cold, turbulent air blasted him. Slowly, he stood, one hand pressed against his throbbing right knee, and gazed at the gateway beneath the overpass.

Seri Reservation, Sonora, Mexico

Lance surveyed the site again: there was nothing but open desert. The soldiers had marched back to the village two miles south-southwest. He nervously approached the site.

The ground had no signs, no fences—just half-buried, haphazardly laid sandstone markers with corrosion-resistant numbers. He stepped carefully between the markers, partly in deference to the dead, partly in wariness of hidden trip wires. The Collaborate and their federal flunkies obviously wanted these graves kept secret, but why did they bury the bodies at all? Why not cremate them, destroy the evidence? *Because they might need a sample*, Lance thought, *like me.*

Marker 43 lay on a freshly patted mound. He knelt, pulled a hand spade from his backpack, whispered a prayer, then dug into sand. Working quickly, he cleared away a fist-sized hole before striking a vinyl bag in the shallow grave. He brushed away sand, exposed the bag, and pulled the zipper down. Cold flesh touched the back of his hand.

He recoiled. *You have to do this!* He shone his flashlight into the bag.

She was, perhaps, four years old, with dark skin with black braided hair, thin, desiccated lips, and dull, gelled eyes. The rest of the face was bloated, distorted.

Had this little girl ever been happy? Was she even capable of it? No, that was bigoted, a question her jailers would have asked. "Forgive me," he said as he took out a four-inch hunting knife and two vials of clear fluid. He cut a half-inch square in her left shoulder, peeled away the skin, freed up the piece of muscle, and placed the sample in a vial. The pungent odor of formaldehyde pounded his sinuses. He sealed the vial, scribbled on its label, and repeated the procedure on the other shoulder. "Tracy, I've got two samples from the girl I saw on the island," he whispered into the pocket recorder. His eyes watered as he zipped up the body bag, covered it with sand, and patted the surface smooth. He offered a moment of silence.

Voices from the direction of the village approached. Lance glanced at a swirling rose sky. Sunrise, soon. Villagers, outpost guards, or marines, it didn't matter. If they found him, they'd kill him, and the Collaborate would win. That frightened him more than dying. His jeep lay hidden behind a mound three miles south of El Desemboque, but the approaching soldiers blocked his path. He gazed to the north: nothing but sterile Sonoran desert hills. Lance gathered his equipment, and headed into the desert. His canteen was almost empty.

Select Procedures Wing
Benjamin Franklin Medical Center (BFMC)
Philadelphia   9:15 A.M.

Dr. Kevin Kincaid scrubbed furiously. Up, down: fifteen strokes per surface, four per finger. Sienna suds plopped into the basin and dissolved in water streaming out the spigot. Beneath the lather, the surgical brush's plastic bristles tore flesh. *Get a grip, Kevin! It wasn't her!* he thought. Systematically, he scrubbed his right wrist and up his forearm as he stared at the featureless wall of the clean room. *Purge the body, purge the mind.*

"Dr. Kincaid, everything all right?"

Kevin looked back over his shoulder at a stout woman in blue scrubs. "Fine, Becky," his surgical mask muffling his reply. Directing his eyes up, "Would you mind?"

She adjusted his surgical cap. "Nothing's too good for our TV star. Think I got a future as a Hollywood hairdresser?"

"Don't hitch your wagon to me. They're just commercials, and only running one week." He glanced down the hall. Holding out wet forearms, he headed toward the operating room.

The OR gleamed, a large chamber that combined a standard surgical suite with high-profile, innovative radiographic and diagnostic equipment. The patient lay on the table, draped in blue, his head shaved. Kevin's team, which included several surgical fellows, scrubbed and unscrubbed free-floating nurses, a magnetic resonance imaging technician, and an anesthesiologist, stood inside a giant metal drum shaped like a wine cask. The hollow drum formed an open-configuration magnetic resonance imaging system, or MRI, enabling the surgeon to peer deep inside the patient's brain, navigate safely past undamaged critical structures, and hone in on life-threatening tumors. Without the open MRI that guided the surgeon's hands and instruments through the brain in real time, the slightest misstep could leave the patient dead, or worse. One laser for digital scanning and two for tissue cutting/desiccation were implanted in the exterior walls outside the MRI magnetic drum. The ungowned tech manned a computer workstation that received and interpreted data, and instantly updated MRI images of the patient's brain on monitors flanking the table. Video cameras covered the room from every angle. Kevin checked the surgical instruments neatly laid on the stand, and the drill beside the tray. The nurse handed him a towel, then gowned him. He thrust his hands into latex gloves that snapped skintight.

"Got a gimp there, Kevin," the anesthesiologist said. "Putting in too many miles?"

"Just a scraped knee, Bransom."

"Try swimming, Nature's most perfect exercise. You can't fall."

"What, and come out looking like a prune?"

"Beats looking like a stick."

Kevin grinned at the anesthesiologist, then returned his attention to the patient. Because of his height, he had to duck his head and crouch forward inside the drum to avoid blocking part of the imaging system. Performing surgery for hours while stooped over often left him with a sore back that required periodic trips to the chiropractor. He gazed down at the shaven head of the man lying anesthetized on the table as a nurse raised the table. "How's my patient?"

"Doing fine," Dr. Bransom stated.

"Everyone, I hope you've got big smiles under your masks, 'cause today you're on camera," Kevin said to the team. Calling to the video engineer in the master control room via the intercom system, "Ed, we all set to record?"

A deep voice answered from the loudspeaker, "Standing by."

Kevin said to the surgical team within the magnetic drum, "The procedure we're taping today is going to the National Institutes of Health, and is also going to be used as a supplement for Continuing Medical Education credits in neurosurgery. The public relations people are also itching to get their hands on it, probably to cut some promotional pieces for the center here. So we'd all better watch our language. And there's one word that we absolutely, positively must not use."

"All right, I'll bite," Bransom said. "What word is that?"

"Oops!"

The loudspeaker voice said, "Five, four, three, two, one. You're on, doc."

Kevin looked directly at a camera. "I'm Dr. Kevin Kincaid. This videotape serves to document Benjamin Franklin Medical Center's ongoing commitment to excellence and research. Today's procedures are in conjunction with human gene therapy protocol number 1103-112 as designated by the National Institutes of Health, Office of Recombinant DNA Research, and have been reviewed and approved by the FDA." He introduced his surgical team, then said, "The surgical suite here in BFMC's Select Procedures Wing has been certified to meet NIH guidelines for biosafety of research involving recombinant DNA molecules, as described in Appendices G-2A and I-1A for physical and biological containment of host-vector systems."

He glanced down at the man lying on the table. "We will refer to this gentleman as 'Patient 24,' a 46-year-old white male with a Grade IV astrocytoma on the left temporal lobe of his brain. The tumor has proven resistant to surgery, chemotherapy, and radiation therapy. The prognosis for survival is three to six months." His mind started replaying the morning run—the image of Helen speeding out of sight. "This morning, we're going to fight Patient 24's battle on two fronts. First, we'll identify, isolate, and excise the tumor that grew back in the patient's brain since his last treatment. And second, using somatic gene therapy, we'll try to destroy the remnants of that tumor without damaging surrounding brain tissue. We'll do that by injecting special genes into the site. These genes are HSV-TK, short for herpes simplex virus thymidine kinase gene, and MDES, short for multiple drug-enhanced-susceptibility gene. Both genes will hopefully incorporate only in tumor cells, making these cells especially susceptible to the drug, ganciclovir, which we'll inject into the patient several days from now. This should kill the remaining tumor cells without harming surrounding brain tissue."

His knee brushed against the table. The irritation reminded him of the morning run, of Helen lost. He continued, "Now the biggest problem in gene therapy to date has been finding a way to efficiently get genes into cells. We do that by stuffing these genes into packages that can penetrate cells. We call these packages *vectors*. Vectors are the key component in gene therapy. One could have the most perfect gene in the world that could fix any genetic problem, but without a vector to insert it into the nucleus of a damaged cell, that gene is useless. It's like a young lady dressed for the prom, but without a ride." Gazing back at the camera, "BFMC's contribution has been the development of a unique vector named BFV.Syn108." Turning from the camera, "Diminish ambient lights to one-quarter, then initiate laser scan."

A laser activated. Thin red streaks appeared on the patient's shaved head. Each streak represented an anatomical structure lying deep within the skull. A projected green blob abruptly appeared on the patient's right temple. Kevin touched it with a pointer and checked the MRI-monitor screen just outside the drum. "That's our target. Mark the time: 09:31."

As Kevin stared at the green light on the patient's head, a surgical nurse placed a handle and blade between his thumb and index finger. Kevin ran the knife across the patient's scalp. A streak of blood followed. An assistant patted the site with a sponge, then retracted the skin edges, exposing bone. Another nurse handed him a drill with a tiny metal ball bit resembling a melon scoop. He revved the drill, then applied it to the skull. Chips of bone dissolved in a stream of sterile saline as he gently sculpted a perfect circle one centimeter in diameter. Resilient tissue appeared at the base of the tiny well. "We're now at the dura, the envelope surrounding the—"

"Amy, I told you last week to make certain that all of Dr. Kincaid's project records were ready for today's visit," said Joan Tetlow, the Senior Administrator of the Benjamin Franklin Medical Center. As always, she wore her hair tightly curled to hide the thinning from premature baldness that had plagued her since her late thirties and a conservative suit, selected from her narrow preference range of plum to amethyst and cut so as to minimize her pear-shaped figure.

"Ms. Tetlow, you told me to give the year-end reports top priority," her assistant, Amy, said. "Every one of BFMC's general ledger files, earnings and losses, quarterly reports, payables, accounts receivable, inventories, budget projections, all on your desk by nine this morning. Well, it was. And it took me and the accounting department the entire weekend to do it."

"Dr. Kincaid's project files were top priority, too."

"But when everything's top priority, nothing is," Amy muttered to herself.

"You want to move up in this world, Amy? Learn to anticipate." She scoured the bustling hospital lobby, but there was no sign of the VIP.

"Is there anything else, Ms. Tetlow?"

"No, you've done quite enough. You can go."

As Amy headed for the elevators, Tetlow quickly checked herself in a lobby mirror. Her suit and signature floral silk scarf draped around her neck and shoulders were perfect, offsetting the hatchet jaw she'd inherited from her father and had learned early in life would keep the boys away. Who needed them anyway? She was Senior Administrator of a major hospital; most of the boys in her high school class were probably still working on assembly lines. She declared herself presentable for the President of the Benjamin Franklin Healthcare Network, while trying not to think about her failure to update Kincaid's files. She knew the meeting would be unpleasant, at best. But she had survived the feeding frenzy of mergers, consolidations, sell-offs, and layoffs. She had survived, thrived through the early, volatile days of the Benjamin Franklin Healthcare Network, revived this once-dead hospital on Lombard Street, and turned it into BFHN's flagship medical center. Ten years ago, she had recruited an unproven Kevin Kincaid to direct the new Department of Molecular Genetics and Engineering, a move that had proved wildly successful and eventually used to maneuver her own ascent to BFMC's Senior Administrator, and had firmly held the post for years—not bad for an RN-program washout. Yes, the president would be pissed, but as always, she would think of something to mollify him. She grabbed the arm of a brawny guard passing through the lobby. "Have you seen Mr. Grayson?"

"No, ma'am," the guard replied.

Tetlow headed toward the elevators. "I'll kill that driver if he took the expressway again." She respected Frederick Grayson: As President of the Benjamin Franklin Healthcare Network, he controlled an integrated healthcare system of twelve hospitals, 150 community medical practices, and 2,300 doctor-providers servicing close to a million consumer members. The only president BFHN ever had, Grayson had deep ties, unusual ties, to Mr. Loring, the CEO, who, according to several reliable sources, had a strange nickname for him.

A white limousine pulled up to the entrance.

She hurried through the main lobby. Wide glass doors parted for her. Her breath condensed in the cold as she waited beneath the marquee. Frederick Grayson stepped out of the limousine. He was trim, wore narrow, round, black-rimmed glasses, and had slicked-down, thinning red-brown hair—very Ronald Reaganesque with surprisingly little gray for a man in his mid-seventies. He also had severe scoliosis, a hump in his back due to a prominent curvature of the spine. He used a cane as he shuffled forward—which the doctors called an 'ataxic gait'—and always made certain that he kept his center of gravity directly over his feet. His cane wasn't constructed from the usual metal alloy, nor did it have the traditional curved handle. It was rattan, like a multifired stick used by martial artists, and had a bulbous end with two intricately carved birds: a dove and a falcon. At times, the cane made the man seem wise, almost grandfatherly; other times, it made him seem more like the aged emperor from *Star Wars*. He greeted Tetlow with a single, formal shake. Cane in hand, he slowly made his way across his lobby.

"Staying long in Philadelphia, Mr. Grayson?" asked Tetlow, respectfully trailing him.

"A few hours. I've business in the District tomorrow," Grayson whispered in his gravelly voice over his shoulder. "But I'll be back on Wednesday night. Mr. Loring is throwing a soiree at one of his residences to which you are invited. Now, I'd like to chat with Dr. Kincaid."

"He's finishing up in surgery, but he'll be done in time for the news conference."

"He is prepared?"

"Completely. With his intellect and that eidetic memory of his, he'll dance rings around the media. He'll provide them with a great story."

Grayson stopped in front of the elevators, slowly removed his glasses, and huffed hot air onto the lenses. "Ever noticed a certain dichotomy in the word *story*?" Wiping his glasses with a cloth from his jacket pocket, "A story can be a child's fable or a Pulitzer prize expose. Truth and deceit, described by the same word."

"The only story here is House Bill 601."

Grayson delivered a white-lipped smile. "Actually, there're three stories. First, the controversy behind the House of Representatives Bill 601 and its implications. Second, the Association to Cure Genetic Disabilities, of which BFHN is a prominent member, and the $300 million media blitz it launched this past week in support of HR 601. Culminating in a two–minute commercial during this Sunday's

Super Bowl. And third, Kincaid himself, a leading researcher thrust overnight into the spotlight as the Association's spokesman, appearing nightly on all the major broadcast and cable networks." Grayson cupped his hands around his cane and pointed both index fingers at Tetlow. "The media has its inside-the-Beltway correspondents for politics, its financial correspondents to investigate the Association, and its science correspondents to explain the medical ramifications. But what the media doesn't have is a good grasp of Kincaid himself. That, Tetlow, is why the press is here. Now, how's he bearing up?"

"He doesn't care for the publicity, but accepts it because he knows it'll help funding."

Grayson pressed the *up* button. "I'd intended to inspect Kincaid's primary project files after chatting with him, but since he's tied up, perhaps now would be a good time to—"

"Why don't we go to the observation suite? It's equipped with closed-circuit monitoring, so you could talk to him while he's operating."

"Let's go straight to the files." Grayson noticed her pursed lips. "But then we can't, because they're not in order, are they?"

She hesitated. "They will be."

"I see." The elevator doors parted. "Then, the observation room it is."

The room looked like a hotel suite with rows of TV monitors. Tetlow flicked one on as Grayson sat on a brown leather couch. Dr. Kincaid appeared, center screen, holding a long, slender syringe, penetrating the patient's skull as he checked the needle's plotted position on an MRI-monitor. "He's injecting the vector complex now," she said. "He's almost finished."

Grayson leaned forward. "That's not the new vector, is it?"

"Absolutely not. That's BFV.Syn108. High-profile, NIH-approved. Been quite successful, too. Thirteen of fifteen patients followed have survived at least a year, which is remarkable considering that normal survival time is four to six months."

"Have him play that up for the press."

She nodded. "I'll make a note of it."

"What parameters have you set for disclosure at the press conference?"

"He's permitted to announce that he's currently working on a series of innovative vectors that may be ready for testing soon. He can tantalize the audience with a few of their properties, primarily vector efficiency and DNA-payload size. He's welcome to speculate how these new vectors will revolutionize gene therapy, and is, of course, encouraged to make the transition into the importance of HR 601." She adjusted her scarf. "But, he knows not to comment on any specifics, structure, or synthesis of the new vector class, because BFHN considers that strictly proprietary."

"How close is he to completion?"

"He's just waiting to dot the *i*'s and cross the *t*'s."

"If his organization skills weren't so poor, we'd know now," Grayson said. "How well will he perform?"

"He's convincing in the ads. Even better one-on-one."

"That's not what I asked."

She glanced at the screen, at Grayson, at the screen and back. "He's brilliant, dedicated, arguably the best in his field. When he puts his passion into his work, his excitement is contagious. If he stays focused, he'll wow them."

"In truth, you're wondering why we chose him as the Association's spokesman instead of hiring an actor?"

She smiled. "Probably because of the very qualities I just listed."

A corner of his mouth upturned. "Yes. That and circumstance."

Tetlow nodded and checked the speaker. "Mr. Grayson, they've stopped recording. You can now talk directly to him."

He nodded. Projecting his voice, "Dr. Kincaid. Frederick Grayson here."

On the monitor, Kevin glanced up from the surgical table, then resumed the procedure. "Good morning."

"What do you have to say for our new $30 million OR?"

Without looking up, "Why, thank you."

The surgical team exploded in laughter.

"Mr. Grayson would like to talk," Tetlow called out. "ASAP in the cafeteria."

"Okay, Joan. We're far enough along. My senior fellow can close." Stepping away from the table, Kevin mock-whispered, "You watch. After that crack, they'll bill me for the room!"

Still in surgical scrubs, Kevin descended the open-air staircase from the lobby to the cafeteria filling quickly with the lunch crowd. Weaving his way through diners carrying trays, he found Grayson and Tetlow sitting at a table and sat next to BFHN's president, who was eating a bowl of minestrone. Kevin looked up at the lobby overhead that ringed the dining area.

"Want some soup?" Grayson asked. "It's surprisingly tolerable."

"No thanks. The news conference is in ninety minutes," Kevin said, scanning the crowd.

"You look nervous," Grayson said between spoonfuls.

"I've lectured more times than I can count."

"It's not a lecture. Think of it as talking to sixth graders . . ."

Jessica would have been in sixth grade, Kevin thought, struggling against the image of her charred body, presented in perfect clarity by his photographic mind. The reek from burned flesh filled his nostrils.

". . . unruly, undisciplined, often hostile, they instinctively smell weakness . . ."

What do they teach in sixth grade these days?

". . . could ask you something completely unrelated . . ."

She had her mother's face. If she'd had her mother's intelligence . . .

"We'll be there to back you up, if you need us," Tetlow said. "But you won't."

Grayson handed him a sealed envelope. "This is for you."

Kevin opened it:

MR. E. D. LORING REQUESTS THE PLEASURE OF YOUR
ATTENDANCE WITH A GUEST AT HIS RESIDENCE ON
WEDNESDAY, JANUARY 22, AT 7 P.M., SHARP.
BLACK TIE. DIRECTIONS ENCLOSED.

"Naturally, you'll be attending," Tetlow said.

"I can arrange a limousine to pick up you and your guest," Grayson said.

"Don't bother," Kevin said. "I'll be coming alone."

"That can be remedied."

"Very kind, but—" Kevin stood, tipping over his chair. His eyes fixed on a spot in the lobby overhead.

"Dr. Kincaid, is something wrong?"

She strode by the railing overhead. Her hair, silken mahogany, cascaded over her back and draped her petite frame. The woman glanced absently at a mural on the dining area wall. Kevin honed in on her eyes.

"What? What is it?" Tetlow asked.

The woman turned to her right. Disappeared from view.

Kevin leaped over his chair and glanced against a resident in scrubs, who careened into a pair of social workers carrying trays. Salad and pie flew across a nearby table. Shoulders turned, he blew through the crowd, his large frame like a bulldozer, knocking patrons left, right. Indignant squeals and curses followed him. At the steps, he waved his arms, parting the crowd, and bullied his way up the final few steps. Standing at the top, fists clenched, he scanned the lobby: the circular main desk, the elevator banks, the gift shop, the chapel entrance, the reception areas. Nothing—no sign of her.

Tetlow stumbled up beside him.

"She was right here!"

"Who?" Grayson asked, hobbling up the last step.

"Helen. My wife. It was her. At least, I thought—it sure looked like her."

The BFHN president shrugged, then patted the surgeon's shoulder. "So many people pass through here every day, you almost might expect to see someone who looks familiar. Don't concern yourself. Ms. Tetlow will accompany you back to your office and ready you for the conference." To Tetlow, "When you're done, stop back at your office before you head to the auditorium together."

"I—I'm sorry. That was really—" Kevin hesitated. "I'm fine now. Fine."

Sonoran Desert

Lance squinted. The harsh morning sun peeked over another scrub-and-cactus-covered mound of rock sticking out of the desert floor. Surely this had to be the place. He scrambled up the slope, his empty canteen jangling on his hip. His planned escape route had been simple: circle southeasterly away from the village, then head south toward the jeep, hidden safely between two rock mounds. But somewhere along the trek, he'd become confused. Twice he'd trudged into mini-valleys where he'd sworn he had parked his jeep—and found nothing.

He slipped and scraped his knee raw on a jagged stone. His blue eyes had grown increasingly sensitive to the radiant sun. If the jeep wasn't over this peak, then either he was lost and had a sixty-mile trek south through the desert, on foot, without water, to Hermosillo—or they had found it. He caught his breath, stood, then assaulted the summit, shimmying through rocks and loose dirt up the slope. Groping the final fifty yards with cracked palms and shredding fingernails, he peered over the summit.

Across the ravine, tucked into the shadow of a giant saguaro cactus at the foot of a mound, sat the black jeep and the empty trailer he'd used to haul his powerboat. "Thank God." Lance charged down the hill, as if fighting knee-high drifts of snow. The hill tugged him down. He stumbled, face-first, onto the desert floor. Sand splattered against his tongue. He tried to spit out swarms of grain burrowed tight between his cheek and gums as he lifted his head. Staggering across the valley, he lunged into the delicious shade protecting the black jeep. He pulled out a plastic gallon of water sheathed in cool sweat from beneath the passenger seat, and greedily drank, washing away the desert in his mouth. Satiated, he looked back at the ravine. Heat waves arose from the desert floor, distorting the distance, though it was not yet noon in the coolest season of the year.

This hidden dry valley seemed unfamiliar. Only thirty-six hours ago, he'd parked the jeep between desert foothills after having dumped his powerboat south of El Desemboque—the powerboat that had sunk in the treacherous strait and forced him to make a desperate escape from Isla de Tiburon aboard an abandoned Seri reed boat. Something about this valley should have seemed familiar. Nothing was. Yet, here lay the jeep, undisturbed.

Jumping into the front seat, he put the key in the ignition. The engine purred. Relieved, he leaned back against the driver's seat before putting the vehicle into first gear. A sharp edge scraped his back. Lance turned around. The seat upholstery had a fine, two-inch slit in its back. He ran his fingers along the fabric. Nothing. Pivoting himself around for a better look, he pressed against the fabric. A pointed, red-tipped stone protruded through the upholstery. He touched his back, then inspected his fingers. Blood.

His eyes ached. He pressed his hands against his throbbing temples. He began shivering. *The stone blade. Is it poison-tipped?* He fought to fill his lungs but slumped forward. Shapes in the desert shadow stirred.

Two men dressed in desert camouflage and carrying automatic rifles walked up to the jeep. One man lifted Lance's head from the steering wheel; another seized Lance's backpack, rummaged through it, and pulled out a sealed, bubble-lined envelope.

Lance reached for the package.

The big man at the front of the jeep shoved Lance back against the seat.

Lance felt the stone blade in the upholstery drive deep into his back. His veins, his blood grew icy. The desert spun furiously around him blurring beyond recognition. He could not feel his feet, his legs, his chest. His hands shook a moment, then grew still.

Benjamin Franklin Medical Center   *1:02 P.M.*

Tetlow followed Kevin into his office. The room contained a great oak desk, computer workstation, leather couch, and rectangular Formica-top conference table buried beneath layers of printouts, disks, and CDs. Kevin pointed to the right corner of the conference table. "Pages twenty-six, twenty-eight, twenty-nine of the Principal Investigator's Quarterly Report and AEs, Protocol 1103-112. Draft four and five modifications are underneath." Pointing at the couch, "Earlier versions of $HACV.V_7$ outer layer synthesis, now outmoded." Pointing to the desk, "And I know every inch of that mess. Comes with having a photographic memory."

Tetlow studied his face. His eyes weren't dilated, his face wasn't flushed. There were no signs of psychosis or delusions, as far as she could tell. He appeared to be his same, sane, rooted, rational, brilliant self. But she had staked her career, her future, perhaps everything on him. And if he was cracking, she needed to know *now*, while the situation was still salvageable.

"I *did* see her." He took a suit hanging in the closet and laid it on the desk. "Twice." He told her about the runner along the river.

"Chasing women on the street? You're lucky there wasn't a policeman around." She leaned against a corner of his desk. "As for the woman in the lobby, Grayson's right. Lots of people pass through here. She could be an employee, a visitor, even a reporter."

A rap on the door. Tetlow turned to the man in the doorway: Peter Nguyen, PhD. The postdoc was skinny and had a round face and slightly cocked dark eyebrows that looked as if they were permanently frowned. His plain plaid shirt and slacks hung loosely on his frame beneath his oversized white coat—a reflection of workaholism, and a still-youthfully exuberant metabolism that happily burned Snickers bars and pizza without adding an ounce to his weight. He clutched a stack of stereographic molecular diagrams. "Sorry to interrupt. Doctor, we must talk."

Tetlow slid off the desk. "Dr. Kincaid has a press conference at two."

Nguyen nodded. "Yes, ma'am, but this is import—"

"It'll wait."

Kevin tried to signal his young postdoc to shut his mouth, but Tetlow blocked Nguyen's view. Nguyen said, "Ms. Tetlow, I just need a moment with—"

"Later!"

Nguyen stepped around her to Kevin, who was rolling his eyes and shaking his head. "Doctor, please don't go without seeing me first." He left.

Kevin picked up his white shirt. "Joan, unless you intend to watch me dress—"

"See you later," she said, then quickly departed.

Tetlow found Grayson back at her office. He was sitting behind her desk and smoking a foul-smelling cigar. Layers of rich smoke hung in midair as he tapped cigar ashes into a Styrofoam cup. "Mr. Grayson, this is a hospital. The alarm—"

"Has already sounded. What happens if Kincaid spots another 'ghost' at the conference?"

"Nothing is more important to him than his work."

Grayson smirked. "Mr. Loring has pledged the reputation and financial resources of this hospital, this health network, and himself to the Association to pass HR 601. There's behind-the-scenes lobbying. A very public advertising campaign in excess of $300 million, just for ads this one week, excluding the two-minute ad during the Super Bowl. And let us not forget Mr. Loring's biotech and allied research companies eagerly anticipating the bill's passage. New industries await birth, Joan." Grayson plunged the lit cigar into the cup. It hissed. "You've made noises for some time about moving up BFHN's hierarchy. It is within your grasp." He tossed the cup into the trash receptacle. "I must know whether Kincaid could jeopardize Mr. Loring's investment."

"We should have a contingency plan to divert the media's attention—just in case."

"See to it. And let's minimize our risk over the next few days. What's Kincaid's schedule?"

"Mr. Loring's party on Wednesday, of course. And a major presentation at the NIH campus on Friday. Should we cancel?"

"No, we want that kind of controlled environment. I mean interviews. Small, uncontrolled environments."

"Nothing like that."

"Keep it that way. No interviews, public or private."

She checked her watch. "It's getting late. Shall we go?"

"Not so fast. Four weeks ago, I left specific instructions for you to have Kincaid's files in order. You've done nothing. Has he perfected it?"

"I believe he is only days away."

"Without Kincaid's breakthrough, Mr. Loring's fledgling industries cannot come to fruition," he said, lowering his voice.

"I know the doctor. He's almost finished."

"How can you be sure? His work habits are sloppy. His notes are jumbled. There's no central file, on disk or hard copy, with the synthesis protocol. And no one, including his staff, seems to know the whole picture."

"Mr. Grayson, Kevin Kincaid can memorize virtually anything, instantly. His associates bring him pieces of the puzzle, and using that great brain of his, he assembles it. He's like a mainframe."

"Except that there's no backup. Joan, what if our 'central computer' was hit by a car? Or decided to sell his product to the highest bidder? Or," leaning in, "had a nervous breakdown?"

"It's not easy dealing with true genius."

"That's not my problem. You either get Kincaid's project files in order or you get him to re-record everything—from scratch. I'll give you one week." Grayson folded his arms. "And remember, Mr. Loring has partners. Some who tend to weigh life in terms of cost."

Rockville, Maryland

Anna Steitz stopped in front of a tiny storefront squeezed between a pizza joint smelling of grease and oregano and a sparse but trophy-laden Kung Fu studio. A computer-printed paper sign filled the storefront's window:

THE ANTIGEN ACTION COMMITTEE
JOIN THE FIGHT TO STOP GENETIC ENGINEERING!

Anna had suggested that Trent change the organization's name: *Antigen*—which was a common medical term for a foreign substance that stimulated antibodies. Trent had countered with a sardonic smile that it was appropriate that his organization's name could be confused with infection.

The storefront's worn wood and glass door stuck, then swung

wildly open. The front room's peeling beige walls were covered with provocative blowups: dissidents in Athens who dressed like tomatoes to protest research permits for genetically engineered vegetables; protesters in Hamburg who sported bunny suits to challenge imports of genetically engineered soy; marchers in Ottawa who donned biohazard suits to protest standards for accepting genetically engineered food; activists in Milwaukee who dumped snack chips from genetically engineered corn in front of the local FDA office. A sullen woman with frizzy bleached blond hair sat behind an old gray metal desk. She inspected Anna's diminutive frame, from the short black bangs to the size-two shoes, then gazed into Anna's dark brown eyes. The woman shook her head. "You just made it," she said and buzzed open the back door.

The corridor beyond, utterly dark and only slightly wider than her shoulders, stopped at the foot of a staircase. By memory, Anna took the seven steps up to another door on the landing and entered without knocking. The room beyond was a cybertech garage: a concrete floor with computers piled on boxes and light filtering from monitors dangling from shelves. Four men and a woman sat on folding chairs around a partially collapsed bridge table. A wiry man chewing on peppermints pointed to an empty chair.

"I did not yet miss the phone call, did I, Trent?" Anna asked, her Bavarian accent still strong.

The man flicked another mint into his mouth, then focused on the telephone and accompanying scrambling equipment on the table. She decided to wait in silence, like the others.

Trent McGovern was the AntiGen Action Committee. He carried a resolve as prominent as his cleft chin. In his late thirties, tall, with wavy but thinning russet hair, his turtleneck sweater outlined his sinewy build. The muscles in his shoulders, chest, and arms were trained, tight, trim. For a big man, his movements were surprisingly quick—a cross between ballerina and puma. Anna had seen him full-contact spar with the master at the karate studio next door, and down the instructor with a vicious hurricane kick. At rest, Trent had a confident warrior's composure. Anna remembered how he'd been so very charming. He'd recruited her from Germany's Green Party. She'd been arrested in Hamburg. Broke and alone, she had been bailed out by Trent; they'd dined on bratwurst at a lovely little cafe, and he'd convinced her to join him. How different he'd been, then. As for the others, Trent had recruited Cameron from the Australian

Gene Ethics Network, Penang from the Third World Network, van Helding from the Dutch Coalition for a Different Europe, Johnson from NOCLONE, and, of course, Mason and Morgan. Trent himself had spent years with Greenpeace before becoming irreparably disillusioned. The team around the table belonged to him; he, alone, controlled funding. Penang believed that their leader was wealthy; Johnson, that the man had built a blackmail network. None dared investigate those conjectures.

The phone rang. Trent lifted the receiver and activated the scrambler. "Yes?" His brows furrowed, then slowly relaxed. "Will he be there?" He paused. "We'll be up tonight." He hung up and announced, "The team's ready, but Loring's not there. And isn't expected."

"Where is he?" Anna asked.

"His jet's on the ground, so he's probably still in Wyoming."

Anna had never met any of AntiGen's shadow cadre that tailed Loring. From what van Helding had told her, they weren't people she would have wanted to meet.

"Too bad." Sylvester Cameron gave a big smile that featured two wide gaps between saffron-colored teeth. "Could've picked 'em off."

"Loring's the most prominent of the bunch, not the most powerful," Trent said. "Kill him, and another takes his place."

"One less to worry 'bout."

Trent swiveled toward Cameron. "You'd bring the full force of the Collaborate down on us. We're a mosquito on the lion's back. Bite too hard, we get swatted."

"It has been two years, Trent," van Helding said softly, his eyelids naturally droopy. Seeing Trent's jaw tighten, "I do not say to question, but when?"

"Soon." Trent said. "They'll be vulnerable through Kincaid. Any questions for now?"

Anna needed to ask—for her friend. "Have you heard from Lance?"

"Not in three days. Last I heard, he was in Mexico."

"Why?"

"He wouldn't say. He's a loose cannon."

"Has she been told?" Anna asked.

"Not yet. You're closest to her. Come with us tonight and tell her yourself, unless you think telling her will jeopardize the mission."

"*Nein, nein.* She is totally committed. Such news will probably make her stronger. But she will be very—what is the word?—apprehensive?"

"She has good reason." Trent glanced around the table. "We all do."

Benjamin Franklin Medical Center

Kevin distractedly drummed his fingers on the table as the auditorium filled with reporters. A liver-spotted hand from behind immediately covered his fingers. Another covered his microphone.

"Please don't do that, Dr. Kincaid. The mike will pick it up," Grayson rasped. "I have every confidence in you. But if the questions become too difficult, look to me." He patted Kevin's back and, cane preceding him, slowly moved toward the podium.

Stragglers clutching gourmet cookies sneaked into the smattering of empty seats. Kevin surveyed the assembly, hoping to catch just a glimpse of the woman with Helen's face.

"Cheer up, Kevin," Tetlow whispered in his ear from behind. "This is probably your last press conference till the bill's passed."

To Kevin's left, at the other end of the stage, was a podium and whiteboard. As the last of the seats filled, he searched the faces in the audience. She was not there.

"Good afternoon. I am Frederick Grayson, president of the Benjamin Franklin Health Network. I'd like to thank you all for coming today," he delivered in a deep, broadcaster's voice over the microphone. "Dr. Kevin Kincaid will be available for questions in just a moment." He scanned the audience. "The Association to Cure Genetic Disabilities is a not-for-profit alliance representing more than fifty companies in the biotechnology, manufacturing, and health service sectors—an alliance that seeks to promote germline gene therapy, so that one day, our children may never suffer from genetic diseases that cripple their bodies or minds. An alliance that wants to rid children of the genetic time bombs they carry—diseases like cystic fibrosis, sickle cell, Tay-Sachs. The Association, and the alliance of companies it represents, wants to eliminate genetic disease from the face of the earth, in our children's lifetime." He paused. "The Association wholeheartedly supports the U.S. House of Representatives Bill 601, which lifts the ban on germline gene therapy imposed in the years following legislation against human cloning. HR 601 will enable research for new medicines that may eliminate genetic diseases forever. More than thirty different grassroots organizations representing different genetic diseases support our efforts. A list is available in the lobby. Now, some people have criticized the Association for conducting a media blitz to pressure the Senate into passing HR 601. To this, we plead guilty." Holding up a finger, "But if it eliminates genetic disease in one child, it will be worth it.

"The Association asks only for the opportunity to allow companies to conduct *research* in germline gene therapy—to have the right to submit these new medicines to the Food and Drug Administration, the same as any pharmaceutical company. It will be years before we have cures, but if we don't have the courage to start the journey, we'll never arrive! And so, I'd like now to introduce Dr. Kevin Kincaid, the Neiman-Stepfield Professor of Neurosurgery here at Benjamin Franklin, and Director of Genetic and Molecular Therapy. Dr. Kincaid?"

Kevin buttoned his jacket and walked to the podium, freeing the mike. "Thank you. Back in 1995, W. French Anderson, the father of gene therapy and an innovative giant, once wrote in *Scientific American* that we live in the fourth revolution of medicine. The first was public health measures like sanitation to prevent rapid, widespreading disease. The second, surgery with anesthesia to help doctors actually cure illness. The third, antibiotics to fight infections and vaccines to eliminate viruses. And the fourth, gene therapy, with its potential to deliver genes into a patient's individual cells, to cure diseases otherwise considered incurable." He paced in front of the whiteboard. "We've come a long way. The discovery of DNA in 1942. Watson and Crick's elucidation of its structure in 1953. Gene splicing in the early 1970s. Rapid sequencing of DNA in 1977. The first patient undergoing gene therapy in 1990. Construction of the first human artificial chromosome, the HAC, by Harrington et al at Case Western Reserve in 1997. Cataloging of the entire human genome ten years ahead of schedule, made possible by J. Craig Venter, the brilliant scientist who kicked NIH's Human Genome Project in the butt to get it moving. The pace is dizzying. The technology, confusing."

Kevin drew a double helix on the whiteboard. "This represents strands of deoxyribonucleic acid molecules, DNA." He drew a circle around the double helix. "This is the nucleus, the heart of a cell." Drawing an outer concentric circle, "And this represents one of the 100 trillion cells of our bodies, each containing a complete set of blueprints, written on twenty-three pairs of threadlike, double-helix structures which we call chromosomes. Each chromosome is just a huge DNA molecule containing some 60 million to 250 million chemical bases, all built by just four chemicals: adenine (A), thymine (T), guanine (G), cytosine (C). A-G-C-T, a four-letter alphabet encoding the 30,000 or more information packets on these chromosomes—the genes—that define human beings to the smallest detail. Genes give rise to proteins. DNA designs life; proteins express it. Everything from brain cells to skin cells are all ultimately built from proteins specified in the DNA blueprint, using an RNA intermediary. Although DNA is correctly translated into proteins 99.999 percent of the time, just one wrong chemical base in one gene of one chromosome can condemn a child to a wheelchair, or lead to cystic fibrosis or muscular dystrophy. The only true long-term solution is to fix those genes.

"When your transmission's broken, new upholstery doesn't help. Creating replacement genes that can supplement, replace, or usurp malfunctioning ones is just the first step. Inserting these replacement genes into the proper place on a human chromosome is quite another. The daunting challenge is finding a vehicle, a way to carry the replacement genes into the heart of the cell, the *nucleus*, and insert those genes where they belong. We call vehicles that carry genes into the cell nucleus *vectors*. Vectors are the key to any successful gene therapy. But there are problems.

"Researchers have tried piggybacking human replacement genes onto inactivate, non-disease-causing viral vectors. Like retroviruses. Or lentiviruses, similar to inactivated AIDS virus. Or adenoviruses, like those causing common colds. Or adeno-associated viruses, that help other viruses. Or inactivated herpes viruses. Some vectors have been known to cause mutations. Some work only on growing, dividing cells. Some are very inefficient. All existing viral vectors can only carry a few very small genes, often too few to be useful. Some are toxic. In years past, there have been significant setbacks, even patient deaths. Some at other institutions right here in Philadelphia."

He paused, looking over the audience. "Then there's nonviral vectors that are based on synthetic chemicals. A few have reasonably good rates of carrying replacement genes into human cells, a process called *transfection*. Yet none consistently carry their gene payload into the cell nucleus. And if the gene payload isn't delivered into the cell nucleus, then the gene therapy is doomed." He walked across the stage. "But, using a new vector developed here at Benjamin Franklin, BFV.Syn108, we've been able to insert two sets of genes into patients with brain cancer—genes that make the cancer more susceptible to chemotherapy. Early results look promising."

Kevin looked out across the audience. Compared to his new vector, BFV.Syn108 was as archaic as dinosaurs. But he'd been premature once before with another promising vector. That mistake had never become public. He would not risk it again. "The human body has two basic types of cells: *somatic cells* and *germline cells*. Somatic cells are nonreproductive cells, like those in your muscles, skin, lungs, liver, heart. Germline cells are reproductive cells: sperm or eggs. Fix somatic cells by somatic gene therapy and you cure the patient. But that patient will still carry that same genetic abnormality in the genes of their germline cells. The result? That patient's child may *still* inherit that genetic disease. On the other hand, with germline gene therapy, you cure the child before it's born, *and that child's descendants*. Now, we have several options for germline gene therapy. One is to modify the genetic composition of a patient's sperm or egg cells so that the genetic defect is not passed on to the next generation. Another is to modify the genetic composition of a pre-embryo or fertilized egg, and then place that back in a mother's womb. Both methods can cure the child, before it's born, as well as that child's descendants. These methods are all well and good for planned pregnancies, such as in vitro fertilization.

"But for 99.99 percent of the world's pregnancies, that sort of therapy would be just plain too late to do any good. So, for the rest of us, there is a third, more innovative approach—germline gene therapy *for developing fetuses while still in the mother's womb*. New breakthroughs in vector research are coming—breakthroughs that may enable us to perform this miraculous new type of germline gene therapy in fetuses, theoretically up to the end of the second trimester. Expectant parents would have months to identify and treat their unborn child's genetic disease. Radical, yes, but perhaps the most *human* way, the most *humane* way to eliminate genetic diseases forever." He stopped, center stage. "I'm proud to represent the Association to Cure Genetic Disabilities. I urge you to support House Bill 601 to lift the ban on germline gene therapy. Let's give our children a chance!" Half expecting applause, "I'll happily field your questions now."

A man with a graying goatee asked, "It seems to me that using germline gene therapy puts future generations at risk. So why do it, when there's scientists making progress on other gene therapies that don't carry that risk and can actually *cure* diseases like hemophilia?"

Kevin said, "Hemophilia is the exception to the rule. We can correct the biochemical abnormalities in hemophilia by producing clotting factor VIII, which only requires a single, tiny gene replacement. But single-gene replacement is rarely enough. Sometimes, the problem is overproduction of gene product, meaning that you'd need to fix *trillions* of cells. That's just not practical—now, or in the foreseeable future. So, in special cases, somatic gene therapy may work, but certainly not most of the time."

A man in a silk suit asked, "Isn't modifying genes before birth against God's will?"

"It seems to me that if God gave us the tools to fix things that are broken, aren't we carrying out His divine will when we do? Germline gene therapy is an example of man using the magnificent machinery that God gave us to work with." Kevin turned away from the questioner to the rest of the audience. "And while we're on the subject, let me emphasize that such thinking is an extremist view not shared by most of the religious communities. As far back as 1986, the National Council of Churches adopted an extensive policy statement on 'Genetic Science for Human Benefit,' approving genetic descriptive research. Now, while not specifically mentioned, I believe that germline gene therapy falls within the spirit of that statement. It's only natural for people to be afraid that fast-paced developments in genetics could outstrip common sense and moral values. In fact, the National Institutes of Health have been spending more than thirty million dollars a year for decades to examine precisely these ethical, legal, and social implications of genetic research."

"That's one view," the man followed. "But suffering is part of life. If genetic therapies eliminate suffering, they remove a natural condition that builds human character."

Kevin walked toward the man. "Bubonic plague, smallpox, malaria, typhoid fever, tuberculosis, influenza, ebola, AIDS. Do they build character?"

"Many of my readers believe that if there exists a gene for something like—like Down syndrome, then perhaps it's God's will, and that He had a reason for placing it there."

At the side table, Tetlow rolled her eyes. "Oh no."

Kevin stopped at the edge of the stage. "Have you ever spent time with someone with profound Down syndrome?" He glared as the man shook his head. "Well, I have. And let me tell you, it sure is hard to see God's divine will there!"

Tetlow and Grayson exchanged nods.

A woman on the far side of the auditorium asked, "Don't human cloning and germline gene therapy go hand in hand?"

"Absolutely not," Kevin declared. "Cloning is genetically *duplicating* physically identical human beings. I find it morally abhorrent to clone an entire human being, not to mention some very significant technical difficulties and, of course, the congressional ban in the opening years of this century, making it impossible to conduct the research to perfect whole-body cloning. Germline gene therapy, on the other hand, preserves every child's uniqueness, eliminates genetic disease, embraces individualism. Cloning destroys all of that."

A clean-shaven young man asked, "Won't passing this bill increase the abortion rate?"

"I see the opposite. Because parents may have the option to prevent genetic disease in their unborn children, they'll be far less likely to seek an abortion for that reason."

Another reporter: "What about introducing dangerous new dominant genes that take over genes that occur naturally in people?"

Kevin faced the entire audience and smiled. "You see it all the time in science fiction movies and books: 'dormant' genes becoming 'dominant' and taking over. Amazing how you always have advanced civilizations that travel a light-year a minute, but can't seem to figure out how to fix flaws in their DNA—which is something we'll be able to figure out in the next generation or two. Warp travel is going to take considerably longer, don't you think?"

"Dr. Kincaid, both the UN and EC have declared germline gene therapy unacceptable," a man with gray hair and a thick German accent said. "Why should the United States not follow such policy?"

"Which documents are you referring to? The UN's Educational, Scientific and Cultural Organization meeting in Paris, 1997, that denounced human germline gene therapy? The EU's recommended ban? The Council of Europe's Recommendation 1100 expressly forbidding it? EuropaBio's declared moratorium? The AAAS—"

"All!"

Kevin paused. "No disrespect, sir, but traditionally, America's always been a leader in scientific research. NIH has funded vector research of new vectors *on healthy volunteers* for years . . ."

Tetlow smiled and whispered to Grayson, "Going well, isn't it?"

A man in a black suit said in a squeaky voice, "The Defense

Advanced Research Projects Agency, DARPA, funds one billion dollars a year on genetic research." Turning to the audience, "For those of you who don't know, that's the Department of Defense, DoD. Now there's this big push to lift the ban on germline therapy so we can change our children's genes. It's a government conspiracy to keep us in our place. What do you say to that, Doctor?"

Kevin grinned. "I like *The X-Files,* too."

A woman with red hair stood. "Before you said that we're years away from suitable gene replacement therapies. Yet ACGD is pressuring Congress into passing HR 601 right now. Why?"

Camera flash bulbs lit the silent room. *It's time,* Kevin thought. He said, "It's a bit premature, but our team here at BFMC is very close to developing the ideal vector. It's a quantum leap in vector technology. Safe, inexpensive, easy to administer, specific for any desired cell. But the key is the payload it can carry." He paused. "Every other vector I've previously described only carries at most a few thousand DNA bases into the cell. Enough for a couple of genes. But our new vector will be able to carry a payload a thousand times larger. Up to four hundred *million* bases. Enough to carry a full-sized pair of human chromosomes! We call our new vector $HACV.V_7$. HACV stands for human artificial chromosome vector. V_7 is the batch designation. $HACV.V_7$ will be able to carry a pair of artificial chromosomes that could supplement or replace not just one damaged gene, but a slew of faulty ones. With vector $HACV.V_7$, we may, one day, completely eliminate many inheritable genetic diseases in our lifetime!"

Cameras clicked. The room buzzed. One reporter shouted, "When?"

"Soon." He hesitated. "Naturally I can't disclose everything about it at this point, but I can give you a heads-up on some of our early work with animals. Specifically, *pxr1* knockout mice."

"Knockout mice?" someone shouted.

"I'll explain all that. Just please hold off your questions till I'm done." He stepped to the whiteboard, completely erased it, then drew a stylized mouse complete with oversized whiskers. In the mouse's belly, he drew a circle with a pair of squiggly lines. "As you've no doubt noticed, I'm no da Vinci. So let's pretend that this is a mouse, that the circle inside it represents the nucleus of a typical cell, and the squiggly lines represent a pair of chromosomes."

He wrote $pxr1^+$ beside each of the lines. "The *pxr1* is a particular key gene in mice. All mice need at least one healthy *pxr1* gene," pointing to the *pxr1⁺* label, "on one chromosome to survive. Without it, they develop severe neurological problems that may include profound mental retardation, massive nerve injury and early death. In our lab, we removed healthy cells from a mouse embryo and cultured them." He drew a test tube in the corner of the board and connected it with lines from the schematic cell. "Now at the same time, we generated faulty *pxr1⁻* genes, which are *pxr1* genes that don't work properly, and injected them into other embryonic mouse cells." In a separate diagram, he drew a squiggly line with *pxr1⁻* beside it in another test tube. Then, in the center of the whiteboard, he drew a large mouse and connected it to the diagrammed test tube with the *pxr1⁻*. "We then injected the cells with the faulty *pxr1⁻* genes into different, healthy, pregnant, foster mother mice." Kevin drew two smaller mice beneath the central mouse and labeled each as *pxr1⁺/pxr1⁻*. "Next, we identified all offspring mice that had one functioning *pxr1* gene and one faulty *pxr1* gene." He pointed to the *pxr1⁺/pxr1⁻* label. "We can call these *knockout mice,* because one of their genes has been knocked out."

"After that, we crossbred our knockout mice." He connected the two with lines, and then drew three new mice beneath the pair he'd already drawn. "That yielded three different types of mice offspring. Some mice inherited two healthy functioning genes," he said, writing *pxr1⁺/pxr1⁺* beside the mouse on the left. "They were healthy as could be." He wrote *pxr1⁺/pxr1⁻* beside the middle mouse. "Others inherited one healthy gene and one faulty gene. These mice were physically okay, because they had at least one functioning gene. But they were disease carriers, because they had one damaged gene." He wrote *pxr1⁻/pxr1⁻* beside the mouse on the right. "And still others inherited two faulty genes. The mice with two faulty genes all died within three days."

He pointed to the two mice labeled *pxr1⁺/pxr1⁻* in the row above. "Now let's go back to the knockout mice. We crossbred another batch and took chromosomes containing healthy, functioning *pxr1⁺* genes that we'd previously cultured." He pointed to the test tube with the *pxr1⁺* label. He drew a big circle that he labeled *HACV.V₇*. Inside the circle, he drew a chromosome labeled *pxr1⁺*. "We stuck those chromosomes on our new special vector, HACV.V₇. In a controlled experiment, we injected one hundred pregnant mice with our vector V₇ carrying chromosomes with healthy *pxr1⁺* genes and another hundred pregnant mice with a worthless placebo."

He stood back and paused, allowing the audience a moment to

digest the information. "Here's what happened. Every mouse born with two faulty *pxr1⁻* genes whose mother had been injected with the placebo died within three days, as expected. But *none* of the pregnant mice injected with our V₇ vector—gave birth to any offspring with two faulty *pxr1⁻* genes. And that's because our vector V₇, containing the life-giving, healthy *pxr1⁺* gene on a complete chromosome, found its way, in the womb, to the mice who would have died without it. And to accomplish that, our new vector had to have some remarkable properties that I can't discuss here. But the experiment undeniably proved that our vector was able to insert a complete chromosome into the nucleus of an animal's cell."

Another: "When will it be available to the public?"

"Sorry, but I'm not at liberty to disclose anything further."

Grayson smiled at Tetlow, then turned back to Kevin.

A woman with a recorder protruding from her hand asked, "Doctor, once we start using germline therapy for genetic diseases, won't we wind up trying to make our children smarter, stronger, or *better*?"

"That's a rather pessimistic view—assuming that the benefits we gain from any developing technology also must bring harm—a kind of 'slippery slope' leading to pure evil. What you're saying is that when we try to cure sickle cell anemia, eventually, we'll only be making children with blue eyes or whatever our ever-changing concept of perfection might be. It presupposes that we'll never recognize the difference between good and evil. I don't agree at all! The slippery slope is more like a broken-down staircase. Take a misstep and we'll feel it in our rump. The gap between restoring health by germline gene therapy and inheritable genetic modification, often called genetic engineering or eugenics, is enormous. *We will know the difference.*"

"How do we guarantee that?" a man ten rows back asked.

"Abstinence, antibiotics, vaccines—we make those choices every day. Each shapes future generations. Banning germline therapy today because we can't guarantee the safety of children two hundred, five hundred, a thousand years from now is like saying that people can't have children because they can't guarantee how their great-great-grandchildren will turn out."

A woman from the back of the auditorium: "What happened to the vector you worked on?"

"Hmmm?"

The woman emerged from a track-light shadow. "For years you

worked on another promising vector, HACV.K$_4$. Could V$_7$ have the same problem as K$_4$?"

Kevin suddenly felt light-headed. Trembling, he leaned against the podium for support. His hands trembled.

"How does that woman know about K$_4$?" Grayson snapped. "Nobody's supposed to know!"

Tetlow stared at the woman by the exit. "I've seen photos of her."

"Who is she?"

"Kincaid's wife."

Kevin steadied himself and fixed his eyes on the woman's. "Helen!" The fire alarm screamed shrilly. Hospital security guards burst through the back doors and began emptying the room.

The woman disappeared through the back of the room. Kevin leaped off the stage after her.

A man in the audience screamed, "It's a bomb!"

Alta, Wyoming

The limousine wound cautiously along Ski Hill Road. The rugged, snow-covered summits of Mt. Owen and Grand Teton Peak loomed overhead. Kristin Brocks stared out the back window of her limousine. This terrain unnerved her: so sparsely populated and much, too much open space. And so high up. Was that why Loring had chosen to meet in such godforsaken country? Possibly, but her touch of agoraphobia and acrophobia had never appeared on any psych eval. She'd made sure of that. "How much longer?"

"We're there now, ma'am," said a guard riding shotgun in the front seat.

Signs reading "Grand Targhee Ski & Summer Resort" flanked the road as the limousine wound up the base of a mountain and, a half-mile later, stopped beside a booth. The driver held up credentials, drove up a private lane, and parked in a prime reserved spot beside the main lodge. "Ma'am, we walk from here."

Brocks had blond hair cropped unflatteringly short, white skin bordering on albino, and deep, glacier blue eyes shining from a face that had no makeup to enhance the remnants of her ancestral Danish beauty. She zipped up her parka, buttoned down the hood, put on her thick gloves, and glanced at her men. They surrounded her as she exited, their eyes constantly searching as she headed toward the lodge. Cold air bit her face and burned her lungs as she trudged to the staging area behind the main lodge, lined by antique Western store-fronts. The aroma of croissant and Belgian chocolate wafted through frigid air. The woman's wary entourage deposited her at a tree-lined path with a gate marked "Snowcat Powder Skiing Only, Closed Today."

"The arrangement stipulates that we can't accompany you beyond this point," Brocks's lead escort said.

"Where's Loring?" she asked, her breath forming iced air.

"Waiting there now."

"Deployment?"

"Twelve sharpshooters confirmed on his side. We have fifteen, but numerical superiority isn't a tactical advantage here. You'll be totally exposed." He hesitated. "If I might speak freely, ma'am, why are you agreeing to meet him here?"

"Mutual assured destruction." She scanned the terrain. "Neither side can take out the other's director without sacrificing its own."

"Ma'am, that's not what I meant."

She squelched a smile. "By meeting him here, in an environment that he finds comfortable, we may create a false sense of security. One we can exploit."

"Risking the queen for a bishop is a poor gamble."

She looked at frost forming on her subordinate's brows. "We're out of time."

He nodded. "The lift will stop midway for precisely ten minutes. To extend that time, raise your right hand. To end it, raise your left. Director, if the situation deteriorates while—"

"I know."

"A chopper will be waiting for you at the summit." The man then spoke into a palm-sized transmitter. After a crackled response, the gate slid open. "Best of luck, ma'am."

Without looking back, she trudged along a wide, snowy path between towering evergreens. For weeks, she'd analyzed what she'd offer Loring if they met face-to-face: trades, concessions, bribes. What could one offer people who had everything? There was always the threat of exposure, but that would also expose the underbelly of her own organization's activities.

He stood at the end of the path by the chairlift: tall, vigorous, wearing a commissar-style fur hat atop gleaming silver hair, long woolen coat to his ankles, his hands clasped inside leather gloves. She focused on his weathered face, his dark brown eyes. Crow's-feet deepened with his smile. "Edwin Dixon Loring," he said, his voice rich and resonant. "Friends call me Dixon. Perhaps, when we reach the summit, you will, too."

The hard-looking, fortyish face that protruded from the parka hood cautiously smiled. "Kristin Brocks. Director, S and I, DARPA. You, on the other hand, may *not* call me by my first name, no matter what we've decided by the time we reach the summit."

Loring tisk-tisked. "I do so hate posturing."

"And I the cold."

"Among other things," he said with a wink as he scanned the mountain. "Lovely up here. *Open*, unoccupied, untamed mountains. So different from the warm confines of buildings and towers. And the view from so high in the sky, almost touching the clouds."

Rubbing it in my face, she thought, painfully remembering how, at age seven, she was lost for two days in Yellowstone. "You're very well informed."

"You sound overstressed, Ms. Brocks. It's no wonder, what with the intradepartmental rivalry and interdepartmental pressure in your agency and DoD. And without the love and support of a good man at home. I can only imagine how painful it's been for you since your divorce. Someday, I'd like to meet that fool ex-husband of yours, who treated you so badly."

His comment confirmed her long-standing suspicions. She fought the urge to glare at him, and instead looked toward the chairlift. "Let's get going."

The chairlift started. Red, two-seat benches suspended by overhead cables whipped around the pole.

"Ever been on one of these?" he asked. Answering his own question, "Of course you haven't. All you do is stand a few feet in front of a chair as it rounds the pole, crouch a bit, and let the chair scoop you up. We go together. Which side would you prefer?"

She chose left.

"True to a knight's form. Keep your enemy by your sword hand."

They stood abreast as a chair whipped around, touched the back of their knees, cradled them, and began ascending the mountain. In seconds, they were half the height of great trees lining the ski trail. As the mountainside fell away, Brocks grabbed the strut joining the chair to the cable track. Her legs dangled over the edge of the chair. She dared not move.

"Don't be afraid."

She wanted to scream. "I'm—not."

Loring scanned the slope. "You know, Kristin, it cost a pretty penny to rent this mountain for the day, at the height of the season. In all fairness, DARPA should defray some of the expense."

Trying to ignore the openness, the mind-numbing height, she released her grip on the bar. "This was your idea. You can afford it."

"Yes." He beamed. "Yes, I can."

Brocks studied his face, a latticework of creases, each crease like a mark of success, built layer by layer, culminating in a quiet arrogance.

"As a sign of good faith, I thought we might start with a simple question," Loring said, gazing at her fingers clutching the strut. "We had an experimental facility in Mexico—"

"Which violates your organization's post-termination clause of the agreement with us that forbids you from using shared technology in facilities outside of U.S. borders."

Loring grinned. "The lab was developing new strains of—perennial wheat."

"But of course. Where?"

"Tiburon Island. In the Gulf of California."

"I thought that was a wildlife preserve. It must've taken some doing to get the Mexican government to cooperate with your *research.*"

"There was an incident this morning. A trespasser might have obtained some potentially compromising information."

"We're not the only ones upset with you," she said.

"If you plan to release that information, think again. The facility's been dismantled, and Mexican officials paid off. The cover story will likely appear on the evening news." He shrugged. "Tiburon was obsolete, anyway."

"It was a crime against humanity."

"Let he who is without sin cast the first stone."

The chairlift halted. Their forward momentum caused the chair to rock gently.

"You've changed the rules of the game," Brocks declared. "We don't like it."

"Bureaucracy makes rules. Rules are poor substitutes for common sense."

She repositioned herself to face him directly, the chair swinging with her motion. "We want your media campaign stopped. Immediately."

"The public should be educated."

She ground her teeth and wrapped her arm tight around one of the bars. The chair gently swayed. "For years, both sides have kept quiet—to our mutual benefit."

"Change now is in *our* best interest."

"Any change should be gradual, preferably over at least one full generation. Not with a media blitz and Super Bowl blowout!" she barked.

"We're working within the system. Using the First Amendment. Aren't you proud of us?" He grinned as she glared. "There are precedents, Kristin. In the early 1990s, when Clinton first came to power proposing the government-run Universal Health System, the Health Insurance Association of America sponsored a series of ads. A working-class couple sitting at the kitchen table, 'Harry and Louise,' bemoaning how government health care would tear into their savings, wreck their lives." He unzipped his coat and reached inside.

"Easy!" she warned as her right hand reached for her automatic.

With two fingers, he withdrew a silver, insulated flask and opened it. A slightly sweet aroma wafted through the cold air as he poured a golden-colored liquid into the lid. He raised the tiny cup to his lips, and drank. "Darjeeling tea. Custom blend." He poured another cup, and proffered it. "Please. It will warm you."

"I don't want to be warmed." She watched him finish the tea. "Loring, we have the resources to reimburse you."

"It's not the expense. It's our commitment to working for the betterment of man."

The chairlift started moving.

"Think we can't get to you, Loring? All of you? Antitrust, IRS, SEC, OSHA, NSA, tar—"

"Look over the horizon, Kristin. You can see Idaho. I own a biotech company in Boise. It's small, but community-oriented." Leaning back, folding his arms across his broad chest, "I have a feasibility study on my desk showing that it's more cost-effective to relocate that facility in Malaysia. Which I'd prefer not to do, but if I'm pressured, well—first, I'd get a call from the governor, and I'd explain my position. He, in turn, would call the senior senator, who'd call the Secretary of Defense, who'd call your boss, who'd call you."

"We deal with pressure."

He raised his eyebrows. "Our members outright own or control close to $300 billion. When we speak, both White House and Wall Street respectfully listen."

"If provoked, we can deal with you more *directly*."

He whispered, "We pay our assassins better."

The summit approached. Less than thirty seconds to dismount.

"Let me phrase this as politely as possible," she said. "We strongly urge you to reconsider. You know that we cannot allow this to continue without response."

Loring swiveled toward her. His eyes were like cannons. "You are the ones who've changed. We have always been on this path. That should have been clear to you from day one. You're in this up to your necks. So ally yourselves with us and benefit, step aside and watch the future pass you by, or get in our way and be dismantled!"

Brocks waited until their feet touched powdered snow. "You may be better funded, but we move in technological vistas you cannot imagine. And if you think I'm bluffing, remember that it wasn't Al Gore who invented the Internet—*it was us!*"

Lombard Street, Philadelphia

Sirens. Fire engines. Police directing people away from the medical complex. Kevin followed the crowd outside the hospital. His audience had spilled onto Lombard Street, snarling traffic. The mass of slowly surging bodies insulated him from the cold. Taller than most of the crowd, Kevin frantically looked out over the sea of heads. *Where is she?*

He spotted her: fifteen feet ahead and to his right was the back of a woman wearing a leather coat. Her hair, silken mahogany. "Helen!"

She drifted farther right. Kevin reached out and began shoving people aside. He closed in. Twenty bodies between them. Ten. "Helen!"

His fingertips touched her soft, calfskin coat. His hand clasped her slender arm. Heat shot through him as her body pivoted toward him. "Helen!"

Her gray-green eyes twinkled, a smile amplifying their glimmer.

"Dr. Kincaid, delighted to meet you. I'm flattered that you know my name!"

She had smooth, supple skin, eyes bright as a kitten's, and seductively sloping cheeks. Beneath her coat was a slim physique with hauntingly familiar curves. Kevin brought trembling fingers to her face. The eyes, the hair—perfect. But her cheekbones were too high, her jaw too angular, her breasts too large. And her voice, too soprano, that of a woman in her late-twenties. Beautiful, but not his Helen Brewster Kincaid. *Of course it isn't her. I must've been crazy to even think it was possible.* "I'm—I thought you were—Helen. Stupid mistake. Sorry, sorry."

"But I am. See?" showing him her ID. "Helen Morgan. *Idaho Falls Post Register.*"

Eyes glistening, "Sorry again. I, uh, have to go."

The crowd surged, knocking her off balance. She tottered backward, wildly swinging her arms. Another shove sent her hurtling to the pavement beneath the stampede. Kevin seized her arm just before she disappeared, yanked her back onto her feet, and pulled her close. Nearly a foot and a half taller, he effortlessly shielded her with his body. "Let's get away from this." Tucking her into his arm, he plowed through the crowd and ducked into a driveway between sets of red-brick townhouses. Free from pressing bodies, he released her, but she clung to him. "Better?"

"Yes, thank you. Lucky woman—the one you mistook me for." She looked up before slowly, slowly separating. "Was that you by the river this morning?"

"Yes." He turned back to the crowd.

She touched his shoulder. "Don't go. We can talk."

"I—don't think we can."

"Because you can't, or you won't?"

"What would we talk about, Ms. Morgan?"

"Human artificial chromosome vector K_4."

He looked back. "HACV.K_4 is a secret. How'd you learn of it?"

"I have my sources."

"We buried that work years ago." He started away.

"Sometimes, things you bury come back."

He stopped. "No, Ms. Morgan. What we bury never comes back."

She stepped in front of him. "Dr. Kincaid, my career's on the line. The only way I could get here was with a one-way ticket and a promise to my editor to bring back an exclusive."

"You can forget that. Nobody's getting an exclusive. I signed a nondisclosure agreement with the Association and the Benjamin Franklin Health Network."

"Why would you do that?" she asked.

"So I could be ACGD's spokesman. Do some good. It's a standard contract and I understand their position. And as spokesman it's wise to be careful what I say and who I say it to. After all, the media is always looking for the cloud behind the silver lining, isn't it?"

"So you traded your rights so you could be their spokesman."

He cocked his head. "What's that supposed to mean?"

"You let ACGD tell you who you can and cannot talk to," she said.

"Nobody tells me that, Ms. Morgan. Nobody!"

"Apparently your contract does, Doctor. You just said so."

"It doesn't say *that*. And I'm not concerned anyway. What could they do—sue me? They wouldn't dare."

"Then there's no reason why you can't talk to me, is there?" She smiled. "It doesn't have to be an interview as such—just two people talking. Over coffee?"

"Some other time. Discretion, valor, and all that." He started walking away again.

"As important as you are, as independent as you think you are, you're still just their little compliant poster boy, afraid to stand on his own," she called.

Kevin turned back. Slowly released a faint smile. "Are you daring me?"

"Dares are good for us. They push us beyond what's comfortable and secure."

"Sometimes, right over a cliff."

"Which makes the thrill. As a scientist, you know the consequences of complacency."

He grinned. "So now I'm complacent?"

She crossed her arms. "Can you prove you're not?"

He studied every facet of her face. It wasn't his Helen, but it was close—so close to the image of his wife branded in his thoughts, living in his dreams. Fate was offering her face, or at least a reasonable facsimile of it. Why? "I'll give you fifteen minutes."

"An hour."

He smiled. "Twenty-nine minutes—with one stipulation. You agree not to compromise, malign, cheapen, or sensationalize my work in any fashion."

She beamed. "Absolutely."

In an alcove with Tetlow beside him, Grayson emphatically waved at the towering security guard in the surging crowd. The man recognized him, channeled his way through the exodus, and shielded his pair of superiors.

"The audience wasn't that large," Grayson mumbled.

"The entire hospital's being evacuated, sir," the guard said. "Bomb threat. We think the call originated in the auditorium lobby."

"We'll deal with that later. Have you seen Dr. Kincaid?"

"No, sir."

"And that woman who knew about K_4?"

"Her either, sir."

"If they're together—find Dr. Kincaid, immediately!" The guard disappeared into the crowd. "The conference is ruined," Grayson told Tetlow.

"Not necessarily. A bomb scare at a hospital during a press conference with the Association's lead spokesman guarantees solid network coverage this evening. And the media hates being victimized, so we might get a double-positive slant, both pro-Association and anti-activist. We could pick up five to seven points in the polls just on sympathy. And raise the dander of one or two straddling senators."

"Perhaps, Joan. I want you to find that woman. Who she is, who sent her."

"I'll get on it." Her teeth chattered. "It's getting cold."

His jacket was open to the whipping wind. "Fewer bodies, less heat. A guiding truth to remember as you rise through the ranks."

"Yes, Mr. Grayson. I'm wondering, though, if could she be Kincaid's wife. It's my understanding that the woman's body was—"

"No, his wife is dead!" He removed his fogged glasses and wiped them hard. "But whoever is posing as her ghost threatens all of us."

They sat in the back of the luncheonette behind crammed tables and a stenciled window looking onto Twenty-first Street. Hand wrapped around steaming coffee, Kevin stared at the woman as she poured artificial sweetener into her tea, then quartered her cranberry-walnut muffin—exactly as his wife had done. Could she have made herself up to resemble Helen to gain his confidence? Maybe, but the resemblance could never be more than superficial. She could never *be*

Helen. But while drinking in her face, his mind modeled it, like clay: working, reworking, shaping, softening, trying to make the transformation complete. If only it were Helen. Barring that, he would have been satisfied if he knew where his wife's body lay.

"They said there was a bomb."

"A hoax, Ms. Morgan," Kevin said, his eyes narrowing. "Do you reporters believe *every* inflammatory lie you hear?"

"You sound pretty cocky, Doctor," she snapped back.

"Haven't heard the boom, have you?"

"Maybe that's yet to come."

"Look, I know you reporters sensationalize your stories to sell advertising—"

"An old and very worn generalization, Doctor. I'd've expected better from someone with your intellect."

He leaned forward and thrust an accusing finger at her. "You journalists have fanned the flames at both ends—religious fanatics on the right, Greenpeace and anti-gene activists on the left. What's the angle of the week: a secret society purifying the racial gene pool? A government plot to mix our genes with aliens'? Do journalists take some kind of perverse pleasure out of feeding people's natural paranoia, so that when science pushes us forward, you gleefully lead the charge back into the eighth century? Or does it all just come down to the almighty advertising buck?"

"Why did you abandon human artificial chromosome vector K_4?"

Kevin slammed his hand down on the luncheonette table. Ignoring the startled stares of the other diners, "What do you mean, *abandon*? It wasn't a baby left on some doorstep in the snow. It was an experiment. It didn't work. I tried something else. We call that science."

"Sorry. Poor choice of words."

"K_4 was supposed to be a secret. How did you find out about it?"

"A reporter can't divulge her sources."

"You'll have to—if you want anything more out of me."

Batting her eyes at him, "There's no need to be hostile."

"I am *not* being hostile. But it's not as if I didn't have good reason. You embarrassed me in front of the media."

She scribbled a few notes hastily on a pad. "Then I take it that you want me to go with what I already have on vector K_4, without your input."

"What do you have?"

"I'll remember to send you a tear sheet." She clicked closed her pen. "I hope you'll forgive any inaccuracies, large or small, that might appear."

"Hey! You're reneging on our agreement!"

She closed her pad. "Hardly, Doctor. I'm doing my utmost best not to compromise, malign, cheapen, or sensationalize—did I get your words correct?—based on what you're willing to reveal. Now if I release any erroneous information about your old K_4 vector which might lead to any unfounded rumors that could potentially jeopardize work on your new vector—V_7, was it?—then that wouldn't be my fault, would it?"

"Hiding behind 'absence of malice'?" *Not only does she use logic the same infuriating way that Helen did, she uses the same tone when she does it!*

"Make you another deal," Helen said. "I can't tell you who my source is, but I can tell you who it isn't—in exchange for information about K_4."

"There are legal and ethical limitations on what I can disclose."

"I can live with those limitations. If they're legit—and reasonable."

Kevin folded his hands. "How do I know that you won't give me the short end of the stick? You could tell me that Abraham Lincoln wasn't the source."

"Somebody around here has to show a little trust. It may as well be me." She sighed. "My source wasn't anyone who works or worked in your lab, or for that matter, anyone who is or ever has been affiliated with the hospital or any of your projects."

K_4 *was a secret. Virtually no one outside of those directly involved knew about it. If she's telling the truth—*

"How long were you working on human artificial chromosome vector K_4?" she asked, reopening her pad, clicking on her pen.

So much like Helen. Even the way she holds her pen!

"Come on, Dr. Kincaid, you agreed."

"Oh. Umm, uh, five years. I worked on K_4 about five years."

"And you started when?"

"A year or so after I came back East. About nine years ago."

"Which means you abandoned K_4 about four years ago? Why?"

He hesitated. "K series vectors work by transfection. That's a non-viral-mediated method for transferring genes into cells. What made the K series vectors unique was that not only were they capable of transporting complete, intact pairs of human artificial chromosomes, instead of small pieces of DNA, into a cell, they could transfer entire human artificial chromosomes, HACs, directly into the cell *nucleus.*"

"What's the difference?"

"DNA in the cell cytoplasm, that is, outside of the cell's nucleus, doesn't last long. When the cell divides, inserted DNA that's outside of the cell nucleus generally is not reproduced. It's lost. But when chromosomes are inserted, intact, into the cell nucleus, they become part of the cell's genetic structure. When the cell divides, the new chromosomes are carried into the next generation. The cell's blueprint, and the blueprint for that cell's descendants, have been changed, forever. K_4 was the culmination of that vector series." He watched her face grow warm, enthralled, like Helen's.

"Why did K_4 fail?"

"Because, Ms. Morgan, the inserted chromosomes tended to denature, that is, break apart when transfected into the cell nucleus. That left random-sized chunks of chromosomes, containing genes, floating haphazardly in the cell. In some cases, those chromosome chunks contained whole expression genes—genes that ultimately code for proteins. Worse, some of the chromosome chunks contained expression genes and pieces of regulatory genes that control expression genes. The 'on-off' switch, if you will."

"What would that do?"

"All too often, the genes coding for proteins had their 'on switch' left permanently on. This led to overproduction of some proteins that overwhelmed the host."

"I don't understand."

"Suppose you transfected a cell with an artificial chromosome that contained an important gene, say 'insulin'. Now, suppose that this chromosome broke into chunks in the nucleus. Suppose one of those chunks contained the gene coding for insulin, but that it contained only part of the genes controlling insulin production. The result? Without proper regulation, insulin production could run wild. A hundred times the normal quantity of insulin is lethal."

"So patients who received K_4—"

"No patient ever received K_4," Kevin declared.

She stared at him. "I don't understand. You just said—"

"All of our studies were performed in vitro, Ms. Morgan." She looked confused. He added, "Cell cultures grown in test tubes, in

Petri dishes, or in tiny wells on a plate. All K_4 studies were performed on collections of cells. Animal cells at that. It's part of what we call the preclinical trial process."

"You're sure?"

"Don't you think I know the difference between cells growing on a plate and a living, breathing human being?"

"There's no chance that it could have ever been used on human subjects?"

Putting both elbows on the table, he leaned forward. "Wondering whether I run a horror show? Maybe mixing human and alien DNA?"

"Of course not, but—"

"I discontinued the project. Destroyed all the samples *myself,* according to standard operating procedures and guidelines set down by NIH and CDC." He realized that her question was legitimate: she obviously wasn't a clinical researcher and she had no way of knowing the details of the K_4 studies. Why was he so angry with her? Because she wasn't his Helen?

She rubbed her right eye.

"Are you all right?"

"The dry air's bothering me." A tear from irritation formed. "So why all the secrecy?"

"Some principles in K_4 also apply to the new vectors. BFHN's Board of Directors was concerned that if we released our findings on K_4, we'd tip off competitors."

"Your breakthrough vector, V_7, the one you hinted at in the conference. It's finished, isn't it?"

He shrugged.

"Your announcement at the conference made that an open secret." She smiled seductively. "You could send a poor girl from Idaho home happy. Which is not necessarily a bad thing."

"I made a mistake with K_4. I thought I'd perfected it. I spoke too soon. It was a debacle. So this time, Ms. Morgan, I'm keeping my mouth shut and all of the information," tapping his forehead, "stowed securely up here. That's where V_7 stays, until I'm certain that it works."

Helen leaned close to him. "I think that's an excellent idea."

He hadn't expected that. "Why?"

Her handbag rang. She opened the flap, removed a wireless phone, and answered it. "How long?" she asked. She nodded and hung up. "Dr. Kincaid, I have to leave." She stood, threw her notepad into her handbag, and slung her coat over her shoulder. She started toward the exit.

"Wait a second! You didn't answer my question."

She looked back at him. "Because more than your career depends on it."

Kevin abruptly stood. "What do—"

"Don't tell anyone—and I mean *anyone*—what was said here."

Kevin shook his head. "What a mistake it was talking to you. You might look like my wife, sound like my wife, even have some of her mannerisms, but you sure as hell aren't her!"

Helen glanced at the door, but took a step toward him. "If you had the guts to get your head out of the sand and look beyond your own little protected world, you might see that I'm the best friend you're ever going to have." She dashed out of the luncheonette.

Senior Administrator's Office
BFMC   *5:15 P.M.*

Joan Tetlow found Grayson smoking another cigar when she entered her office.

"What did Kincaid have to say?" he asked.

Trying to ignore the smoke that wafted across the room and into her face, "The woman he met was Helen Morgan. She's certainly no ghost, but she does bear a striking resemblance to his dead wife, which Kincaid insists is just a lucky accident."

"I don't believe in serendipity," Grayson said. "Neither should you."

"He says that this Helen Morgan is a reporter for an Idaho newspa—"

"Who knew of K_4's existence. Not exactly public knowledge."

"That's all that Kincaid says she knew—when she came, and when she left."

Grayson took in a mouthful of smoke. "And HACV.V$_7$?"

Tetlow pulled out a pocket recorder, hit the *rewind* button, and waited a moment before stopping it. She put the recorder to her ear, listened briefly, and again stopped the tape. "This is what he said when I pressed him on the issue." She hit the *play* button. Kevin's voice said: "Who the hell are you to tell me who I can and cannot talk to? You may sign my checks, but you don't run my life. Just remember, there are institutions that would kill to have me. Some within walking distance."

She clicked off the recorder. "I've known him ten years. Kevin Kincaid has always seemed like a burn victim, encased in scar tissue, utterly incapable of touching or being touched by anything or anyone—except for his work. I've never seen him behave this way."

"We can reasonably assume that the reporter is the source."

"I believe most of his story," Tetlow said.

Grayson blew out a smoke ring. "Even so, he is covering for her."

"Why?"

"That, Joan, is what *you* are to discover. Kincaid is the only one who fully knows how to synthesize the new vector. Which makes it imperative that you get his files in order. I've already warned you once, I won't do it again."

"Consider it done."

"And find out who leaked K_4." Grayson straightened his collar. "I'll be back day after tomorrow to check on your progress. At which time I'll expect answers."

Adam's Mark Hotel, Philadelphia

Room 601. HR 601. Helen Morgan wondered whether the coincidence was a good omen as she slid her security key into the lock and opened the door. She flipped on the light switch. Nothing happened. "Crap!"

Hands outstretched, she groped across the dark room. A minty aroma filled the air—chocolate mints on her pillow?—as her fumbling fingers found her bed and guided her to the nightstand lamp. She turned it on.

"In for the evening?" asked a deep voice behind her.

She dropped her handbag, and slowly turned. Trent McGovern sat beneath a floor lamp, his feet propped on a table, his hands folded like a choirboy's. To his right stood Sylvester Cameron, his gap-tooth smile chilling, his dancing snake-tattooed arms flexing. To Trent's left, Howard Straub, her silent partner at the conference, vigorously chewed gum. And Anna Steitz swayed, jittery, by the TV halfway across the room.

Helen rasped, "I hadn't expected you here."

"Neither had I," Trent said. "Until Straub called."

Helen glared at Straub. She'd asked him, begged him to keep his mouth shut. The assignment was hers, not his, and she needed to complete it her own way. "Weasel!"

"Asshole," Straub returned. "Just like your brother."

"Children, stop fighting!" Trent snapped. Facing Helen, "We're all family—*my* family." He smiled, glancing at Cameron, at Anna, at Straub. "Each of you was facing long imprisonments." He turned back to Helen. "Or death."

"You've found me useful," Helen said.

"Journalistic and auto theft skills, an eclectic mixture. Not nearly worth the trouble I went through rescuing you, and giving you sanctuary and purpose." He looked away. "And for what, Helen? So you could treat me like this?"

Helen gazed into Trent's eyes. She thought she saw disappointment, but Trent's mood shifts were notoriously erratic. The empathetic Trent often preceded the vicious version of him—sometimes changing on a single word. "Trent, I can ex—"

"It was too late to stop you." Trent popped a mint in his mouth. "The question now is whether it's too late to pick up the pieces."

That explains McGovern's presence, Helen thought. *Cameron's been brought in for additional muscle. But Anna? Why is she here?* She said, "Trent, it's going as plan—"

"You were supposed to seduce him. The man hasn't screwed for ten years. He'd have told you anything. All it called for was a little feminine guile." Slamming his fist on the table, "And you fucking wave a red flag in his face! Who gave you permission to announce K_4 to the world?"

"It was necessary."

"Bloody moron, she is," Cameron spat.

Trent strode across the room, holding his head as if it would explode. Anna dodged out of his way while Straub melted into the background. "When you trumpeted K_4, you blew your cover. You forced Straub to improvise, phone in a bomb threat, and disrupt the conference to prevent *them* from capturing you. How would you have escaped if Straub hadn't made that call? Or warned you during your little coffee break?" He approached her. "You've tipped off the Collaborate. Now, unless you're very, very careful, they'll use you to get to us." He pulled back his jacket to expose an automatic in its holster. "If this mission wasn't so critical—What's one to do with such a mischievous family member?"

"Kincaid may be naive, but he's not living in a fantasy world," Helen said. "He'd never have confused me with his wife. The trick was to use her face as the in. But that's not enough. We have to appeal to his intellect, too."

He put his face close to hers. "You're a clever liar. What's your real reason?"

"I'm telling you. It's the right way to get to him."

"Looks like you need a little disciplining." Trent looked across the room to Cameron and nodded. Cameron wheeled around and viciously slapped Anna with his open palm. Her head glanced against the bed. She fell to the floor. Cameron lifted her up and dropped her on the mattress. Anna sobbed. Her right eye was red, angry.

"You bastard!" Helen rushed at Cameron, who effortlessly pivoted around, swung his forearm beneath her chin, and locked her in a choke hold.

Trent shrugged. "We can't risk damaging your face now, Helen. But your friend, Anna?"

"She's one of us!"

"It's hard watching someone else suffer for your mistakes, isn't it? So, for Anna's sake, I ask you again: why did you make a spectacle of yourself at the conference?"

She struggled against Cameron's grip. "Because I had to know."

"Know what?"

"Whether he knew what the Collaborate had done with K_4. Whether he's one of *them*."

AntiGen's leader shook his head.

"Kincaid doesn't know. Trent, he really does not know!"

"A bomb doesn't know who it blows up, either. It just does."

"He's a doctor trying to stop disease!"

"He's responsible, Helen. Why should you care?" He looked deep into her misty eyes. "Of course. I see." He turned to Cameron. "Get the team. Go with the alternate plan."

"No!"

"Cameron, we go tomorrow. Two teams. One takes Kincaid when he's isolated after nineteen hundred hours. The other seizes the lab after twenty hundred hours. If he hasn't talked by morning, we kill him, then destroy the lab and computer system."

Cameron threw her to the floor.

"You've left us no choice," Trent continued. "You're too involved."

"You need me!"

"Not anymore."

"You're missing our best opportunity." She grabbed his jacket. "I know where V_7 is!"

Trent pivoted back to her. "Where?"

"In his head." She nodded. "He said so."

"Great! We'll pick him up tomorrow and—"

"Suppose he won't talk. Suppose he dies under torture first? Then what?"

"At least *they* won't have it."

Helen folded her arms. "Can you be sure?"

"What do you have in mind?"

"Let me bring Kincaid into AntiGen."

"Out of the question."

"Not only would he deliver us the vector, but think of it—their own poster boy speaking out against them. He could kill 601. Expose the Collaborate. It's what we've worked for!" She took a deep breath. "But take him hostage, kill him, and you solidify the public against us. HR 601 becomes law. Maybe even gives the Collaborate time to redevelop V_7."

Trent hissed through his teeth. He glanced around the room. Straub stepped away from the wall and tilted his head. Anna stopped sobbing, sat up sluggishly, pressed a hand against her swollen eye, and nodded.

"Could work, mate," Cameron voiced.

Trent shook his head. "The Collaborate will be watching."

"Yes, but they'll be cautious," Helen said. "As long as I'm out there *by myself*, I pose no overt threat. The risk to AntiGen would be minimal."

"But not zero." Trent bit on a peppermint. "Two teams will tail—"

"No! They'd be spotted. The Collaborate would clamp down around the doctor, pick off our people, and go straight for our carotid artery."

"Can you really prove to our angel of mercy that he actually serves the devil?"

"Yes." She wet her lips. "Have you heard from Lance?"

Trent looked to Anna, who said, "I am sorry, Helen. We do not think we will."

Helen's eyes started to tear. Her contacts burned.

"We heard it on the news. An 'accident,' they say. A toxic chemical spill," Anna continued. "Tiburon is quarantined, their cover story."

"Was Lance there?"

"His last reported position was in the Sonoran Desert, across the strait from Tiburon," Trent answered.

Helen's legs quivered, weakened. "But you don't know. He could still be alive."

"Don't count on it. And Helen, you still haven't explained just how you're going to prove your case to Kincaid."

Slowly, she whispered, "That's my problem, now, isn't it?"

Grinning, "I like your answer. So be it. You have forty-eight hours to bring in Kincaid. Fail, and he'll suffer an unforeseen accident by Friday. And if the Collaborate's on your tail, so will you."

Trent headed to the door before signaling his entourage to follow. Anna dragged herself off the bed, a hand still pressed on her eye.

"Let her spend the night with me," Helen suggested. "I'll put her on a train in the morning."

Trent said, "Straub will check on you both later." Patting Anna's shoulder, "It wasn't personal. I hope you understand. Keeping a family together sometimes requires discipline."

The door closed behind them. Helen listened, waited, then opened the door, peeked out, and checked the corridors and elevator bank. They had left. "Is the room bugged?" she asked Anna.

"*Nein.*"

Helen crossed to the minifridge, wrapped ice in a washcloth, and placed it on Anna's eye. "I'm sorry. Trent is an animal." She sat beside Anna. "How did we become so submissive?"

"We both know. He is effective."

"Anna, I need your help. Aside from Lance, you're the only one I trust."

"You are my friend."

Helen patted Anna's hand. "We have to go to the District. Tonight."

"Why?"

"The patent attorney. But if Trent learns of this—"

"I know. He'll kill us."

Loring Jet

E. Dixon Loring sprawled across his couch and stared out his cabin window to the hiss of rushing air. Low cabin lights cast a glare on the window as he gazed at the dark Rockies below.

How far Karbonville was: the old town was 20,000 feet below, 2500 miles to the east, and forty years away—but it seemed farther than that. Such an ugly place: mountain streets, corner bars, black-brick churches, small-thinking people whose lives consisted of hourly wages, brood-rearing, drinking, and brawling. He'd seen and fought his future early, at first by selling magazine subscriptions to people struggling to pay their electric bills. Later by learning to kick a football higher, straighter, and farther than classmates who bullied him for his frail physique. Placekicking: that was the revelation. Fresh, well-rested, he'd trot onto the field in the final moments to kick while the others, bruised, bloodied, and beaten, would drag themselves back for just one more play. He'd kick the field goal, win the game, and soak in the adulation, while the others who'd fought on the front lines the entire game were forgotten. Let others do the work. Reserve the killing blow for yourself. That was showmanship. That was power. It had bought him a scholarship to Penn State. An early career in investment banking that led to founding Comline Venture Capital, which financed successful biotech, software, and research companies that he leveraged. All the while, enhancing his showman image, surrounding himself with the beautiful and buxom, creating an image that focused on him so as to leave the rest of the Collaborate free to work, unencumbered by publicity. He put another pillow beneath his head.

"Excuse me, Mr. Loring," said a strikingly attractive woman with pale blue eyes. "Mr. Grayson is on the line."

"I'll take it here," he said, only glancing at the form-fitting skirt curved over her tight rear, swooshing as she left.

A six-foot screen snapped on with the satellite image of Frederick Grayson, his hands cradling his cane as he sat in the back of a limousine. "How was your tête-à-tête, Dixon?"

"Merlin, they're pathetic," Loring said.

"It would be a catastrophic mistake to underestimate them."

"That's near impossible." Fixing his pillow, "I caught a replay of the press conference."

"There's more." Grayson summarized the past ten hours.

"Disturbing, in light of the Tiburon incident," Loring said.

"The Agency could be involved."

"I didn't get that impression from Brocks. She knew about it, yes, but I don't think she's responsible. Besides, the foray at Tiburon reeked of amateurs."

"So does setting up a woman to impersonate Kincaid's wife."

"Good point. You know, Brocks said that there could be a third player in all of this."

"Do you believe her?"

Loring sat up. "This is a delicate time for us. The closer we come to Implementation, the more vulnerable we become. Add in a wild card, you have the formula for disaster. Merlin, we've got to find the connection. That woman's the key."

"I suggest we observe her, discreetly. She'll lead us to her cohort."

"What if she doesn't appear again?"

"She will. She must." Grayson waited as Loring poured a gin. "Dixon, whatever Brocks said, whatever impression she gave, I do not believe that, as the time draws near, she will stand by and do nothing, no matter how strong our position. You might want to convene a Quorum."

"What for?"

"To accelerate the timetable."

Laboratory for the Research of Genetic and Molecular Therapy at BFMC

Kevin swiped his key card through the slot and put his thumb on the screen. The security system recognized him. The metal door clicked open as the LCD on the wall flashed: Personnel in Lab: 0.

The door closed behind him, immersing him in a silent, temperature-controlled darkness. Gradually, sounds of high-pitched hums from incubators and freezers filled the room. He'd spent the last few hours walking alone on the streets, trying to crystallize his thoughts. He needed a familiar place to think. This place was home.

The Helen he'd met certainly was not his wife. What had she meant by saying more than his career depended on keeping V_7 in his head? And the way she'd left just seconds before Grayson and Tetlow showed up? As if she'd been warned. As if she feared them. Tetlow and Grayson were bureaucratic obstructions, but menacing? They'd been generous to him over the years: unlimited equipment, manpower, funding. But then again, that was for his *work*, not for him. And the way Tetlow had questioned him about Helen Morgan, as if he had no life and weren't entitled to one. Maybe he had it wrong: maybe it was Tetlow who feared that reporter, not the other way around.

He flipped a series of switches on the wall. Banks of fluorescent overheads snapped on, and surged in progressive waves to the lab's distant recesses. Kevin's Laboratory for the Research of Genetic and

Molecular Therapy was a three-storied temple of biotechnology. This floor, the second, was dedicated to isolating and identifying genes, and characterizing unique proteins. The floor above, for synthesizing expression vectors like HACV.V$_7$. The floor below, an animal lab where research products of the other two floors underwent preclinical testing in mice, rats, and, rarely, gibbons or chimpanzees. He looked out across a maze of workbenches, computer stations, and delicate free-standing equipment: biological safety cabinets for handling powerful chemicals; robotic arms for culturing cells; plate dispensers and universal microplate readers for assaying; fluorometers for measuring unique colors cast by specially tagged genes and proteins; and microscopes connected to computers and mounted cameras for analyzing and photographing specimens. There were automated DNA sequencers, little tan boxes that shot lasers at fluorescent-dyed DNA fragments in an applied electric field, making it possible to identify thousands of chemical bases in minutes. There were reagents for analyzing and manipulating DNA genes and proteins: plasmid kits for inserting isolated genes into cell cultures; probes for forming hybrids with experimental DNA; polymerase chain reaction (PCR) kits to duplicate DNA; fluorescent dyes for tagging different human chromosomes; and blot kits for identifying DNA fragments and proteins. And, of course, software programs to analyze it all and compare it with databases from around the world. The physical and intellectual fruits of this floor were sent upstairs, where vectors were designed. All under his control.

Kevin stared at a workstation that contained a program for predicting protein structure. Uncle Dermot had boasted that he'd designed the ultimate program for that task, but did such a program ever exist? It had been ten years, and Kevin had never seen anything remotely resembling his uncle's claim.

"I thought you might be here," said a voice behind him.

Kevin froze, caught his breath, and turned. Behind him stood Peter Nguyen, his gifted postdoc out of the University of Pennsylvania, across town on the other side of the river. "Working late? And in the dark?"

"Where else would I be?" Nguyen said. "I'm surprised you didn't come here after the press conference."

"I had other things demanding my attention. Any problems here?"

"I'm not sure. After the bomb scare in the auditorium, security checked this place thoroughly. Very thoroughly. As if they were look-ing for more than a bomb."

"Such as?"

"I don't know, Doctor. They didn't take anything. Didn't disrupt anything, either. But they were definitely looking for *something*."

"Is that why you're still here? To see if they were coming back?"

"Maybe, in part."

"Well, apparently they're not. So it's late and you can go home." *And I can have some quiet time to think.*

"You hired me to be thorough," Nguyen said.

"I hired you because you're brilliant and have real insights into transfection processes." *That, and you're the only one in the lab I com-pletely trust, because you've never asked for anything.* "So now that you've been suitably complimented, you can go home happy."

"There's nothing for me there."

Kevin sighed. "Man, do I ever know that feeling." Seating himself at a workstation, "It's been a year. Is there any chance she's coming back?"

"Divorce papers haven't been filed. So I suppose there's a chance."

"I don't know what's worse—knowing that there's a chance or knowing that there isn't."

Nguyen shoved his hands in his pockets and looked away.

Kevin remembered that reaction from Nguyen, just before learn-ing of the K_4 debacle. "You said that you were still here *in part* for security. What's the rest of it?"

"We have a big problem downstairs." He hesitated. "With the *pxr1* knockouts."

Kevin charged the elevator at the far end of the floor, Nguyen three steps behind him. He pounded the *down* button. "Come on."

The *pxr1* gene knockout mice were the first animals that had suc-cessfully undergone germline gene therapy with vector V_7. From there, Kevin had used the vector to carry larger genetic payloads, building success upon success. But the *pxr1* knockout mice had been the first; they'd survived longer following V_7 germline therapy than any other living creature.

The elevator doors opened onto the ground floor. Kevin burst down a glazed brick–lined corridor, turned the corner, and opened a door into a room lined with cages. The odor of urine, feces, impend-ing death assaulted him. Hundreds of cages were stacked against walls and in islands in the middle of the room. Many were empty. Most housed frail white mice, staggering blindly, limbs twitching, or convulsing violently.

"Many are dead," Nguyen said. "The rest will be soon. It started while you were in surgery this morning."

Kevin stuck a finger between the bars of a cage and touched a quivering, furry ball. The mouse curled tighter. "All of them?"

"Like clockwork."

"You should've isolat—"

"There's no pathogen, Doctor. It's not viral. It's not bacterial." Nguyen stepped dolefully between the cage stacks. "I've taken random tissue samples. The pattern's the same: massive cellular lysis—as if the cells in their bodies are literally exploding." He dug his hands into his coat pockets. "At this point, I think we should assume the worst."

Kevin picked up an empty cage, wrapped his fingers between the bars, and pulled until its metal sides warped. "Damn it! All this time wasted!" He flung it aside and picked up another empty cage and hurled it at the brick wall, but it bounced off and only fueled his rage. He picked up a third cage and heaved it at the large window partition. The window shattered, showering the room with glass shards.

Nguyen retreated to the far wall and watched the large man's rage slowly dissipate.

Spent, Kevin surveyed the ruins surrounding him. Slowly, his hands covered his face. It was the end of everything. "V_7 doesn't work!"

ACGD Commercial #2—

"Germline Gene Therapy: Fix the Problem, for Good"

The following commercial aired on all major broadcast and cable networks the evening of Monday, January 20, and late night/early morning Tuesday, January 21:

> [VIDEO]: Opening shot of a typical, middle-class suburban street of single-family houses. Close-up on one driveway: a frustrated man working under the hood of a new car. Dr. Kevin Kincaid walks on camera.

DR. KEVIN KINCAID (TO MAN UNDER HOOD OF CAR): What's the problem, Sam?

SAM: Something's always going wrong with this lousy engine!

KINCAID: What is it this time?

SAM: The distributor.

KINCAID: Why don't you give the car a new paint job?

SAM (LOOKING UP FROM THE HOOD): Are you nuts? What good would that do? You have to fix the problem!

KINCAID (TURNS TO CAMERA): Ridiculous, isn't it? You can't possibly expect to fix a car's engine by painting the hood . . .

> [VIDEO]: Switch to sick child laying in hospital bed. Kincaid standing bedside.

KINCAID: . . . any more than you can cure many genetic diseases by giving chemicals and radiation. To cure the disease, you've got to fix the body's engines. You've got to fix the problem in each and every cell.

> [VIDEO]: Transition to Animated Sequence: CGI (computer-generated imaging) of cell and center of cell (nucleus). Zoom in on center of cell, with crumpled white strings (chromosomes) and one black, misshapen string (deformed chromosome).

KINCAID (VOICEOVER [VO]): In the center of every cell in our body is a nucleus. The nucleus contains strands of DNA, called chromosomes. Each chromosome contains hundreds or thousands of genes made of DNA. These genes are the blueprints for our bodies. But sometimes, something goes terribly wrong.

> [VIDEO]: Animated Sequence: Focuses in on misshapen black string.

KINCAID (VO): Just a few mistaken DNA molecules on one gene of one chromosome can mean a lifetime of suffering.

> [VIDEO]: Split screen. Animated Sequence on left. Montage of sick
> children on right.

KINCAID (VO): Sickle cell, Tay-Sachs, beta-thalassemia, the list goes on. No matter what medicines we give these children, we'll never fix their engines—their genes. And the worst part is, if these children survive, *their children* will either suffer from, or carry the disease, too. Unless . . .

> [VIDEO]: Full-screen CGI Animation: A bubble-enclosed white string
> (new chromosome) enters the cell and penetrates the
> nucleus. The white chromosome replaces the misshapen
> black chromosome.

KINCAID (VO): Unless we get rid of disease-causing genes in every cell. Replace them with healthy, working genes. "Why don't we?" you ask. Because, by the time we are born, it's probably too late. There are just too many cells in our bodies to fix. To save these children, we have to fix their genes *before* they are born.

> [VIDEO]: CGI Animation: Pull back to reveal many cells with
> deformed black chromosomes replaced by healthy white
> chromosomes. Then hundreds of cells. Then the outline of
> an arm. Then the outline of a recognizably human fetus.
>
> Transition to Live Action: A pregnant woman receiving an
> injection in the hospital. She smiles as a doctor withdraws a
> needle (not seen clearly on camera).

KINCAID (VO): It's called *germline gene therapy*. It will fix her baby's cells before it's born. And her grandchildren will be saved from the disease, too.

> [VIDEO]: Live Action: Wide-angle shot of healthy babies in nursery.

KINCAID (VO): But there are those in Congress who want to *deny you and your children* access to germline gene therapy.

> [VIDEO]: Healthy babies replaced by stills of children visibly suffering
> from genetic diseases.

KINCAID (VO): Call your senators! Tell them you want to permit research for germline gene therapy!

> *[VIDEO]: Stills of suffering children replaced by healthy babies.*

KINCAID (VO): Demand that your senators *support* House Bill 601!

> *[VIDEO]: Transition to pregnant woman, from previous scene, now smiling in her hospital bed. Freeze-frame of her cuddling a healthy newborn.*

KINCAID (VO): Give our children a chance!

> *[VIDEO]: End Tag: Add supered letters to lower third of screen.*
> *SUPPORT HOUSE BILL 601!*
> *GIVE OUR CHILDREN A CHANCE!SM*
> *Paid for by the Association to Cure Genetic Disabilities.*
> *Hold image for five seconds. Fade to black.*

4

TUESDAY, JANUARY 21
Washington, D.C., NW   *12:08 A.M.*

Helen drove the silver Pontiac down Connecticut Avenue. Anna squirmed nervously beside her. Street lamps marched along the avenue, each briefly and dimly lighting the car as it headed deeper into the city. Helen knew it was risky to steal a car for an unsanctioned operation, but she'd been careful to wear gloves with the fingertips sanded down, to use her homemade Lemon Pop to unlock the car's door, and to use a standard combination slide hammer and screwdriver to start the engine. She had no time for further precautions: it was four hours to Washington with a stop at Anna's Rockville apartment to pick up equipment, two hours for the mission itself, and three for the return. She had to be back in Philadelphia before dawn.

"When all is settled with Herr Doctor Kincaid, I am finished," Anna said, touching her swollen cheek. "When Trent recruited me, I accepted because I thought he was visionary. When did he change? Or was he always this way?"

Helen couldn't answer for herself, let alone Anna. Trent had found her two years ago: rudderless, bitter, running. He'd arranged for plastic surgery, a new identity, a channel for her rage. But he'd never fully assimilated her brother. What telltale signs had Lance seen that she had missed?

"Helen, are you certain of what we do?"

"I know Kincaid. His habits, his needs, his pain. I know how he'll respond to change."

"In playing the part of the doctor's wife, could it be that you have become too close to him?"

Helen looked to Anna, then turned back to the road. Supplied with hundreds of videotapes, voice recordings, and detailed documents, she'd spent the last year perfecting the image of Helen Kincaid: hairstyle, dress, gait, preferences, peeves, mannerisms, expressions, diction, personal philosophy—all that made Helen Kincaid unique to Kevin. All to enhance the natural physical resemblance that plastic surgery had provided. All to complete her mission. Was Anna right? Had she allowed herself to be drawn too close to him? She'd recklessly announced K_4's existence to prove to herself, not the mission, that she was not falling for a prince of the Collaborate. And now, here in the District, she was risking everything, again. "I know who I am," she said. *I just don't know what I am.*

Anna frowned, then reached under her seat, withdrew a laptop computer, and booted it. "You know him best. Will the Program convince him?"

A block behind them, a navy blue Toyota cautiously followed.

Laboratory for the Research of Genetic and Molecular Therapy at BFMC (Kincaid's Lab)

Peter Nguyen had watched Dr. Kincaid sacrifice three mice—two dying and one apparently healthy—remove the vital organs, section and stain them, and study the slides under low- and high-power microscopes. Cardiac, bone, lung, liver, striated muscle, nerve, kidney cells—all looked like tiny jelly-filled balloons dropped from a roof onto a sidewalk. "Massive cellular lysis," Kevin said, lifting his head from the eyepiece. "You're running cultures, aren't you?"

"Sure. But I don't think there's a pathogen."

"On what basis?"

"I found ten mice from another batch that had been mislabeled and mistakenly put in the same room as the knockouts for two weeks. They'd received the same diet, been examined by the same handlers, yet none of them have come down with the disorder. So if there is a pathogen, it isn't airborne. Other transmission modes seem even less likely." Nguyen shifted on his stool. "It must be associated with the vector expression system."

"But that was administered while the animals were still embryos. They're fully developed adults. Why would they be dying *now*?"

Nguyen hopped off his stool. "Maybe I could answer that if I knew V_7's full structure."

"I'll figure it out in time," Kevin said. He put another slide under the microscope.

"And what are the rest of us supposed to do till then? No one likes being left out."

Kevin rubbed his eyes, then put another slide under the microscope. "Everyone in the lab gets credit." He studied the slide. "We work together in teams, each tackling separate components of the vector. The harpoon, the cochleate cylinder, transport proteins—"

"But they're assembled in only one place, Doctor. *Your* mind."

"That's my job."

"But it's not good science, and honestly, Doctor, it's very disheartening. None of us working here ever gets to see the big picture. It's like working an assembly line without ever seeing the final product. There's accountability, but no personal satisfaction. None of us has ever seen $HACV.V_7$'s full design." He paused. "The morale in this lab has never been lower. The line at the copier is so long, you have to take a number to photostat your curriculum vitae."

Kevin looked up from the slide. "Look how much we've accomplished!"

"The feeling is more 'Look how much *Dr. Kincaid* has accomplished.'"

"There's no reason people should feel that way."

"Forget the assembly line image. Here's a better one. Imagine working on a submarine: you're isolated, cramped, living in close quarters with no luxuries, no privacy, and you don't see anything other than pipes running through your tiny bunk or instruments at your duty station. You never see where you're going. You never know for sure where you've been. Except you, Doctor. You're the only one who gets to look through the periscope."

"If that's true, then why hasn't anyone come forward and told me? Ever?"

"You really don't know?"

Nguyen hesitated. "You're unapproachable."

"My office door has always been open—to everyone. At any hour for any reason."

"No, that's not it. You're unapproachable because you're—too brilliant."

"Peter, I'm not some egotistical bast—"

"You're always three steps ahead of everyone. Before anyone finishes their first sentence, you've analyzed their argument, formulated yours, proposed and analyzed their counterarguments, and devised your own winning rebuttal. It's intimidating."

Kevin remembered in perfect detail an early November morning recess: the caustic smell of burning leaves, the wind chilling his chest as it sliced through his skimpy cloth jacket. He was in fourth grade and standing inside the school's gates, where cracked asphalt met the school yard's only patch of grass. He watched nine boys play touch football with a makeshift ball of plastic and black tape. They'd let a new kid play, even though he was gawky and wore a tweed coat that hampered his running. There might never be a better time. Kevin felt his feet slowly shuffling over the bumpy, hard grass toward the boys. This time, *this time*, it would be different. He neared their line of scrimmage. They stopped. Jimmy Farber, the tall boy with the crew cut, turned toward him. He grinned. "Dumb-ass book-boy!" he yelled. Two of the other boys joined in. Then the new boy with the tweed coat. Then all of them. Kevin glanced down to his left: tucked under his arm was *A Primer on Solid and Plane Geometry,* a blue bookmark protruding from page 273. The image faded. His mind began showering him with painful memories, forcing him to relive shunnings that stretched from elementary to high school and a procession of college roommates who'd ignore him after the first week. Always alone: the curse of the gifted child. "I had no idea."

"Once the other staffers find out that V_7's failed, they're going to leave in droves."

K Street, NW
Washington, D.C.

"Are you in?" Helen asked.

SIA Security Systems' home page popped on Anna's laptop screen just as the car turned onto K Street. "Not yet," Anna replied.

Helen looked out the passenger window as the car passed an

alabaster and glass building on a city block dominated by high-powered attorneys and lobbyists. "There it is." She slowed the Pontiac, peered at a small red sticker on the building's thick glass doors marked "Protected by SIA Security Systems," turned the corner, and parked between two minivans.

Anna typed in the building's address, and on-screen, pulled down a trio of small windows: a closed-circuit-TV view of the building's front lobby, a detailed schematic of the first floor, and a lock on the front-door security pad. "We have direct access to the building's security system, courtesy of SIA's mainframe."

"Oh, you're good."

"Trent thought so, too. He provided all my equipment. Strange it is that he has not called on me more often to use it."

"No stranger than him knowing where the Program is, and doing nothing about it." Helen put on tight, black gloves, then reached into the backseat and grabbed a canvas bag.

"You understand that I cannot guarantee overriding all security measures."

"Anna, we already agreed. If necessary, you're to cut me loose."

A gust of wind whipped through Helen's leather jacket as she opened the door. Traffic was sparse. The street deserted. She turned the corner and ducked into the target building's alcove. Thick glass doors sealed by magnetic locks led to the lobby. Satisfied that the lobby was empty, she stepped to a keypad on the wall. Eyes scanning the street, she knelt, unzipped the bag, withdrew a portable headset, and pressed it to her ear. Anna's voice came through. "Got it," she answered, then punched in an eight-digit code. Magnetic locks released the right glass door. She slipped inside then slinked across the building's lobby while trying to muffle her footsteps, echoing on the tiled floor. Bolts slammed behind her, their echoes reverberating across the atrium ceiling. She whirled around to the front door. A surveillance camera swiveled slowly in her direction—and stopped.

"Don't worry. It is me," Anna's voice sounded in Helen's headset. "I sealed the main entrance. The building is empty."

Down K Street, behind the wheel of a navy blue Toyota, a man placed a call on a scrambled digital phone. "She's entered the building." He listened as a distorted voice responded. After that, he asked, "And if she's discovered?"

Helen exited the stairwell on the fourth floor. The corridor had maroon carpeting, matching walls, and was flanked by recessed doorways with decorative windowpanes. A surveillance camera panned the hallway, then focused on her.

"Suite 407. Third on your left," Anna's voice sounded in her headset.

The camera followed Helen to a suite with gold relief on an oak door:

DIEHL, TEASDALE, & WILCOX
PATENT ATTORNEYS

After disarming the office's alarm system with the PIN number Anna transmitted, Helen unzipped the canvas bag and pulled out a hand-sized cordless cylinder with a needlelike projection, and an electric pinch gun. She plugged the projection into the top lock and turned on the power. The device vibrated in her hand as the projection, the rake, struck up and down within the lock, opening pin and disc tumbler cylinders. Ten seconds later, the lock clicked. She repeated the process on the second lock, then swung the door open. Light from the hallway faintly lit a receptionist's desk. She took out a pair of night-vision goggles.

"There are no defense systems inside the office," Anna said.

Helen put on her goggles and cautiously entered. The suite had three offices, two conference rooms, and a bathroom off the reception hub. All doors were open, except for the one marked "Robert Diehl, JD." "I'm inside. No problems."

"Only Diehl's station will have the Program."

Helen went to Diehl's door and turned the handle. It was unlocked. She started to swing open the door, but stopped. It felt wrong, dead wrong: the Program was one of the Collaborate's key components. Certainly, the patent attorney needed a confidential copy, and according to Trent, the man had used it for years. But protecting such a critical piece of software with just a mundane security system? "Anna, it's too easy. We missed something."

"But SIA Security Systems does not—"

"I'm telling you there's additional security. I can feel it."

"Very well. Do precisely as I say. First, open the door, very slowly. No more than seven centimeters a second. Then gently, gently peer in."

Helen carefully turned the handle and pushed the door in, imagining a ruler along the floor, ticking off inches. The hinges released a long, guttural creak. "I'm in. What am I looking for?"

"Photoelectric cells. Motion detectors. Temperature sensors. The first two we manage. But there is nothing in your bag to defeat a temperature-sensitive sensor. First, scan floor and molding. See any small rectangular attachments to any wall, perhaps a few inches above the floor?"

Helen surveyed the room: a desk, chairs, couch, coffee table, and computer station against the back wall. Nothing along the molding.

"Now check the walls. Any unusual wall hangings?"

"Uh, no."

"Check electrical sockets. Sometimes they can be disguised as plug-in room fresheners."

"Nope."

"Check the ceiling. There should only be an overhead light, a smoke detector, usually round, and a sprinkler head. Anything else, tell me."

"Looks innocuous." Helen scoured the ceiling. "Nope, everything looks—wait! I see a small block pasted against the ceiling, but it also has a—looks like a cylinder embedded in it."

"A motion detector. A full 360-degree access with look-down. Probably quite sensitive."

"You can beat motion detectors with radio frequency interference."

"Not high-performance ones. It would take an expert. But you are there. I am here."

Helen clenched the door. "I'm going through with it!"

Anna exhaled. "You will have to move at the same slow pace. Two to three inches at a time. No sudden moves. How far is it to computer?"

"Oh, forty feet."

After hesitating, "You cannot cross the room in less than six minutes. Then, at the same pace, you must attach the CD-burner, access and download files, and erase signs that files were copied. Then, you have the same six-minute crawl back to the door."

Helen stared at the computer on the wall as if it were on the far side of Death Valley. Slinging one arm through the bag, she lay on her stomach and began the long, tedious crawl. Her fingernails bit into the

Berber carpet, each stunted pile loop a guidepost. She moved forward, thirty loops at a time. First one hand, then the other—maddeningly slow. Part of her mind concentrated on the systematic, autonomic crawl across the floor; part wandered, reflecting on how she'd come to this place. All roads led to Trent. How did he know so much about the Program? Why had he shared that knowledge with the rest of the Committee, yet forbidden them from stealing it, especially with the Collaborate so close to victory? What was Trent saving it for?

She grasped the base of a leather chair. Palm over palm, she pulled herself up, slithered into the seat, and buried herself in its contour. "Anna, I'm at the computer." Panting, "I don't know if I can keep this up."

"Boot the system. I will do the rest remotely."

"I thought we needed to attach the CD-burner to copy the Program files."

"I will download all Program files and remotely perform proper file wipes from here."

"If it's so simple, why didn't we plan it this way? What's the catch?"

"My laptop cannot accommodate two separate connections. To access Diehl's freestanding system, I must terminate the connection to building security system. I cannot download and watch your back at the same time."

Helen quickly pressed the PC's *power* button. "Do it."

Anna had stormed past Diehl's pitiful security measures, and was watching the last copy of his files float from his system to hers. When it finished, she eliminated any trace that the files had been copied. "Helen, you can shut it down, but do not power off until the computer says it is safe to do so. Otherwise, when Diehl boots his system, he will get a corruption reading." After Helen acknowledged, Anna terminated the link to Diehl's computer, then reestablished the connection to SIA Security Systems. "Oh my God!"

The observer in the blue Toyota watched two men in long woolen coats pull up in front of the building, punch in the proper codes on the exterior keypad, and enter. He'd already called his superior.

Instructions would be forthcoming, he'd been told, so stand by. Another thirty seconds, and it would be too late. There was no choice: he opened his laptop.

Helen flowed from the chair to the floor, then spread herself across the carpeting and prepared for the tedious crawl across the room.

"Oh my God!" Anna blared in her ear. "You must have set off the alarm. There are two men in the lobby. They will be there in seconds. Get out! Now!"

Helen jumped to her feet and ran out of the office, slamming the doors behind her. She ripped the night-vision goggles from her face and scanned up and down the corridor. Elevators? No, she'd be trapped. The stairs? No, they'll come that way. Duck into another office? And risk setting off another alarm? She looked back at the elevators. "Anna, are they still in the lobby?"

"Yes."

"Take control of the elevators. Lock one at the lobby and send the other to the fifth floor."

"But—"

"Do it!"

Seconds later, the left elevator display changed from "L" to "2."

"Are they still downstairs?" Helen asked.

"Yes. Watching the elevator."

"Good." She opened the stairwell door. "I'll wait on the stairs, by the third-floor landing. Tell me if they enter the stairwell. When the elevator reaches the fifth floor, hold it there a few seconds, then send it back to the lobby."

"Why?"

"They'll think I'm taking the elevator down from the fifth floor. They'll naturally wait in the lobby for me to deliver myself right into their hands. But when the elevator comes back empty, they'll both take it to the fifth floor. With luck, I'll be able to walk right out of the building."

"Trent is right. You are the most dangerous of us. Am sending the elevator down." A moment later, "As you predicted, they are waiting."

"Disable the fire alarm," Helen whispered, trying to keep her voice from echoing in the stairwell. "This way, I can just scoot out the stairwell onto the street."

Anna paused. "They are taking the elevator."

"Now's my chance. Is the fire alarm disabled?"

She listened to pounding on the keyboard. "Damn! I cannot disable fire alarm!"

"It's okay, Anna. Anyone waiting out front?"

A long hesitation. "I do not know. The cameras do not look that far onto the street."

Helen faced the dilemma. Continue down the stairwell and exit onto the street, and she'd set off the alarm, removing any doubt that someone had breached Diehl's office. Exit the front lobby, she risked capture. "I'm coming out the front." She slinked down the stairwell, exited, and headed across the lobby. She checked her footsteps, her back, then hurried to the keypad and punched in the sequence. The magnetic locks released. She pushed open the thick glass door.

Two men in black coats stepped off the elevator. Each checked opposite ends of the corridor. "Nothing here," said one. "You check the stairs. I'll take the office."

Helen peered at K Street from the building alcove, but saw no parked cars, except for a blue sedan at the far end of the block, across the street. She bundled her coat and dashed down the street. Around the corner. And into her car.

"I looped the video in the surveillance cameras and inserted new time stamps," Anna said as they sped off. "There will be no photographic evidence of break-in."

"Great. Thanks for everything."

"You will drop me off at my apartment, and I will copy the Program to CD, yes?"

Helen glanced at her watch. "We just might make it."

The man stood, arms akimbo, surveying Diehl's office. Computer, files, furniture, all appeared undisturbed. He looked up at the motion detector. "If only you were a goddamn camera."

His partner entered the room. "Didn't see nothing. You?"

"Same. Think anyone was here?"

"Dunno. But don't touch anything. I'll order up a forensic team. And a system analyst. They'll find—"

A whooping, high-pitched siren rang through the air.

Water rained from the ceiling and began dousing the computer, the desk, the carpet. The man glanced up at the overhead sprinkler spraying water onto the room. "The fuck did you do?" he screamed at his partner.

"I didn't do nothing!"

"It's all ruined. They'll blame us, you know!"

The partner wiped water from his face. "My story is that thing," pointing to the motion detector, "went haywire. Like the alarm."

"Works for me."

Helen turned onto Connecticut Avenue and noticed Anna staring out the window and mumbling to herself. "Problem, Anna?"

"I do not understand why I could not disable the alarm system."

"You were under the gun. We both were."

"No. I was locked out."

Kincaid's Lab

Kevin started, "You wanted to know the details of V_7? I'll show you."

Nguyen closed the conference room door then sat at the end of the long rectangular table.

Kevin, black marker in hand, was at the whiteboard on the far wall. "We begin with basics. The mouse: murine cells." He drew two concentric circles: a thin outer ring and a thick, double-layered inner one. "The outer cell membrane and the inner bilipid layer nuclear membrane," he said, pointing to each. Within the innermost circle, he drew pairs of squiggly lines. Beside them he wrote the number "20." "The murine cell nucleus, with its normal contingent of nineteen nonsexual chromosome pairs and one sex chromosome pair. This mouse is condemned to death because it's missing the critical functioning *pxr1* gene. We rescued these mice not just by supplying a functioning *pxr1* gene, but by inserting it on an *entirely new pair of chromosomes,* artificially generated here, in this lab. And by getting those synthetic chromosome pairs into the murine cell nucleus, where they became part of the mouse cell's genetic blueprint."

Nguyen listened attentively. Though this information was far beneath him, the preamble heightened his anticipation.

"Here are the five enormous hurdles our vector had to overcome." He wrote on the board:

HURDLES FOR VECTOR:
1. Carry a big DNA payload
2. Penetrate cell barrier membranes
3. Deliver DNA payload without disrupting cell
4. Have a 100% transfection rate
5. Deliver *ONLY ONE* payload per cell

"First, V_7 had to be able to carry a very large payload. Now, existing vectors can only transport twenty thousand to fifty thousand DNA bases, which is only enough for a few genes. We wanted our vector to lug entire chromosomes, which contain *millions* of DNA bases."

Nguyen crossed his arms. "Through both membranes? Quite a feat."

"Of course. For any vector to be effective, it has to be able to get the pair of artificial chromosomes through both the outer cellular membrane, and the even more formidable inner nuclear membrane surrounding the cell's DNA. If it can't get the payload DNA, whether it's genes or chromosomes, to penetrate both membrane barriers, it's a failure. Naturally, it also has to deliver that payload without destroying the cell," Kevin said, underlining point number three.

"You expect one hundred percent transfection? That's ten times more efficient than any other vector developed. You're demanding that a vector insert chromosomes into *every* cell."

"But if it fails to do so you can wind up killing the organism—or patient."

"You need at least one vector with a DNA payload for each and every cell you target."

"Exactly, Peter. But the last point is the most overlooked and most difficult hurdle to overcome. The vector has to be 'smart enough' to deliver only one chromosome-pair payload to each cell—and one pair only. If, for example, four or five individual vectors each delivered a pair of chromosome payload to the same cell, that cell would wind up with too many copies of a chromosome."

"Setting the stage for a cascade of genetic defects like—"

"Like Down syndrome, where patients have too many copies of Chromosome 21."

Nguyen considered the implications of the specs. "Somehow, the vector has to distinguish between cells that have been infused with the payload DNA and those that haven't. Otherwise, some cells will wind up with too many copies of chromosomes, and others won't receive any. V_7 overcomes all of these hurdles?"

Kevin planted both palms on the table. "This, Peter, is the work of art to which every person in this lab contributed. I was just lucky enough to assemble the pieces." He turned to the whiteboard and began drawing furiously with three colored markers. "This is what you've all built," he announced as he finished, "HACV.V_7."

Nguyen stared at the drawing and shook his head.

"Not what you expected, huh?"

"It looks like a burrito with a pointed tail and an oversized pea in its belly."

"V_7's design is an amalgam of concepts borrowed from nature, an MIT-AT&T collaboration, material researchers at Scripps Institute and UC-Santa Barbara, and NASA."

"NASA?"

"Think of V_7 as being like the old Saturn rockets, a three-stage delivery system, except that its payload is a pair of new chromosomes instead of astronauts." Turning to the whiteboard, "The first stage, a viral-like 'harpoon,'" pointing to the green tail, "developed by Pratt's team. And the attached cochlear cylinder," pointing at the red burrito, "developed by Gensini's team."

Nguyen studied the board.

"The harpoon resembles the tightly coiled proteins in HIV and influenza viruses. It has a barbed end that attaches into the cell's outer membrane, like a whaling harpoon. This, in turn, is attached to a cyclic peptide nanotube. The nanotube, in turn, is attached to a cochlear cylinder, which is a sheet of lipid rolled up like a crepe. The harpoon pierces the outer cell membrane with a small, temporary opening provided by the nanotube. The cochlear cylinder unwinds, exposing a small capsule," he said, pointing to the blue pea. "The capsule plunges through the cell membrane opening created by the harpoon and nanotube. And voilá, the capsule, containing the chromosome payload, is in the cell cytoplasm, and is ready for stage two."

"What prevents different vectors from harpooning the same cell?" Nguyen asked.

"The harpoon stays behind," Kevin said. "The nanotube collapses. The cell membrane seals around it. And," pointing to the red cylinder, "the rolled-up cochlear cylinder has sites on its exterior that are repulsed by the harpoon. In short, the cylinder won't unfurl and release the capsule if the cell has already been implanted by another individual vector."

Nguyen's eyes widened.

"The second stage is the capsule." Kevin drew a dotted line from the blue pea and extended it into the cell, just outside the inner circle of the nucleus. "The capsule, or shell, containing the artificial chromosomes, is composed of copies of a single protein, bound together to form an icosahedron—a crystal with twenty triangular faces, like those in adenoviruses and polio virus. Except that this shell was designed to be broken apart by the cell's enzymes. A brilliant piece of biochemical wizardry, courtesy of DeVries's team." He wrote on top of the capsule in black marker.

"And that releases the capsule's contents, the synthetic chromosome pair, intact?"

"Right. Now, for the third stage." Kevin drew a convoluted pair of chromosomes in blue, and speckled them with black, green, and red dots. "Inside the capsule are V_7's payload chromosomes, neatly compacted, with the assistance of nucleosome proteins designed by Kanami's team," pointing to the black dots. "Once the capsular proteins are degraded, the DNA strands tend to uncoil into their natural state in solution. This stresses the nucleosome proteins holding the DNA taut, and ultimately, dislodges the nucleosomes." In blue, he drew a pair of classic, recognizable double-helix chromosomes.

"What are those?" Nguyen asked, pointing at the green and red dots on the previous picture.

Adding green and red squiggly lines to the chromosome pair he'd drawn in the outer portion of the cell, "The keys to it all. As we know, getting man-made materials through the cell's inner, double-layered nuclear membrane is tough—real tough. But the nucleus is constantly transporting its own molecules in and out of that membrane through its own complex pore system. Well, we've found a way to temporarily hijack the nuclear membrane's own pore system to get our artificial chromosomes inside the nucleus. We did it by attaching two essential proteins to the artificial chromosomes." Pointing to the green dot, "This one. A nuclear localization signal, NLS—a short sequence of amino acids that acts like a key to open the nuclear pore 'door.' And," pointing to a red dot, "the importin-gamma protein that drags the DNA right up to the nuclear pore. The artificial chromosomes are drawn into the nucleus like a kid slurping spaghetti. The last two proteins are courtesy of Chin's group and Horowitz's team." Kevin cupped his hands. "And there you have it. That new chromosome pair is now permanently part of the mouse cell's blueprint. When that cell divides, it'll make a new line of cells with twenty-one, not twenty chromosomes. Forever."

"Stunning!"

"You all made the music. I just conducted." Kevin stared at the drawing of the cellular nucleus. "So what the hell went wrong?"

Loring Estate
Santa Fe, New Mexico

Loring stared out his French windows. The 20,000-volume library in Santa Fe was the smallest on his estates, yet had the best view: a high desert plateau with uplifted jagged peaks to the horizon. He'd arrived before sunset and would be departing before sunrise. No time for anything but work as the last component of the Plan neared completion. Perhaps he'd see full Implementation in his lifetime. If not, well, he had the rare opportunity to both write and right history.

The grandfather clock chimed. The library doors automatically sealed. Two sets of dark drapes flew across and covered the glass vista. Soft, low-frequency music flooded the chamber to mask sensitive communications. Loring walked to a mirror on the far wall, tightened his Windsor knot, then placed his index and third finger beneath the right lower corner of the frame. A red light behind the mirror scanned his face from top to bottom, left to right. The lower half of the mirror grew opaque. A second later, white lettering flashed across the bottom:

FACIAL CAPILLARY PATTERN SCANNED. EDWIN DIXON LORING RECOGNIZED. INCOMING TRANSMISSION: 1 min 28 sec

He poured himself a sherry, then seated himself in a settee opposite the bolted doors. Red, blue, green lights scanned him. In the background, a faint A-minor chord chimed.

A rotund man with a silhouette reminiscent of Alfred Hitchcock's appeared sitting in the far corner of the room.

Loring respectfully nodded. "Mr. Bertram." He never knew where the transmission originated: London, Istanbul, Sydney, Kuala Lumpur, across town? The holographic intranet system kept transmission and receptive sites secret. Similarly, a projection of Loring's figure was appearing in one of Bertram's facilities, somewhere in the world. The difference: Loring's projection was real; Chairman Bertram's, a sham.

No one had seen Eric Bertram in more than twenty-five years. Loring had met him once almost thirty years ago, at a SciScan stockholders meeting. Bertram had been engaged in a hostile takeover, vilified by company management, investment bankers, and shareholders before he'd taken the podium. The man was obese, and had waddled to center stage amid catcalls and boos. But in a calm, melodic voice, he'd asked the audience seemingly innocuous questions, each answered by a simple, straightforward yes. Question after question, the answer always yes, yes. *Yes.* A half hour later, the podium had been transformed into a pulpit, the stockholders into a joyful chorus singing his praise. Three months later, he broke the company apart and extracted its assets.

Eric Bertram, a flamboyant and spectacularly successful investor and entrepreneur with more than $40 billion in assets, had been a lavish philanthropist until suddenly retiring from public view. Loring never understood why someone with so much power, so much wealth, wouldn't want to trumpet it to the world. The holographic image of the rotund figure was Bertram's appearance thirty years ago. Loring doubted that it bore any semblance to him now. Plastic surgery, weight reduction, hair transplants, the man could look like anyone.

"Your meeting with Brocks?" asked the holographic Bertram from speakers in the library ceiling.

"As projected, Mr. Chairman. They're terrified of implicating themselves." He sipped his sherry. "Their next move will be to step up surveillance. Probe for weakness."

"DARPA's forte is and has always been communications. Despite all our safeguards, they could penetrate our intranet. Which is why, for the next few weeks, we should minimize virtual conferences and rely on the couriers," Bertram said. "Your overall assessment?"

"The bill will be on the Senate floor next week. The ad campaign's in full swing. They've missed their window of opportunity."

"Buying large, expensive blocks of network airtime draws attention. DARPA should have known months ago. Why didn't they?"

"I don't know."

"We are *concerned* about the Tiburon Island incident."

"Mr. Chairman, I broached the matter with Brocks. I don't think they're responsible, but they may know who is. The investigation so far has shown nothing to disprove preliminary findings: a lone male intruder on the Seri reservation was detected and eliminated, but the helicopter carrying his body crashed in the sea. It was a shame we had to destroy the lab. We still don't know for certain whether security was sufficiently compromised to warrant that action. Nonetheless, it's done. At least we still have Delphi."

"I'll consult our contacts within DARPA."

"We could lose those operatives."

"Once 601 passes, we won't need them."

"Mr. Chairman, I suggest moving up the primary branch's timetable twenty-four hours."

Bertram's silhouette remained silent for a moment. "I don't think we need a Quorum to approve that adjustment. Proceed." Then added, "And the secondary branch?"

"I'll be checking on Kincaid tomorrow night. Personally."

Kincaid's Lab   4:47 A.M.

Nguyen lay sprawled across the conference table rhythmically snoring while Kevin stood with his eyes fixed on the whiteboard and his mind writing, erasing, reevaluating failed modifications. With V_7's intricate three-stage delivery system, the permutations for failure were enormous. But karyotyping had proven that the mouse cells contained the artificial chromosome pair transfected by V_7. Why then, after so many cell divisions, after such a long period in the mouse's life cycle, had there been such a catastrophic failure? Finding the cause could take years of testing. The flute began playing "Amazing Grace." His photographic memory again flooded his brain with agonizing images from which he could not escape. He looked at the clock: almost 5 A.M. Yes, a morning run would help. He tiptoed past the sleeping Nguyen. *Purge the body, purge the mind.*

Kevin's arms pumped. His feet pounded the West River Drive's frozen asphalt. Each stride carried him farther down the leafless tree-lined drive. A few yards to his right, the river flowed sluggishly. Freezing air that permeated his lungs brought pain, not euphoric release. Was it too much to expect his run to expunge the image of Helen and V_7's failure—if only for a moment?

The street lamps faded.

The sun appeared, bathing his path in light, in warmth. Trees grew thick, fragrant leaves. Clashing birdsongs arose from their branches. The air smelled warm, moist, lazy. And the river, now a tight, rippling stream, danced over a clear, pebble-laden bed filled with fat fish. Kevin stopped running. A towering man with short red hair, matching beard, and checkered shirt appeared beside him. "Can't catch fish with yer hands," he said, with a light brogue.

"Dad?"

Donnelly Kincaid, Sr., looked down at his sneakers. "I'm not wearin' hip boots, boy. Neither're you," he said. "No sport in catching fish with a net."

"I don't want a net, Dad. It's been so long. Can't we just sit? Talk?"

Donnelly slowly turned his head as if taking in a panoramic view. "I know you're just dyin' to fish, but look around."

Kevin sighed. "You can't hear me, can you?"

"Beautiful, isn't it?"

He gazed up at his father. Proud, strong, defiant, brilliant—before life had pummeled him into submission. "This is Miller's Point. I'm eight. Donny's already—away. This is the last happy time the two of us will ever spend. Mom will die next month."

"Appreciate moments like this, son. Life goes fast," the elder Kincaid said. He produced a rod and reel. "Let's you and I get down to some serious fishing." He lifted the rod. "It's all in the wrist. First you slowly pull back, then you flick forward." Line and lure sailed into the creek. "Now reel it in." He demonstrated, bringing in an empty line. He placed a rod in Kevin's hand, "You try."

"I don't want to fish."

The man's great hands guided Kevin and his rod, but the line flew back. The lure snagged onto a branch behind them. Donnelly tugged gently at first, then began yanking. After a few tries, disgusted, he dropped the rod, traced the line to the branch, and tried to disentangle it. Instead, he pricked his fingers. "Sorry, son, it's hopeless."

Kevin stared at the leafy branch.

"We've got to cut it loose. I'll get the knife." The elder Kincaid took a pocketknife from his jeans and began cutting the line. "Sorry, son. Guess I'm not much of a fisherman."

Kevin's eyes never wavered from the tree. "That's it!"

The light faded. Leaves on the branch withered. Disappeared.

Puffs of warm, condensed breath floated across his view of barren branches. Kevin found himself lying prone on the icy asphalt. "That's it! That's it!"

Adam's Mark Hotel

Helen scrambled into her hotel room and checked the phone: no messages, fortunately. She dropped her coat and gloves on the floor, stretched out on her bed, and eyed the CD containing the copy of the Program she'd downloaded from Anna's laptop. Every AntiGen member knew that the Program had something to do with proteins. But now she and Anna suspected that it harbored significantly more information.

In seven hours the doctor would be in his usual Tuesday afternoon place—a place where he'd be vulnerable, open. That left her five to crack it.

She went to the desk, hooked up her laptop computer to the phone line, booted her system, and turned on the tiny camera atop her monitor. On-screen, icons popped onto a cirrus-cloud background. She clicked on the icon designed for file directories, slid the CD into a slot on the laptop's side, and began running the program. Setup "*.exe" files began downloading onto her hard drive. She minimized the file screen window as it worked, then established a link with her ISP, and entered: www.uspto.gov.

Ten seconds later the link was established. The banner across the top of her screen read "U.S. Patent and Trademark Office" with options below it for searching the U.S. Patent Bibliographic Database. She chose "Patent Number Search." From the middle desk drawer, she pulled out a list of numbers: patent numbers processed by Diehl, Teasdale, & Wilcox. She entered 9,408,571.

The screen answered:

Protein Kit for Analyzing Rat Membranes
Inventor: Walters, John
Assignee: Handot Biosystems

A slew of complex references followed, capped by an obtuse abstract.

She minimized the Internet browser window and restored the file managing window as the Program's setup elements finished downloading. The phone rang, a twirling trill of annoyance. She picked it up on the second ring. "This is your wake-up call," a whiny voice said to her.

"Straub, you weasel."

"That's no way to talk to your partner," Straub replied.

"Some partner. Ratted me out to Trent. Almost had me thrown off the mission."

"Trent told me to check in on you and Anna this morning."

"In the morning, not the crack of dawn. I'm going back to bed."

"Put Anna on."

She had dropped off Anna and the equipment at Anna's apartment—in Maryland. "She's asleep, nursing Trent's lesson. Let her alone."

"I don't trust you. You think you're smarter, better than the rest of us, just because you're a whiz at searching on-line. Big fucking deal. As far as I'm concerned, you're just some bitch Trent picked out of the gutter. Now, put her on. Or would you prefer I pay a house call?"

He doesn't know, she thought. *If he did, he'd have been here, gloating.* "Just a minute. I have to wake her." She had no time to conference-call with Anna on the same phone; Straub would know anyway. The only other phone in the room was her wireless. If she used that, Straub and Trent would trace it. Frantically she scanned the suite. The laptop! It might work—if Anna was on-line.

Helen cut the connection to the patent office, clicked on the outreach application icon, and hastily sent an instant message to Anna's mail address. *Come on, Anna. Be there!*

"The hell are you doin'?" Straub screamed.

A bleary-eyed Anna Steitz appeared on the laptop screen. Her movements were stiff, disjointed, a consequence of transmission inadequacies. "Hello, Helen. What did you—"

"*Wake up*, Anna," Helen said, picking up the phone, holding the receiver in front of the mini-camera. "Straub's on the line," she shouted, waving the receiver at the screen.

Anna made an *oh* sign with her mouth. "Uh, tell him to let me sleep!" she yelled.

"Satisfied?" Helen asked Straub.

"Yeah, I guess so. Trent wants to remind you that you have thirty-six hours."

"I can tell time," she said. Then slammed down the receiver.

"Do you think he knows?" Anna asked.

"No, not yet. Get some sleep," she answered and ended the transmission.

On-screen, Helen opened the window and folder containing the Program files, and clicked the executable file. Her machine hummed briefly, then the screen flashed: *Fully Installed.*

She clicked "OK." A 15-item menu of unfathomable references appeared on the screen. Most of the choices, she suspected, were search engines for sophisticated biotechnology and/or genome data-bases. One, however, intrigued her. She clicked on the choice "U.S. Patent Office Interface." The screen replied: *Program running.*

Helen waited. Nothing happened. She shrugged, minimized the window with the Program supposedly running, reestablished her Net connection with the patent office, and entered the first number on the list: 9,408,571. "Stupid. I already searched that one."

But this time, the screen displayed radically different search results.

Kincaid's Lab

Kevin exploded into the conference room. "Up, Peter!"

Nguyen lifted his head and peered through sleep-encrusted eyes. "I'm not sleeping."

Kevin attacked the whiteboard. His surgical scrubs whooshed as he erased the last traces of HACV.V$_7$'s design, then began to draw a set of concentric circles representing a cell and its DNA-packed nucleus. "We've been sloppy fishermen." Not hearing Nguyen's "huh," he drew a barbed arrow into the cell membrane. "The problem is V$_7$'s harpoon. We designed it to latch on to the target cell membrane and use nanotubules to create an opening sufficiently wide to inject the capsule enclosing the chromosome through the outer cell. We also designed the harpoon fragment to remain behind, stuck in the membrane, so that other V_7 complexes carrying chromosomes would recognize it, and therefore, not latch on to the same cell. Like a careless fisherman." Nguyen was staring blankly at him. "Don't you see, Nguyen? It's like carelessly casting your hook and line. Sooner or later it will snag. If you can't untangle it, you have to cut the line. But the *hook* just doesn't disappear. It's there, stuck where you left it waiting for someone or something to prick themselves."

"I just woke up. My mind's operating on a very simple level."

Kevin drew a line through the harpoon. "That represents the tip of the harpoon sticking through the cell membrane. It was designed to stay in place—apparently, too long, like a slow leak."

"But that wouldn't account for the massive cell destruction. The target cells have divided at least twenty times. Meaning that only a few percent of the cells in those mice were originally transfected by V_7. The vast majority of the affected cells are descendants of those original cells."

"Which means that *this* part of the harpoon," circling the portion of the harpoon outside of the cell membrane, "is responsible."

"How? An autoimmune reaction?"

"No, it's more mechanical than biological. I suspect that in a relatively uniform time frame the exterior portion of the harpoon dislodges, floats through interstitial tissues, encounters another cell, and punctures that cell's membrane. Then it moves on and punctures another cell—and so on. Like 'micro-daggers.' These 'micro-daggers' accumulate in the bloodstream and lymphatic system, causing widespread destruction over a prolonged period."

Nguyen's head tilted from side to side, as if weighing the theory. "Sounds bizarre. But if that's the case, what's the solution?"

"Redesign the harpoon. Make its protein structure less resilient, its amino acid sequence more easily degraded. The harpoon need only be effective for a few days, not a lifetime. I already have some ideas for new harpoon structures developing in my head."

"Is this another Kevin Kincaid–only solution?"

"Oh, I want—no, I need your help. You and everyone else in this lab." He erased the board. Forcing a smile, "You're going to the NIH conference, aren't you?"

"Think I'd miss your speech?"

"Okay. We'll start a fresh slate on Monday. Full staff. I'll open up the problem to the floor. But in the meantime I want you to conduct serum assays and Western blot analyses in the mice for harpoon polypeptide sequences. Establish the validity of my theory and begin assays for possible antibodies to harpoon sequences, in case it is an autoimmune response. That should keep you busy for—"

"Ever," Nguyen finished. He nodded and left.

Kevin stared at the scribbling on the whiteboard. His mind had already begun synthesizing a modification of the harpoon that could potentially solve V_7's problem. But until then, how many more children would be waiting for a cure that might come too late?

Someone rapped on the door behind him. "Kevin?"

He turned around: Joan Tetlow stood in the doorway. "You're up early," he said.

"Busy week." she said, uneasily tightening her scarf. "I want to apologize about yesterday. I've been under a lot of stress. Grayson's pressuring me, and I supported him over someone who's put ten years of dedication and excellence into this institution. We've worked so well together for a long time. I don't want to jeopardize that."

"You went too far."

She took two steps toward him. "I, uh, I've been in touch with the Association's board. They're all very pleased with your news conference. We expect a strong boost in public opinion polls."

He stiffly clapped his hands. "I'm so happy for you."

"*Me?* You're responsible."

"It's *your* success. Yours—and Grayson's."

"You shouldn't feel that way." She touched his shoulder awkwardly. "We care about you, Kevin. All of us, especially me. Look at all I've done for you over the years."

"You did for me? For me? I'm not sure you *ever* did anything for me. For my work, yes, but not for me. And let's not forget that you and BFMC have done pretty damn well by me, haven't you?"

She sighed. "I already said I'm sorry."

Kevin folded his arms.

Tetlow softly said, "Kevin, I'm in trouble. I need your help."

"Your timing stinks."

"Loring and the board are demanding to see your progress. I know that V_7's files are in disarray, but—"

"There's just too much going on for me to handle that now. In a couple of weeks I can—"

"I need those files by the end of the week. Monday, the latest."

"Joan, you're asking the impossible."

Tetlow fixed her scarf again. "You remember that request you made last month for an additional five million in funding, over and above your budget projections? I believe you said you needed it for additional soft- and hardware, another full research team, new equipment?"

Kevin put his hands on his hips. "You said to talk to you in four months, around the start of the fiscal year. You weren't overly optimistic."

"We have a—special endowment. I can arrange for you to have whatever you want within ten working days—if I have those files."

"All of a sudden you can get the funding," snapping his fingers, "just like that? What's the hospital's general counsel supposed to do while you're sticking your hand in the cookie jar?"

"The funds involved are discretionary and justifiable, particularly in light of your recent publicity. I'm asking you—please."

He stared at her. "You really are serious."

"My job is on the line!"

"Which justifies bribing me?"

"Kevin, please, you and I have had our problems, but," faintly smiling, "it took you almost ten years to break me in. Who knows how long it'll take for my replacement?"

He grimaced as he considered her offer. "All right. I can't do it myself with the conference this week at NIH, but I'll put Nguyen right on it."

"Nguyen? But I thought you were the only one who knew the formulation."

"I am," he said, rubbing his eyes, "but Nguyen and I were working on it this morning."

"You must have been up real early," she said. "Did the run help?"

He lifted his head and stared. "How did you know I went on a run this morning?"

"I saw you from my office. I've been there since four A.M."

Kevin remembered glancing back at the hospital shortly after beginning his morning run. Tetlow's corner office on the tenth floor had been dark when he left—and dark when he'd returned. *She's lying. How did she know? Did she have me followed?*

"So, I can count on receiving those files—"

"Peter'll have them on your desk by Monday afternoon."

"Great! What's your schedule for the rest of the day?"

"Rounds this morning. Then some time in the lab before seeing Donny."

"Yes, of course. It's Tuesday. I forgot." Tetlow stood and graciously smiled. "Thanks for being so understanding."

Kevin waited until Tetlow left the lab, then summoned Nguyen back to the conference room. "Peter, who have you told about V_7?"

"No one, Doctor."

"Good. Organize the files for Ms. Tetlow. She needs them by Monday."

"I can't do that and work on the harpoon problem simultaneously."

Kevin paused before answering. "Your work on the harpoon will have to wait for now."

"Are you sure?"

"Yeah. Right now I've got to get our Ms. Tetlow off our backs. A couple of days on the harpoon won't make that much difference with the conference coming up. In the meantime, I can continue laying the theoretical groundwork for a fix. After all, that's my forte. You can start laboratory testing once I've worked out some possible approaches."

"Tuesday, then?"

"You bet." As Nguyen started to leave, he added, "And don't tell anyone about the design flaw."

"Uh-huh."

Kevin grabbed his arm. "I mean it, really. Not a word!"

"Okay, okay. Are you worried about PR fallout?"

Kevin released Nguyen's arm. "Yes, that's it. Bad press."

Dirksen Senate Office Building
Washington, D.C.

"Your eleven o'clock is here," the secretary's voice sounded over the intercom.

Senator Jordan DeRay checked his calendar and scowled. His appointment's mission was hopeless, but in deference to requests from some prominent contributors, he'd promised the man fifteen minutes. However, the senator from North Carolina had spent thirty-four years in Congress's Upper Chamber, served as a committee chairman, and, at his age, was obligated to no one but himself. Nothing on God's earth was going to make him change his mind. "Send him in."

An elderly man with round, black-rimmed glasses and a cane entered, his right hand extended, the other holding a notebook computer.

"Mr. Frederick Grayson, President of the Benjamin Franklin Healthcare Network, and representative for the Association to Cure Genetic Disabilities," the secretary announced.

DeRay stood, allowing the glare from the window overlooking Massachusetts Avenue behind him to blind his guest. He smiled, shook hands, and offered a seat. DeRay tilted his head and squinted. "Sir, have we met previously?"

"Not that I'm aware of," Grayson answered.

DeRay adjusted his steel-rimmed glasses. "Twenty-five, maybe thirty years ago. A fund-raiser in Charlotte?"

"I've never been to your beautiful state."

"No matter. Mr. Grayson, I appreciate your stopping by and hope we can come to a mutual understanding."

Grayson smiled politely. "Translation: I've as much chance of procuring your support for HR 601 as God taking pity on a prayer from hell."

DeRay said, "I sponsored the ban on germline gene therapy in the first place."

"Times change, sir. People do not."

"Of course people change." DeRay half smiled. "Just not this one, when he doesn't have to—and knows he's right."

Grayson placed both hands on his cane. "Forgive me, sir, I misspoke. By people, I meant the human race as a whole. Essentially, human beings are the same today as they were two hundred thousand years ago."

"Mr. Grayson, I'd be happy to discuss anthropology with you some night at a fund-raiser, but right now, I'm a busy man."

"Perhaps there's some way the Association can help you find a way to reconsider your current position on 601."

DeRay grinned. "Sir, my coffers are filled, and I do believe my constituents will continue electing me after I'm dead."

"Perhaps one of our member companies can relocate in your fine state."

"The people of North Carolina would be grateful, sir. But not at the cost of their immortal souls."

"You make me out to be a devil, sir."

"Your next step would be to threaten to move one of your companies *out* of our fine state. You can, you know. But with Cary and Research Triangle Park, our bucket's already quite full."

"Senator DeRay, all we're asking is the opportunity to prevent genetic disease in children, as the March of Dimes does."

"No! You want to change the genes of unborn children while they're still in the womb! My God, haven't we done enough damage to the unborn in the last fifty years?"

"We just want the opportunity to fix Nature's mistakes."

"By introducing our own?"

"Senator, have you ever seen a child with cystic fibrosis?"

DeRay folded his arms. "HR 601 isn't about fixing genetic defects. It's about controlling people. Eugenics. And if tight-asses like the Germans and Swiss are scared of it, then by God, so should we."

Grayson glanced around office walls filled with photos of the balding senator with presidents in the Rose Garden, with chairmen of the Joint Chiefs of Staff, receiving awards and honors from universities and right-wing support groups from Cape Hatteras to Point Barrow. Grayson stood and extended his hand. "Thank you for your time, sir." After shaking DeRay's, he used his cane to slowly make his way to the door. Halfway there, he turned back. "Senator, after six illustrious terms in the Senate, wouldn't you like to leave behind a legacy?"

"I already have."

Glancing around the room, "More than scholarships, or awards, or buildings bearing your name. A real living legacy to the people of your state. Or, more properly, to the demographic groups who overwhelmingly vote for you. But demographics has a certain, oh, *color* to it, doesn't it, Senator? And certain *colored* demographic groups tend to feel that you don't represent them. And these particularly colored demographic groups tend to reproduce more rapidly than those groups a little less colored who do vote for you." He whispered, "Maybe not during your tenure, Senator. But inevitably your electoral base will become the minority."

DeRay gazed deeply into Grayson's eyes. They seemed familiar, as if housing a powerful truth. "And you possess something that reverses this trend?"

He hobbled over to a photograph of DeRay kissing a baby. "HR 601 is worded so as to permit germline gene therapy to restore normalcy. But no one has ever adequately defined *normal*, not to mention that it's politically incorrect to do so. That leaves the difference between *normal* and *enhancement* as a semantic interpretation suitable for exploitation."

"And just how does this benefit my preferred constituency?"

"Think ten years down the road, Senator. The middle class will be able to purchase certain advantages for their unborn children. Increased intelligence, strength. These will be expensive, probably beyond the financial means of *less desirable* groups. In time these advantages should more than compensate for the numerical superiority of those less desirable. In some districts one may correlate such differences along ethnic and/or racial lines."

DeRay whistled through his dentures. "Think I'm a fool?"

"This is no trap, sir. I am not wired. Have me searched if you wish. But remember, Senator, you can do more to shape the future in your favor with this one roll call than all of your previous votes combined over the last quarter century."

"There is a flaw in your demographics argument, Grayson. In theoretical terms, that is." DeRay swiveled his chair toward the window. "My base constituency, the folks who've sent me back here term after term, are good people, but poor, living off the land, never having the means to buy what you're hawking. They are *my* people."

"Precisely, Senator." Grayson sat down. "And that can be your true legacy."

DeRay patted his fingers before answering. "You make an interesting case but—"

"But not sufficiently compelling," Grayson finished. He again glanced at DeRay's numerous plaques and certificates adorning the office walls. "You've had quite a career in the Senate. I'm sure this room is but a small sampling of your many honors."

"That'd be a fair assessment."

"Thirty-four years on the Hill. Soon it'll be time to start campaigning again, assuming you plan to run for a seventh term."

"I'll never leave the Senate."

Grayson leaned on his cane. "More like you *can't* leave."

DeRay stared at his visitor, then chuckled. "I had no idea you were such a loyal fan."

"Senator, various investigative agencies are always dipping into people's pasts. These agencies, however, are easily intimidated by a six-term U.S. senator chairing one key committee and highly-ranked on several others. Now, we know that just in the past two years, you've squashed investigations into contract awards for the new interstate construction project around Charlotte and the collapse of two of the nation's largest banks, both headquartered in your state."

DeRay folded his arms. "I agreed to meet with you as a favor to some of the other party elders. I don't believe there's anything further to discuss."

"But they haven't yet looked into the Malaysian computer chip deal. What do you stand to gain for your part, two hundred thousand dollars?"

"I don't respond well to threats."

"Neither do we, Senator. But we haven't made any. Nor do we intend to. You don't build lasting relationships on fear." He sat back and slowly crossed his legs. "Sir, you're seventy-two years old, you've spent half of your life in the Senate. Despite all of your public protests, we know that, privately, you want to retire, travel, enjoy the rest of your life without the politics, the media, and the annoyances that go with them. You have considerable influence, but that decays with loss of power. Once you leave the Senate those investigative agencies will grow emboldened and begin looking into your past indiscretions. You become vulnerable. And if your enemies want you bad enough, they will get you."

The senator grimaced. "Sounds like retirement isn't an option."

"Quite the contrary, sir. The Association's influence extends to the highest levels. We will continue to protect you long after you've left office."

DeRay sat quietly a full two minutes before answering. "Not enough."

"Did you think that was all we were offering?" He motioned toward the desk. At the senator's nod, Grayson opened his notebook computer on the desktop, the cover facing his host. "Just a moment, please, to boot up and make the connection."

Three minutes later, when Grayson's knobby fingers had finished working the keyboard, he turned the notebook around. The senator studied the screen. It appeared to be an account summary statement.

"An account at the Zenstrasse Bank in Bern channeled through a dozen unbreakable dummy shells. Untraceable and safeguarded by our many security interests." Pointing at the bottom of the screen, "Notice the amount."

DeRay furrowed his brows at the figure: $102,843,711.40.

"The figure is correct, Senator. With that, you can establish a substantial charitable trust to see that *your* people have the financial wherewithal to purchase our—wares, and still have a very large retirement fund for yourself and your lovely wife. We consider it a worthwhile investment in America's immediate future. We would hope that you might convince others to see such possibilities, as well."

But why such an odd number?

"You don't recognize the figure, sir?" Grayson placed his cane across his chair. "It is ten times the amount that has found its way into your personal accounts over the last thirty-four years. To the penny, sir."

DeRay clenched his jaw, then slowly smirked. "Were such a thing to be true."

"I am a busy man as well, sir. Do we have an understanding?"

DeRay put his fingers to his lips. "I'll give your proposal the consideration it's due."

"Then the proposed legacy intrigues you?" Grayson asked.

"Yes."

"And it is desirable to make this your last term so that you can travel and enjoy your remaining years with peace of mind?"

"I suppose so."

"And is the figure you've seen adequate?"

DeRay nodded.

"Then the answer's obvious, isn't it?" Grayson shifted in his seat. "You'll undoubtedly want to verify this information through personal sources. Fine. However, the site will need to hear a confirmation from me by midnight, its local time, in order to fulfill this—order." Grayson checked his watch. "That gives you six hours to make your decision." He snapped closed the notebook and gathered it under his arm. Handing DeRay a card, "A secure number, where questions can be answered. I believe we've already shaken hands." He turned to leave.

DeRay waited until his visitor nearly reached the door. "Who exactly are you?"

Without looking back, "I believe I've introduced myself."

"No, you have not." He stepped around the desk as Grayson opened the door. "I never forget a face, sir. Yours will come to me, sooner or later."

Chester County, Pennsylvania

Subdued sunlight filtered through barren trees as the Buick headed down the narrow two-lane road. Kevin knew every dangerous turn of this portion of Route 100; he'd driven it every Tuesday afternoon for ten years. The ride was quiet, comforting, and without traffic, he had a few uninterrupted moments for reflection, insights he might share with Donny. After many years, and after a fashion, he'd learned to interpret signs from Donny, signs that had to fight their way through miles of chemically unbalanced neural pathways.

The car approached a three-way intersection. To the left was an old narrow bridge across the Lenape creek. As he stopped at the sign, Kevin glanced at the passenger seat: it was empty. "Must've fallen under the seat." He threw the car into park, checked under the passenger seat, and pulled out a flat rectangular box wrapped in green and gold. A car let loose a jarring beep behind him. He checked the rearview mirror: a fat man in a black Mercedes was pounding on the wheel. Kevin warily turned his car left and drove slowly over the bridge while glancing behind him in the mirror. The Mercedes shot straight ahead, paralleling the creek, and disappeared around the bend.

The road led up a steep hill to a gentle plateau. After a quarter-mile he saw the familiar green sign swaying in the wind: Halloran House. He turned onto the long driveway. In spring and summer the grounds smelled like honeysuckle, with a garden boasting finely sculptured hedges, manicured croquet lawns, and long, lazy swings strung from tree branches. Now all was barren, dormant.

The main building, atop a small knoll, had white colonnades supporting the lower roof, which formed a long front porch, and sturdy, stucco walls surrounding its great wide old windows. It seemed more inn than institution. Kevin pulled into the deserted visitors' parking lot, took the gift-wrapped box, and walked briskly up one of the switchback ramps flanking the stairs.

"Hi, Karen," he called to the receptionist at the front desk. "Has he had lunch?"

"Uh-huh. He's in his room."

"I'll head right up."

"Oh, Doctor, *you* have a visitor." She pointed to a recessed, poorly lit waiting area behind him.

Kevin pivoted around: a woman stood, removed her overcoat, and walked out of the shadows. As the light touched her face, her gray-green eyes glimmered.

Genfutures Inc.
Gaithersburg, Maryland

Last night's break-in had drained Anna. As computer code swam across her screen, the flashing pixels taunting her bleary eyes, all she wanted was a quick nap, something her cubicle couldn't accommodate. Genfutures Inc. wasn't a bad place for a day job: flexible hours, good pay, work that honed her skills and kept her informed of developments in molecular genetics. All arranged, as a cover, by Trent.

The envelope icon appeared on the lower left corner of her screen, signaling a new e-mail. She clicked on the icon. It expanded to a window containing a message:

> Anna, please see me on the fifth floor ASAP. Problems on the Korban project.
> Steve Reynolds
> VP Marketing
> Genfutures Inc.

She deleted the message, yawned, then headed through the cubicle maze to the elevator. Eyes downcast, she waited. The doors whooshed open. She stepped on.

A powerful hand clamped down on her shoulder. Shaking, she slowly turned around. "Trent! What are—"

"Come with me."

The elevator opened onto the top floor. Trent, with index finger pressed into Anna's back, guided her to the stairwell and up the final flight to the roof. He slammed the door behind them. Cold air, channeled along the building's huge heating-ventilation-air conditioning unit, whipped across the rooftop and sliced through her dress. Ominous gray clouds hung low. He led her toward the Capitol in the distance—toward the roof's edge.

"What are you doing?" She straightened her legs, planting her feet in the soft gravel surface. Trent's thumb pressing at the base of her neck sent sharp, painful bolts down her spine.

Thirty feet to the edge. Twenty.

"Trent!"

Ten feet. Five.

"I think this is far enough," he said.

Her pain eased. She craned around. Her eyes teared from the cold as she watched him place his hands in his pockets. The wind flapped the tails of his coat. "Trent, I have to get back. Reynolds sent me an e-mail—"

"*I* sent it." He took two steps forward. "You're looking tired, Anna. Did you have a fitful night?"

"Yes."

"Spend the whole night with Helen, did you?" As she nodded, he approached. "What time did you get in?"

She retreated dangerously close to the precipice. "Almost nine."

"Anna, I care about you, just as I do for everyone in my AntiGen family. But if you keep lying to me—"

"I am not lying."

"Anna, I entered you into my world. I can exit you as easily." Taking a half-step, "Where was Helen last night?"

She glanced at the edge behind her. "In town. At Diehl Teasdale."

"You have the Program?"

"Helen could not convince Kincaid without it. And I trust her."

Trent bit down on a peppermint and inched closer. "The only reason your sloppy attempt worked was because *I* backed you up. Who do you think set off the fire alarm?"

She stepped back, lost her footing, and started slipping over the edge.

Trent snatched her as she screamed, dangling over the pavement sixty feet beneath her. "I should drop you on principle alone."

"Trent, help me!"

"The only reason you're not splattered now is because you pulled it off without alerting the Collaborate." He grabbed her forearm and strained. She slipped. He pulled harder. She reached out and clutched both of his arms. He yanked her up. Deposited her on the gravel roof. "Tell Helen she can show Kincaid the Program. Afterward, I expect it and any copies surrendered to me."

She expelled a sobbing, gasping *yes*.

He squatted beside her, reached out, and lifted her chin. "Wondering why I didn't want you to steal the Program?"

"*Nnnnnein.*"

With the back of his hand he caressed her, cheek to chin. "Smart girl. I'll be in touch." As he turned away, he called back, "And remind her that she now has only thirty hours."

When he reached the stairwell, a gust of wind blew in her face, carrying with it Trent's mumbled words: "Because Kincaid will be dead shortly after."

Halloran House
Chester County, Pennsylvania

Helen studied Kevin's face as he moved ominously toward her. He stopped at the edge of her personal space and gazed down at her, taking full advantage of his height. This was her last chance for rapprochement. If he rejected her, he'd belong to Trent.

"What are you doing here? This place is way off the beaten track," he snapped.

"That's what the cabdriver said." She inched closer. "Sorry I had to leave like that. An emergency came up."

"Life or death, no doubt."

"But it did pique your interest, didn't it?"

"That remains to be seen. So why are you here, Ms. Morgan? The truth, please."

"To finish the interview."

"You're wasting your time. I've said all I'm going to say about K_4 or V_7."

"Actually, I was hoping to find out more about you personally: your motivations, drives, goals, reflections, past, those sorts of things."

Kevin smirked. "I'm not exactly the human-interest type."

"Oh, but you are the story. Down syndrome is your noble crusade. My readers would love to—"

"I don't give a damn about your readers. Donny's not a crusade. He's my brother and what's left of my family."

"I'd like to meet him."

"To put him on exhibit?"

"Haven't *you*, Doctor?"

"Now just what the hell does that mean?" he growled.

"Why, putting him in one of your public service spots for the Association, of course."

He stared at her. "How do you know that? Nobody knows that. The commercial hasn't been aired yet."

"Did you ever think that your brother might like to—" She stared beyond Kevin's right shoulder. A woman with smartly styled frosted hair and a fiftyish, luminous face headed across the main foyer. Her head sat atop a neck held obliquely six inches above a polished wood tray. Her right hand, palm forward, poked through a slot in the tray beside her ear while her left forearm was rotated ninety degrees behind her. Her spine was twisted backward so that her legs were positioned over her head, as if some enraged giant had seized her body and twisted it beyond undoing. Or she had been permanently fused in a bizarre yoga position. Helen had never seen someone so afflicted. She wanted to turn away but could not. Her eyes burned. She blinked rapidly.

From an optically directed control chip on a band around her head, the woman guided her motorized cart toward them. "Hey, doc!"

Kevin turned. "Wendy! How'ya doing?"

The woman looked to the box tucked beneath Kevin's arm. "There's chocolate-covered cherries in that assortment. Donny doesn't like chocolate-covered cherries. Be a shame to let 'em go to waste."

Smiling, "I'll leave instructions."

"Thanks." To Helen, "Hi. I'm Wendy Reymer."

Helen managed a raspy introduction.

Wendy motioned to Kevin with her eyes. He walked to her, bent down, and listened attentively as she whispered in his ear. He nodded, smiling at Helen.

"Got a Ping-Pong game coming up. Nice meeting you, Helen."

Throat thick, eyes watery, Helen watched the motorized cart chug to the back of the foyer. "What happened to her?"

"There's so many steps that can go wrong in the transition from embryo to infant. In Wendy's case, defects originated in her neural tube. Such a nice lady. She was condemned six months before she was born."

"But she's not, uh—"

"Mentally impaired? No."

Helen whispered, "Almost be better if she was."

"Why?"

"Because then she wouldn't have the capacity to understand what happened to her. I mean, how can you look at her and not be—when I looked at her, I didn't know whether to thank God that I've been spared or curse Him for screwing her over." She turned away.

"It's one thing to talk about genetic deformities in the abstract as 'vector target sites' or 'morality issues,'" Kevin said quietly. "Quite another when you glimpse the courage of the victims. Whatever story you're writing, Wendy belongs in it." He added, "So does Donny Kincaid."

She shut her eyes an instant in silent gratitude. Instead of the CD with the Program, she withdrew a pocket recorder from her handbag and turned back to Kevin.

Bypassing the ground-floor elevators, he led her up the main staircase. There were no institutional odors of urine, alcohol, and antiseptic; or vacant-eyed, partially robed patients wandering halls; or wild screams from locked, padded-wall rooms. The air smelled springlike. The walking or wheeled residents she passed along pastel-colored halls were well-dressed, alert. Sounds wafting through the halls were of laughter from private rooms, the upstairs game room, and off-key singing of "Sweet Baby James" in the auditorium.

"Let me give you a little clinical background of Down syndrome for your story. It's a genetic disorder characterized by the presence of an additional copy of the twenty-first chromosome. Instead of the normal two copies of chromosome number 21, people with Down syndrome have three. It's also called Trisomy 21. It's the most common cause of mental retardation and begins in the embryonic stage. It eventually results in reduced muscle tone and facial distortions, the most recognizable being an enlarged forehead. Much of this ties into the disorder's association with monocarbonic acid metabolism and CAF1P60 gene on chromosome region 21q22.2. Did you get all that?"

She checked her recorder and nodded. "Don't people with Down syndrome generally live at home, become educated, employed, even—"

"Most, but there's a spectrum of severity. Many have IQs between fifty and seventy-five, mildly to moderately retarded. With training they function semi-normally. But Donny's retardation is profound—rare, even for Down's. He's in the bottom percentile. His IQ's below thirty. He can't feed or dress himself. He also has other neurologic complications, unrelated to Down's, from circumstances I don't want to get into." Continuing down the hall, "I brought him here—"

"After the fire that killed your family," she finished.

He stopped. "How did you know about the fire?"

"It's not exactly a state secret. Please continue."

He stared at her a moment, then resumed, "Here, Donny gets the best care available, but more important, he's part of a community. That's something he'd never get just being with me." They stopped at the last room on the right, a sign marked "Mr. Donnelly Kincaid Jr." Kevin looked down at her, then at her recorder. She turned it off and put it away. "Two rules," he continued. "One, while you're in the room, you can talk to Donny, or to me, but not *about* Donny as if he wasn't there. His speech is slurred, but sometimes he'll surprise you. Wait here," he said, ducking into the room. She heard an excited squeal. Then Kevin poked his head out the door and motioned her inside.

Donny's place was more hotel suite than hospital room: a fully furnished sitting room and furnished with a couch, dining table, and large flat-screen TV next to an adjoining bedroom with braces and assist bars in the walls.

"Donny, this is Helen Morgan. She's come here to talk to us. Say hello."

A squat man rocking vigorously in a chair chewed gleefully on a chocolate from the open box on the table beside him. The face that gazed at her was Kevin Kincaid's, though younger, stretched, flattened, with a Jupiter-sized receding forehead. The face bore a radiant smile reminiscent of Kevin from his old family movies—the movies she'd seen too many times.

"Hello, Donny," she said uneasily.

The man mumbled indistinguishably before opening his mouth for another chocolate. Kevin fed him a nougat.

"I'm sorry, Donny. I didn't hear. Could you say that again?" Helen asked.

Donny mumbled, his eyes wandering around the room. She smiled blankly as he spoke. Kevin sat down and massaged his brother's arm. Donny's head tilted as he uttered collections of vocal sounds. Kevin whispered in his ear, received a babbled return, then whispered more emphatically to his brother.

Helen slowly drifted closer to Kevin as she watched him interact with his brother: one of the brightest men on the planet showing no condescension toward one of the least intelligent. An instinctual warmth filled her, like the kind she felt at seeing a father carrying a daughter on his shoulder, or pushing his son on a swing. His back to her, Helen found herself reaching out to touch him, as if physical contact with him would somehow boost that warmth, would make that vision real.

Kevin glanced back at her as he was saying, ". . . Isn't that right, Ms. Morgan?"

Helen quickly pulled her hand back. "Uh, uh, yes. Sure." She glanced at her watch. He'd been talking to Donny more than half an hour.

Kevin patted his brother on the back and fed him a chocolate-covered caramel. "You can't understand him, Ms. Morgan, can you?"

"Sorry. Not a word."

He tilted his eyes up to her. "The speech pathologist assures me that the sounds he makes are just rudimentary attempts at spoken words. I've been told that, basically, when I listen to Donny, all I really hear is a projection of myself." He looked back to Donny. "I know better. If you listen carefully, you can understand him."

"You broke your own rule," she whispered. "You're talking *about* him."

He frowned. "That's what happens when I let down my guard."

She thought of the Program in her handbag, of her mission. But as she gazed at Kevin, at Donny, the Program grew less important. "I'll wait outside."

"Please, I want you to stay." Then added, "*We* want you to stay." He looked out the window. "My wife was very good to Donny. Like the mother he never really had. She was far better to him than I ever was. Ever will be." He drew in a shuddered breath. "Even I didn't think he was capable of remembering."

"Remembering what?"

"He's very happy to see you *again*. But he's also disappointed."

Helen Morgan returned his gaze. "I don't understand."

Kevin bit his lip. "He said that the last time you visited, you promised to bring the new baby."

Delphi

Marguerite Moraes looked around the empty gymnasium. Less than a year ago this playroom had been filled with toddlers running wildly in the creative dances, their laughter reverberating from the high steel-beam lattice overhead. Now it was silent, sterile, morose. She gazed through one of the great, iron-barred windows, beyond the helipad to the distant snow-covered hill. It was thirty miles from the school grounds to the nearest town, but it might as well have been three thousand. Though Marguerite was slim, athletic, once a marathon runner, she'd never made it anywhere near town before Delphi security officers had brought her back.

The surveillance camera in the far corner of the room swiveled toward her. The one in the near corner followed. It was unwise to stare out the window too long.

Loud grunting sounds echoed around the gymnasium. Marguerite turned to the little boy at the far end of the polished wood floor. "No, I haven't forgotten, Ethan."

He answered by grunting louder and emphatically pointing at the red rubber kickball tucked beneath Marguerite's arm.

Using a broad, toothy smile, Marguerite tried to mask her anguish at the sight of him. Ethan was so beautiful: almost four years old with gorgeous brown locks and adorable dimples. Three months ago the boy had an IQ beyond what the Stanford-Binet or WISC tests could measure. But the last seizure-induced stroke had ravaged his speech center. She prayed that it had also taken the last vestiges of his spectacular intellect so that he could no longer remember what he once was. Flicking her long, dark hair back over her shoulders, she knelt and slowly rolled the ball toward him. "C'mon Ethan. Kick as hard as you can."

Ethan looked intently at the red ball. His eyes suddenly lost their sharpness as if a black cloud had descended behind them. His head gently shook. His eyes rolled back. His arms, his legs grew tight, rigid. He fell to the floor. His entire body quivered.

"No! Not again!"

Chester County, Pennsylvania

"Thanks for driving me back to the hotel," Helen said as Kevin turned his Buick from the country road onto the main highway. "Have you and your brother always been that close?"

"Only after Helen—" He swallowed the rest of his words.

I have to pull him back onto familiar ground, before maneuvering him forward, she thought. She began with a question to which she knew the answer. "So Dr. Kincaid, are you hoping that germline gene therapy can correct Donny's condition?"

"No, you're confusing germline and somatic gene therapy," he said, eyes fixed on the road. "Germline cells are egg and sperm cells that unite to form a new organism. Somatic cells are nonreproductive cells, which is everything else: heart cells, nerve cells, whatever. In somatic gene therapy you change the genetic structure of nonreproductive cells—an area of lung or brain, such as for fighting cancers. In somatic gene therapy, no matter how many genetic changes you make to these organs, the children of these patients are still predisposed to inherit the same genetic disorder. But in germline gene therapy, you genetically alter the individual's egg or sperm cells, either directly or inadvertently through spillage."

"Spillage?"

"A vector that can't differentiate between germline and somatic cells. It alters both types."

"And in germline therapy?"

"The individual's offspring will carry the gene therapy's alterations so a patient won't pass on the genetic disorder to his children. Or by altering their unborn offspring, just after conception, in the embryonic stage. Or when the embryo is just a ball of undifferentiated cells, a blastosphere. Or while the fetus is still in the womb, perhaps as late as the end of the second trimester. Obviously, the earlier you intervene, the easier the process and the greater the likelihood of success. But any type of germline gene therapy can prevent genetic disorders from ever occurring."

She studied his profile: the muscles along his jaw and temple had firmed but the pain had evaporated from his eyes. "So somatic gene therapy would be the answer?"

"Yes. One strategy is gene augmentation therapy. In that case, the patient's cells are missing a gene encoding for a key enzyme or protein. So with a vector you supply the cell with the missing gene. A second strategy is targeted gene mutation correction. In that case the patient's cells have a mutated gene that's creating havoc. With a vector you insert the correct gene and remove the mutated one. A third strategy is targeted inhibition of gene expression. There you use a vector to carry a gene into a patient's cells that prevents mutated genes from being translated into faulty proteins. Of course, each strategy has enormous logistic and technical problems."

"Which would work for Donny?"

The car slowed as it approached a red light at the bottom of a hill. Stopped. "None."

"Why?"

"Donny has more than just an extra couple of genes. He has a whole extra *chromosome*. Short of inserting a vacuum cleaner into the cell nucleus to suck it up, I have absolutely no idea how to cure his disease at a genetic level. I'm not sure anyone ever will." He sighed. "There are drugs being developed that may one day counteract his biochemical imbalances, and studies have shown serious deficits in genes critical to proper neuronal development. But Donny is what he is. *I'll* never be able to change that. Maybe someone someday might find a way to build upon my work with expression vectors."

"*Expression* vectors?"

"Basically there's two categories of vectors. Cloning vectors, designed to insert a piece of DNA into a cell strictly to reproduce the new DNA over and over and over, like a virus. And expression vectors, used to insert the DNA into the host cell to make that cell function like normal."

"Like your V$_7$?"

"You know that I can't tell you anything about V_7."

"Have it your way. Frankly, it's irrelevant to my story."

He glanced at her. "Just what *is* your story?"

Helen repressed a smile: she'd made *him* ask. "There's a maelstrom swirling around you, Dr. Kincaid. Germline gene therapy is evolving into an across-the-board divisive issue. It's worse than the abortion issue because this one could destroy the foundation of civilization." Kevin chuckled. "It's true," she countered. "I've been out there ten months."

"And I've been out there ten years. You may have splinter groups on the righteous right and radical left who oppose germline therapy for any reason. But people are starting to support it."

"With the abortion issue, religious and conservative groups oppose it while liberal-minded groups support it. But on the germline issue both extremes oppose it basically for the same reason. And that's only what you see aboveground. My story's about what's below." The car changed lanes. "Doctor, this theater has three other players. To start with, the government."

"You working with the reporter at the press conference? The *X-files* fan?"

"You laughed when he said that DARPA had spent a billion dollars on genetic research. Well, I have documents obtained through the Freedom of Information Act that show that the government's spent more, *a lot more* than that. DARPA in particular! And then there's eugenicists looking for racial purity. What they've lost through intermarriage they intend to restore by the kind of selective breeding germline gene therapy might one day make possible. From neo-Nazi Aryans to African-American purists, they're all well-funded and waiting for the technology to become available."

"Does your story get the front page all by its lonesome or do you have to share it with alien invaders and JFK clones?"

Helen turned, touched his arm, and whispered, "Something else is out there, Dr. Kincaid. Something a lot scarier than the government, the lunatic fringes, or even terrorists for that matter. What exactly it is, I don't yet know."

He shook his head. "You're chasing a shadow."

"There are times when I think you're right." She closed her eyes. "God, I've been on the road so long for this story! I don't even have a home anymore. I'm broke. And you know what the worst part is? The loneliness. Dinner at McDonald's for one. The not-being-touched.

And the only man who's looked at me in God knows how long, only did so because I looked like somebody else." Feeling his eyes on her, she lay back in silence, allowing the *clump-clump* vibration of rubber on asphalt road to filter through her cushioned seat. Tears formed in her eyes as she realized that she'd said it more for herself than the mission.

"Ms. Morgan, do you have—plans for tonight?"

"I'm supersizing at Mickey D's."

After a long silence, he said, "I can get you in someplace nicer."

"Another table for one?"

He cleared his throat. "Let me rephrase. Would you like to go to one of the world's finest restaurants, tonight, with me?"

She opened her eyes. Turned to him. "Because I remind you of your wife?"

The car slowed, stopped at a red light. His mouth dry, he gazed into her eyes. "Because you remind *Donny* of my wife. He was more animated today than, well, that's worth the price of a decent meal."

"How about I trade that in for more info on V_7?"

"Don't push your luck."

Her mind played a collage of his faces: from continuously looped home videos with his family, from photos at schools and in professional societies, from his first gaze at her. *It's working.*

BFMC

"Table for two. This evening, first seating," the voice said.

"Thanks again for fitting me in so impossibly late," Kincaid's voice responded.

Tetlow clicked off the recorder on her desk. At last, the tap on Kincaid's office line had proved useful.

Le Bec-Fin
Philadelphia   7:59 P.M.

Crystal chandeliers, like diamond-studded broaches, reflected and refracted their light, bathing the restaurant in brilliance. A great mantled fireplace overlooked the elegant room of Louis XVI furniture and tables with Bernardaud china, Schott Zwiesel stemware, and exotic flowers. A delicate Mozart selection masked the sounds of tuxedoed waiters and busboys pampering patrons. Ornate mirrors provided the illusion of size for the intimate twenty tables. Helen sat beside Kevin. Her long, silken mahogany hair framed her small nose, high cheek-bones, and gray-green eyes. A tight, black, shining satin dress with a low, square neckline accentuated her figure. Bringing a forkful of *galette de crabe* to her lips, she said, "This is scrumptious." Pointing at his full plate. "Your meal alone is a hundred and fifty dollars, and you haven't touched it."

"I'm not hungry."

"You'll excuse me if I am." She touched the corners of her mouth with her napkin. "You might be looking at me, but you're seeing her."

"I've read that people choose prospective mates based on subconscious appraisal of symmetry. What we interpret as beauty is really just facial and body symmetry, which our minds interpret as measures of health and vigor."

She demurely smiled. "Deciding how symmetrical I'll be in bed?"

"No two symmetries are the same. No matter how subtle, there's always imperfections."

"Care to list mine?"

"What I'm trying to say is, when I look at you, I see Helen Morgan, not Helen Kincaid."

"Because of my imperfections?"

"Because of your differences."

She interlocked her hands like a bridge and balanced her chin on them. *"Pour exemple?"*

"The resonance in your voice. The way your jaw skews to the left when you chew. When you look at just the right angle, a hint of melancholy in your eyes."

"Maybe that's a reflection of your own."

A busboy appeared beside Helen and took her plate. As he removed Kevin's plate, he accidentally touched the china to Helen's water glass. The stemware tipped over, spilling onto the table. The busboy apologized profusely, dabbed a damp spot on the tablecloth, and hastily departed with Helen's glass. He returned a moment later with a fresh glass for her. With a tiny brush, he whisked crumbs from Helen's side of the table into a tray and exited just before a waiter presented a plate of *filet de boeuf* to Helen and *mignon de veau au citron* to Kevin.

"So, Ms. Morgan, what is your story?"

"I thought we weren't going to talk shop tonight."

Drawing a glass of Merlot to his lips, "No, no. Not what story you're reporting on—I mean what is *your* story."

"Me, personally?" she said, touching her chest. "Basically, it's a testament to dedication, naivete, stubbornness—the cocktail for disenchantment and ruin."

There was a long, uncomfortable silence. "Go on. I'm listening."

"You've said that there's nothing more to you than your work. What makes you think that there's anything more to me than my story?"

"You say I'm seeing my wife when I look at you. Maybe you're right."

She slowly lowered a forkful of rare filet to her plate and gazed at him. "Told you."

"But if you insist that I *know* that I'm looking at Helen Morgan, I have to know something *about* Helen Morgan." He touched her hand. His pulse quickened.

Helen withdrew her hand, opened her eyes wide, then, squinting, looked up and around. "Excuse me." She opened her handbag, withdrew a tiny fluid-filled vial, held it over her upturned head, and released two drops into each eye. She blinked, then turned to Kevin with glistening eyes. "Contacts. The dry air here plays havoc with them."

Kevin stared at her as if calculating different approaches for his next move. "Let's start with an easy question. Where are you from?"

"Everywhere. Nowhere. My father worked for the government. We moved around a lot. Before college my life was a series of two-year stints at research stations from Anchorage to Atlanta. By the time I was ten I'd learned to stop making friends."

"Until college."

"I was a broadcast-journalism major at NYU. Minored in theater." She hesitated. "For the first time my life was stable. You can't appreciate how wonderful it is to wake up in the morning and know that you'll be in the same place, and that the people you meet and care about will still be there, too." She pushed a slice of meat across her plate. "I was exactly where I wanted to be: New York. I was going to be a network anchor."

"You certainly have the drive and the intelligence. And," gently smiling, "you wouldn't look bad in front of the camera, either."

"That dream died when my father did."

"I'm sorry. Money problems?"

Her fingers stiffened. "Among other things."

"It must have been difficult. But you're still in the business. Don't count yourself out."

She looked away from him—in part, a strategic move, but in part because it was difficult to face him. "I wound up interning at KIFI-TV in southern Idaho. It didn't work out, but I managed to get a job at the *Idaho Falls Post Register*. Which has led me to this increasingly pleasant dinner."

He raised his glass to her. She speared her filet.

From within the safe confines of her limousine's tinted rear window Joan Tetlow, hands rigidly clasped, stared at the entrance to Le Bec-Fin. A man carrying a box dodged across Walnut Street, slid between parked cars, and rapped on the limousine's rear window. Her driver released the lock. The man jumped into the seat beside her.

Carefully, he opened the box. It contained bubble sheets wrapped around a sealed jar with crumbs and a water goblet. "Will this do?"

A sixtyish woman with tight silvery hair, teardrop diamond earrings, and husband-on-arm approached Kevin. "Dr. Kincaid? We saw you on TV. We wanted to tell you that what you're doing is wonderful. Years ago, we," glancing at her man, "lost a child to cystic fibrosis. No one should ever have to go through that." Her smile evaporated. "No one."

Helen studied Kevin as the couple moved on. She knew she had to maneuver ever more carefully. "Enjoy being in the spotlight?"

"You're the reporter. That's where *you* want to wind up."

"I'll take that as a yes."

"Then you'd be wrong. The only reason I ventured in was to dismantle the legal roadblocks hampering my work." He sat back. "I have absolutely no desire to see my private life, such as it is, plastered on tabloids by the checkout aisles."

She sighed. "You, Dr. Kincaid, are afraid of opening up to anyone. Especially me."

He tossed his napkin on the table. "Bullshit. You've seen me with Donny."

"That's hardly revealing. I could've been watching that commercial—excuse me, public service announcement—tonight on TV."

"You still haven't explained how you knew the content of the Association's PSA *before* it was aired. That was a closely guarded secret. Only a few senior officials at the Association and the network knew what was being aired. Now if—" Kevin stopped speaking. He appeared to be listening to a delicate classical piece being played in the background. After a handful of notes, he called the maître d' over and slipped him $100. "Please change the music. Something less—airy."

The maître d' looked perplexed. "Sir?"

Kevin slipped him another $100. "I don't care what. Just as long as there's no flute."

The man shrugged and left. Thirty seconds later, a neutral Bach piece played.

"Why did you do that?" Helen asked.

"How did you know about the commercial?" Kevin shot back.

"Trade you. Even up."

Kevin crossed his arms.

"Oh, all right! My editor may run a small-town newspaper, but more than a few network execs have started out in the boonies."

"Somehow I don't think that's the whole truth."

"Impugning my word is a poor defense for going back on yours."

"Okay, okay. At the funeral, my sister-in-law insisted on a flutist. The damn bastard played 'Amazing Grace.' It seems like I hear it all the time, but it's especially bad when I hear a flute solo. Changing background music is easy. But there're times when I have to be a bit more resourceful to drown out the sounds."

"Such as?"

"I studied Kung Fu a few years, as if I could learn to parry and punch the pain. But the only thing that ever helped silence that god-awful flute was work." He poured himself another glass. "And running. Endorphins, for a short time, purge my mind."

"Purge it for what?"

"Work," he said.

"Catatonia may seem a blessing, but you miss the highs, as well as the lows."

"I've had my share of both the last two days. Personally and professionally."

Could he be having doubts about his employers? Helen reached for the CD in her purse, then decided not to pursue it. "Kevin, when was the last time you felt exhilarated?"

He smiled. "Are you asking when the last time I was in bed with a woman?"

"Down, boy. I mean, when was the last time you felt—free?"

He leaned back, stared up at the chandelier. "I was standing on an old railroad trestle over the Perkiomen River, maybe eighty feet above the water. We were camping for the day, and some kids had dared me. I stood on the edge, looked down at that brown water—and I jumped." Slowly, a grin emerged. "There's this embracing, electrifying, terrifying delight. Your mind tricks you, tells you that your feet are just about to touch the ground the next instant. The next. Then the next. With each lie, you become more alive."

"How'd it feel when you hit the water?"

"I struck the river, legs stiff, but angled a bit forward. It wasn't a hard smack, I just kind of slid in and shot down, but at an angle that redirected the force of the fall to drive me back to the surface. I remember opening my eyes. The river was so murky, I couldn't see my hand in front of my face. I fought my way up, hands groping for the surface. I held my breath, using the same mind trick, promising myself that the surface was just an instant away."

"Boys! How old were you?"

"Eight. I remember because it was the last time before—" He stopped.

If only I can get him to open up. She stroked the back of his hand. "I'm listening."

"My father worked late, sometimes seven nights a week. He'd had an affair shortly after I was born. That ended, but my mother never fully trusted him again. She'd regularly greet him at the door with accusations. And before you ask whether she was right, the answer is—who knows? But this," holding up and swirling a glass of wine, "was her solution." He finished the glass. "Then Donny came and things really went wrong."

"How so?"

"Donny was 'unexpected.' Halfway through her pregnancy my mother knew that she was carrying a child with Down syndrome. When he was born he also had severe neurologic problems, which the doctors promptly attributed to her drinking. My father blamed my mother. My mother blamed herself. And me, I blamed Donny."

"Why?"

"My family may have been dysfunctional, but at least it was a family. Donny shattered that." He shrugged. "One morning I tried to wake up my mother. Her arms were cold." His jaw muscles flexed. "You know, people really can will themselves to die."

Helen's fingers caressed his hand. She blinked rapidly. "I've ruined your evening."

The waiter presented him with the bill. Kevin placed a platinum credit card in the book and handed it back without looking. "Remember Wendy? The woman you met at the hospital? Well, over the years, she's seen many pictures of my wife. Know what she whispered in my ear?"

Helen blew her nose. Shook her head.

" 'Second chances come only once.' "

Helen Morgan returned his gaze. "Take me back to my hotel," she rasped. "I've something to share with you."

Tetlow's fingernails digging into the seat, "Move your people into position. We may only have this one opportunity."

The man in the front seat relayed her orders. A moment later he said, "Don't worry, Ms. Tetlow. My people have all the angles covered."

Kevin and Helen appeared at the restaurant's front entrance. Kevin signaled the valet to bring the car.

"I don't see any of your men. Where are your men?" Tetlow snapped.

The valet helped Helen into the car. Kevin tipped the man and drove off.

"Did they get it? Did they get it?"

A man in a short leather jacket hurried across the street, walked up to Tetlow's car, and handed a disk to the man in front. "Here they are, Ms. Tetlow," he said, "your photos."

Adam's Mark Hotel
Philadelphia   *10:01 P.M.*

Helen entered her hotel room with Kevin close behind her. Her dress swishing, she took his coat and hung it in her closet. "That was a wonderful dinner."

"Glad you liked it."

She approached him, her eyes just above his shoulder level. She ran a finger up and down the outside of his firm upper arm. His warm breath glided over her hair, down her back. The beat from his pounding heart jumped the narrowing gulf between them, burrowed into her chest. Eyelids drooping, she gazed up into his face, brushed back an errant lock of his hair, then touched tiny beads of perspiration on his forehead. *I must divorce mission from passion*, she thought, taking his hand, leading him into the bedroom. Placing her hands beneath his jacket, she pushed it up over his shoulders and onto the floor, then slithered her third finger beneath his collar and loosened his tie. "Let me share something precious with you," she said. "Close your eyes."

Kevin's eyes fluttered shut.

Helen pulled back. So tall, strong, tight. Yet quivering. From anticipation? Fear? She had to know whether payment should be made in advance. She took her handbag from the floor, and exposed the precious CD inside. *I have to be certain.* "Tonight, I can be your—"

"No. Don't say it. I," stifling a laugh-cry, "want *you*, Helen Morgan."

She, too, hushed a cry, closed her handbag, and gently kicked it away.

He opened his eyes, touched her chin, and raised her face to his.

She reached back, unzipped her dress, let it slink onto the floor, and stood, her body open. Errant strands of her long hair flowed over breasts billowing from her satiny chemise. "Show me."

"It's been so—such a long, long time."

For us both.

He followed her lead, undressing to taut, baby blue briefs stretched to bursting limits.

She massaged her palms in sweeping, circular motions across the tops of sparse hairs on his muscular chest. Each chest hair stiffened, aroused in synchrony to his thumping heart as she blew a stream of warm, steamy breath over them. She removed her panty hose. Let her slip fall.

He removed his briefs, released a long, shuddering breath, and trembled.

Extending her arm, she took his hand, led him to the side of the bed, and directed him to sit near the edge. She sat between his legs, her back to his chest, and brought his arms around her midriff. "Hold me." His chest warmed her chilled back. His hot breath, his desire to please her, heated her in places she thought long dead. Tucked against her back, his burning stiffness grew hotter, thicker. Stronger.

She turned her face to him. Their lips met, at first, closed. She widened hers, and felt his tongue gently trace their inner lining. Then pull back, waiting. She gave a long, lingering glance at the strong man who wanted to please her, and responded in kind. Their mouths spread in unison, their tongues meeting, exploring, playfully dancing around each other, entwining, battling to be with and within the other. She guided his hands across her abdomen. Up and beneath her breasts. He held them in adulation, as if they were precious, fragile treasures. Adoring fingertips glided up over their curves, pausing gently over her nipples before they touched in ever-tightening circles. The burning engorgement in her back grew hotter. Wanting more. It was time.

Her right hand caressed his. She led it away from her breasts—down across her belly, her pelvis, along her right thigh, and inward. She released his hand. It skipped to the other thigh, slowly slid inward, and again skipped the sensuous center. His fingers glided back and forth between her legs, each pass denying the touch to desirous flesh that needed, screamed for it. She could not wait.

As if hearing her body's screams, his fingers touched her tender flesh. Stroked it gently. It was already wet, sticky with excitement. Slowly up, slowly down. Her body swayed to each stroke. His strokes increased in strength, in speed, in intensity to her desire. More, she wanted. More.

He followed the changing rhythms of her body. Her skin gleamed with sweat. Her tongue no longer able to dance, her mouth needed to be open, to moan. She needed his rhythmic strokes higher, to touch her incarnation of ecstasy. He could not know; she had to show him.

But his hand moved, so slightly up and in. To her place of purest pleasure.

"Ohhh!" She felt him stroke her anew, following the movements of her body, whispering in her ear of her beauty, of delicious promises, of unquestioned, unrestrained fulfillment of her most hidden desires. She grimaced with pleasure, feeling him grow beside her as her body rocked, holding back for that one lost moment before absolute ecstasy. One last second.

Her body erupted. She convulsed in rapture.

His arms tightened around her middle as her body writhed from aftershocks. He kissed her cheek, her neck, her shoulder, and hugged her again. Her ecstatic tremors slowly, slowly receded, though they burned as strong.

He started again.

As his fingers tenderly caressed between her legs, she knew it would again be wonderful. But she needed to transcend that level. She brought her hand around to his face and lightly kissed his lips. "Come, face me."

He picked up his leg and swiveled around to face her, his fingers continuing ever-heightening strokes. She touched his shoulder. He folded, kneeling before her.

She whispered, "If you'd rather not—"

"Shhh!" He kissed her knee, touched his tongue to her thigh, and drew a long, wet curve inward. He lifted his head, and began again. First one leg, then the other, then back. Never coming home.

Her fervor rose. What was he waiting for?

He touched his tongue to her most tender spot. She wriggled as wave upon wave of electricity surged through her. He changed his rhythm to match the slowly strengthening beats of her body. She whined in expectation. He suddenly stopped.

"Please," she panted. "Please!"

He touched the barest tip of his tongue to where she cried out.

She erupted. Stronger, so much stronger than before. And deeper. But not deep enough.

She motioned him onto the bed. He scrambled to her. They sat facing each other, legs spread wide. They gazed a moment into each other's eyes, then she shimmied between his legs, his thighs. Drenched in perspiration, her skin tingled from waves of heat that arose from the tip of his erectness. Closer, she moved. It touched her. She quaked with anticipation. They leaned into each other, kissing wildly, devouring each other. She grabbed his fullness, growing in girth, and hot, scorching hot. Its swelled underside pulsating, she felt his heart beat in her palm.

His lips broke away. He reached out and caressed her cheek. Helen gazed at him. He was not looking on her as conquest, but with empathy, with genuine desire to fulfill her. She knew he would be happy to bask in whatever warmth she would give back.

Half lunging forward, she guided him inside. She rocked as his burning filled her, the bed thumping to the ferocity of their rhythm. Deeper, expanding, he filled her. Overfilled her. His pulse pounded within her, joining his heart to hers. Her insides, permeated with pleasure. More—she wailed to his driving, thrusting expansion— more. More! She had to have him!

He furiously convulsed within her. She exploded with euphoria. He convulsed again. Her body responded in spectacular kind. He rumbled again inside her, a mini-burst of exhilaration.

The powerful fullness within her slowly deflated, retreated. His matted chest hairs pressed against her as she tried to squeeze out the last drops of his fullness. He raised her chin and softly touched his lips to hers. Skin tingling, pelvis reverberating with ghostly echoes of his rhythm, her mind lazily swam through a choking ecstasy.

Never before had she—never before. "Were you making love to me or your wife?"

Stupid! she thought. *Stupid! Why did you do that? He'll—*

". . . was you. *You* were the one who brought me back."

She still felt his heat inside her, strong as ever. Out of the corner of her eye, she saw her handbag strap protruding from beneath the bed. There'd be plenty of time in the morning to show him the Program. It could wait.

DARPA (Defense Advanced Research Projects Agency)
Director's Office, S&I (Security & Intelligence)
Arlington, Virginia

Kristin Brocks took off her reading glasses and dully stared at the small holographic-image projector on her desktop. She'd already played the Collaborate's last intercepted communication twenty-five times, hoping to discover some hidden nuance she'd missed. On her 26th playing, she focused on the image of the silhouette. The apparition said: "I'll consult our contacts within DARPA."

After two years of investigations with surveillance satellites, hidden operatives, and planning, they'd finally said openly what she'd feared all along: the Agency had been compromised. But the intercepted communication told her more: the Collaborate was going to ground. Thinking back, her meeting on the ski lift had been a mistake. Loring's carefully crafted comments about her divorce had caught her off guard and neutralized her edge. And she'd compounded that blunder with an ill-conceived closing bravado. Brocks chided herself for allowing her shattered feelings to disrupt the focus of her life.

Her computer beeped and displayed a tiny phone icon in the center of her screen: it was an incoming call. Immediately, she down-loaded the holographic message onto one of the Agency's ultra-high-density transparent data crystals, pocketed it, deleted and destroyed the parent file on the network, then put the call through. A man appeared on her monitor: Dr. Quentin Hicks, Director of the Defense Sciences Office. DSO was DARPA's largest technical office and its technological conscience, charged with developing the most promising arenas of basic science and engineering research and bringing them into DoD. DSO generally handled cryogenics, holo-graphic data storage systems, virtual integrated prototyping model-ing, and biomimetic systems—but there were notable exceptions. The DSO Director, though not her superior, required some measure of deference. "Good evening, Dr. Hicks. You're up late."

"They wouldn't listen to you?" Hicks asked.

"Loring laughed in my face."

"Why are they being so unreasonable?"

"Because they can."

Hicks wiped his sweaty forehead. "One of my sources verified that Kincaid has, indeed, produced a vector capable of transport-ing full sets of artificial chromosomes in animal cells with one hundred percent transfection efficacy and one hundred percent specificity. We want it. We're entitled to it under the terms of the collaboration."

"They don't see it that way. Their agreement with us was dis-solved years before Kincaid perfected his vector. Even before our tête-à-tête, Loring facetiously invited me to bring it up in open court."

Hicks rapped his index finger on the table. "Who cares what they think? I just want to know how *you* are going to get it!"

She tried to rub the exhaustion from her eyes. She didn't want to argue, but knew the next place that finger was going to point was at her. "Quentin, I've spent every waking hour of the last few years try-ing to clean up your mess."

"My—"

"You were project manager."

Dr. Hicks smiled nastily. "All this time and you still don't under-stand the System. This agency is dedicated to high-risk technology research free from bureaucracy. We're small, flexible, autonomous, unconstrained by conventional thinking, a bunch of freewheeling zealots pursuing unconventional goals, willing to accept failure *if* the payoff is sufficiently high. Here we develop long-term projects that require extended focus. Here we employ 'Technology Push' by identifying technologies that could make a difference, working them through to their limits and translating them into what this country will need—*tomorrow*. Now, should I repeat that, Kristin, or just put it in big, easy-to-read typeface?"

Brocks put on her reading glasses. "By all our SOPs, that Controlled Biological Systems project should have been kept *wholly within the government*. You set in motion a disaster by subcontracting to private industry, not to mention fully collaborating with them."

"That's what we do here, you overpriced security guard! We set up innovative agreements with the private sector outside of federal acquisition regulations. Projects likely to support both commercial nonmilitary and military applications. We cost-share with these companies, and then forecast what they'll do with our shared technology."

"Well, your former collaborators have used these shared resources to implement a program that not only threatens national security, but the foundation of western civilization. You made a deal with the devil." She tossed her glasses back on the desk. "And he still has plenty of silent disciples listening within this agency!"

"So, damn it, bring in the FBI! Or NSA! Or Homeland!"

"Your former friends would consider that provocative. Dr. Hicks, they have copies of the files on your special Controlled Biological System's project. If threatened they'll dump the entire contents onto a slew of websites. Need I go into the far-reaching consequences? As Project Manager your name would appear at the top of the indictment." He emphatically shook his head. "Think again," she continued. "You deliberately covered up that some of your industrial partners were not—American. On a project such as this, that's more than enough."

He buried his head in his hands. "I thought you supported the Project."

"I do. Which is why I'm keeping this matter internal and tight. So," putting on her glasses, "shall we refrain from finger-pointing?"

Adam's Mark Hotel

Beneath warm sheets in darkness pierced by the blue LCD digits of her alarm clock, Helen cooed as Kevin's hand slowly, slowly ventured toward the underside of her breasts. Her back tingled from his tender kisses moving down her spine. The phone rang. Reluctantly, she answered.

"It is Anna."

Helen brushed Kevin's roaming fingers from her chest, turned on her side, and clamped the receiver against her ear. "I have—company."

"Kincaid, yes?" Anna hesitated. "Trent knows that we copied the Program."

Helen felt Kevin's hand glide across her shoulder. She stepped from the bed. The covers fell away. "How?"

"Trent has many people hidden in many places. This is the first chance I have had to talk to you since—" Anna's voice cracked. "He almost killed me."

"Oh my God! What did he do?"

"Push me off my office building roof."

The bipolar bastard, she thought. "Are you okay?"

"Ja, ja. I am unhurt. He has a message for you. He says that you may show the doctor your evidence, if we return every copy to him later."

"I don't understand his about-face."

"Nor I. But Trent said that your time is running out."

Helen smiled reassuringly at Kevin. "Not a problem."

"He is in bed with you?"

"Oh, yes," she rasped.

"He—pleased you?"

Helen turned away from Kevin. "You're a good friend, but that's none of—"

"You have been trained to confuse him. Do not become confused yourself."

Covering her mouth, whispering into the phone, "He wants *me.*"

"Helen—Kevin Kincaid is going to die."

The room began spinning. She felt light-headed, suddenly cold.

"Trent intends to kill him by Friday."

Helen's right contact felt dry. "Maybe you're wrong."

"Perhaps. But if you have not convinced Kincaid to join us by then, Trent certainly will."

Her eye started to burn. She rubbed harder. "Talk to you later." And hung up the phone.

"Who was that?" Kevin asked.

"One of my sources," she said, blinking against her contact lens.

Kevin tossed off the sheets. Nude, partially erect, he turned to her.

"You're trembling." He touched the hand over her mouth. "What is it? Are you in trouble?"

Massaging her pained eye, she nodded.

"Helen, let me help." He held her arms.

Her irritated eye suddenly felt better. "Oh, no!"

"What? What?"

"My contact just popped out." She dropped to the floor and began scouring for it with extended fingers. "Don't move."

"I'll get the light."

"No!" She continued groping in the dark.

"Helen, this is silly. Let's turn on a lamp."

"Kevin, don't—"

He flicked on the nightstand light—and caught a full view of her face. One eye was green, the other pure, intense blue. His look turned pained, as if he'd just been struck.

"I've, uh, I've always worn colored contacts," she whispered. "I love green."

He recoiled from her. "My Helen's eyes were gray-green. Not something you'd find on the shelf. Those lenses had to be custom-made."

"Kevin, let me ex—"

"Your resemblance to my Helen was no accident! You made yourself up to look like her. Talk like her. My God, you even had her mannerisms, her likes, her—You used me—used me to get close enough to steal V$_7$."

"It wasn't that at all. You don't under—"

"Who's behind it? Radical extremists? Fundamentalists? Some greedy CEO?

"Kevin, please—"

"Shut up!" He gathered his tousled clothes. "Was it fun playing dress-up? Playing on my loneliness—my longing for the only woman I ever loved?" He slapped on his shirt, pants, shoes. "Tell me, what did they pay you to hurt me like this?" His eyes watery, "What the hell kind of person are you, that you could do this?" The door slammed behind him.

Helen staggered to the bathroom and looked in the wide mirror. The face that stared back had one blue and one gray-green eye. Half Helen Morgan, half Helen Kincaid. She was a nothing, a nobody, an amalgam of dreams: her own submerged nightmare and Kevin Kincaid's fantasy. She collapsed onto the tiles and curled up, her knees to her chest. She'd failed for her father, for her brother, for herself, and for the rest of humanity.

ACGD Commercial #3—
"Germline Gene Therapy: What Might My Brother Have Achieved?"

The following commercial aired on all major broadcast and cable networks the evening of Tuesday, January 21 and late night/early morning Wednesday, January 22:

> [VIDEO]:   Opening shot of Dr. Kevin Kincaid.

DR. KEVIN KINCAID: I'm Dr. Kevin Kincaid. For the past few nights, you've kindly let me into your homes to tell you about the promise of germline gene therapy. You've let me tell you how, one day, germline gene therapy may not only prevent genetic diseases in our children, but actually eliminate such diseases from the face of the earth. Now, let me give you a very personal reason.

> [VIDEO]:   Camera pans back.

KINCAID: My brother, Donny.

> [VIDEO]   Camera reveals Kincaid standing beside his brother, Donnelly Kincaid, in a wheelchair in a home.

KINCAID: A hundred years ago, people would have called Donny a "mongoloid idiot." Today, we know his condition as Down syndrome, or Trisomy 21. Now, in many cases, people with Down syndrome can lead nearly normal lives. A few, like my Donny, are not so lucky. Donny also has other genetic disabilities.

> [VIDEO]:   Camera pushes in for close-up of Donnelly.

KINCAID: Normal cells have twenty-three pairs of chromosomes.

> [VIDEO]:   CGI (Computer-Generated Imaging) Animation: Graphic of a human cell with twenty-three pairs of squiggly white strings (chromosomes) in the center (nucleus).

KINCAID (OFF-CAMERA VOICEOVER [VO]): Unfortunately, Donny's cells have an extra chromosome number 21.

> [VIDEO]: CGI Animation: Appearance of an additional red squiggly string (chromosome) beside one of the chromosome pairs. Close-up of the chromosome triplet: one red intertwined with two white.

KINCAID (VO): The only way we can ever hope to cure his genetic disease would be with gene therapy.

> [VIDEO]: CGI Animation: The red chromosome breaks apart and disappears.

KINCAID (VO): But it's too late for Donny.

> [VIDEO]: Transition to close-up of Donnelly.

KINCAID (VO): Even if we knew how to get rid of the extra chromosome that causes his genetic disability, we could never change all of the many billions of cells in his body. We needed to cure him *before* he was born. He needed germline gene therapy.

> [VIDEO]: Transition to CGI Animated Sequence: View of cell and center of cell (nucleus). Zoom in on center of cell, with crumpled white strings (the chromosomes) and one black, misshapen string (deformed chromosome.)

KINCAID (VO): In the center of every cell in our body is a nucleus. This nucleus contains strands of DNA, called chromosomes. Each chromosome contains hundreds or thousands of genes made of DNA. These genes are the blueprints for our bodies. But sometimes, something goes terribly wrong.

> [VIDEO]: Animated Sequence: Focuses in on misshapen black string.

KINCAID (VO): Just a few wrong DNA molecules on one gene of one chromosome can mean a lifetime of suffering.

[VIDEO]: *Split screen. Animated Sequence on left. Montage of sick children on right.*

KINCAID (VO): Down syndrome. Cystic fibrosis. Sickle cell. Tay-Sachs. Beta-thalassemia. The list goes on. No matter what medicines we give these children, we'll never fix their genes. Their disability will be carried on, generation after generation after generation. Unless . . .

[VIDEO]: *Full-screen CGI Animation: A bubble-enclosed white string (new chromosome) enters the cell and penetrates the nucleus. The white chromosome replaces the misshapen, black chromosome in the cell.*

KINCAID (VO): Unless we get rid of those disease-causing genes in every cell and replace them with healthy, working genes *before* there are too many cells to fix.

[VIDEO]: *CGI Animation: Pan back. See many cells with deformed, black chromosomes replaced by healthy white chromosomes. Then hundreds of cells. Then the outline of an arm. Then the outline of a recognizably human fetus. The fetus morphs into a young man resembling an idealized version of Donnelly Kincaid, without the physical characteristics of Down syndrome.*

KINCAID (VO): It's called germline gene therapy. And it might have prevented what happened to my brother.

[VIDEO]: *Dissolve to Donnelly's actual facial appearance. Camera pans back to Kincaid standing beside him.*

KINCAID (ON CAMERA): I love my brother. He's special. I wouldn't trade him for the world. But, sometimes, I wonder what he might have achieved if he had been given the same chance in life as me. Maybe you know someone like that, too.

[VIDEO]: *Freeze-frame of Donnelly.*

KINCAID: Call your senators! Demand their support for House Bill 601. Lift the ban on germline gene therapy. Tell them to vote *for* House Bill 601! Give our children a chance!

[VIDEO]: End Tag: Add supered letters to lower third of screen.
SUPPORT HOUSE BILL 601!
GIVE OUR CHILDREN A CHANCE![SM]
Paid for by the Association to Cure Genetic Disabilities.
Hold image for five seconds. Fade to black.

5

WEDNESDAY, JANUARY 22
Delphi   *12:32 A.M.*

Marguerite Moraes pressed her face against the OR theater's plastic
dome. Far below, the emergency team worked furiously, fighting the
ventricular tachycardia that had turned the little boy's heart into a bag
of wriggling worms. Marguerite wiped away her tears. So much
potential wasted. She wanted to beg God to at least let Ethan taste life,
but obviously, He had scorned them all.

Delphi had no graveyard. What would they do with the boy afterward? After Ethan, only one child remained. When the last one
went—she tried not to think of what would happen to her.

A short man with bulging forearms and wearing surgical blues
approached her. He said, "We've stabilized the boy."

"What now, Doctor?"

"We've tried everything. His seizures have progressed from partial
type, located in discrete areas of the cerebral cortex, to severe, generalized, tonic-clonic type, spreading across his higher centers. We've
titrated him with front line therapies, then adjunctive and second-
lines. We've tried drugs in four experimental families in addition to a
unique formulation synthesized by Dr. Ambrose downstairs. Nothing's worked. The child is progressing through to status epilepticus.
The seizures will begin lasting longer than thirty minutes, piling up
on each other without time for recovery. Before long, standard therapy for status epilepticus will fail. It might be weeks or days, perhaps
only hours." He folded his arms. "You've been through this before."

"Can't you do *anything?*"

"The autopsy may tell us why he survived longer than the others."

"Might it help Meredith? She's the last survivor, you know."

"I've said too much already. We'll inform you when the boy's status changes." The doctor spun on his sneakers and left.

He knows what's killing them! she thought. *I'm going to get Meredith out of here before they kill her, too!*

Adam's Mark Hotel

The face in the mirror that stared back at Helen Morgan was a hybrid of her shattered self. She'd thrown away the gray-green contacts, leaving her with her natural, blue eyes. Her cheeks had returned to their sallow shade, but her hair was now dyed obsidian black. For her own safety she could never allow her hair to return to its natural blond color. She turned off the bathroom light. Her half-packed suitcases lay strewn across the bed and couch, but she had nowhere to go.

The red light on her telephone blinked: a message, probably from Trent, or his sniveling sycophant, Straub. She phoned the front desk.

"Package for you, Ms. Morgan," the clerk said.

"Who from?"

"There's no return address. Should I have it sent up?"

"Yes, please." Then she hung up. *What's in the package? Who sent it? Trent? No, unmarked packages aren't his style. Kevin? Not likely, after the look in his eyes. Who else knows where I am?*

Helen answered the knock at her door. A messenger stood holding a sealed brown, bubble-lined envelope. She absently handed him $10 then closed the door in his face.

The package was dirty and mail-worn. She cradled it, backside up. A mail bomb? She held her breath and flipped it over. It was addressed to Helen Morgan, care of the Adam's Mark Hotel. And written in familiar block lettering. She dropped to her knees, ripped open the package, and spilled out the contents: a note, dated January 20; a mini audiocassette; a camcorder-sized videocassette; and two vials with spongy, pinkish-white tissue suspended in clear liquid. She seized the letter and began reading:

Tracy,

I found the Collaborate installation. It's on Tiburon Island, Mexico. I've been inside. You can't imagine what they've done to the Seris! I almost broke down. I've caught it on audio and video. The world's got to see this. But the Collaborate's so powerful and people are so cynical that I'm afraid this will be dismissed along with UFO sightings and alien autopsies. So I included two specimens. They're tissue samples from a little girl they mutilated. Take it to someone you trust. Have them do a full work-up. Make sure they do a 'KARYOTYPING.' It may be our only proof. You can fake pictures and sounds, but you can't fake DNA.

Tracy, whatever you do, KEEP THIS AWAY FROM TRENT! I'll try to meet up with you in Philly or D.C. If I don't show up in the next week, try looking at the old place in Virginia. But, whatever happens, promise me that you won't come after me! Because if I'm not there, I'm probably dead. I love you, Sis.

Always, Lance

Helen wiped her eyes, took the videotape, inserted it in the camcorder lying on her suitcase, and opened its viewer. She began to play the tape.

BFMC, Kincaid's Office

Kevin sat in his office, his mind at war with itself. On one side intellectual centers used pure logic to predict the complex interactions of biochemical electron shells. The problem with V_7 was the stiffness of the harpoon used to penetrate and tag the cell membrane, a problem attributable to its constituent sequence of amino acids. Painstakingly, his mind plucked possible amino acids from the air and ran them through a reconstruction algorithm to see whether they would fit the growing chain that slowly was becoming a new harpoon. A charged polar amino acid here. A substituted basic amino acid for an acidic one there. A less rigid uncharged polar amide-group amino acid with a hydroxyl group replacing a more rigid amide one. Only a handful of people in the world could use eidetic imagery to perform so many complex chemical reactions so quickly. But the root of his brilliance, that unswervingly perfect memory, was also the source of his anguish. So often it had turned against him by flawlessly immersing him in the sights, the smells, the senses of his personal tragedies, forcing him to relive those moments again and again. Only discipline and constant work had checked the flood of memories and the pain.

The solution to V_7's problem was coming together in part of his mind—while the other part displayed a montage of blue- and gray-green-eyed Helen-faces, plastered on darkness, each image begging his forgiveness. She'd left him raw, bleeding, wanting to die. He fought harder to modify V_7, even as Helen-faces were being incorporated into the harpoon's new amino acid sequence.

BFMC, Cafeteria

Joan Tetlow shoved her spoon deep into her grapefruit, the breakfast she'd been denied because of the paper mountain that had accumulated on her desk the last few days. The grapefruit squirted her. She rubbed a burning eye clear, then glanced up. A woman with long, silky-black hair, carrying a man's overcoat, strode quickly across the lobby. *Was that her?*

BFMC, Kincaid's Office

Kevin felt the solution coming. Amino acids were dropping into the new harpoon protein sequence like the last few words filling a cross-word puzzle. The new harpoon slowly transformed. Slowly, it was becoming a living, twisting, stereoscopic ribbon twisting in his mind. Soon, he'd have the harpoon's preliminary sequence. Perhaps next week his coworkers could begin synthesizing and testing.

Heated voices from outside his door touched the edges of his con-sciousness, like fragments of overheard conversation in a crowded mall. One was his secretary. He couldn't clearly hear the other.

There it was—his mind presenting it with perfect clarity: the fix for V_7's flaw! Kevin turned to his computer, opened the protein sequencing program, started a new file, and began entering one-letter amino acid codes:

```
 1  MAGQLRTPKWESYLGFFEFDWQEIVGSAFEDNPPQTGVNICAYDQWSLEG 50
51  FKLKQVINSEDDNH—
```

A woman with long black hair and hot blue eyes burst into the office.

His eyes locked on to hers. "Helen, you've changed the face that launched a thousand ships. So who do those blue eyes belong to?"

"They're mine."

"The black hair, too?"

She folded his overcoat and laid it on a chair.

"Thanks for returning it. Now that that's done," voice trembling, "so are we."

"Kevin, you're a brilliant, sensitive man. But sometimes you're so myopic, so naive that—"

"So now it's my fault?"

"I risked my life coming here to save yours."

"No more cloak-and-dagger!" Pointing, "Door's unlocked."

She glanced at the monitor and VCR on a cart in the corner, then opened her handbag and withdrew a videocassette. "Here's the Ghost of Christmas Future." She turned on the monitor and VCR and put the tape in the slot. Shaky images, seemingly from a jostled handheld camera, appeared on the TV of a somber, granite-block building rising out of marshland enclosed by a high, barbed-wire fence. The image jumped to out-of-focus figures, children, moving around the compound. Not clustered together, playing, but walking erratically. "This is Isla de Tiburon, Mexico."

"Camera work's not very good," he said.

"The cameraman may be dead."

The picture zoomed in on three children. One child had distorted neck muscles that twisted his head three-quarters backward. Another had massively enlarged chest muscles on the right side, with atrophied muscles on the left side. A third, swollen legs like tree stumps. Each hobbled.

"I've never seen such a collection of neuromuscular asymmetries. Did you get this from the island of Tiburon or *The Island of Doctor Moreau*?"

The picture jumped to a tiled lab with old equipment: biological safety cabinets, orbital shakers, cell-culture incubators, low-power microscopes. Seemingly shot from an exterior window, the picture panned to a back room, then zoomed in. Two men in white coats knelt alongside a dark-skinned little girl in chains. Her head bulged on its left side, hideously distorting her face like a cut-away diagram in an anatomical atlas. Her left shoulder was bloated, covered with oozing ulcers, and dislocated high on her collarbone. The other shoulder was withered, frail. Her left arm, manacled, rattled inch-thick chain links as she squirmed in terror. One man produced a scalpel and approached the toddler while his partner applied a tourniquet to her arm. He began carving through skin to burgeoning biceps beneath. The little girl screamed.

"My God! What's he doing?" Kevin exclaimed, her wails vibrating through his chest. "He's not even using anesthesia! What kind of doctor—"

"One without conscience, testing the muscular strength of his 'experiment' under duress. That's all these children were to those monsters—just guinea pigs."

The man dissected deeper. He isolated a chunk of ultra-dense pink flesh with a pair of pick-ups and plopped it into a fluid-filled vial. Helen froze the tape.

Kevin turned away from the vivisection. "It's a hoax."

"You know it wasn't." Helen shut her eyes. "It gets worse."

"Why are you showing me this?"

"These deformities didn't occur naturally. They were induced."

"Induced? By what? Some kind of radiation?"

"You just don't see it, do you?"

"See what?"

Shaking her head, "What your vector can do."

"Oh, no! No way! I'm not responsible for that!"

Helen knelt beside him. Touched his hand. "Oh, but my sweet Kevin, you *are!*"

Loring's Estate
Berks County, Pennsylvania

Loring poured himself a drink from the bar, then seated himself opposite the bolted doors. It had been two years since he'd spent an evening at his Berks County estate. The library, similar to but larger than the one in Santa Fe, afforded a view of his private golf course nestled in rich farmland between rural Lancaster and urban Delaware valleys. Though maintained by a skeleton staff, the house had a faint, musty odor—an odor that had to be removed before evening.

"Thirty seconds to incoming transmission," announced the synthetic voice.

Unlike yesterday's private holographic conference with Bertram, this would be a Quorum Summit, with at least seven of the principal seventeen members participating, though all were rarely in the same hemisphere, let alone the same country. Aside from Bertram, the participants varied from meeting to meeting. Quorum Summits yielded to the chemistry of their participants: sometimes afternoon tea, often trench warfare.

Red, blue, green lights scanned him. In the background, a faint A-minor chord chimed. In the far corner of the room, the pseudo-image rotund silhouette appeared at a desk: Bertram.

Five other holographic images appeared in the room: Floyd Elliston, dressed in jeans and cutting a steak; Andrea Beller, in a black *tobok* in the middle of a Taiji pattern; Euan McDonald, feet propped on a couch and smoking a pipe; Stuart Knorr, slumped in a chair, hand propping up a sleepy head; and Wolfgang Vorpahl, in an impeccably tailored suit, and sitting at attention. The Americans and the Australian were principals in biotech industries; the German brought vast holdings in communications and banking to the table. In the Collaborate's early, formative years, many members had pushed to include representatives from the Middle East and North Africa, citing their potentially enormous financial assets. Bertram had steadfastly refused to allow a citizen of any Muslim state to join—which particularly puzzled the membership, considering Bertram's extensive travels throughout Asia and Africa. The Collaborate had nearly disbanded over the issue. Then came the atrocities in New York. After that, no one ever questioned his decisions.

"We have a Quorum," the Bertram silhouette began. "First on the agenda: Tiburon. As you all know, the facility had to be dismantled due to a security breach. There was insufficient time to call for a referendum."

"Breached by who? The government?" Floyd Elliston asked between bites of beef.

"You've all received, by courier, Mr. Loring's report on the meeting with the DARPA security chief," Bertram said. "They knew about Tiburon, but kept their distance."

"Doesn't answer my question," Elliston said.

Bertram answered, "The matter is under investigation."

"Estimated loss in U.S. dollars?" Wolfgang Vorpahl asked quietly.

"The facility was antiquated," Bertram said. "The final tally, allowing for discounting, less than $150 million American, excluding graft to Mexican officials. Sustainable."

"Total loss, ya mean," Elliston spat, slamming down his fork. "What the hell did we get out of that place anyway?"

"Data, Mr. Elliston," Bertram said slowly, emphatically. "We know that the new genes synthesized for musculoskeletal structure are fully effective. Don't we?"

"Yeah."

"And we know that the chromosome carrying them can, in theory, be fully inserted into human cells. Don't we, Mr. Elliston?"

"Yeah."

"And we know, from autopsies of female subjects, that induced genetic alterations are present in subjects' egg cells and are, therefore, carried into the germline and passed from generation to generation. That was our intent, was it not, Mr. Elliston?"

"Uh-huh."

"And through creative cost sharing, the bulk of funds for establishing Tiburon came, unwittingly, through DARPA. Did it not?"

"I know, I know."

"Then certainly you must agree that Tiburon has proven itself cost-effective."

Loring smiled at the beauty of Bertram's signature sales tactics: little yes's leading the buyer into a final acceptance.

"With the final component, facilities like Tiburon and Delphi will take on lesser importance. Beta testing, primarily," Bertram said. "Item closed. Which brings us to the next order of business. The new vector, Mr. Loring?"

Loring finished his drink. "Kincaid has virtually completed formulating and testing the new vector. I hope—anticipate—presenting it to this body within two weeks."

"What about the woman at the news conference?" Andrea Beller asked, then snapped out her right hand as if delivering a punch. "Who is she?"

"The matter is being investigated."

"Why doesn't that comfort me?" Beller sneered.

Loring stared at his empty glass. "We have photographs, fingerprints, DNA samples. We're running her through every database on Earth."

"The woman knew about K_4."

"We're investigating possible leaks from Kincaid's lab and other sources."

"Like what?"

Loring put down the glass and glared at Beller's holographic image. "Like this virtual room."

The others shouted protests and accusations. Bertram banged a gavel.

"The Feds're involved," Elliston voiced.

"They're breast-beating," Loring said.

"Dixon, could there be a connection between Tiburon and that woman?" Euan McDonald asked, smoke wafting from his pipe.

Loring looked to the silhouette of Bertram. "Possibly."

"I realize that it is the policy of this organization *not* to employ extreme force against the outside world, as any such use presents a substantial risk to the Plan. Nonetheless, I believe this Quorum should grant Mr. Loring the authority to use such force as required," Bertram said. "The Chair votes yes on this matter. And the rest of this Quorum?"

The five others raised their hands.

"It's passed. Mr. Loring, I trust you'll use *discretionary* force."

Loring nodded graciously. His assignment offered a rare opportunity.

"Third order of business," Bertram resumed. "Progress on passage of U.S. House of Representatives Bill 601. Some of you have concerns regarding the handling of this matter, Herr Vorpahl."

Vorpahl adjusted his collar. "I understand the importance of this legislation. America is unrestricted by social and political restraints in European Union. Developments in United States lead to perceived inadequacies in Europe. But a $100 million bribe to a senator?"

Bertram paused. "A small sum, considering our expenditures to date, and it assures passage of Bill 601. But it will also buy other key votes that will be needed in time. In addition, I would not be surprised if much of this expenditure finds it way back into our coffers."

"*Danke.*"

"Last order of business." Bertram hesitated. "Owing to the delicacy of progress on House Bill 601, events at Tiburon, possible security breaches, and the probability of stepped-up pressure from U.S. agencies, we will refrain from holding summits for at least a fortnight. Communications will be maintained by the courier system—with the Chair, as usual, serving as focal point."

"I don't like being left out in the cold," Elliston declared.

Bertram cleared his throat. "Let us now consider suspending all noncourier communications for the next two weeks. The Chair votes 'yes'. How does the rest of this Quorum vote?"

Loring raised his hand, as did the others, except Elliston.

Bertram whispered, "In matters of security, a unanimous vote is always less complicated."

Elliston slowly raised his hand. "I think it's a mistake to hamper free communication when we might need it most."

"So noted," Bertram said. "This session is ended. Thank you all for your time."

The holographic images disappeared.

Loring raised both fists triumphantly before smugly striding to the bar for a celebration. Seventeen years of plans and plots had culminated in an almost casual Quorum vote. *For the next two weeks, I am the Collaborate!*

BFMC

Kevin continued to stare at the blank screen after Helen removed the video. In the ten years following his residency, he'd performed more than 5,000 surgeries, cut deep into people's innards, and held living brain tissue in his hands. But to see such torture on young, horribly afflicted children. His mouth tasted vile from his churning stomach.

"You're doing better than I did," Helen said. "First time, I threw up."

"Who? Who would—"

"Your employers." She returned the tape to her handbag. "And you, Kevin."

"*Me?*"

"In the coffee shop, you said you'd only used vector K_4 on cell cultures."

"K_4 was a prototype. It wasn't ready for clinical trials on human beings!"

She sat on a corner of the desk and leaned in. "Apparently someone thought that it was."

"I don't believe you."

"Lance," stifling a sob, "my brother, the one who took these pictures, knew it, too." Opening her handbag, "So he sent these." She held a pair of vials with spongy, pinkish-white tissue suspended in clear liquid. "Tissue samples from one of the children. Proof that K_4 was used."

He took one of the vials. "Won't work. If HACV.K_4 was used in human germline therapy it would've been used to transfect genetic material in those children when they were embryonic, most likely while they were still little more than a blastula, a ball of cells. Any traces of K_4 would have long since been cleared."

"You told me that you abandoned K_4 because it often broke the chromosome it carried. So wouldn't that leave behind some characteristic pattern in the cells?"

Kevin reexamined the vial in his hand. "Let's see. K_4 tries to insert a new chromosome into embryonic cells. For some it succeeds, creating cells with a new extra pair of chromosomes. When those cells divide, generation by generation, they give rise to a line of cells with the new extra chromosome. For some cells it fails, inserting only fragments. In most cases those fragments aren't viable and when those cells divide, those chromosome pieces are not replicated for the next generation. For a few cells, though, it just might partially fail and—"

"Partially fail?"

"In order to be replicated when cells divide, chromosome pairs need two key segments. A centromere, that's the central portion separating the long and short arms of each chromosome. And telomeres, those are the caps at the tips of the chromosomes."

"So a few early cells had chromosome pieces with a centromere and telomere?"

"In part. So what we're left with is collections of hybrid cells. Some containing an extra chromosome, some containing the normal number of chromosomes, and a few containing viable pieces of an extra chromosome."

"Would that show up under a microscope?"

"Possibly. K_4's never been used on living higher organisms." He stared at the blank TV. "At least, not to my knowledge." Horrific images of distorted children flooded his consciousness. He parried the pain by clinically sifting through their deformities. A pattern emerged. In most cases, the deformities appeared to follow lines of human embryonic development. Something had happened to those children while they were embryos, as if an artificial chromosome carrying genes for super-muscles had been effectively inserted into some areas of the embryo, but not into others. The pattern was consistent with failed experiments on K_4.

"Kevin, I need your help. Can you analyze them? Now?"

He sat straight up, turned to the desk, picked up the phone, and punched in a series of numbers. "It's me. I'm in my office," he said into the receiver. "I need you up here, right away. Alone." He paused. "Don't tell anyone where you're going." He hung up.

"It's not safe for me to be seen in your office," Helen said.

"I want answers! Who at this center would use K_4 to—"

"Oh, it's much bigger than the hospital. Bigger than BFHN, too."

"The Association?"

"That's just their PR invention," she said, heading toward the closet.

"They?"

"The Collaborate."

"Who's collaborating to—"

"I'll explain later." She stepped into a closet and closed the door. "Shhh!"

He heard a light rapping on his office door. "Come in," he called.

A haggard Peter Nguyen shuffled in. He surveyed the room. "I thought I heard voices."

"I hope that's not from sleep deprivation because I have a new top-priority task for you." Kevin placed the pair of vials in his postdoc's palm. "Analyze these. Just you, Peter."

Nguyen studied them. "What would you like?"

"The works. Karyotyping, FISH, Western blotting if you find any unusual proteins, sequencing if you can. Anything else, let curiosity be your guide."

"What am I looking for?"

"You tell me."

Nguyen scrutinized the vials. "Give me a week and—"

"You've got ten hours."

"That's barely enough time to run one test, let alone—"

"Get the results tonight and I'll buy you dinner in Chevy Chase tomorrow."

Nguyen shrugged. "Guess I'll have to take the deal."

"Oh, and Peter, keep this strictly between us."

"There is a problem: Tetlow. She wants all V_7 files in order and ready to ship on Monday."

"Ship? Where?"

"She didn't say."

"You just analyze those samples. Let me worry about Tetlow."

Helen emerged from the closet after Nguyen left. "Can you trust him?"

"Can I trust you?"

She stiffened. "What by the way, is a fish?"

"FISH, *F-I-S-H*. Fluorescene in situ hybridization. A way of labeling DNA with fluorescent markers that show up under ultraviolet light. Basically, there are special labels that you can attach to each human chromosome. Like painting each specific chromosome a different color. If there's a new, artificial chromosome in any of the specimen cells, it'll stand out like a sore thumb, because there won't be any chromosome paint for it."

"Thank you. I'm so sorry about—"

"You'll get your information. Just go."

"It's only natural to want to run away from this. I know, I've tried. But you're in, and you're going to have to choose sides. Ours, or theirs."

"What is your side?"

She pointed at the monitor. "The alternative."

"You're asking me to accept that the people who've supported me all these years—"

"I can show you—on your home computer."

Delphi

Marguerite Moraes glanced out the window. Snow covered the glen and the aboveground portion of Delphi complex. Beyond lay a barren forest ringed by an invisible security system. Quickly, she locked her office and pressed her back against the door while clutching a piece of paper in her hand. If they knew, she'd vanish.

In California she'd had a promising career in elementary-level teaching—until a disturbed boy in her second-grade class publicly announced that she'd forced him to fondle his genitals. She was virtually certain that the boy's father had trumped up the accusations because she'd refused his sexual advances several times. The legal nightmare that had taken three years of her life had declared her not guilty, but had also left her friendless, broke, unemployable. Then, like a miracle, the headmaster of Delphi had appeared, promising her a very generous salary to teach some of the brightest young minds in the world at a secluded private school. At first it had been idyllic: a magnificent complex in a pastoral setting and thirty brilliant, attentive children. Still in diapers, the toddlers blew through a year of elementary language arts in a week, algebra within a month, and surpassed the limits of her knowledge within a year. She'd brought in specialized tutors carefully screened by Delphi administrators. Along the way she'd learned never to ask too much about her special charges. But after two years, she noticed one child abruptly stop work, stare into space for a minute, then return to work, unaware of the lapse. Once, twice, then ten times a day. Delphi's doctor confirmed her suspicions: epilepsy, petit mal. A second student fell victim. It spread through her class. Then the violent seizures. First-line, second-line, adjunctive anti-epileptic medications worked temporarily, but the children's seizures rebounded quicker, more violently. No established or devised treatment by Delphi's brilliant clinicians could stop the plague rampaging through the children. Neither, it seemed, could earnestly offered prayers. Her class disintegrated. The children retreated to private rooms. The tutors disappeared in a single night. The children began dying. It was beyond tragedy to lose just one of these special children. But to lose them all? What was *really* striking them down? There were no funerals, no ceremonies. It was as if when they died, they had never existed. She cried for them. She cried for humanity, which would never know the potential that *her* children offered. She cried for herself.

Marguerite dropped her window blinds. Looking back, it was clear why Delphi had chosen her: she was without home, family, friends. No one would miss her if she disappeared. Only in the last few months, with nearly all of the children dead, did she recognize her precarious position. Too long she'd denied the danger to herself. And though she'd tried to escape, she'd acted too late. Now, uneasily beginning to accept that she would probably never leave Delphi alive, she made one last promise to herself: she would sacrifice her life, if only to save just one child.

She peeked at the scrap of paper containing the username and password she'd stolen earlier from Dr. Stevenson, the pathologist. Now, she could access Delphi autopsy files, under his name—unless they monitored such intrusions, or traced it back to her terminal. Wiping perspiration from her forehead, she booted her computer, entered Stevenson's username and password when prompted, and searched for files containing the word "autopsy." The computer presented her with a list of files, one for each of her students. As she scanned the list, each file evoked a memory: an eagerly raised hand, a beautifully subtle question, a cherubic face. All gone. "Mortuis paresdium et vocem dare necessee est," she whispered. *The dead must be given a voice.*

Marguerite pointed her mouse to the file for Orson. The most difficult of her students, a wild, red-haired three-year-old terror prone to violent outbursts and vitriolic diatribes, Orson had died in horrible convulsions eight months ago. Marguerite opened the file. The computer offered three options: text only, video only, and text-plus-video. She chose the last option. Her monitor split-screened: report text on the left, autopsy video on the right. Text rolled up the screen. At first she read basic demographic information followed by summary findings of internal organs and tissue cell analyses before stopping on the cause of death. But her eyes were drawn to the autopsy video.

Orson's little body lay face up, naked on a tilted aluminum table with raised edges, spigot, and drain. Standing at the side of the table a husky man, Dr. Stevenson, placed a block beneath the boy's body while another man, gowned, gloved, and wearing a clear plastic face shield, checked his surgical instruments. Stevenson positioned himself over the body and made one deep incision from the boy's right shoulder to the bottom of his rib cage, followed by another from the left shoulder. Where the two incisions met, Stevenson made a third cut deep through the abdomen, down toward the boy's genitalia. Deepening the Y-shaped incision, he began peeling back skin until the chest wall was exposed. Then he cut through the rib cage along the flanks with mammoth bone cutters resembling pruning shears. After snapping the last rib, he removed the boy's breast plate, and began dissecting the body cavity, tying off neck veins first, then proceeding toward the chest and abdomen. A moment later, he'd removed all the organs of the trunk in a single, messy block that he handed to the man with the face shield.

Marguerite leaned to her side, seized her trash basket, and vomited.

The wrenching odor mugging her, she reopened the autopsy report to the text-only option. This time, she tried to focus directly on the conclusions:

FINAL SUMMARY
- The subject expired from respiratory failure due to an imbalance of neurotransmitter activity, attributable directly to faulty and/or incomplete insertion of neuroreceptor enhancement genes on Chromosome 23, sites 23q11 through 23q18, by vector HACV.K_4.

PROSECTOR/PATHOLOGIST: Roderick Stevenson, MD, PhD

Marguerite did not understand what neurotransmitters and enhancement genes and chromosome 23q11 and HACV.K_4 were. But Delphi had an extensive library. It might be too late for Orson, but, damn them, it wasn't going to be for Ethan. Or Meredith.

BFMC

Helen followed Kevin across BFMC's lobby. His strides were long, strong; hers, short, measured, and cautious. Soon she'd reach the relative safety beyond the sliding glass doors. Changes in her hair and eye color had not long fooled the multiheaded beast—the Collaborate had found her before. Only with Trent had she found relative safety.

Joan Tetlow emerged from the gift shop. "Kevin, heading out to lunch?"

"No, Joan," he said. "I've got work to do."

"You might want to get a little rest before the party tonight." Tetlow turned to Helen and extended her hand. "I'm Joan Tetlow, senior administrator here."

"Helen Buchman." She lightly accepted Tetlow's hand, noticing the administrator covertly appraising her: the dilated pupils, the flushed cheeks, the clenched jaw.

"You look *very* familiar, Ms. Buchman. Have we ever met?"

"I have that kind of face."

"Helen's an old friend. Now if—"

"Are you from Frisco?" Tetlow asked.

Helen politely smiled. "The Bay Area. First time I've been east in a dozen years. Thought I'd spend a few days reminiscing with Kevin."

"How nice." Tetlow nodded. "Mr. Loring, our esteemed CEO, is having a very exclusive soiree tonight at his estate. Kevin's the guest of honor. Why don't you come?"

"She's tied up," Kevin answered. "Business."

To Helen, "Mr. Loring is well connected. I'm sure a single phone call would free you up." Smiling, "And Mr. Loring's exclusive and rather extravagant parties are always memorable."

"Love to," Helen shot back.

Tetlow beamed. "Great. See you both there." She marched away.

Once they reached the street corner, Kevin grabbed her arm. "If the Association is what you claim, why the hell are *you* going to the party?"

"The woman's already suspicious. Refusing her invitation would have made her more so."

"Back up a second. Tetlow's just one of those annoying bureaucrats you learn to live with."

The light changed. "Hardly. She's one of them!"

Delphi

An hour of rummaging through Delphi's enormous intranet library had left Marguerite more bewildered than ever: what was 23q11? It sounded like some sort of genetic code, but human beings didn't have a Chromosome 23. True, they had twenty-three chromosomes, including a pair of sex chromosomes, but not one labeled "23." And what was HACV.K$_4$? She'd never seen any designation like that anywhere.

Her phone rang. The caller ID said it was Dr. Roderick Stevenson—the physician whose password she'd swiped, who'd cut open Orson.

They know! she thought. *No, no they don't! If they knew, they'd be breaking down the door, not calling.* She picked up the phone on the fourth ring. "Yes?"

"Marguerite, you said to call when—I'm sorry. The boy, Ethan, just passed on."

Kincaid Residence
Philadelphia   *2:28 P.M.*

Helen trailed Kevin the six-block walk from the hospital to a street flanked by immaculately kept, four-story, nineteenth-century brownstones. He stopped beside a maple tree protected by a wrought-iron enclosure, pointed to a town house with cherry-red shutters, then hurried up a set of stone steps to a high, arched door. She checked both ends of the street.

For Helen, for a moment, it was Sunday morning, Upper East Side, eleven years past. She was leaving her ground-floor apartment in an old converted brownstone and heading out to meet her friend Claudia for a leisurely brunch. What had ever happened to Claudia?

"Coming?" Kevin asked, motioning her inside.

After depositing their coats in a closet, Kevin opened a pair of great, sliding wooden doors beyond the foyer to the left of the stairs. Photographs of his wife and children ringed the room. An exquisitely painted burgundy Chinese table and chairs occupied one corner. Along one wall, lit glass curios contained delicately painted pots from the Southwest, glazed vases from China, ancient oil lamps from the Middle East. From fireplace mantel to deep pile carpeting to couch, the room was virginal white. *Very white,* she thought. *For a billion people, the color of mourning.*

He led her into an oversized sitting room lined by medical tomes and bound collections of neurologic and molecular biologic journals. A computer desk with a fully loaded PC swallowed the tiny room. He removed papers from a metal folding chair and motioned her to sit. Then he plopped into the captain's chair in front of the monitor and booted the system. Shielding her from the keyboard, he entered his password. Program and application icons jumped onto the screen.

Helen opened her handbag. Lance's audiotape leaned neatly against the Program CD. It was so tempting. The tape would have been a stirring narration of the videotape horror, but would have too soon exposed her personal connection to the Collaborate. That in turn would have inevitably led Kevin to ask questions about *his* connection—questions too dangerous for him to pose at present. And if Kevin posed those questions too soon and forced her to answer, she was certain he could not hide his anger during the party. Loring would see it, her mission would fail, and the Collaborate would crush AntiGen.

Kevin put her CD in the drive and clicked the "run" application. The screen turned sapphire blue. Three icons appeared in the center: a tangled ribbon, subtitled "Protein X-ACT"; an open book, subtitled "Library": and a box around four horizontal lines, subtitled "BLAST." "It's a program bundle," he said. "Where do I start?"

"Protein X-ACT."

He clicked on the tangled ribbon. The program quickly loaded. The screen displayed:

PROTEIN X-ACT
    Primary, Secondary/SuperSecondary/Tertiary Protein
    Structure Prediction from Amino Acid Sequence
    ☐ (Proposed) New Sequence
    ☐ Existing Sequence
[in box—Submit Query]
Enter input data as pdb
(if applicable)

    _____

Enter sequence (in 1-letter codes for amino acids) or name (in quotations):

    _____

All outcomes to be displayed in stereoscopic structure.
Patent # 15,433,521

"See the patent number," she said. "I checked. The assignee is PolyPepGen, Inc."

"My Uncle Dermot's company. Just before he died he was telling me about a protein-predicting program he'd developed."

"Not according to the patent," she said. "He wasn't listed as inventor. In fact, the patent description doesn't match the program."

"He said the company was burying it. Where'd you get this?"

"A four-point-two-billion-dollar company buries something that would make them a fortune. Odd."

He shrugged. "There are lots of algorithm-based programs for predicting how proteins fold into three-D shapes. Who's to say how good Dermot's program really was?"

"You are, Kevin. I need you to tell me how this program works."

He cracked his knuckles, then clicked the mouse on the "(Proposed) New Sequence" button, and began entering letters in the large box: MAGQLRTPKWESYLGF . . .

"What are you doing?" she asked, leaning over his shoulder.

"I'm entering a new sequence of amino acids as a test. Something I was working on this morning, before you interrupted."

"What are those letters?"

Continuing to type, "Proteins are made up of one or more chains of amino acids. Each letter here represents one amino acid. *M* for methionine, *A* for alanine, *G* for glycine, *Q* for glutamine, *L* for leucine, and so on." When he completed 120 letters, he pressed the "Submit Query" button. A tiny hourglass appeared on screen. "Depending on their chemical interactions, chains of amino acids can twist, bend, or distort into sometimes bizarre, sometimes beautifully symmetrical shapes. Predicting the precise shape can be a mathematical nightmare. Sometimes I've winged it in my head, but getting a true stereoscopic shape can take hours, sometimes days for—"

The hourglass disappeared. Within a 3-D grid lay a ribbon that looked like a bisected spear at one end and tightly coiled pigtails at the other.

"Man, that was fast!" Kevin exclaimed and began rotating the 3-D model.

Helen watched the elation on his face slowly replaced by—disappointment? "What's the matter?"

"The program's great. It's just that the model here isn't what I expected."

"What did you want?"

"I wanted this part," pointing to the coiled tip with the mouse, "straighter."

"So take the pointer and do it."

"It doesn't work that way, Helen. There are complex calc—"

She grabbed the mouse, pointed to the curly-Q tip, and dragged it out. The coiled end straightened. She double-clicked the mouse. The bottom of the screen flashed: Resequencing. "There, I'm straightening out the protein for you."

"How did you know you could do that?"

The screen flashed: Resequencing Complete. The monitor displayed the original screen, except that some of the amino acid sequence letters had been changed.

That was the correct fix for V_7! Kevin devoured the sequence alterations. "Amazing! Amazing! Let me try one more test!" He touched the "Existing Sequence" button, cleared the box, and typed in "titin_1." Then pressed "Submit Query."

The computer responded: Accessing Protein Database.

"I'm ordering it to search the government's database and bring up the structure for titin," he told Helen. "Titin's a key muscle component. It's also one of the largest proteins ever found—more than thirty thousand amino acids long."

A second later, a stereoscopic view of a tightly woven yet flexible cord appeared within a rotating 3-D grid: the titin protein. He pointed the mouse at one end. "This part of the titin protein, called PEVK, is like a bungee cord, and allows muscles to stretch. Now, we'll just see what my uncle's program can do." With the mouse pointer he twisted the tip of the giant molecule into a semi–square knot and double-clicked. The on-screen hourglass appeared. "If the program transforms this molecule, it'll work for any protein."

Moments later, alterations in the protein appeared, amino-acid letter by letter.

"This program is light-years beyond anything. Ten thousand man-hours compressed into two minutes. Do you know what this means? DNA may be the blueprint in the architect's office, but proteins, they're the steel girders, the concrete blocks that actually make us. Whoever possesses this program can custom-design proteins in hours! For example, with titin, maybe you could make stronger, more resilient muscles." He looked absently at a corner of the room. "Or, like Uncle Dermot had proposed, faster nerve cells."

"How much would that be worth?" she asked.

"What price could you put on a tool that custom-designs life?"

"So, it might be more profitable for PolyPepGen not to market it?"

"If they used it in-house to design new proteins, it'd keep them years ahead of any competition."

"Now exit Protein X-ACT, go back to the main menu, and enter the Library," Helen said.

He restored the three main icons and clicked on the book icon. The computer displayed a new screen titled simply "Available Proteins: 540" with a "Submit Query" button. Below that were a list of titles, each underlined, arranged in reverse chronological order:

Scatter Factor Substitute 32

Calcium-channel Alpha 2 Subunit Enhancer

p53 Synthetic 12

IGF-1A Neural Adaptor

Hybrid Immunoglobulin Test 47

Relaxin Substitute 1

N-methyl-U-aspartate Receptor Enhancer 7

Gamma-aminobutyric acid (GABA) Receptor A, Version 7.3

He scrolled down ten pages. "These are synthetic substitutes, enhancers for naturally occurring proteins. They appear to be designed to improve what Nature provided us."

"Improve on what?"

"Muscles. Nerve cells."

"Kevin, have you ever heard of these synthetic proteins?"

"Not those listed here. So what is this?"

Helen cupped his shoulder. "Ten years' worth of protein designs from Protein X-ACT. From your uncle's program. All patented."

"I've never seen a paper published on any of these proteins."

"You never will. Click on something that looks interesting."

He rapidly scrolled the list. The pointer came to rest on an entry marked: NMDA-Receptor (1 & 2) Enhancer 7. He double-clicked. The screen displayed:

N-METHYL-D-ASPARATATE (NMDA)-RECEPTOR (1 & 2)
ENHANCER 7
Developer: Protein Syngate, Inc.
U.S. Patent Number: 15,428,609
Summary: NMDA-Receptor (1 & 2) Enhancer 7 is designed to

facilitate NMDA receptor subunits at post-synaptic neurotransmitter receptor sites to allow overall faster transmission of glutamate neurotransmitters.

Additional Background Material

Related Links

Sequence:

1   EEEEEDSFTIGKSVWLLWGIGEGQNPKDAQAATVRNVANNDTVQQDSGKQP 50

51   SYLKAPHTFTIGK

"Wow! This protein's designed to speed up neurotransmission of glutamate."

"I don't understand."

Turning to her, "Your brain and spinal cord are made up of nerve cells that, in a sense, conduct tiny electrical currents. Every thought, every movement you make comes from tiny electrical currents passing from one nerve cell to the next along fantastically complex nerve pathways. Now, in order for the electrical current to pass from one nerve cell to the next, the signal has to find a way of making the jump to the next nerve cell. It does so by chemicals that create a potential electrical difference between them—like a battery sets up an electrical current by using chemicals that create a potential difference between its parts. In nerve cells, the signal reaches the tip of the nerve and causes chemicals, called neurotransmitters, to be released from tiny storage pockets. The neurotransmitters then jump across the gap between the two nerves, called the synapse, latch onto special chemical receptors on the receiving nerve, and change the tip of that nerve by making it more permeable to key ions, sodium in particular. Some ions penetrate the receiving nerve, setting up a potential electrical difference—just like a battery. So, the signal gets transmitted to the next nerve. Then the next nerve. And so on."

"If you say so."

"Just think of neurotransmitters as chemicals essential for transmitting nerve impulses." He paused. "Anyway, so this synthetic protein here makes receptors in the next nerve cell more eager to accept the neurotransmitter glutamate. Glutamate is one of the most common neurotransmitters in the brain. It's excitatory—key to what you might call thought processes." He sat back and squeezed his temples. "This protein looks as if it's designed to speed up nerve impulses in the brain. Potentially, it could make people think faster."

"You mean make them more intelligent?"

"It would be tricky, exceedingly tricky. But theoretically, yes, it could make people smarter."

"How much smarter?"

"Is there a limit?"

BFMC

Tetlow entered her private office. Grayson sat back in her chair, as if carved into it. Cigarless, eyes downcast, legs heavy on the floor, he appeared grayer, older. Worn. He ignored her. "Sir, you don't look well."

He winced as he shifted in his seat. "Northeastern winters play havoc with my joints. My left arm is killing me, and—no matter. We have the fingerprints, photos, and DNA samples of that woman. Good job."

"Thank you. Any word on her identity?"

"Not yet. The usual sources and databases are dry."

"Could her records have been expunged?"

"Woman is too amateurish to be a federal agent. A highly skilled hacker with connections would cover her trail. So?"

"Sloppy tactics. Superficial resources. I'd say we're dealing with some sort of activist group. Anti-genetic, anti-transgenic."

"Where is she now?"

"Kincaid's townhouse. I'm giving her an opportunity to play her hand."

"A shame you didn't bug his house."

"But I did tap his phone."

Restraining a smile, "Anything useful come of it?"

"Not yet. But in the meantime, I invited her to the party."

"You what?" Grayson stood. "Why would you do that?"

"Keep your enemy close. She very well might make a mistake, exposing herself and/or her associates. If so, you and Mr. Loring will be right there to make the appropriate decisions."

Grayson, precariously balancing on his cane, slowly approached.

"Sir, I can assure you that she found my invitation perfectly innocent."

He beamed. "Grand."

Wanting to raise her hands in triumph, "She's changed her appearance. Darkened her hair. Changed her eye color. She looks a lot less like Kincaid's wife now. Why the change, I don't know."

Kincaid Residence

"Helen, this is astounding! If this one protein works, then you could extend—"

"Kevin, do you remember the patent numbers you saw?"

"I remember everything," he said. "Everything—and always."

"What was the first protein you looked at?"

"(NMDA)-Receptor (1 & 2) Enhancer 7. Patent number 15,428,609."

"Put this screen on hold, and access the U.S. Patent Office through the Net."

He minimized the window containing the Collaborate library then established an independent connection with his ISP—a connection completely separate from the CD program. He accessed the Net. The home page for the U.S. Patent and Trademark Office appeared on-screen.

"Now, search under the patent number."

He clicked on the search option. Then "Patent Number Search" on the following screen. Two seconds later, the result appeared:

PROTEIN ISOLATE FOR THE TREATMENT OF ALZHEIMER'S
DISEASE
Inventor: Jurgens, Kenneth
Assignee: Protein Syngate, Inc.
Patent Number: 15,428,609

"That's wrong," he said. "I mean, the assignee and number are right, but the patent info is wrong. According to the 'Library' database you showed me, that protein is a neurotransmitter enhancer, not an aid for treating Alzheimer's."

"Try again."

He did. Seventeen times. The patent number and assignee always matched. The patented protein never did. "Helen, where did you get that CD?"

"From a patent attorney whose firm represents every company you've seen listed here."

"Could the Library be a fake?"

"Every inventor listed in those patents is either dead or missing. No, these companies have friends in the patent office."

"I doubt it. It's beyond the patent office's expertise and manpower.

For years, they were inundated with meaningless chunks of DNA sequences. The same's probably true for amino acid sequences of proteins."

"Then how do we prove that these patents were obtained under false pretenses?"

"Well, you'd need to show that the amino acid sequence doesn't match anything similar. For example, a key muscle protein fiber would have an amino acid sequence reasonably similar to other muscle types. But if you compared that protein with, say, a piece of brain tissue, they wouldn't."

"And how do we compare these different proteins?"

"With BLAST."

"A blast?"

He restored the "Library" screen window. Returned to the main menu. One icon remained untouched: a box around four horizontal lines, subtitled "BLAST." "See." He minimized the window and returned to his Net connection, independent from the CD program, and typed in: www.ncbi.nlm.nih.gov/BLAST. His request began churning through cyberspace.

"BLAST is the Basic Local Alignment Search Tool. The NCBI, the National Center for Biological Information, set it up and runs it. Basically, BLAST and megaBLAST are very sophisticated pieces of software that compare millions of DNA, protein, and vector sequences in seconds. They've been used to analyze virtually every piece of DNA or protein that's ever been sequenced. As hubs of the world's storehouse of molecular biology, they're linked to every major relevant database in the world. If there's an answer, it's through BLAST or megaBLAST."

The basic BLAST homepage appeared. He requested program "blastp," the search program for proteins. Then entered the sequence for patent number 15,428,609, and pressed the "Submit Query" button. Seconds later, a series of black lines appeared beneath the query request.

Helen watched him scroll down row after row of gibberish: meaningless letters peppered with "score bits" and "E-values." She picked up confusion in his eyes. "What's the matter?"

"See these?" he asked, pointing to a series of black horizontal lines. "They represent low-probability matches with isolated segments of proteins."

"Which means?"

"That the patent office is telling the truth! Your Library program is a fake!"

"That can't be!"

He whipped around. "BLAST can't lie! There's too many safe-guards in it. Tens of thousands of people a day access it. The world's biological community depends on it!"

"They must've gotten to it. Nothing's beyond—"

"Get out!" His chair launched back as he jumped up. "Take your doctored video and your fake programs and your imaginary lists and your conspiracies and get the hell out of my life!"

How could they have faked it? Helen thought. *And now—Wait a second! That's it!* "Shut down your direct web access."

"Another game?"

"Shut it down, then reopen the main menu window on the Library program."

"What good will that—"

"Do it!"

He did. A sapphire blue background reappeared, with the BLAST icon untouched.

"Access BLAST through the Library program."

He clicked on the icon. Moments later, the basic BLAST homepage appeared, except outlined in sapphire blue. "Now what?"

"I'm betting that while you and I and everyone else in the world sees one thing, the Collaborate sees the truth. Repeat your search, please."

He entered the sequence for patent number 15,428,609 and sub-mitted the query. Enduring a long, cold silence, she held her breath and glanced around the room.

"Helen, look." On-screen, beneath the amino acid sequence query, lay five bright red horizontal lines stretching the width of the screen—a radically different view from the short black lines dis-played in the previous BLAST search. "The red lines indicate very high alignment scores. They're very similar to sequences in NMDA neuroreceptors. The odds against such matches are astronomical. You were right. I can't believe it."

She nodded. "The Collaborate's infiltrated government biologic databases to protect its investments. From the patent office to NCBI and the National Institutes of Health."

"The statistics. The permutations. It's inconceivable that anyone could have compromised so many critical, sophisticated databases," he whispered. "Biotech people couldn't have done this alone. It'd require extremely adept computer scientists and programmers, people with inside access through national security levels." Looking directly into her eyes for the first time in hours, "The government is involved."

She stared blankly at the first stirrings of a hideous clarity.

Kincaid's Lab

With each magnification, Peter Nguyen grew more confused. He'd rushed Dr. Kincaid's specimens to Microscopy and had fed several pieces to the automatic processor. A robotic arm had quickly frozen them in liquid nitrogen, sectioned them with a guillotine blade into slivers microns thick, mounted them on specially prepared slides, rotated them systematically through the electron microscope, and projected images of tissue magnified 36,000 times, 53,000 times, 120,000 times.

On the surface the tissue was obviously striated skeletal muscle, the kind attached to bones of the lower and upper extremities. Definitely mammalian, probably primate, possibly human. The first few slides had shown normal muscle, each contractile unit a pattern of cross-striations with light and dark bands. But in the last few slides, the muscle patterns had been bizarre. There were too many contractile units, too many cross-striations and muscle filaments. The units were twice as thick as normal. Some were scalloped or gnarled at the ends. Normal and bizarre muscle, mixed in the same specimen?

Nguyen focused on the distorted, thick muscle filament, and magnified. Tiny knobs appeared scattered across the thick filament. Was that the key? He ordered the automated system to double-magnification power, then looked at the muscle unit, blown up 255,000 times its true size. He compared it with a magnified view of one of the normal-looking slides. "Must be a glitch."

He ordered another set of magnified views: one normal-looking and one bizarre-looking slide. Side by side, they appeared on-screen. "That's impossible!"

Kincaid Residence

"Move over, Kevin," Helen said as she produced a diskette from her handbag and shoved it in the slot. Seconds later, a list of biotech and med-tech firms appeared in the left-hand side of a new window on the monitor. She highlighted "Benjamin Franklin Healthcare Network." "Corporate members of the Association. I'll correlate them against firms listed in the Library," she said, then clicked on the "run" button at the bottom of the screen. The results appeared instantaneously:

CORRELATION (R) = +0.998
PROBABILITY = 99.99%

The Association to Cure Genetic Disabilities and the patent holders of custom-designed proteins were the same.

Helen turned to Kevin as he sank back into his chair. "They call themselves the Collaborate." Taking his hand, "You've been working for them since you came back East. They're wealthy industrialists—E. Dixon Loring is one. They've been pooling resources for 17 years."

"What kind of resources?"

Helen took a deep breath. She'd been running from and fighting the Collaborate for so long that it was challenging to describe its activities in anything but a rant. "Kevin, the Collaborate funds on three levels: prominent, corporate, and clandestine. Prominent funding goes to places like BFHN, your lab, places where they want to publicize advances in gene therapy. The U.S., unlike Europe and much of the world, is open to genetic and transgenic research. There are seventy-nine major labs researching truly new, innovative vectors in this country. The Collaborate partially or totally controls almost half of them. Yours was always most promising. And did you ever deliver." She paused. "Their corporate research is what funded your uncle's Protein X-ACT program and made it possible to build a library of custom-made proteins intended to *change* people." She pressed forward on her knees. "Kevin, if you know the amino acid sequence of a protein, how difficult would it be to determine the DNA sequence that codes for it?"

"Each amino acid is coded by a codon, which is a triplet of RNA molecules. Some amino acids are coded by several different RNA codons, but basically, when you know the RNA code, it's relatively straightforward to figure out the DNA code that generates it. Essentially, if you know the protein sequence, you can deduce the DNA sequence for its gene."

"How difficult would it be to synthesize a gene, once you know the DNA sequence?"

"You can order DNA sequences cheap from reputable labs. Why?"

She wet her lips. "My brother, Lance, believed that the Collaborate wasn't just building new proteins in a lab. He was convinced that they were beta-testing them—*on human subjects*. The video you saw from the Tiburon lab was proof of their testing new muscular proteins. He thought that there was another facility, somewhere, where the Collaborate was using your K_4 vector to insert new nerve cell proteins into developing fetuses."

"I didn't know." Kevin hung his head in his hands. "I didn't know. How could I?" He felt a red wave of heat suffuse his face, momentarily blinding him as he realized how his research had been misused. How children had suffered because of his work. Slowly he clenched and unclenched his fists. Blood drained from his face, leaving him pale, gray.

"Poor Kevin, they're still using you." She ran her fingers through his hair. "Ever since that sheep, Dolly, was cloned, the public and the Congress have been terrified of genetic research, especially genetic engineering. For the Collaborate to expand beyond just beta-testing subjects in secluded bases it had to find a way to counteract years of public paranoia and mistrust. So it created the Association to Cure Genetic Disabilities to promote support for technologies that ostensibly could fix genes responsible for Huntington's disease or cystic fibrosis, or eliminating genes responsible for inheriting cancers, like BRCA1 and BRCA2 for breast cancer. And do it by adjusting genes in people's germlines. Their children."

"601," Kevin muttered.

"Yes. Ambiguous, badly written, House Bill 601 reopens the door to less altruistic applications of germline gene therapy. ACGD's been ramming it through Congress. And there you sit, Kevin, center stage, ACGD's marionette. Not just providing the Collaborate with the vector to implement its plan, but lending your face and integrity to nightly commercials playing before a hundred million people."

Kevin threw his head back. He gazed at the dark ceiling. "What happens if 601 passes?"

"The possibilities terrify us."

"Us?"

"The Anti-Genetic Action Committee—AntiGen."

"What agency—"

"We're not part of the government. We're private—"

"Radicals!"

"After what you've just seen, Kevin? You tell me who the radicals are!" She released a long, exasperated breath. "Kevin, join us."

"Groups like yours have been trying to shut me down for years!"

"We're probably the only ones who can stop the Collaborate."

"The police could—"

"Stop a global conspiracy to genetically engineer children based on a few largely incomprehensible entries in a database and video from a concentration camp that never existed?" She snorted, "Yeah, that'd work!"

"The government—"

"Or a faction of it is in collusion with them. You proved that yourself."

"What can AntiGen do?"

"Prevent the Collaborate from getting the last key component of its plan—V_7. We cannot allow the Collaborate to gain sole possession."

"That sounds like a threat."

"You've seen what the Collaborate will do."

"How do I know you're any different from *them*? What if I don't work with you? What then? Kill me?"

She brushed at watery eyes. "You're already living under a death sentence."

"With you as assassin."

"I've been trying to save your life!"

He turned away. "Suppose I said that V_7 doesn't work. Would that solve your problem?"

"People know you're too smart to make the same mistake twice, especially after K_4. The Collaborate would assume that you're holding back. They'd torture you, extract the information, then kill you. Our leader, I'm sorry to say, is almost as brutal." She hesitated. "V_7 does work, doesn't it?" He said nothing. She cupped her hands around his face and brought it gently to hers. "Put in with us. Put in with *me*."

"Why should I trust you?"

"Because I'm the only friend you have. Because I've risked my life for you. And because I'm the only one who can help you get through this night alive."

Loring Estate
Berks County, Pennsylvania

Loring sat opposite Grayson as the butler silently crossed the library, placed a tray with a sterling silver tea set on the eighteenth-century table, and withdrew. Loring poured a golden, aromatic tea into a cup and handed it to his guest.

Grayson sipped. "Excellent Darjeeling. I taught you well."

Pouring himself a cup. "Who taught you?"

"Experience in the Darjeeling district."

He put down the cup with a clatter. "Merlin, I've known you hell knows how many years and never once have you mentioned traveling through that region of India."

"A quest of self-discovery. The Aborigines call it a 'walk-about.' "

"Spiritual journeys are for directionless kids and indecisive weaklings. I knew what I wanted. I worked hard." Holding up his palms, "Here I am."

Grayson gazed out the library window at the rolling off-green hills. Tiny beige ovals dotted the land. "How many times have you told me about being too poor to play the public links around Karbonville? How you swore you'd build one, just for yourself? There it is, yet when was the last time you played it?"

"Two years ago. And it's not the playing. It's knowing that you can."

"Yet now, you never play."

Grayson winced as he lifted the tea to his lips. "No Quorum has ever bestowed so much power, even temporarily, upon anyone other than the Chairman."

"I couldn't have done it without you."

Grayson winced again as he tried to put down his cup and saucer. Seeing the concern on Loring's face, "It's just arthritis, flaring up again."

"Bullshit! Did you think I wouldn't find out? You need a new heart!"

Grayson nodded. "There are those who would argue that I have never owned one."

"I'll arrange for a transplant."

Grayson stared out the window. "I'm tired, Dixon. I've begun to think more on that quest of self-discovery I began forty years ago." Turning to Loring, smiling, "I need to complete that journey while I still can."

"You'll go farther with a new heart."

"Then it would no longer be just my journey."

"You still have fifteen or more good years ahead of—"

"I'm tired of plots, of power plays, of anonymity, of assassinations. *I want to retire!*"

"You know that's not permitted."

"You can grant me an extended leave."

Loring crossed his knees. "No."

"I'll find a replacement. Train a replacement. Whatever you want."

"No. Maybe later when—"

"I've run out of 'later's, Dixon. I have been your servant, occasionally your mentor, but always your friend. If that means anything to you, let me go."

Sighing, Loring poured another cup. "If I said yes—if—would you stay until 601 passes?"

"Assuming our enemies on the Hill don't drag it out."

"No one can ever replace you." Loring nodded, painfully. "But I will need recommendations for a successor."

Grayson beamed. "I'll let you know soon. And thank you." His smile evaporated. "Now regarding the matter at hand, we need more information on Kincaid's girlfriend."

"One of my firms, Rysound Security Systems, developed a prototype subdermal transmitter. It's a bug a quarter of the size of a pinhead that's injected under the skin. Undetectable, made of a platinum-iridium alloy that the body won't reject, just a pinprick to inject, and it turns the subject itself into a microphone-transmitter for seventy-two hours. Prototype I developed it years ago to track people entering the country on visas—before civil libertarians nixed the idea. I can have one here before the festivities." He noticed Grayson subtly lower his eyes. "You disapprove?"

"She'll be in a hostile environment and wary."

"I see where you're going. Good idea, Merlin." He leaned forward and softly patted Grayson's right shoulder. "Unfortunately, it's time to bring in someone capable of running an unpleasant but necessary operation. Someone effective."

Loring Estate   *6:55 P.M.*

". . . and, Kevin, it's critical that you don't let on, or else—"

"I know, Helen," he said as he pulled the Buick around the circular fountain of the Three Fates and stopped in front of the mansion's grand Roman Doric column facade. He turned to Helen, a beauty reinvented: long black hair up and attractively coiffed, radiant new blue eyes, and lips, moist and inviting. She smelled like an orchid.

An attendant opened her door. She gracefully exited as he handed his keys to the valet. Rock music from behind the mansion charged the air.

Together they entered a circular vestibule adorned by a ceiling of leaded-glass designs and a swirling-pattern floor of black-and-white marble. A butler escorted them down a grand hallway paved in crimson tile and adorned by wall sconces and Queen Anne sideboards. The bricks reverberated to bass guitars rocking the house. Kevin felt the percussion through his feet as the servant led them up to a flying staircase, past a vaulted-ceiling antechamber, and into a reception room dominated by Norwegian-spruce panels, hand-carved console tables, and a Chinese pediment over a mantel flanked by Corinthian columns with grape-leaf capitals. An ashen Grayson, cane tapping, shuffled into the room. "So glad you could come, Dr. Kincaid."

Kevin shook the cold, sickly hand. "Is Mr. Loring here?"

"He'll be along momentarily." Turning to Helen. "And who is this ravishing lady?"

"Helen Buchman," she answered.

Grayson took her hand and sandwiched it between his. "And what is it you do, my dear?"

"Video," she said.

"How interesting, Ms. Buchman. What, specifically?"

"I'm a director."

"Fascinating. I've never seen your name on any credits."

"I do commercials, mostly."

"What agency are you with, if I might ask?"

"I freelance."

Grayson looked at Kevin. "Dr. Kincaid, you should have told us. The Association certainly could have thrown some work this beautiful lady's way."

Laughing, Edwin Dixon Loring burst into the room. Tall, distinguished, gentle gray at his temples, he had an overpowering grin, a half-filled highball, and two exquisite-looking women, both clad in extravagant, revealing gowns, trailing him "Dr Kincaid, such an honor to finally meet you," he said, vigorously shaking Kevin's hand. "And this enchanting woman?"

Helen again introduced herself.

The background music swelled. "Ms. Buchman, your friend here, more than anyone else, is responsible for changing the course of medical history!" Loring declared.

Helen looked from Loring to Kincaid, and back. "I know."

"This party is just a small thank-you from the Association." Loring disengaged from his escorts and put his arms around Kevin and Helen. With Grayson and the ladies trailing, he led his guests out the exit on the far side of the mantel, down a cream-colored hallway and onto an elevator lined by bouncers. The party grew louder as they descended. Elevator doors parted. Roaring vibrations greeted them. Bouncers on either side snapped to attention as the entourage stepped out onto a mezzanine thirty feet above the spectacular dance floor. Below, hundreds of guests in tuxedos and evening gowns danced to the music beneath spinning laser lights. A seven-piece band on an elevated stage belted out an old, hard-driving Stones tune that sounded loud enough to taste. Guests milled along the dance floor's edge and around tables filled with Bries, pâtés, exotic fruits, lobster tails, quails, and exquisite pastries. Two bars had liquor stacked from floor to ceiling. "Most of the house was so staid," Loring said, waving his hand, "So I added *this*."

"Can't hear you!"

Loring turned to a guard in a tuxedo, pointed to a small box on the wall, and snapped his fingers. The guard respectfully nodded, opened the box, and pressed one of three buttons inside it. A yellow light flashed by the band's lead singer. The band immediately cut the volume. Loring led his guests to the top of the grand staircase connecting the mezzanine with the dance floor. An attendant handed him a microphone. He tapped on it twice, then announced, "May I have your attention?"

The band stopped. The ambient buzzing subsided. People gazed up at their host.

Loring's voice echoed across the ballroom. "Ladies and gentlemen, members and supporters of the Association, esteemed guests, friends, I thank you all for coming. I'd now like to introduce our guest of honor. Were I to list his accomplishments, I'm afraid we'd all die of thirst." Scattered chuckles. "So please give a warm welcome for Dr. Kevin Kincaid."

Thundering applause. Spotlights turned on Kevin.

Loring motioned him down the grand staircase. Flushed, floating down the stairs, Kevin absorbed the adulation of business/financial leaders, congressional representatives, charitable trust administrators, and two Nobel laureates. So many distinguished faces, all to acknowledge him. Helen hooked her arm around his elbow and drew him close. He barely felt her.

". . . again explain what a vector is?" Loring overheard the drunken banker ask.

Kevin washed a cocktail shrimp down with champagne, then glanced at his host and Helen with a "let-me-make-it-stupidly-simple" shrug. "Imagine that a cell is an egg with the shell . . ."

Loring forced a smile: his soiree had become boring. The two hours he'd spent leading around party-shy Kincaid was work. But the friend Helen, quietly in Kincaid's shadow, smiling, speaking only when spoken to—she was intriguing. A man handed Loring a sealed envelope. He quickly tore it open: *Dixon, need you now in library. —M*

Pocketing the note, he strode to a private elevator to the left of the grand staircase, took the express to a guarded corridor, and entered the last room on the right. The door locked behind him.

Grayson, sitting in a high-back chair, reached out with the tip of his cane and effortlessly tapped the button on a nearby desk that controlled a holographic projector. "We've identified the woman. See for yourself."

A three-dimensional picture of a blond-haired, blue-eyed woman and a running dossier appeared in the center of the room.

Loring studied the virtual file. "No, that's not possible."

Grayson activated a separate monitor. A camera panned the dance floor, located Helen, zoomed in, and freeze-framed when it captured a full-face view. Pixels assembled a 3-D view of Helen next to the file photo. "Here is the plastic surgery feasibility mapping."

The holographic image of Helen began morphing to match the dossier photo: jaw recessing, nose narrowing, cheekbones raising, eyelids realigning. At the bottom, numbers whirled. When the images matched, Loring read the bottom of the screen: PLASTIC SURGERY FEASIBILITY = 88.9% PROBABILITY.

"Merlin, that just theoretically proves—"

"We matched her DNA. Dixon, it's *her!*"

Loring picked up the phone. "Larson, have all personal items in the cloakroom and bathrooms checked for explosives. Check on any packages or items left unattended. Keep the woman who came in with Kincaid in sight at all times. And don't alarm the guests. And wait until *after* the announcement." He hung up. To Grayson, "Yin-yang. Hard on soft. Soft on hard. If they attack, don't block. Parry, deflect the blow—leaving them open to attack."

Grayson winced in pain, then smiled. "Correct. Keep alternatives open, but concentrate on the most likely prospects."

"Subversives, activists, terrorists—secrecy is their strength, is their weakness. When they go to strike, we deflect their blow to where it will harm them most."

As the band switched tempo, Helen grabbed Kevin's hand. "Come dance with me." Half dragging him onto the dance floor, she pulled him close, wrapped one arm behind his back, and stretched out the other, taking his hand. Slowly, they revolved around their common center. "This is the first time we've been alone all night."

Kevin found her smell intoxicating: flowers and sweat and sex. Her breasts pressed close to his chest, re-creating the memory of last night's caresses, kisses.

Placing her head on his shoulder, "Quite an ego-stroker, being the object of all this."

"It's hard to accept that *this* is the Collaborate."

"Most people here are just ignorant tools. But aside from Loring and Grayson, you can't be sure who knows what."

"How am I supposed to know what's reality and what's not?"

She gazed around the room. "This, Kevin, *this is fantasy*, built on the horror you've seen with your own eyes. And unless you choose wisely, untold millions will suffer."

Microphone in hand, overlooking a piece of his domain, Loring stood on the mezzanine and spied a tall, balding waiter with an empty tray. The man slowly weaved his way through the crowded room toward Kevin. Smiling, Loring boomed into the microphone, "My friends and esteemed guests, in a few short moments, we'll have an opportunity to see one of the Association's nationally broadcast commercials." From his vantage, he watched the ball with laser lights rise to the ceiling while a quadplex of huge screens was lowered into place high over the dance floor. "I'd like to make two announcements. First, according to the latest polls, support for germline gene therapy is up an astonishing *seven points* from last night! Second, and most important, I have it from very reliable sources that there has been a major swing on the Hill. We now have sufficient votes in the Senate to pass HR 601, as is. Ladies and gentlemen, we've won!"

Thunderous applause erupted. Loring watched a congratulatory crowd close in around Kincaid.

The waiter with the empty tray seemed caught up in the crunch as he tried to reach the guest of honor. Loring placed both fists on the railing.

The waiter drew close behind Kevin. Loring held his breath.

The waiter nonchalantly veered away.

Kevin pulled his right arm back over his shoulder, as if trying to scratch a mosquito bite. He whirled around, seemingly confused then resumed shaking hands. From the mezzanine, Loring scrutinized him for three minutes: Kevin did not again try to rub his back, nor did he appear to be in pain. Loring scanned the dance floor for his waiter, and found him at the far corner, by the bar. He tried to get the man's attention.

Another man appeared, said, "It's time, sir."

Loring shrugged, then tapped on the microphone. "May I have quiet, please. Our spot is about to air. Please direct your attention overhead."

The commercial began with an opening shot of a hospital bed with a sick child in an intensive care unit, her head bandaged, her mother and father by her side, holding her hand. Dr. Kincaid appeared, superimposed, off to the side of the screen. "The little girl in that bed is Bernadette Trelaine. Not an actress portraying her, but Bernadette herself. She loves puppies, her first-grade teacher, and Malibu Barbie. I know because she's my patient."

The camera cut to a close-up of Bernadette smiling and talking, despite her droopy eyes.

"She has a brain tumor called a glioblastoma," Dr. Kincaid's off-camera voice stated. "Her older sister had one. And died from it two years ago."

The camera cut to a close-up of Bernadette unconscious, anguished parents by her side.

"I tried conventional gene therapy on her. It worked for a while but another tumor arose with a vengeance. You see, the genes in Bernadette's brain cells were programmed to make untreatable cancer from the day she was conceived."

The sounds of Bernadette's heart monitor grew louder. A shrill alarm sounded. Nurses and doctors burst into the room. A crash cart followed. The camera cut to a close-up of Bernadette's weeping mother then swung to the comatose child. And faded to black.

"Germline gene therapy could have prevented her from being born with the genes that would eventually kill her," Dr. Kincaid's voice resounded from the black screen.

The scene switched to a graveside funeral with mourners laying flowers on a casket. Dr. Kincaid approached the casket, his voice cracking, "Medicine has devoted so much time, money, and energy to ridding the world of diseases. We inoculate our children against smallpox, chicken pox, measles, hepatitis, whooping cough. Why can't we inoculate them against genetic diseases, too?" He laid a flower on the casket. The funeral scene dissolved to home movies of Bernadette playing on a backyard swing. "Tell your senators that your child, and their children, are entitled to healthy, happy lives. Tell them to pass House Bill 601."

The camera cut to Bernadette smiling in her hospital bed. Froze on the image.

"Bernadette's younger brother has been diagnosed with brain cancer."

Superimposed over the lower third of the screen: SUPPORT HOUSE BILL 601! GIVE OUR CHILDREN A CHANCE!SM Paid for by the Association to Cure Genetic Disabilities.

"How's it working?" Loring asked as he burst into the library.

Grayson, slouched in a high-back chair, tapped a panel with his cane. A monitor snapped on and quickly zoomed in on Kincaid talking to a regal-looking woman with a diamond necklace and bracelets.

". . . exciting that my humble contributions may help rid the world of sickle cell . . ." sounded Kevin's voice against the party background noises, in sync with lip movements on camera.

"Subdermal transmitter appears to be functioning perfectly," Grayson said. "Every sound around him is being recorded."

"Any sign that it bothers him?"

"Nothing since the initial insertion. We have a winner." Grayson shut his eyes. He groaned.

Loring knelt beside him. "I'm calling—"

"No. No!"

"Have it your way, Merlin. I'll have your suite prepared upstairs."

"Who could sleep through this ruckus? I'm going back to the hotel."

Loring shook his head and embraced his old mentor. "Obstinate."

"It helped build your cunning."

Helen watched the sharpness drain from Kevin's eyes as they danced slowly across the floor. Men: they were so easily dazzled. Her father had fallen prey to the same tactics. But she felt responsible for Kevin's reaction; had she not ripped him from his deep, emotionless sleep, he'd have looked on the evening as just a boring cocktail party that interfered with his work schedule.

"You are beautiful," Kevin whispered.

The music swelled. For a moment, her mind replayed last night's perfect ecstasy. She allowed herself to forget the mission and the real likelihood that she would never have him again.

"This evening, this place may be fantasy, but I've decided that you are real," he added.

She focused on the video monitor, at the far end of the room, trained on her—just one of sixteen that had been relentlessly tracking her throughout the evening.

Sal, one of Loring's drivers, stood by the stretch limousine and respectfully tipped his cap when Grayson doddered out of the mansion's east entrance, a burly attendant close by each arm. One man held the old man's elbow and gently hoisted him into the rear seat while another handed him his cane. Grayson groaned as he slid across the upholstery.

"Take Mr. Grayson to his hotel," said one attendant.

"Right away." Sal closed the door and hurried around the car.

He wound the limo along the back road that would eventually lead to the turnpike. He glanced in the rearview mirror: Grayson looked ill. He speeded up.

The privacy window lowered. "Please, slow down. And stay off the main highways," Grayson rasped.

"Yessir, but it'll take twice as long."

"I have all the time in the world, Sal." He lowered both rear windows. Cold air blasted through the limousine. "Ever think about retiring?" Grayson closed his eyes. "Don't worry. Your job's not in jeopardy. Please, just answer my question."

"I'll never retire, sir."

"Love your work that much?"

"I enjoy it, sir, but I'll have to work till the day I die. I got two kids in college. I got one who's been out in the world, didn't like it, and came running home. I got another, at home, unmarried, with one child and another on the way."

"Obligations. They dictate our lives. Ever think about what you'd do if you could retire?"

"Naah. Doesn't help dreaming about things you'll never have."

"But what are we without dreams?"

Sal was forced to concentrate on his driving, unable to take long looks at his passenger. When the twisting road dumped into a four-lane thoroughfare, he said, "My father always said that a man *is* his work *and* his family. Guess I'll never run out of either." Shaking his head, "If you don't mind my asking, sir, ever thought of what you'll do when you retire?"

No answer.

He checked the rearview mirror. Grayson lay slumped, his head protruding awkwardly out the open window, air blasting through his thin hair, buffeting his face.

"Sir, are you okay?" *Who could sleep like that?*

No response.

"Sweet Jesus!" Sal jerked the car onto the road's gravel shoulder, slammed on the brakes, ran out of the car, and opened the passenger window. Grayson tumbled onto his legs. He lifted him back onto the backseat. He frantically checked Grayson's wrist for a pulse. Then his neck.

"I know the party's not over, Mr. Loring, but it's getting late," Kevin said, the front vestibule's marble floor still resonating to the music. "And I'm delivering that keynote speech at NIH tomorrow."

"Why not stay here for the evening, both you and Ms. Buchman?"

Loring asked as Tetlow graciously smiled behind him. "A chauffeur will take you down to Bethesda in the morning."

Kevin glanced at Helen beside him. "Some other time, perhaps. Thank you for everything."

A parking attendant handed Kevin his car keys. As Kevin and Helen turned to leave, Loring called, "Oh, the TV network's throwing a bash this Sunday in New York for Super Bowl major sponsors who aren't attending the game. Ms. Tetlow will have passes for you both in her office."

"Thank you."

Loring turned to Tetlow as Kevin's car disappeared into the night. "Mr. Grayson was impressed with your recent performance." He pointed down the main hall. "Join me in the library for a cup of Darjeeling. We'll talk about the future."

Berks County   *11:55 P.M.*

"If it was going to happen it would have by now," Kevin said, his headlights illuminating chunks of hilly road.

"I'm not wrong," Helen whispered, eyes darting.

He checked the rearview mirror again. "No one's following. We're alone." He glanced at her blue eyes bearing down on him. "Why do you always seem to make it so damn hard to believe you?"

"Cause she's an expert liar, mate," a voice barreled from behind.

Startled, Kevin swerved. Fighting the car skidding on the gravel shoulder, he swung the wheel left. The car slid toward the guardrail, bit into asphalt, then jerked back wildly onto the road. Oncoming headlights bore down. A fast-approaching horn blared. He spun the wheel right and cut back across the yellow lines as the oncoming car blew by.

"Don't go doing that again. There's a gun by your ear," the voice warned.

Kevin cautiously turned toward the rearview mirror. A metallic-cold gun barrel pressed into the back of his neck. He glimpsed a burly man with a woolen cap, blacked-out face, and saffron-colored teeth in stark contrast to his darkened skin.

"Cameron, put the gun away," Helen said. "He's with us."

"That so, doc?" the AntiGen operative asked. As Kevin slowly nodded, "She has a way with men, our Helen. Real persuasive-like."

"Where's Trent?" she snapped.

Cameron produced a phone and engaged a preset number. "It's me. Got 'em both." A muffled voice. He responded, "Five, six minutes. I'll signal you." He hung up. To Kevin, "Take a right at this intersection. Follow the signs to the turnpike. Then head west."

"Where are we going?" Kevin asked.

"If Trent's not happy—to the end of the line."

Loring Estate
Library

". . . and that's the essence of it," Loring concluded.

Joan Tetlow finished her tea. "Yes, sir, I understand. But the organizational timetable is a bit unclear. How long after Implementation?"

"Best case, ten years. Worst, twenty-five years. Figure the same sort of time line as it took for one disk operating system to monopolize the software industry back in the early nineties. We have the enormous advantage of forcing the market that we'll already dominate."

"Beyond that?"

"Just time, aided by demographic and socioeconomic changes, legal gridlock, and generational passage. What was once an abomination will become an oddity, then accepted, then commonplace." A chime rang. "That would be him," Loring muttered. "One of the house staff will show you to your quarters for the night. But first, I'd like you to meet someone." Loring touched a button on the control panel beside him. A man with receding white hair, thick glasses, and a wispy, imperial beard leisurely strolled into the room, his hands dug deep in his jeans. "Joan, this is Anthony Blount."

Pennsylvania Turnpike: Eastbound

After passing the tollbooth, Kevin drove down the semicircular ramp and merged left onto the high-speed road. "Where are we going?"

Cameron ignored him. "We're on and clean," he said into his wireless.

"You'll see us in a minute," said the voice at the other end of Cameron's phone.

Cameron put the call on hold. To Kevin, "Watch your speed. Don't wanna get pulled over."

Two pairs of tractor-trailer taillights appeared on the distant ribbon of night road.

"Got ya in sight," Cameron said into the phone. "You can fall in formation now." In the distance the one pair of taillights swerved toward the other and merged. The car quickly approached the lights. "You're coming on two trucks," he told Kevin. "Get in the left lane. Pass the first truck, but stay behind the second."

A moment later the Buick was alongside a long tractor trailer. After passing it, an identical truck lumbered at the same speed a few yards up ahead in the right lane. The rear truck reduced speed, dropping back five car lengths.

"Move over to the right lane. Slow to forty miles an hour," Cameron directed Kevin.

The lead truck's rear doors opened as he did. A ramp slid out.

"Listen carefully, doc. Start up the ramp at *exactly* forty-five. No more, no less. Hit the brake *before* your front wheels touch the back of the trailer, or you'll crash through into the cab."

Kevin looked to Helen, took a deep breath, and inched the car forward. His front wheels touched the ramp, generating sparks on the road. The big rig's cavernous opening prepared to swallow them. His foot reached for the brake, but touched the accelerator. The car shot forward. The compartment's front wall closed in. His foot desperately reached for the brake.

The car screeched. Skidded. Came to rest inches from the container wall.

He took a breath, then looked over to Helen, rubbing her head. "You okay?"

Someone wrenched the door open. An arm unbuckled her seat belt and yanked her out of the car. Another woman, wearing a wig and dress similar to Helen's, jumped inside. Arms grabbed Kevin by his lapels, lifted him from his seat, and tossed him onto the truck's dirty floor. He shoulder-rolled and flipped up just in time to catch a glimpse of his assailant: a man with his physique and wearing an identical tuxedo. The man flashed him a mock salute, got into the car, and backed it down the ramp. The truck door closed, leaving him in total darkness.

Kevin smelled peppermint. "Helen, where are you?"

Weak lights snapped on. Helen stood twenty feet from him. Four men, including Cameron, had pistols trained on him. Kevin raised his hands.

A fifth man appeared—Trent. "Helen, I was hoping you'd bring me a doggy bag."

"He's with us," Helen told Trent.

Kevin asked her, "Are these your friends?"

"We *serve* together."

"I'm offended," Trent mocked. "I thought we were family."

She pointed to a pair of heavyset men to her right. "I've never seen them before. Or my double, who yanked me out of the car."

"Did you really think yours was the only cell in my organization? I've had to mobilize all my resources." Trent added, "I like your hair."

"Where's Anna?"

"In her apartment. Together, you two cause mischief."

Kevin lowered his hands.

"Get those arms up!" yelled one of Trent's men.

"Stand down, gentlemen. Dr. Kincaid is our guest."

The men lowered their weapons but remained at attention.

Trent moved toward Kevin. He held out his right hand. "I'm Trent McGovern. This merry little band of mine is the AntiGen Action Committee."

Warily, Kevin took Trent's hand. He felt a mastery of kinesthetics, of center of body, of hidden strength in that arm.

"Forgive the histrionics, Doctor, but they may have you under surveillance. This was the only way we could chat in private. Decoys are taking your car to your house. If you and I come to an understanding we'll get you there, too."

Kevin glanced at Helen, "And if not?"

"Tell me, Doctor, did you enjoy your evening in the Potemkin village?"

"What the hell's a Potemkin village?"

Trent closed his eyes a moment. "Tsarina Catherine the Great— 1787, the Crimea. Russian Field Marshal Grigory Potemkin, Catherine's lover, conquers the territories of the Crimean Khanate for her. Though having put millions into virtual slavery, Catherine believes her serfs to be happy, prosperous. So, while she sails down her newly conquered domains in a fleet of ships, like Cleopatra, to inspect her newly conquered territories, her lover Potemkin has building facades erected along the Dnieper River, fills the mock villages with impoverished serfs from the surrounding countryside and commands them to dance and frolic. All so that Catherine could glimpse them as she sails by. And after she's passed, Potemkin's mock villages are dismantled. The serfs returned to their miserable existence."

"If you're talking about the party, Helen—"

"The party was window dressing. Everything you've seen or heard or think you know has just been part of the Collaborate's facade—while you've sailed merrily along believing that your noble research would benefit humanity."

Helen moved to Kevin's side. She took his hand. "He wants to help."

Trent looked down at their interlocked hands, then said to Helen, "I thought you said it would take more than *that* to convince you."

"I've seen Protein X-ACT," Kevin said.

"She risked this organization to get it for you. What did you think of it?"

"It could revolutionize biology."

"*Has* revolutionized biology. *Has.*" They lurched slightly as the truck rounded a bend. "Your uncle was a genius. How different the world would be today if you had accepted his offer."

"No one knew about that. How do—"

"I ask the questions." Eyes locked on Kevin's, he held out his hand, palm up, to Helen. "And while we're at it, Helen, did you get Anna's message?" She opened her bag and surrendered the CD. Trent inspected it. "Seen what else is on here, Kincaid?"

"A protein library hidden under false patents. Amino acid sequences for proteins that, theoretically, could make muscles more efficient, speed up neurotransmitters in the brain, or God knows what else."

"God is the operative word, Doctor. Did you see the third option sitting on this CD?"

"BLAST?"

"Exactly. The world's central search engine for DNA and protein sequences. I'm sure you couldn't resist testing it against the Collaborate's protein library. What'd you find?"

"That the sequences don't match. Someone's tampered with the system."

"Someone?"

"All right. The government."

Trent pointed at Helen. "Which is why I told you not to steal the Program." Back to Kincaid, "It's bad enough fighting just the Collaborate. But with the government as silent partner—" He threw up his hands. "What you see before you is humanity's last stand. And you, Doctor, are the linchpin that can keep the wheel of humanity from sliding off the axle into the pit."

Helen said, "Trent, he—"

"Did she tell you where she got this disk?" he asked Kevin.

"From a patent attorney's office."

"Did she tell you that five other patent attorneys have similar program packages, each possessing a different set of protein formulae in their 'libraries'?"

Kevin turned to a surprised Helen. "No."

"Helen, my errant child, surely you didn't think the Collaborate put *all* their booty in the hands of *one* attorney?" To Kevin, "There are close to fifteen hundred brand-new proteins, designed by Dermot Kincaid's Protein X-ACT, synthesized in labs in San Jose, San Diego, Boise, Research Triangle, Gaithersburg. All humming away, constructing improvements on paralogous proteins from animals and homologous proteins from humans. A veritable cornucopia of improvements in muscle and nerve proteins being back-coded into genes, fitted onto artificial chromosomes, alpha-tested in mice, then beta-tested on *higher* forms of life." He approached Kevin. "Yes, the Collaborate's built itself quite a database, a compilation of formulae for new, spectacular genes that code for proteins that could serve as a second genesis for man, or beast, or both. And as you very well know, life is just a coded series of DNA base sequences."

Kevin's eyes narrowed. "You can't patent human beings."

"But you *can* patent the genes that make the proteins that correct a genetic disease—which is how it begins. Imagine the royalties for patenting the future. The Collaborate will come to own us, own our children. The Collaborate creates the Zoo, anoints itself Zookeeper, and," whispering, "in time, becomes God in every sense of the word."

Kevin's mind replayed Helen's video in perfect detail: the hideously mutated little girl, her distorted, manacled arms pulling desperately against chains in concrete, the scalpel cutting into her unanesthetized flesh, the trickle of blood that followed. He closed his eyes, trying to force away the images. When he opened them, the outline of the tortured girl in chains hung behind Trent. "All utterly useless without the vector to carry them into the cell nucleus."

"Germline therapy is the demarcation between gene therapy and genetic engineering. And you are both designer and huckster."

"What do you want, McGovern?"

"Sole possession of vector $HACV.V_7$."

"Suppose I told you that it doesn't work?"

Helen looked quizzically at him.

"Then I'd be forced to kill you and destroy your lab to prevent the Collaborate from ever building on your work," Trent said.

They swayed as the truck took a long, winding curve.

"What will you do once you get it?" Kevin asked.

Glancing around at the others, "Some of us want to destroy it. Others, lock it away indefinitely. A few think we should put it in the public domain so no one has the advantage. The only thing we all agree on is that the Collaborate must never have it."

"And if I refuse?"

"You're a neurosurgeon, Kincaid. You know the power of pain."

Kevin nodded at Helen. To Trent, "I'll get it for you. But not right now."

Trent clenched his jaw. "Helen said that you keep it all in your head."

"V_7's specs call for complicated stereoscopic representations. One misinterpreted chemical bond and you'll have nothing but junk. I need time to get my files."

Trent cocked his head. "How much time?"

"Twenty-four hours."

"Too long."

Kevin felt Helen's eyes tell him: *Now!* "But there is a better way." He faced Trent. "I'm keynote speaker at a major molecular genetics conference at the National Institutes of Health campus in Bethesda. There'll be satellite coverage on six continents. What if I expose the Collaborate publicly? The fallout would kill 601 and force the patent office to investigate the Collaborate's protein library. V_7 will be stopped dead in its tracks."

"And I'm supposed to buy into this because?"

"Because this way you have a chance to win the war, not just the battle."

Trent chuckled. "Care to run that by me?"

Kevin stepped closer to him. "Mine might be the best lab in the country at developing vectors, but it's by no means the only one. Sooner or later someone somewhere is going to figure out how to make a V_7. McGovern, you and your people can't hold your vigil against these scientific advancements forever. You can't know for sure where and when the next discovery will come. Even if you did, you'd have to fight this same battle, again and again and again. Today I'm on center stage across the country. Tomorrow I'll be center stage across the world. I can expose the Collaborate. And if you're still debating whether you can take a chance on me, ask yourself when the hell you think you're ever, *ever* going to get another opportunity like this."

Trent put his hand to his chin. "*If* I were to approve, you'd need to present unequivocal proof to those skeptical, thick-headed scientists."

Kevin glanced at Helen. "We have proof."

"Namely?"

Kevin pointed at the disk.

"You can't hold our only—"

"Then let Helen keep it. She's guarded it safely so far."

Trent looked to Helen. "This was your idea, wasn't it?"

"Everything's worked so far, hasn't it?" she said.

The truck struck a bump in the highway. A scowl racked Trent's face. "Tell me I'm not making a mistake." Slowly he handed the CD back to Helen. "Keep the CD with you off-site, just in case. One of the usual meeting places."

"Georgetown Mall?" she asked.

He approved. To Kevin, "Understand this, Doctor. I've been fighting the Collaborate for ten years. Most of that time alone. I'll do whatever it takes to stop them, whether that means killing you, destroying your lab, or blowing up that conference at NIH."

What did the Collaborate do to him? Kevin wondered. *It couldn't have been worse than what they did to me.*

"I'll arrange for escort and transportation back to your house," Trent said.

"What if it's being watched?"

"Not your problem." Trent turned and spoke to his men a few minutes. "You know, Doctor, you showed a lot of restraint at the party," he said as the truck slowed. "Had it been me, sooner or later, my hands would've been around Loring's throat."

"Trent, don't!" Helen pleaded.

Trent glanced from Kevin to Helen and back. "She hasn't told you?"

"Told me what?"

"Trent, please. Don't!"

"Tell me, McGovern!"

Trent held up his palms as Helen shook her head. "The lady's asking me not to."

Kevin grabbed Trent and rammed him into the trailer wall. Guns trained on him as he pinned AntiGen's leader by the shoulders.

"Put him down, mate," Cameron shouted.

"Don't harm him. It's all right," Trent yelled to his people. They slowly backed off. To Kevin, "Since you insist."

Kevin eased his grip.

"Flashback ten years," Trent started. "The fire at your uncle's wasn't an accident."

"You're not going to hand me the crap that investigator in Marin was circulating—that somehow my wife was responsible?"

"Your wife was a victim. She had nothing to do with it."

Kevin shifted his forearm firmly under Trent's throat. "Then what are you trying to say?"

"That your family was murdered."

"Yeah? Who by?"

Incredulous, Trent looked at Helen. "He *still* doesn't get it!"

"Trent, please, don't!" Helen pleaded.

"Who by?"

"Loring. Loring murdered your family."

"What!"

"Loring had your uncle killed because he was going to take Protein X-ACT public and form his own company. They must've thought you'd come to his house alone. Wife and children in the back of the van, the tinted glass—I guess the hit team didn't see them enter the kill zone. Unfortunately, by the time Loring's people set the fire, it was too late. I'm sorry, Doctor."

"No! No! That can't be! Loring's people hired me!"

"Even then, they saw your promise. And what better way to keep you under their thumb?"

"You're lying!"

"Remember the psych tests you took before taking your position at Benjamin Franklin?"

Kevin replayed that September afternoon nearly a decade ago. In an isolated, soundproofed, six-by-eight-foot room with a wall-sized mirror, he sat by himself in front of a chipped, pressed-wood desk. For more than five hours, he'd answered hundreds of drilling psychological and behavioral questions in a grueling series of multiple-choice tests. The questions seemed trite, or repetitive, or contradictory, or just plain unanswerable. They weren't like any psychological test he'd ever seen. Afterward, as he'd walked the six blocks through the rain to the suite the hospital had rented for him he wondered why the hospital had conducted such exhaustive testing for just a research position. He remembered entering the suite, feeling dizzy, and collapsing onto the soft king-sized bed with a heavy down quilt.

"That was the Collaborate's way of confirming that you hadn't repressed memories of the incident that could prove compromising," Trent resumed.

"No!"

"I can show you copies of the evaluation."

Kevin released Trent. "What about my wife?"

Trent fixed his collar and cleared his throat. "If you're asking me whether she's alive or dead, we assume she's dead, but the real answer is, we don't know."

Releasing a shuddering sigh, "If she is dead, then why haven't we found her body?"

"We don't know that, either."

His mind ablaze, Kevin whirled around and glared at Helen's glistening eyes. "You knew!" He seized her shoulders. "Why didn't you tell me?"

"Kevin, look at you now. Could you have made it through the evening convincingly playing Loring's golden boy if you'd known?"

He shoved her aside. She looked dolefully at him. "Go on," he snapped. "Leave me alone."

Trent said, "The two of you have to spend the night together at the doctor's town-house for appearances' sake, so you'd better come to an understanding." He whispered in Kevin's ear, "Just as long as you understand that your future rests with me."

Loring Estate
Library

Blount rewound the tape and replayed the last minute of Trent's conversation. "Yes, sir, I'd say you've got yourself a shitload. You should've let me burn Kincaid years ago with the others."

"In which case we wouldn't be here, on the brink of completing the final component, now would we?" Loring briefly shut his eyes. "The leader has given me an idea."

Kincaid Residence

Kevin nearly closed his living room's sliding doors on Helen's face.

Their doubles had been unnecessary. The Collaborate did not appear to have them under surveillance, which had both pleased and worried Trent. Kevin and Helen had been whisked to his abandoned Buick four miles outside the city, where together, silent, they'd driven back to his townhouse.

"Kevin, I—"

"Did Loring murder my wife?"

"Trent's afraid that I have too strong a hold on you. That might upset his plans."

"Did Loring murder Helen?"

She whispered, "Yes."

He shut his burning eyes. "Jessica and Kathy?"

"I'd have told you sooner, but think, would you have been able to hide it from Loring?"

"I trusted you." His mind replayed in perfect clarity the image of Helen in her hotel room: her supple nude body, her long, flowing mahogany hair, and her shocked face—with one eye hidden behind a gray-green contact lens designed to mimic his wife's and the other eye exposing her natural, pure, intense blue. "*Again!*"

"It takes years to wall off that soul-ripping pain. Kevin, I know firsthand because—"

"Shut up! McGovern said that we had to spend the night together for appearances' sake. Fine. Sleep anywhere you like, except my bed." He spun around. "Nguyen should have preliminary results on your specimens." He slammed the door to his study and slipped into the cramped space behind the computer and monitor with minicam attachment, and checked his e-mail: Nguyen had left an urgent request three hours ago promising he'd stay online no matter how late the party.

Three minutes later Kevin established a video link. "You've analyzed the specimens?"

"It'll take years to fully analyze them," Nguyen answered. "Where'd you get—"

"What've you found?"

"Nothing that makes sense. I'm going to transmit some visual records so you can follow for yourself." Nguyen leaned off-screen. A few seconds later, "It should be coming up on your screen now."

On Kevin's monitor the image window of the haggard Nguyen shrank to a quarter of the screen. A set of blue and pink slides of longitudinal stripes with tiny clumps appeared. The stripes of the bottom slide were far thicker than those of the top slide. "Looks like muscle."

"Striated skeletal muscle. Color-enhanced."

"They look radically different."

"They came from the same specimen."

Kevin studied the images. "Human?"

"The top one, yes."

"And the bottom?"

"I'll start slow. Then you can tell me where I screwed up." Nguyen sighed. "The basic contractile unit of skeletal muscle is made up of myofibrils, right? Normally these myofibrils are nice, neat, stacked lines, like carpeting. They're involved in muscle contraction. Essentially, there's two types of myofibrils: thick filaments called myosin, and thin filaments called actin. And there's stripes, striations that run perpendicular to these fibers. Each muscle contractile has an M-line running down the center and Z-lines running along its edges."

Kevin compared the top slide with the bottom. "The top view looks pretty normal. There's the typical cross-striations running perpendicular to the normal muscle-fiber bands." Scanning the lower slide again, "The cross-striations are still there in the bottom view but much tougher to see."

"That's because the thin muscle protein bands, the actin, are abnormally thick. And the thick muscle protein bands, the myosin, are whoppingly thick. Now, we know that muscle contraction is basically myosin fibers sliding past actin fibers. The overlap of these muscle protein fibers is what creates muscle contraction." Nguyen interlocked his fingers to demonstrate. "The greater the number of chemical bonds between the actin and myosin filaments, the greater the muscle's tension, and its power. As the myosin and actin fibers of muscle slide past each other, and overlap, they establish chemical bonds that show up as muscle tension. Strength." He sighed. "Now, take a look at this." New slides appeared to the left of Nguyen's image. "These are actin and myosin fibers magnified a quarter-million times."

The top slide had normal, relatively smooth thin and thick fibers. But on the bottom slide, the thin, actin fiber had neatly spaced spherical projections lining its surface. And the thick, myosin fiber had correspondingly spaced indentations.

"What the hell are those things, Peter?"

"Damn if they don't look like ball-and-socket joints."

Kevin swiveled in his chair. "What do you think?"

"I think since thin and thick fibers slide by one another, overlap, and chemically bond for strength, these ball-and-socket joint adaptations could fantastically improve muscle strength. It's like two mountain climbers. One scales a perfectly smooth rock face. The other, a craggy surface with neatly positioned crevices and outcrops. It's a no-brainer who can climb faster with a more secure grip." Nguyen shrugged. "Somebody with musculature like that could probably lift a locomotive."

"I believe you."

"That's not the half of it." Another pair of close-up slides appeared on Kevin's screen: on top, a partially unwound ribbon dominated the screen; on the bottom, a highly coiled spring. "These are close-ups of titin. It acts like a bungee cord—"

"To enable muscles to extend. Yes, I know."

"Well, regular titin, in the top slide, can let muscle fiber stretch four times its normal length, but the titin in the bottom slide could let a muscle stretch ten times that. Dr. Kincaid, you don't need an expert to tell you there's not a mammal on earth with this muscular configuration. Where did you get this?"

Kevin heard objects clattering, banging from the living room. *What the hell is she doing?* "Theories, Peter?"

Nguyen's image glanced from side to side. "This is where it gets really strange. Microscopy indicated that the actin, the myosin, and the titin fibers, all had extra proteins wrapped around them— as if these muscle cells had extra genes encoding these new proteins, which accentuated vastly improved muscle strength and flexibility."

"Did the two slides come from the different specimens I gave you?"

"No, the same specimen! Which meant that the organism—and that's what I'm calling it—had cells with improved muscle mixed with cells from normal human muscle. Some parts of the specimen were dominated by new muscle cells. Others, by normal muscle cells."

"Chimera?"

"A fusion of two organisms? Or a fusion of two different fertilized eggs? Germlines?" Nguyen shook his head. "That's what I thought at first. Then imagine my surprise at this." The muscle slides disappeared and were replaced by the familiar photo of a cell nucleus with its tiny pairs of rods: chromosomes. "At first glance, this looks normal: twenty-three pairs of chromosomes. Typically human. Until you study the lower right corner of the picture." At the far edge of the cell nucleus was a small pair of joined black rods. "I'll magnify." It was another pair of chromosomes, smaller than the others, but perfectly formed. "A 24th pair of chromosomes!"

Kevin stiffened. His last refuge of denial was being stripped away. The nightmare, his culpability, was being proven in his own, private court. "Mutation? Genetic disorder?"

"Not with a *pair* of chromosomes. Not a duplicate Chromosome 21 or duplicate X chromosome. It's not Down or Klinefelter or any other genetic disease with an extra piece of chromosome. That's a real *pair* of chromosomes—with centromere and telomeres—as valid, as functional as any other in the cell."

"You're certain it's not just a pair of duplicate chromosomes?" Kevin asked.

"You gave me the idea when you asked for FISH analysis. I performed chromosome paintings." A series of chromosomes against black backgrounds appeared on Kevin's screen: some light orange, one bright yellow. "Right now, you're looking at a nucleus with Chromosome 9 painted. That's the one glowing bright yellow." Another cell-nucleus photograph appeared: the same chromosome positions except that another chromosome was glowing. "Chromosome 21." A new photograph. "And Chromosome 6." Nguyen continued transmitting new, fluorescent photographs of the cell nucleus. With every new photograph denoting a different tagged, glowing chromosome, a tiny pair of chromosomes remained the same: uncolored. After finishing the series, "Notice, doctor, that the chromosome paints never attach to that unknown pair of chromosomes."

"Say it, Peter."

"They're human artificial chromosomes—HACs. I believe those HACs contain the genes ultimately encoding for proteins that improve muscle strength and flexibility." Nguyen hesitated. "I think somebody genetically-engineered those proteins, designed the genes that code for them, stuck them on artificial chromosomes, and inserted them, transfected them, into the nucleus."

"Proof?"

"Clumps of abnormal muscle cells all contained HACs. Clumps of normal muscle cells didn't."

"Have you started DNA sequencing the HACs?"

"I haven't had time."

Kevin took a deep breath. "Any sign of the vector used to transfect these artificial chromosomes?"

"Thirty percent of the cell nuclei had intact HACs. Sixty percent didn't. But the last ten percent had DNA fragments—fragments that appeared to be pieces of the artificial chromosome. Some DNA fragments actually seemed viable. I found the pattern familiar so I checked it against the lab's historical records." Nguyen leaned out of camera.

"Spit it out."

"The decay pattern was identical to vector K_4. Dr. Kincaid, somebody's been using our failed vector on human beings."

The Tiburon video again appeared in his head. The deformed girl's face, screaming in agony. Until that moment he'd been able to partially shield himself from blame. Though he believed the video, the link to his work had been circumstantial. But now, undeniably, his vector was responsible for that little girl's living nightmare. He turned away from the screen and clenched his fists. The mouse in his right hand cracked.

The floor gently vibrated. Outside the door he heard scraping sounds. Something being pushed across the living room? Was Helen barricading him in? *I'd deserve it,* he thought. *I've been thinking only of myself. People were tortured, murdered because of my work. Helen, you were right. I am responsible. Maybe you were right not telling me about the fire, too.*

"Dr. Kincaid, what's going—"

"Coming to my lecture at NIH?"

"I'd like to. The rest of your staff is."

"Bring the samples with you. They're evidence."

"Evidence of—"

"It's not safe to know yet, Peter. Don't tell anyone."

"All right. Doctor, I've also built a meta-file on the specimens. It contains my findings, graphical representations, the works. Should I bring that, too?"

"Sure, great. Smart kid. Download me a copy. Oh, and if this stuff is on the hospital network, delete it."

"Okay, Doctor. I'll attach it to e-mail. You'll have it in a few minutes. And don't worry. I know how to purge e-mails from the hospital's server."

Kevin terminated the connection, but left the system on. Before reaching for the door, he rehearsed three opening apologies to Helen.

Something banged on the living room floor.

He swung open the door. "Helen, I—" Her legs dangled at eye level. His head craned up. She swung from the chandelier, a bedsheet wrapped around her neck.

Loring Estate
Library

"At least it's not DARPA," Loring said evenly as he leaned back and turned down the speaker. Kevin's voice clicked off.

"You're sure you don't want Kincaid killed?" Blount asked.

Eyes locked on Blount, he lifted the cup to his lips. "We do not as yet have V_7."

"So, I'm to pull all of this off within twelve hours."

Loring checked his watch. "Closer to ten."

Kincaid Residence

Kevin leaped onto the table that Helen had slid into the center of the room, grabbed her torso with one arm, and lifted her, relieving the pressure from the strangulating sheet around her neck. His other hand struggled to loosen the knot. The sheet fought him, twisting tighter. His grip on her slipped. The noose around her throat tightened. His fingers dug into the sheet, but couldn't loosen it. Desperate, he scanned the room for something sharp. He dared not release her: the sudden drop this time would snap her neck.

He looked up. Yes, it was the only hope. Tightening one arm around her waist, the other around the sheet, he yanked. The chandelier shook, but held firm. He yanked again on the sheet. The fixture swayed, but didn't weaken. He momentarily released his grip on the sheet, reached up, locked his hand directly on the chandelier, and yanked. He could feel his shoulder being torn from its socket.

The ceiling bolt weakened. He pulled again. The fixture bent toward him. Plaster fell to the floor. Repositioning himself, he pulled. His shoulder on fire, he cried out.

The fixture snapped. They flew backward.

His shoulder slammed onto the floor. Helen crashed onto his chest. The chandelier smashed beside them, three of its crystals ripping his forehead. Blood poured from a gash on his temple onto the carpeting.

Quickly he checked her neck: there was a bright red streak across it, but her airway was open. She was breathing. Apparently, the sheet had wrapped directly under her jaw. When she'd dropped, her weight must have shifted and she had hung by her jaw instead of her throat.

She suddenly made throat-clearing, rasping sounds. Then took a deep breath, and coughed.

Loring Estate
Library

"It's not the money," Blount said. "It's the timing. A multifaceted operation like this? I'd need ten days minimum to prep. You're asking me to go in stone cold in as many hours." He pushed his empty teacup and saucer toward his host. "Seven million."

"I don't appreciate being gouged, especially by a single-source contractor." Loring placed his teacup on the table. "One million."

"I don't like being forced on a suicide mission. Six."

"One point five million. For you *and* your team." The phone rang. Loring picked it up. As he listened, his complexion grew ashen. For a moment Blount thought the man would keel over. Loring turned off the phone and collapsed back into his chair. "Frederick Grayson is dead."

"Sorry to hear that." Blount's head bobbed. "I hate to rush, but I'm pressed for time and we were still deciding my fee."

Loring flashed a frigid smile. He touched his teacup. "This is cold." He swung his arm and slung the tea set off the table. China flew across the room and smashed onto the floor. Shards of porcelain exploded in mini-bursts, leaving liquid splatter trails coalescing on the carpet. "That was two-hundred-year-old china. It was irreplaceable," he said quietly. "Are you?"

Kincaid Residence

Kevin stroked Helen's hair and rocked her. Slowly, her breath began to return. He felt her body slacken from exhaustion. He waited until she lay quiet, sedate. "Why, Helen?"

"I'm all used up. Trent thinks I'm useless—useless in the fight. Worthless to you as—that's why he told you that Loring killed your family."

"He's wrong. On both counts."

"I spent so much time training to become your desire. To have the right face, the right body, the right words, the right actions. To learn you. To become your dream. In time, I couldn't help but want you. But it's all learned, Kevin, like freshman math. Learned, just to steal your secrets." She pulled away. "Now that the moment's passed, I'm left with nothing—not you, not a cause, not even the real me."

He whispered, "As much as you've hurt me I can't deny that I have feelings for you—"

"*Helen*," she finished. "It will always be *Helen*, until your wife comes back to you, or you can lay her to rest."

"Is it so impossible to believe that if you are my dream, I could feel as I do for *you*?"

"Listen to yourself. I'm a dream. I'm fiction. You don't know the real me."

He laid his head on her side. "Are the two of you so different?"

"There's nothing left of the real me." She shook her head and sobbed.

"Helen, you don't learn to love someone from photographs or file folders or briefings." He caressed her back. "You experience it from some inborn call of kinship."

"The only kinship we share, Kevin, is pain. You can't trust me."

"Show me that I can."

"You won't want me, then."

"Maybe I'll want you more."

"The Collaborate killed my family, too."

He held her tight. "Helen—"

"Not Helen. Tracy. Tracy Bergmann."

He loosened his arms.

"See? I said you wouldn't—"

"You just surprised me, that's all. I've come to think of you as—go on, please."

"My father was Wyndom Bergmann." She paused. "Ever hear of him?"

"Oh, yes. Yes, I've read several of his papers. Growing human tissue, in vitro, outside the body on synthetic polymer scaffolds for replacing diseased tissue—mostly regenerating liver tissue. Last I'd heard, he'd been working on growing nerves."

"Ten years ago, Wyndom Bergmann was the country's leading tissue engineer. My father's work was a generation beyond his published papers." She draped his arm around her waist. "He was gifted, loving, and arrogant. With my mother and brother I spent my childhood being dragged by Daddy about the country, while he went from lab to lab trying to find someplace that could tolerate the aggravation that came with his genius. Two years, a resignation, and he'd be off in search of a more understanding opportunity. And of course the limitations on stem cell lines and research made Daddy's search for work increasingly difficult. That was until ReGenerix Tech—one of Loring's firms." She rolled onto her back and opened her eyes. "My God, you're bleeding!"

Kevin dabbed his cheek. "It's not bad. Go on."

"He was appreciated there. We were stable for the first time, a happy family. We even had a weekend retreat up in the Blue Ridge Mountains. My brother went locally to college. For the first time I had friends. I finished high school and started at NYU as a broadcasting major."

"So you did really want to be a network anchor."

She nodded. "But in those final months Daddy became erratic, sullen. At first we all thought that he was ready to move on, but it wasn't dissatisfaction with people, it was with his *work*."

"What exactly was his work?"

"He never really said. Except once, Daddy mentioned in passing that he'd created some sort of bottle. It had a Russian name. Polish, maybe? Began with a *B*, I think." She shrugged. "Near the end, my mother called me at college. She was frightened. Daddy had been ranting for days about some 'treatise' he'd seen. About how his work was the 'first component' in some grand nefarious scheme. At the end, he called my brother and me back from college, and told us about contingency plans he'd made—false identities, money, escape plans in case something happened to him." She stared past Kevin. "Daddy blew up Loring's lab—and himself. Two weeks later they found my mother sitting in bed, a bullet in her brain. Suicide, they said."

"I'm so sorry."

Her eyes moist, "People watched me from doorways, street corners, black vans. My dorm was broken into three times. Lance's apartment, twice. Someone was after us. Lance and I took the fake passports my father had provided and fled to Europe. We drifted together awhile. In a way, it was the happiest time of my life."

"Why did you come back?"

"The money stream dried up. Our IDs were suddenly no good. Neither Lance nor I knew who they were, just that they were coming. So we split up, separately made our ways back to the States, and established new identities more times than I can remember. But it didn't matter. After a few months, someone would come around asking questions." She took a deep breath. "While at NYU, I learned how to hack."

"To augment your journalistic skills, no doubt."

"I was a pretty fair at it, too. Though certainly never nearly as good as Anna."

"Who's Anna?"

"Later." She continued, "Hacking came in useful when I went underground. Of course, my clients weren't exactly 'corporate'. But they paid in cash. And it helped keep me one step ahead of the Collaborate—that and stealing cars."

"You? A car thief?"

"Learned through years of running. Saved my life more than once. That is, until—" She reached up. Touched his cheek. "Trent McGovern found me in an alley, my face slashed, ribs fractured, dying. He repaired me. Gave me and Lance unbreakable identities and a way to fight back. All just for seducing you. For what he offered, I'd've French-kissed the devil."

He cupped her face in his hands. "Do I call you Helen? Or Tracy?"

DARPA
Arlington, Virginia

"All hell's going to break loose," Kristin Brocks muttered as she sat in her office and watched yet another replay of the Collaborate's last holographic message.

E. Dixon Loring was now apparently in charge. The Quorum Summit, at Bertram's urging, had temporarily anointed him emperor: a dangerous transition in Collaborate evolution. Though Loring was a showman and skilled manipulator, the man was haunted by his roots. Still proving and re-proving himself to his old mountain town. Still susceptible to seduction: in ten years, three unfaithful mistresses had disappeared. One, planted by her Agency predecessor. No, Loring was not the cool, shrewd intelligence directing the Collaborate. Why had they given him so much power?

As always, all answers pointed to Eric Bertram, through his legions of well-paid agents and global contacts. Nonfinancial information on the man was sparse: his background had probably been demagnetized clean from cyberspace. That left only Quorum communiqués and a fragment she'd uncovered from his past. At one time, Bertram had been a world traveler, interested in the ancients of the Middle East, India, Himalayan Asia. What had changed him? Had he gotten religion? Did he envision himself a latter-day prophet? Only once had Bertram ever let any such reference slip—a meaningless term derived from Middle Eastern metaphysical nonsense: *Qutub*.

6

THURSDAY, JANUARY 23
Delphi   *10:33 A.M.*

"Meredith, please open up," Marguerite Moraes begged. She had
the authority to override the lock, but what would that accomplish?

The door finally unbolted. She opened it wide enough to slip
through. The room was austere. In its center stood three simultaneously running PCs, surrounded by whiteboard walls filled with multicolored Greek letters in enigmatic equations. A tiny bed, sheets
disheveled, was tucked in the far corner. "Meredith?"

No answer.

Marguerite tiptoed to the computers and peered around the
back. A girl not much larger than a toddler with braided, flaxen
hair sat at a console, her tiny fingers dancing over the keyboard as
she whizzed through algorithms flying across the screen. Marguerite knelt beside her.

Meredith turned, exposing round, bloodshot aqua-blue eyes.
"Ethan's dead, isn't he?"

Marguerite rubbed a warm hand across the girl's back.

"My turn, soon, Aunt Margie. I know the signs."

Marguerite held the girl's face close to her. "No, it's not."

Meredith pushed away and walked over to the near wall, contem-
plating an equation on the whiteboard:

$$|\psi> = |\phi_1>e\otimes|\chi_1> d + e^{i\Delta\alpha}|\phi_r>e\otimes|\chi_r>_d$$

"Are you close to finding an answer? Could that," pointing at the
equation, "be it?"

The little girl stared blankly. "That's just an entangled wavefunction of an interferometer and detector used for dephasing in an electron interfer—"

"Meredith, I thought you were working on a cure?"

"There is no cure!"

"Child, you must not—"

The girl's body grew flaccid, unresponsive. Her face, her eyes, vacant.

Marguerite had seen that too many times: petit mal seizure. The child would resume normal mental and physical activity in a few seconds, unaware that she'd just had a seizure. But it could happen a hundred times a day. Marguerite liked to believe that during such moments, Meredith's mind was visiting some enchanted, happy place. Soon, the severe seizures would start.

Meredith's muscles tightened. She blinked, then resumed, "I was reading a story, *Flowers for Algernon*. It's about a retarded man who was given an injection that made him brilliant."

Marguerite shut her eyes, afraid to ask how the story ended.

Natcher Conference Center
National Institutes of Health (NIH) Campus
Bethesda, Maryland

Cold drizzle fogged Peter Nguyen's glasses as he hurried across NIH Campus's Center Drive to Natcher Conference Center. He stopped beneath the building's portico, put down his briefcase, and placed his foot on the handle as he wiped his glasses. Beside him, a man self-consciously dragged on a cigarette. "Dr. Kincaid speak yet?" Nguyen asked him.

The smoking man shook his head. "After lunch. But why bother? Just watch tonight's commercial."

Nguyen shrugged, glanced down at his briefcase, and imagined that he could see the specimen samples of hybrid muscle tissue and the meta-file CD. "Oh, you might be surprised," he said before proceeding through heavy glass doors.

Natcher Conference Center was a soaring cathedral of tinted glass. Wall panes of polarized glass thrusting eighty feet over the polished floor drank in natural daylight. Nguyen felt as if he walked through clouds, his steps echoing along the great atrium. Beyond an unattended black marble security desk he spotted a sign—"Twenty-eighth Conference on Molecular Genetics and Advanced Expression Vectors"—with a red arrow pointing to the left. To the right was the cheerfully decorated entrance to an open-air cafeteria pushing pizza, deli, and salads, but there wasn't time to eat. Briefcase tight in hand, he headed for the conference registration and entered another atrium with a great glass wall offering a hemi-panoramic view of manicured grassy knolls dotted by the campus's Colonial-style red-brick buildings. Small auditoriums and meeting rooms were perched on a mezzanine above the conference's ground floor. Below, people chatted and sampled pastries in the lobby outside the grand auditorium. He descended one of the two open-air staircases leading to the ground level. Though the main floor was windowless, light streaming through the glass atrium made it bright, airy. Bypassing the self-serve cloakroom and private meeting rooms, he wound slowly through the crowd to the registration table guarding the grand auditorium entrance. At the desk, an attractive woman with curly black hair and a blue cashmere sweater smiled at him.

Nguyen smiled back. "My name is Nguyen. Peter Nguyen."

She looked up his name on a list. "Ah, I see it. Welcome, Dr. Nguyen." She handed him a badge and loose-leaf binder. Widening her smile, "Do enjoy the conference."

Nguyen flushed. Was she just being pleasant or giving signals for him to make a pass?

Someone jostled him from behind. He quickly turned around. There stood a stout man with long jowls and a tieless shirt: Dr. Gregory Pratt, one of Kincaid's team leaders. "You're just about the last," Pratt said, holding a styrofoam cup.

"Who else is here?" Nguyen asked loudly above the crowd's noise.

"My team. Plus Gensini, Horowitz, DeVries, and their teams. But not our fearless leader. Maybe he won't show."

"Why wouldn't he?"

Pratt leaned in with his coffee breath. "You tell me, kid. Animal lab's been sealed off and cleaned out. And Kincaid hasn't spoken to anybody in the lab in days—except you."

"He's under a lot of stress."

"Something's going on, and I don't like being kept in the—holy shit, here she comes!" Putting on a toothy smile, "She's got a bee in her bonnet for you." Pratt slapped Nguyen's arm and pretended to laugh at a joke. "Call me if you need a reference." He disappeared into the crowd.

"Nguyen!" A voice pierced the din. Joan Tetlow, with her trademark oversized scarf, was cradling a stack of papers against her chest, and bearing down on him. "Good morning, Ms.—"

"Dr. Kincaid put you in charge of assembling the files. Just look at this!" she said in a low, emphatic voice while shoving her pile of papers into his stomach.

Taken aback, Nguyen dropped his conference binder on the registration desk beside him, knocking a cup of pens and a stack of flyers onto the floor. The receptionist looked dismayed. "Let me get that," Nguyen offered, putting down his briefcase.

"It's all right, Doctor." The receptionist smiled warmly. "I'll take care of it." She leaned under the registration table.

"Never mind her." Tetlow tapped on the papers. "Look at these files!"

Nguyen scanned the top few pages. They appeared to be schematics of the cochlear cylinder configuration, but degraded, with its original crepe shape twisted. Accompanying data for synthesis was garbled, as if four files had been printed simultaneously. "It looks like one of V_7's outer—"

"It's junk!"

"I think it's encrypted. Ma'am, did I send you this file?"

Maintaining her low, stern voice, "I took them off the system myself." Before he could object, "It's Thursday, Nguyen. Three days, and I still don't have Dr. Kincaid's files. And here I find you lounging at a conference, on hospital time, paid for with hospital funds."

"Dr. Kincaid gave me until Monday to assemble his files for you. I promise I'll meet the deadline."

"You'd better. Postdocs are a dime a dozen. Why, I could send you back to Philadelphia this minute—and I ought to, except that the conference is already paid for. But," holding up a finger, "when I get back to BFMC, you'd better be hard at work assembling my files. Now, give me those." She scooped her papers in her arms and stormed away.

The receptionist smiled sympathetically. "Supervisors—they're so frustrating."

Nguyen returned a sheepish shrug and gave her a long look-over.

With a radiant smile she said, "Enjoy the conference, Doctor."

Eyes fixed on hers, he leaned down and reached for his briefcase, but missed. He glanced down. There it was, locked, but at least three feet to the right of where he'd left it—or remembered leaving it. He looked at the receptionist, but she was already busy servicing another attendee.

Lister Hill, NIH Campus

Blount stood at the window, his hands clasped behind his back like a Napoleon as he surveyed the NIH campus. The Lister Hill Building, the tall glass tower connected by tunnels to the National Library of Medicine, offered a near-perfect vantage. Even through drizzle and enclosing fog, he still had a high-ground view of Natcher Center, from the glass colonnade in front to the elevated ramp in the rear. While scrutinizing the target site with binoculars, he coordinated his teams throughout the NIH campus and Washington via a headset with earphone in his right ear, while simultaneously monitoring Kincaid and Bergmann through a separate earjack in his left ear.

"This is registration desk," a woman's voice broke in on his right earphone. "I have it."

"Good," Blount said into his mouthpiece. "Watch him. See that he doesn't open that briefcase." He put his hands on his hips, pressed tighter on his left earpiece, and listened intently.

Exit 34 (Wisconsin Avenue/Rockville Pike/NIH)
Interstate 495, Maryland (The Beltway)

Rain splattered the windshield as Kevin drove down the Beltway. Two and a half hours behind repetitively sweeping wipers was too much time—time to think about children suffering from Collaborate experiments with K_4. Time to think about what the Collaborate might do with V_7—the twisted possibilities made him shudder.

"What's the matter?" Helen asked.

"Nothing, Tracy."

"Call me 'Helen' until we're safe."

Will we ever be safe? No matter what happens, my career is over, Kevin thought. *Denounce my own work, and I'll spend years testifying at investigations, defending my integrity, avoiding the press, fighting legal battles. I'll be a vilified informer.* He looked at her morosely. *Sometimes I wish I never met you.*

"Exit thirty-four," she said. "This is our—"

"I know the way." The car slid into the right-hand lane and turned off the Beltway onto the busy, lighted Wisconsin Avenue. "Last night it all seemed so clear. Stand before the global scientific community and denounce the Collaborate. Present the clinical evidence from your tissue specimens. Show that the world's key biological databases have been subverted." He stopped at a red light. "It won't bring my family back—or yours. Helen, these people have power. Power manipulates perception."

"Your audience will believe you."

"They'll ask the one question I cannot answer: 'Why?'"

As the light changed, "We know the answer. Global domination."

"If you wanted to rule the world, you'd amass wealth, raise armies, build weapons, buy influence, manipulate heads of state. You wouldn't spend decades and billions of dollars on genetic engineering."

"Unless you wanted to *reshape* it," Helen said.

"Reshape into what? I've spent the last few hours imagining what they'd do. But without a clear motive, they'll paint us as paranoid conspiracy freaks." Glancing at her, "We're missing a vital piece." Under his breath, "Just like V_7."

She met his gaze. "Last night, you asked what would happen if V_7 didn't work. Was that hypothetical? Or did you mean it?"

"Here we are." He turned the Buick to the right, past a black sign announcing the National Institutes of Health, and onto Center Drive, leading through the sprawling complex. They wound past the National Library of Medicine, a squat structure with concrete-slab walls designed to collapse inward and protect its contents if struck by a nuclear bomb. He glanced to his left: there was the Lister Hill building, home of the National Center for Biotechnology Information (NCBI). Someone in that great tower had compromised the world's most sophisticated genetic database. "This is it." He turned right up a wide, tall ramp behind the sculptured-glass building and parked the car in a reserved space with his name strung on a placard covering a parking meter. Raindrops quickly covered the windshield. "Do you want to wait around front?"

"Anna said she'd meet us here in the back."

"I don't see anyone."

"She'll appear when she's sure no one's watching." Helen looked deep into his eyes. Her breaths grew deliberate. "We have a few minutes."

He returned her gaze. "There are times when I wish I'd never met you."

She slowly smiled. "Is this one of them?"

Mirroring her long, labored breaths, his mind replayed in perfect clarity Helen standing nude in her hotel room, her long hair tousled over her shoulder, errant strands flowing over breasts billowing from her satiny chemise. The image slowly shrank. Almost the size of a thumbnail, it pulled away and dropped into the left side of a balancing scale held by a blindfolded Helen. He began reliving another memory. He felt Helen's smooth, supple abdomen beneath his hand as she lay beside him. She got up from bed and left him cold and exposed in the dark. He switched on the light and saw the face of betrayal: one eye gray-green, the other blue. The memory shrank and receded, but this time dropped into the right side of the balancing scale, tipping it to the right. Then again he was in bed with Helen, his fingers feeling the wet stickiness of her tender flesh, the smell of her excitement bursting into his thoughts. The memory receded and tipped the scales left. He was again in the tractor trailer, listening to Trent explain how she'd with-held the truth about Loring murdering his family. This memory receded and tipped the scale far right. His photographic mind began deluging him with more memories. Though Kevin desperately wanted to replay only pleasant ones, his gift seemed more determined to remind him of the anguish she'd caused. Was it telling him that desire, no matter how powerful, how seductive, could not balance out betrayal?

Helen's smile faded. "Guess it must be one of those times."

A new, vibrant memory ignited in Kevin's consciousness, crowd-ing out the others. He found himself rocking Helen's body in his arms. Only moments before, she'd been dangling from his chandelier. Now, as life slowly returned to her body, he tasted her perfect warmth, drank in her intense blue eyes looking up at him, and felt her melodic voice reverberating within him, saying *In time, I couldn't help but want you.* The memory cycled again and again, growing clearer, growing stronger with each replay.

Helen turned away.

He slowly reached out. Gently, he drew her to him.

Her lips parted.

He moved closer.

A fist rapped on the passenger window. Helen pulled away from Kevin and wiped away condensation on the glass. Beneath a black umbrella, a woman with dark features framed in short black hair was motioning to her.

"That's Anna. I have to go. I'll be waiting for you in Georgetown."

He nodded. "If anything happens—"

"It won't."

Lister Hill, NIH Campus

"The hell it won't," Blount snickered. He watched the umbrella protecting Helen and Anna slowly progress toward the main visitors parking lot, but could not overhear their conversation. *Loring's mistake. I'd've implanted subdermal transmitters in them both.* No matter: she would be waiting in Georgetown.

Main Visitors Parking Lot, NIH Campus

"You do love him," Anna said, starting her car. "It is destructive to hope that you can have a future with him."

"You're wrong. Kevin will have exposed the Collaborate," Helen said, looking at the CD in her handbag, "Trent will have his Protein X-ACT. So you see, there's—there's no reason for Trent to kill him."

"You are not convinced."

Helen turned to the rain beating on her window. "Why would Trent do that?"

Anna turned her bruised eye to Helen. "He has some personal need to take Kincaid's knowledge, then kill him. At times, I think it is more important to him than the mission."

Helen sank in her seat. "I've condemned Kevin to death. Anna, what am I going to do?"

Anna turned onto Center Drive. "You Americans have a saying about a carrot and stick."

After a moment, Helen perked up, and began rifling through her bag. "Yes." As they stopped at a red light at the campus's main entrance, she held up her brother's video. She handed it, with a pen, to Anna. "Here. Label this 'Family Picnic' in German."

"Why?"

"We're burying the carrot."

At the first red light, Anna shrugged and scribbled on the label.

"Make a left," Helen said, taking back the tape.

"But we want to go right, down Wisconsin Avenue into the District."

"First, we drop the tape off at your place for safekeeping."

"What is this tape?"

"Pictures of hell." The explanation took three-quarters of the trip to Rockville.

"And you think Trent will spare Kincaid's life in exchange for that tape?" Anna asked afterward. "Even if he agrees, I do not think he will keep his word."

"It's how Trent answers that's important."

"I do not understand."

"We've both learned to read Trent. We know when he's lying. When I make the offer, we'll know whether he'll keep his word. If he doesn't, he gets the stick."

Anna pulled up in front of her apartment building. "What stick?"

Helen clenched her teeth. "Loring."

"You cannot mean—"

"Oh yes. If I have to, I'll tell Loring himself that Trent McGovern masterminded their downfall. With luck, they'll get Trent before he kills Kevin. Or us!"

AntiGen Action Committee Headquarters
Rockville, Maryland

"Penang, how's it coming?" Trent asked.

"Not good," said a woman with long, straight black hair who frantically worked a keyboard.

"You swore to me that you could tap into the conference's uplink. What's the problem?" he asked, pacing the cold, concrete floor of AntiGen's tiny Operations Room.

Van Helding, Straub, and five others sat crammed in silence around the bridge table, the converted garage illuminated only by light from one of the computer station monitors. Trent felt their eyes questioning him, again. The computer beeped. Penang threw up her hands in disgust.

Trent spun her chair toward him. "You've got to tap into that uplink. I've got to know what Kincaid's telling the world *in real time!*"

"I cannot." Penang, with dark, bloodshot eyes, looked up at him. "NIH's system is off-line. They cannot link up to satellite."

He thought, *Could the Collaborate have learned that Kincaid's going to expose them and disabled the satellite uplink? No, no. They'd never have let it go this far.* "Keep working." Circling behind Straub, "Go to the drop-off point. Get the disk from Morgan. Steitz probably made a copy. Get that, too. If NIH's system stays down, Kincaid won't be able to live up to his end of the bargain. Maybe he never intended to. In which case, Morgan and Steitz are in on a double-cross. Now get your ass there!"

Straub bolted from the table and left.

Trent whipped out his cell phone and called one of his two operatives at Natcher Center. "Johnson, where are you now?"

"Cafeteria. I've got Kincaid in my sight," a subdued tenor's voice replied. "He's talking with some geek. Looks innocent enough."

"Stick with him. If he gives any sign that he's going back on the deal—"

"I'll take him out."

"Negative! You will *not*, repeat, *not* take him out." Trent hesitated. "In that event, you will take him to drop-off location seven."

"You want me to kidnap him? In front of all these people?"

"You heard me," Trent finished and hung up. He popped a mint in his mouth and crushed it. "And just what the hell is Cameron doing?"

Reception Area, Natcher Center

Cameron weaved through the lunch-thinned crowd outside the main auditorium to the area beneath the open-air staircase. He sneaked down a narrow hallway to a door marked "Video and Telecommunications" adjoining a side entrance to the auditorium. Gently, he opened the door and peeked inside. A large panel of audio and video controls, surrounded by a slew of monitors, dominated the room. Two chairs for technicians behind the panel were unoccupied. He stole to the control panel and noticed a tiny puddle of brown liquid on an inset monitor. He touched it with his finger, sniffed, then brought it to his tongue: coffee, just coffee. Puddles of coffee lay across the control panel's delicate circuitry, but there were no cups.

A spark flew out of the panel.

Bloody thing's been short-circuited by coffee. To his right, tucked in the corner, he noticed a door, ajar, marked "Storage." He stood motionless, listening, and detected faint breathing sounds. He withdrew a gleaming, six-inch hunting knife with a serrated edge. Stealthily approached the open door.

Two bodies lay piled in the corner of the floor—with a man in a dark suit standing over them, running his fingers along the back closet wall. The man knelt, opened his briefcase. A faint caustic odor drifted across the room as he removed a fist-sized doughy wad and shaped it onto the wall.

Bloody hell! Cameron charged at the kneeling man.

Without looking back, the man's left heel shot back and smashed into Cameron's knee. He whipped around and shot a spear hand at Cameron's knife-wielding right arm. The weapon dropped. The man's right hand pinned Cameron's stunned arm against his shoulder like a fulcrum. His left arm wrapped around Cameron's, held it taut, then hyperextended it. With a single twist of his hips, he snapped Cameron's elbow backward.

Cameron screamed. The man delivered a lightning front kick to the throat.

Cameron collapsed, gasping wildly for air.

The man turned his back, quickly finished his work, closed his briefcase, and fixed his twisted tie. He turned around. Cameron lay on his back: mouth agape, throat bruised, eyes bulging, lifeless. The man picked up the knife beside the body. "The last unit's in place," he whispered into a transmitter. After waiting for the confirmation, he said, "Had an intruder. And it wasn't security." He explained Cameron and the knife. "What d'ya wanna do?" He listened, bobbed his head, and grinned. "Gotcha. Out." He opened his briefcase and placed a piece of the putty in Cameron's lifeless hand.

Courtyard Cafeteria, Natcher Center

". . . don't you think, Dr. Kincaid?" Dr. David McKuserk asked.

Kevin looked up from his untouched salad to the robust white-haired man with matching full beard, then around the airy dining area. People at several tables were staring at him, but quickly looked away at his glance. "Is it my imagination, or are people sneering at me?"

McKuserk craned around. "I'm afraid not."

"Why is that, Doctor?" Kevin asked.

McKuserk leaned back. "The Sagan effect."

"Come again?"

"Carl Sagan, you might remember, was an eminent astrophysicist and exobiologist who committed the unforgivable sin of trying to popularize science. The physical sciences community, and many members of the Academy, took a dim view of one of their own parading on nightly talk shows and becoming part of pop culture. Molecular geneticists are cut from the same cloth."

"You agree with that?"

McKuserk squirmed in his seat. "As conference chair, let's say that I'd rather not see one of the country's leading vector specialists doing promos between prime-time sitcoms."

Kevin snapped, "You'll understand after my lecture."

McKuserk stood and pointed toward the main lobby, "Speaking of which. Shall we?" He led Kevin through the great atrium, past seminar rooms to a service stairwell leading to the auditorium's backstage. "Almost forgot. You said you brought no slides. Any A/V needs?"

"I have a CD."

"No problem. You can run it right from the podium."

They entered the backstage of the main auditorium. Stagehands with their crew boss were laying cable across the polished wood floor. Audience murmurings filtered through the closed red velvet curtain.

Kevin nervously ground his teeth. For the first time, he realized that he'd never considered how his audience would react. Would they openly accept his proof? Or, in true scientific fashion, try to tear him apart? "Will that go out over satellite feed, too?"

"Certainly," answered McKuserk. Glancing around, "Speaking of which, a tech should be here now. And why are those men laying cable *now*? They should've finished hours ago."

"McKuserk, honestly, tell me what's really sticking in your craw."

He shrugged. "Have it your way, Doctor. Germline gene therapy shouldn't be permitted for any reason. Not now. Not ever."

"The slippery slope theory?"

"Not theory. The inevitability of human nature. I—"

Blood spurted from McKuserk's mouth. Dazed, wide-eyed, he gurgled, and collapsed face first onto the stage floor.

Frozen, Kevin stared at the gaping bullet entrance in McKuserk's back, oozing blood.

Powerful arms bear-hugged Kevin from behind. A cloth with a dizzying odor covered his nose, his mouth. His head spun. He glimpsed a blurred outline of McKuserk's limp body being carried away on a stagehand's shoulder. Color evaporated. He lost consciousness.

· · ·

Lister Hill

Blount scrutinized the elevated platform behind Natcher where his men hustled a slumped Kincaid into the van abutting the loading dock. He checked his watch. "Gentlemen, we are leaving," he ordered into his headset. "Beta team, withdraw. Gamma team, hold at perimeter until beta team vacates. Is the observer standing by?"

"Yeah," a voice replied in his ear. "He'll let us know the minute it—"

"Place the call exactly three minutes later. Now move. Out."

Blount went to the closet, removed his satchel, and fixed the collar on his overcoat. A bald man, the lead computer scientist who'd overseen and engineered Collaborate infiltration into the BLAST search engine and other NCBI databases, lay slumped in the closet corner with a hole in his forehead. "Thanks for the use of the hall." He slammed the door in the dead man's face, checked the ceiling, and placed his open satchel directly beneath the sprinkler head. Fire would erase any evidence of his presence.

Main Auditorium, Natcher Center

Nguyen leaned against the glass pane separating the control booth from the back of the auditorium. The great hall, dominated by a seventy-foot-high red velvet stage curtain, had nearly three hundred of the world's most innovative minds in molecular genetics buzzing.

"Kincaid's grandstanding," the woman next to him whispered.

"Think he's found the Holy Grail?" asked a man with thinning white hair three rows from the front.

A woman with silver bangs answered, "If he has, you and I go the way of the dino—"

"Interesting speculations, huh, kid?" Dr. Gregory Pratt nudged Nguyen in the ribs. "It'd be a real slap in the face if our fearless leader showed the planet V_7's structure *before* showing us."

Nguyen looked down at his briefcase, standing on edge.

"I overheard you and Tetlow. Why should *you*, a lowly postdoc, be assembling V_7 files for her? I've given Kincaid seven years of my life. What's he planning? And why the hell is Tetlow here?"

"I wish I knew."

"Ahh, you're useless." Pratt recrossed his legs. His foot accidentally brushed Nguyen's briefcase. It teetered to one side, then struck the floor with a dull thud.

Nguyen bent forward and righted the briefcase. Both combination latch locks were set at 9-1-0, the correct combination. But he *always* randomly spun each combination lock whenever he closed the briefcase. "Oh no!" He grabbed the briefcase, set it on his lap, snapped it open, and rifled through the folders and collapsible binders. The disk with the meta-file, the specimens—gone!

"Something wrong, kid?"

The stage shook.

People sitting in the front rows of the auditorium jumped screaming to their feet. Those in the rear of the auditorium couldn't clearly see what was happening. Row by row, they stood, at first trying to find the cause of the commotion, then cramming into the aisle, climbing on top of each other, stepping on those who'd fallen. The great red velvet curtains onstage burst into flames.

A blue-white fireball exploded from the stage.

People in front disappeared, engulfed in an expanding inferno. The blast picked up rows of bolted seats and slammed them into the surging crowd. The shock wave knocked over Nguyen. Glass behind him shattered. A pulse of searing heat scorched his face. The air tasted acrid.

A gaping hole in the concrete floor had opened at what had been the auditorium stage. Remnants of the red velvet curtain burned overhead from a swaying crossbeam. A man ablaze, shrieking, fell into the hole. Others, clothes singed, stood dazed as concrete rained around them. Screaming people climbed over each other, madly dashing down the remains of the center aisle toward the exit.

Nguyen felt himself picked up in the human maelstrom. His body being banged, bumped, slammed, he whirled helplessly. Pressing bodies, like an undertow, pulled him into trampling feet and dragged him into the lobby.

Breathing space suddenly appeared. Like columns of ants avoiding an obstacle, the crowd split, each part heading toward the nearest open-air staircase. Nguyen moved away from the stampede into the middle of the floor and tried to recapture breath forced out of him by the surging mob. He glimpsed Pratt heading up one of the staircases.

A blast behind him. The staircase swayed, snapped. Collapsed.

Pratt lurched and dropped headfirst onto dozens trying to reach the staircase. Concrete chunks fell on top. The mezzanine tilted forward. A woman slid beneath the railing, desperately grabbed onto a strut, and dangled over the rubble as the elevated floor shook. Pieces of mezzanine collapsed in rapid succession like dominoes winding a circular pattern around him, burying the crowd. Dust clouds of pulverized concrete drifted above the wreckage.

There was an eerie silence. Nguyen shook, sensing himself alone in the midst of a field of death. He prayed to awaken from the nightmare.

Another explosion—high overhead. Glass rained around him.

A shard the size of his forearm pierced his abdomen. Drove him down onto the floor. On his back, belly on fire, he felt cold—so cold. He looked up. A part of him long thought buried hoped to catch a glimpse of the face of God. But all he could see was a glass sword hurtling toward his eyes.

AntiGen Headquarters
Rockville, Maryland   *1:48 P.M.*

AntiGen operative Penang pressed the headset against her ear. "No uplink, still. But, I pick up much activity in surrounding area."

Trent punched in numbers on his wireless. Neither operative answered.

Van Helding, one of the four sitting at the bridge table, stared at a wall monitor displaying a closed-circuit view of a green-black van lettered "M&G Plumbers, Heating and A/C" parked across the street from AntiGen's storefront entrance. "Small services, like plumbers, usually have the phone number on the truck," van Helding said. "This one does not. Surveillance I would guess. Yet this truck is much larger than those that have previously spied on us."

"Find out if M&G Plumbers exists," Trent said, checking the monitor of the rear of the building. The alley was clear. Then, he stared at the front monitor: something disturbingly familiar was missing. He dialed the woman with frizzy hair sitting at the front desk. "Barb, how long has that truck been parked out front?"

"Twenty minutes," she answered. "I figured the usu—"

"Any activity?"

"Unh-unh."

Trent hung up, continued staring at the front monitor, and counted to sixty. Not a single vehicle passed the camera. Which meant that traffic had been blocked off.

"No listing by that name in Metro area," van Helding said. "Authorities—or Collaborate?"

Penang stifled a cry.

"What is it?"

She changed channels from the closed-circuit exterior of the building to a broadcasted special news report. The monitor switched from the van to an image of twisted steel and broken concrete. Smoke rose from rubble. Fire engines hosed down the wreckage. Legions of police and rescue workers scurried about the devastation. The camera paused on a long row of body bags. Supered across the bottom of the screen was 'Natcher Conference Center, National Institutes of Health Campus, Bethesda, Maryland.'

"Pipe it in!"

A reporter's voice: *". . . more than one hundred fifty confirmed dead, including many prominent scientists. Survivors are being taken across the street to the National Naval Medical Center. Nearly all the missing or identified dead were attending a lecture on the building's ground floor being delivered by Dr. Kevin Kincaid, who's been seen frequently on TV spots this past week. Kincaid himself is missing, believed buried beneath the mountain of twisted steel out there. Hundreds of federal agents have descended on the campus. Officials are already publicly linking this with terrorist . . ."*

"Let's get the fuck outta here," a thick-set man to van Helding's right declared, pulling out his automatic as he stood.

Trent shoved the man back deep into his chair. "That's what they want. The feds are keeping tabs on every terrorist group in the country."

"But we are not terrorists, Islamic or otherwise," von Helding said.

"Doesn't matter," Trent snapped. "They're watching. If we come out, ready for a firefight, they blow us away, and pin it on the survivors."

The others stayed seated and uneasily placed their guns on the table. The TV continued: *". . . to a series of explosions. That pattern of destruction is consistent with a powerful plastic explosive, like military-issue C4, only home-grown . . ."*

"RDX," Trent whispered. "Like Bergmann."

The TV continued: *". . . are investigating several terrorist groups claiming responsibility for the bombing. But, this is an exclusive, we've learned that a receptionist at the National Library of Medicine received a bomb threat just one minute before the blast. The call originated in Rockville . . ."*

Trent slammed his fist on the table. "The Collaborate set us up!"

The lights went out.

"They cut power!" Van Helding yelled.

Emergency lights flicked on, bathing them in crimson.

Trent said, "People, this is how we survive." He picked up a bridge chair, put it in the corner of the room away from the exits, then sat and crossed his legs. "We do absolutely nothing."

"We can't—"

"The feds'll be coming at us with everything they have," Trent said. "We resist, we die."

The thick-set man picked up his automatic. Van Helding and the others followed his lead. "Let 'em come."

"Here's what'll happen. The emergency lights will go out. Battering rams will smash open the doors. They'll burst in with night-vision goggles and assault rifles." Trent leaned forward. "You'll never see who kills you."

The lights went out. Clicking sounds filled the room: their automatic safeties being released.

"You've got to trust me. Everyone, put down your weapons!"

"Like I always thought, nothing but mouth," one complained.

The doors exploded in.

Mallory's Saloon
Georgetown, Washington, D.C.

Helen speared the crouton on her fork and crushed it in her salad bowl. Like an animal sensing an earthquake, she felt impending disaster tremble beneath her feet.

Anna put down her coffee. "Please to relax."

Helen gazed out the window on M Avenue. There was no sign of Kevin: just passersby peering in Georgetown's trendy shops. She glanced around the saloon decorated with Irish landscapes set against cherry-paneled walls. The place was quiet. The bartender, waitress, and five older men were all crowded around the bar, staring at the TV. "He should've been here by now."

"I am sure there were many questions after the lecture. And traffic—"

"He's just down Wisconsin Avenue. We had time to go to Rockville, drop off the tape at your apartment, get here, and finish lunch. No, something's wrong." She pointed at patrons and staff.

"They've been watching TV for an hour. Nobody's ordered a drink. Our waitress hasn't budged."

Anna pushed back from the table. "Let's see."

Helen hated Mallory's Saloon. This was Trent's place: dark, with a back entrance directly into Georgetown Park Mall, and easy access onto M or Wisconsin Avenue, or the canal behind—plenty of places to escape into Georgetown's narrow streets, back alleys. It fit Trent's paranoia.

Helen followed Anna to the bar. She looked up at the TV: the NIH conference center was a field of twisted, smoking debris amid fire engines, confusion, ambulances, and covered bodies.

Helen's chest thumped, tightened. The room spun. She felt herself falling on her face. Three pairs of hands grabbed her and lifted her up into a seat beside a table. She curled forward, head to her knees, panting.

"You okay, lady?" a man asked in her ear.

"She will be fine," Anna said. "She—knows somebody there."

"Sorry," the man who had helped her to the table said. "Hope they made it."

"Goddamn terrorists," another patron yelled. "We should fucking nuke 'em."

The dizziness subsided, replaced by a creeping sensation of unreality. "Anna?"

"It does not look good."

"I want to go—"

"It is not safe. The Collaborate may still have people there."

"The Collaborate didn't kill him. Trent did!"

"Helen, you do not think that—"

"Why do you think Trent sent Cameron to the conference?"

"Cameron's dead!" answered a high-pitched male voice behind her.

Helen looked over her shoulder. A thin, unobtrusive man with a sallow face stood, a holstered nine-millimeter peeking beneath his overcoat. "Straub, you—"

"Easy." Placing a firm hand on her neck, Straub slid into the seat between the women. "Cameron died in the blast." He scanned the bar. "Man, I could use a drink."

"Come to finish the job?" Helen spat.

"It wasn't us, Morgan. Somehow, they found out. The place went up *before* Kincaid could deliver. If Cameron got hold of Kincaid's formula, he took it with him."

"But the Collaborate doesn't have Kevin's vector. Why would they kill him?"

"The Collaborate would not kill the doctor too soon," Anna whispered. "Have they found his body?"

"Not that I heard," Straub said.

"Then perhaps they will not, for some time."

Helen perked up. "You think Kevin's alive?"

"That's the least of our problems." Straub nodded toward the bar. "Look."

Helen turned to the TV in the corner. Anna gasped. On-screen, AntiGen's storefront teemed with FBI and ATF agents in assault jackets, SWAT teams, patrol cars, bomb disposal trucks. In the chaos, attendants wheeled five body bags into ambulances within cordoned-off police lines. A squad of agents surrounded one handcuffed man as they led him into an armored van.

"That's the bastard!" bellowed a man at the bar.

"Oughta fuckin' cut him open!" another beside him added.

Anna whispered, "Trent!"

"Uh-huh," Straub replied.

"And the others?"

Straub pointed to a body bag on-screen.

"Figures he'd be the one to walk away," Helen said.

Straub drove his finger into the table. "The Collaborate set us up! The feds got a bomb threat from AntiGen *before* it went off. They were on us so fast. Our people never had a chance."

"How'd you get away?" Helen asked.

"I was already heading here to get your CD. I *saw* the blast on my way. So, putting two and two together, I headed back to Rockville, but it was too late."

"But a bomb threat alone—"

"Morgan, the Collaborate used RDX! The same stuff your father used against ReGenerix! And, word is, *you* phoned in the warning!"

"I never—"

"You're a screw-up, not a bomber." Straub rapped his fists. "By the way, the feds cracked your cover. Congratulations, Tracy, you're now America's Most Wanted."

Eyes glistening, she looked down. "Daddy, they've done it to me, too."

"Probably the only reason your face isn't plastered all over the tube is because of the plastic surgery. They don't know what you look like yet."

"Why'd you come here? For the disk?"

"It's our only proof." He hesitated. "I don't like you, but we're all that's left."

"How did the Collaborate know?" Anna asked.

"Maybe they had us bugged," Straub suggested.

"No! It was Trent!" Helen declared.

"Come off it."

"No, think about it. Where did Trent get the money for equipment, computers, recruitment, operations? And operatives from other 'cells'? Where'd that manpower suddenly drop in from? Who else knew so much detail? And now, he walks away while the rest of us are massacred. Don't you get it? He's part of the Collaborate!"

"You're crazy! If that was true, the feds'd be here already," Straub said.

Two men in dark suits entered the bar from the street.

"Unless they were waiting," Helen said, glancing at the rear entrance from the mall, "for you, Straub."

Anna pointed. "Look!"

Another pair of suits appeared in the rear.

Straub cracked his knuckles. "Shit! Feds!"

Helen leaned around Anna and peered out the front window. Impatiently sitting in a car across the street was a woman with a scarf protruding from her coat. "Not FBI, Straub. Collaborate. That's Kevin's boss out there."

"Tell me neither of you are armed." They weren't. "Fuckin' great!"

Anna trembled. "This is the end."

Straub bit his lip. He gazed at Anna, at Helen. "Not for us all."

"You weas—"

"They posed as feds hoping we'll go without a firefight," Straub said. "That means they'll probably hesitate. Maybe, just enough." He explained his plan to them.

"But they will kill you," Anna objected when he finished.

"You don't have to do this," Helen said, grabbing Straub's hand.

"You do have the CD, don't you?"

Helen checked her handbag. It was there, complete with Protein X-ACT and the Collaborate's private door into the world's key genetic databases.

"You and that disk are our last chance. I," wiping sweat off his upper lip, "I should've died with the others. Besides," feigning a smile, "you'll owe your life to a weasel."

"Straub, I'm sorry."

He half grinned. "That almost makes it worthwhile."

He stood, gazed nonchalantly at the TV for a moment, then ambled to the rear of the bar. Collaborate operatives at the front entrance advanced. The enforcers in the rear stiffened, reached inside their jacket pockets. Straub swung to his left toward the men's room, and extended his arm to push it open. The rear enforcers relaxed slightly and, in unison, began lowering their arms.

Straub whirled. Fired.

The first bullet struck the left enforcer's forehead. The surprised face burst. The body slammed into the wall. The second bullet struck the right enforcer's chest. A puff of blood erupted below the left nipple. Wide-eyed, the man gazed down at blood seeping through his vest, tilted his head, as if puzzled, then crumpled onto the floor.

Helen tipped over the table and squatted with Anna behind the makeshift shield.

Enforcers in front reached into their jacket pockets. Moved into firing positions.

"FBI! Everybody down!" one yelled.

Patrons shouted, began ducking beneath the bar.

Straub pivoted forward and locked in a kill shot on one enforcer as another zeroed in on him. But he swung his automatic up toward a corner over the bar. And fired.

The TV exploded. Hot energy burst into the room.

A bullet struck Straub's neck. Blood spewed out like a high-powered fountain as he died.

The blast from the TV showered two enforcers in the energy stream.

Helen grabbed Anna's hand. "Now!"

They dashed to the rear of the restaurant. A shot buzzed by Helen's ear as she leaped over a dead enforcer. Behind her, Anna stumbled as they lunged forward into the spacious mall.

"You lost them?" Blount snapped into his earpiece as he stepped into M Street.

"They're in the mall," a voice answered.

"Units guarding level three exit to M Street, and level two to Wisconsin Avenue and the bridge over the canal—converge. Don't let them out of your sight! We can't risk them hiding the disk."

Helen and Anna burst into Georgetown Park Mall: a bustling, four-level, grand enclosure of olive green trim, bronze metalwork, serene courtyard fountains, and delicate planters framed by expensive boutiques, haberdasheries, and specialty shops. Helen knocked over a woman in a fur coat and sped toward the open-air staircase as Anna ran two steps behind. She seized the top of the railing and slingshotted herself down the stairs. Then running down two steps at a time, she jumped onto the landing between the second and third level. She glanced back: Anna had just started down the stairs. "Come on, Anna!"

"FBI! Stop!" a man with a pockmarked face called from the mezzanine.

Shoppers on three levels scurried from the atrium. The dark suits and white-shirt mall security units converged on the second and third levels. Blount approached the upper railing. Helen's gaze briefly met his.

"Jump, Anna!" Helen yelled, then vaulted over the railing. She fell, feet first, arms spread, for an exhilarating moment, then landed squat on the tiled floor beside a long fountain. She rolled onto her feet.

From twice as high, Anna was falling off balance, twirling her arms. She struck the floor, tumbled, and slammed her shoulder against the fountain. She righted herself, but hunched forward. "Oh, I think I broke my arm!"

Helen grabbed Anna by her uninjured arm and dashed through the mall's ground level. Shots ricocheted off wrought-iron furniture and pedestal planters in their wake. Shoppers screamed, ducking under tables.

They burst into an enclosed court surrounded by Chinese food, pizza, and ice cream stands, all shielded from the upper levels by a low ceiling painted like a serene sky. "Canal Exit" read a sign straight ahead. Helen pushed through the maze of chairs, tables, knocking over anything that might slow the men. They plowed down steps in the rear of the food court, broke through sets of heavy glass and steel doors, and found themselves, outside, in the cold, on a gravel path: the C&O Canal Towpath. Behind them was an old black granite wall laced with sharp, jutting edges. Directly ahead was a fifteen-foot wide canal of yellow-brown brackish water that, through a series of locks, led nowhere. On the other side of the canal stood high, red-brick walls. Up and to the right, a covered bridge joined the mall to businesses across the canal. Anna sank to her knees.

Helen glanced left. Right. "We go left to Thirty—"

"No! I hold you back. Go on!"

"They'll be here in seconds!"

Shoulder hanging, Anna started to her right.

"Anna! That's the wrong way! Come back!"

Anna, hobbling away like a hunchback, raised the fist of her good arm in defiance.

Helen started after her. Hesitated. Hesitated. Then turned away.

Blount descended to ground level in the mall's glass elevator.

Enforcers met him as he stepped off. "They're headed for the canal," the one with the pockmarked face said.

"Only the disk matters."

Anna tripped, scraped her right side against rocks jutting from the black stone wall, regained her balance, and hobbled down the gravel path beneath the bridge linking the mall and the red-brick building on the other side of the canal. The path dumped into an old winding set of wooden steps. She clambered up, lost her balance on the landing, and banged her injured shoulder against the railing. Struggling up the last few steps, she crawled onto a walkway between the mall on her right and a glass-enclosed restaurant on her left. Just a few more yards to M Street.

A navy blue sedan pulled up on the street. Two men got out.

She turned to run. From behind, a burly man spun her to the cold bricks, yanked back her arms, and handcuffed her. She started to struggle. Another man pressed his forearm directly against her throat in a guillotine choke. In seconds, she was on the floor of the sedan with two sets of feet driving her into the carpeting.

"That's not Bergmann," one voice said.

"The disk!" a second voice demanded.

"What disk?" Anna answered.

A foot struck her damaged shoulder. Hands tore off her blouse, reached inside her bra, and yanked her breasts. Then ripping away her skirt, they plunged under her panties, between her legs.

"She doesn't have it."

Helen, running the other direction down the gravel path paralleling the mucky canal water, passed beneath the old arched, stone bridge of Wisconsin Avenue. The path gently sloped up, depositing her at Thirty-first Street. Her choices: left and back onto M Street, where they'd be waiting; straight along the canal towpath, where they'd cut her off; or right, down toward the Potomac. She headed right and dashed down the inlaid red-brick sidewalks. The street grew steep. Her foot caught on a loose brick. She tumbled forward and landed on her back. Taking two quick breaths, she righted herself and ran toward the river. She passed the ivy-covered smokestack of the Georgetown incinerator, beneath the steel pillars of the Whitehurst Freeway, and came alongside an office building complex of curved walls with jutting balconies. She found herself at Washington Harbor by the Potomac River. To her left lay a wide-open boardwalk gravel path that ran, fully exposed, for blocks along the river. In the distance, a woman runner approached. To her right, the path continued as a narrow gravel running strip. There was nowhere to run.

She looked behind her. An old, three-foot-high cement retaining wall ran beneath barren trees and between the gravel path and the river. She glanced up Thirty-first Street, then back to the retaining wall. *They won't see it!*

She climbed over the wall and squatted among broken concrete slabs and hardy trees. Behind her, the Potomac lapped peacefully. She closed her eyes, leaned her head back against the wall, and for a moment, relaxed. Her right hand touched her lap. "Oh my God!" Her eyes shot open. She checked the ground. Her handbag with the CD was gone.

Blount turned the corner onto Thirty-first Street, and met two enforcers proffering a burgundy handbag. He rifled through it, pulled out a CD, and held it up to the light.

.   .   .

Anna felt hands grab her head. Violently twist. For an instant, excruciating pain ignited her world in white fire. Before it ended.

Blount pointed at a woman with black hair running across the gravel path by the waterfront.

The henchman beside him hesitated. "Her?"

"Yes. Do it!" Blount snapped.

"Are you sure that's her? I thought she was wearing—"

"Of course it's her, you idiot! Do it before she gets away!"

Six shots popped. The runner fell back over the retaining wall.

The woman's body crashed on top of Helen. Lifeless green eyes stared at the overcast sky. Helen almost screamed. After four quick breaths, she checked the woman's neck for a pulse. There was none. The runner had the same general build and hair as Helen; for that, they'd mistakenly killed her. Quickly, Helen removed her suit jacket, put it on the woman, pulled the body down to the river's edge, and rolled it, facedown, into the water. Then, she scrambled back up the embankment and huddled against the wall. And waited.

"We can't be sure. The woman's floatin' facedown." She heard one man say.

"I saw her. That's what she wore in the bar," said another.

"It's her," Blount affirmed.

"You know we're not gonna recover the body."

"It's her. We have the disk. Let's go!"

The voices faded away as the body receded from view.

Helen lay curled against the wall. She had only one place left to go.

Safe House
Fairfax, Virginia

The source of the voice drifted through his dream, through his struggling consciousness, calling his name. He tried painting it Helen Kincaid, painting it Helen Morgan, but the colors ran. And the source's shape, no matter how he molded it in the image of his treasured women, always remorphed to its natural form like resilient plastic. "Kevin, wake up."

His eyes fluttered. His head throbbed. The blurry face clarified into Joan Tetlow, smiling warmly. "Shhhhhh," she whispered, laying a gentle hand on his chest. "The drug they used to knock you out leaves you disoriented, so I'm told. When you're ready, I'll help you sit up."

Fighting his spinning head, he forced a series of long, cleansing breaths through his lungs. Female hands helped sit him on the edge of a bed, his head halfway between his legs. A bedpan was shoved into his hands. He dry-heaved. A warm, massaging hand touched his back as a drop of spittle plopped in the pan.

"Here," she said, handing him a plastic cup. "Swish this in your mouth. Then spit."

Minty mouthwash. Cleansing.

"Feeling better?" Tetlow asked, taking the pan and cup.

The room focused: cheap table, lamp, chairs, beige walls, draped window, and tacky wall mirror. A hotel room? "Where am I?" he rasped.

"A safe house. In Fairfax."

"Safe? From what?"

"Give your stomach and head a chance to settle."

"I was preparing to—" He remembered McKuserk spewing blood. "Jesus! You found out! You're one of them!" He jumped to his feet. Head swimming, he staggered across the room and pulled open the drapes. The window, made of thick block glass, distorted street lights.

"Kevin, stay away from the window."

He turned, pointed at the wall-length mirror. "Prepping me for interrogation?"

"It's not a two-way mirror. See for yourself."

He peered behind the frame. It was just a mirror, hanging on the wall. He looked to the door. "But I'm still locked in."

She motioned to the door. Following her lead, he placed his hand on the knob. Expecting resistance, he yanked. The door flew open, exposing a modest upstairs hall. He could hear voices coming from the floor below, just beyond the staircase. "If I'm not a prisoner, then who are those men downstairs?" he asked.

"Your bodyguards."

"I'm free to walk out of here?"

"If you leave unprotected, the Collaborate will find you."

He tilted his head. "*You* are the Collaborate!"

"No, Kevin, I'm not. We're not. Remember the conversation you and I had a few days ago, in your office? I tried to warn you, but you wouldn't listen. Now, we either have to convince you, or deprogram you."

"Brainwash." He wavered, his head still woozy from the drug.

She closed the door, guided him into a chair by the table, propped his feet onto an ottoman, and knelt beside him. "We've had you under tight surveillance since last night's party. We know what you've been through."

"I'm sure the Collab—"

"We're not the Collaborate! We're just people in the biotech industry with common interests. People smell conspiracies in large aggregations of wealth, but, really, there's nothing sinister, illegal, or immoral about the Association."

"I suppose now you're going to convince me that the Collaborate doesn't exist."

"Oh, it most certainly does. McGovern, his associates, AntiGen—*they* are the Collaborate's front. Only too late, we've learned how deep they've been playing you."

"But I've seen evidence."

"*Their* evidence."

"The tissue samples. The slides. The genetic engineering. Proof that K_4 was used."

"*Their* tissue samples. *Their* genetic engineering. *Their* abuse of K_4, which *they* stole."

"The BLAST database interface is—"

"*Their* gateway, Kevin. The Collaborate is in league with DARPA, which rigged NCBI search engines."

"But Protein X-ACT—"

"The Collaborate stole it from PolyPepGen, faked the manufacturers in the Protein Library database that you accessed, and made it seem as if the Association and the Collaborate were the same."

"What about the video?"

Tetlow seemed surprised.

"The video of Tiburon. The atrocities! They didn't fake that."

"You, uh, you don't know where this video is, by any chance?"

"Helen had it." Slowly, his head began clearing as the drug dissipated. "Where is she?"

"They got to her first. Kevin, she's," sandwiching his hand between hers, "dead. I'm sorry."

He pushed away the ottoman and stared out the block windows at points of light, blurred, like the truth that had once been a pinpoint, now distorted. "You killed her."

Smoothing his shoulder, "No, Kevin, *they* killed her."

"I don't believe you! She almost took her life to—" He choked. "She wasn't part of the Collaborate! She was fighting it!"

"She thought she was. That McGovern had her fooled, right until the end."

"How?"

"A lot happened while you were out." Tetlow picked up a remote control lying on the table, clicked on a TV in the corner, and set it to a cable news channel. "You'll need some time alone."

Kevin stared at the rubble that had been Natcher Center.

Tetlow returned an hour later. Kevin was sitting in the chair; still staring at the TV. She clicked off it and poured him a glass of water. "You're dehydrated."

He greedily downed it. "Why?"

"Their twisted, brilliant plan to get sole possession of V_7. Trick you into thinking you'd expose the Association as the Collaborate. Gather together the world's finest minds in molecular genetics. Then whisk you away. Kill off the few people in the world capable of duplicating your work. Blame the tragedy on terrorists. And then, with the world presuming you dead, they're able to extract the process for synthesizing V_7 at their leisure." She stroked his limp arm. "We learned of their plot too late. We barely rescued you in time."

"And Helen?"

She sighed. "Kevin, the Collaborate knows you're alive—and they're going to keep coming. We can't allow them to get hold of your vector."

"Peter Nguyen is—"

"Dead." She held his hand. "Look, I know this is a lot to ask right now, but we need your help. Do you feel up to going back to BFMC tonight and retrieving your files?"

He nodded. Seconds later, a bodyguard entered the room. Eyes still fixed on the blank TV, Kevin did not turn to greet him.

"This is Briggs," she said. "He's in charge of your security."

"Earl Briggs. Sorry for your loss, Doctor," said Anthony Blount.

Approaching Philadelphia   10:21 P.M.

"He's still out," the woman's voice echoed behind him.

Kevin lifted his head. He found his hands lashed to a wheelchair in a room that seemed familiar. The chest of drawers, the mirror—this was Donny's room. "What am I doing here?"

"You gave him too much," the female voice objected, ignoring him.

A masculine voice responded, "Since when did you become an expert on burun—"

"It's a good thing I stopped you from giving him more. We can't risk damaging his mind."

"That was a mistake," said the male voice.

Kevin shouted, but the voices droned on. His fingers reached the spokes of his wheelchair. He pivoted around. And saw the source of the voices: Helen/Tracy. She declared, "I don't care how many times you've used it. A second dose wasn't called for!"

The man beside her was tall, muscular, with a face reminiscent of Kevin's: the sloping forehead, the thickened lips. "Donny! Is that you?" Kevin shouted.

"He's coming around," Donny said, smirking. "Told you."

"Donny, you're cured! I cured you!"

"Donny. The brother, right?" Donny asked.

Kevin's wheelchair disappeared beneath him. He felt himself suspended in midair, tilting forward. Then falling. A hand grabbed his arm. Shook him.

Kevin opened his eyes. Blurry shapes coalesced. Hissing air assaulted his ears.

Tetlow sat belted to a dark blue cushioned seat beside him. "Evening, Kevin. You're in a private jet. You slept the whole trip." She smiled, "We'll be landing soon."

His head pounded. "Landing where?"

"Philly."

He looked out the cabin window. In the distance, rows of blue and red lights glimmered in an island of dark surrounded by suburban-lit grids in the night. "I—my lecture?"

Tetlow glanced at the man seated across the aisle—the man she'd introduced to Kevin as Briggs—whispering to one of the four men seated around him. She touched Kevin's hand. "You're still feeling the effects of the drug those AntiGen terrorists used on you."

"I remember—a room with block windows—and feeling sick."

Tetlow repeated her explanation from the safe house. This time, Kevin sat quietly. He felt no pain at the news of Helen's death, or that so many of his colleagues had died in the bombing, or that he'd been fighting on the wrong side. Only an irresistible, superimposed acceptance of her truths, though a Lilliputian voice inside him objected.

". . . And that," pointing at Blount, "is Earl Briggs, who's in charge of your security."

Kevin gazed across the aisle at the compact, muscular man with tight curly hair, wispy moustache, and powerful, protruding square jaw, and an *L*-shaped scar on his right temple—a scar that he'd seen somewhere before.

"You met him at the safe house," Tetlow said.

No. Before that, Kevin thought. *Long before that.* His mind began systematically sifting through the thousands of faces he'd seen in his life. Portrait profile views that would normally whiz by in his photographic mind now droned sluggishly. A task that usually required seconds could take hours, days. Why?

"You've got to help us get the HACV.V$_7$ files before the Collaborate does," Tetlow said.

He felt something in his mind obsequiously answer for him.

Tetlow patted his hand. "I knew you would."

The pilot announced that they were approaching the airport.

"Joan, what drug did they use?" Kevin rasped. She didn't answer. "Drug," he repeated. "The drug AntiGen used on me?" He noticed the security chief's eyes momentarily flicker.

"C'mon, Kevin. I'm a hospital administrator, not a doctor. You know how bad I am at remembering drug names, especially generic compounds."

The plane dipped forward. A whine, then the long *ka-chunk* of the landing gear lowering. Kevin gazed out the window. The swirling, dizzying patterns of oncoming city lights were like his mind: jumbled. He remembered an old trick his father had taught him after he'd staggered off the Spinning Teacups at a carnival: *Keep focused on one spot, and you'll keep yer head.*

Tetlow handed him an airbag. "Use this, if necessary."

That voice! In the dream, Helen had been speaking with Tetlow's voice! He'd overheard part of her conversation, probably with Briggs, and incorporated it into his light-sleep dream.

Runway lights zipped by the window.

What had Donny said in the dream? ". . . An expert on berun—" Or was it burun—Must be a drug. He remembered the product-names index of the *Physicians' Desk Reference*, which listed every prescription drug trade name sold in the U.S. At an infuriatingly slow pace, his mind searched the directory for every trade or generic name resembling *berun-* or *burun-*something.

The jet's wheels scraped the runway, bounced slightly, then smoothly rolled along the concrete. The decelerating force tried to pull him from his seat. The jet stopped, turned, and taxied toward the terminal. His mind completed the scan; no drug beginning with *ber* or *bur* remotely matched the kind of compound that must have been used on him.

He glimpsed the approaching terminal: an old-style control tower attached to a two-story building the size of a district police station. "You said we were landing in Philly. This isn't the—"

"*Northeast* Philadelphia airport, not International. A small commuter field just inside the city limits," Tetlow said.

"Dr. Kincaid, publicly, you're missing and presumed dead," Blount said. "We can't traipse you through a busy public terminal."

That was Donny's voice in the dream!

The plane stopped before reaching the tiny terminal. Blount's men prepped for deplaning.

Did I mishear the word? Kevin wondered. *Or subconsciously manufacture it? Something dulled my thinking. Could the word be foreign?* He searched for any unusual word that began with *ber* or *bur* in every foreign journal, publication, or notice he could remember.

Blount nodded to a husky, neckless man. "Harris, you ride with us." Looking at the other three, "Dostayev, you ride lead. Hood, Gilman, you two ride backup."

"Where are we going?" Kevin asked.

"Your lab. Remember?"

"But if I'm supposed to be missing—"

"The fire alarm to the north wing emergency exit has been disabled. We'll be in and out before anyone notices," Tetlow finished.

Cold wind snapped against Kevin's face as he stepped off the plane. A mini-motorcade lay waiting: two blue sedans sandwiched around a black limousine. Three men stood at attention beside each sedan, two beside the limo. One man said to Blount, "I-95's jammed. We have to take the long way, Roosevelt Boulevard South to the Schuylkill Expressway."

The men climbed into their sedans in synchrony. Tetlow accompanied Kevin into the back of the limo. Blount seated himself directly opposite them as another man and the driver climbed in. The procession started.

Kevin gazed out the tinted window as the limo passed through an open gate, spilled onto a side street, and turned into a twelve-lane boulevard with wide median strips lined by barren trees. Street lamps hypnotically danced by. In summer daylight it was a pretty thoroughfare. Helen/Tracy would have liked it. "Are you certain, absolutely certain, that Helen is dead?"

Tetlow held Kevin's hand as Blount glared. "I saw the Collaborate kill her."

A page of text exploded on his consciousness: a translated excerpt from *Le Monde*. Serif lettering in the second paragraph expanded. There was that word! "Burundanga," Kevin inadvertently whispered.

Blount leaned forward. "What did you say?"

Kevin read the article in his mind. Burundanga, a poison, a Bogotá specialty rarely seen outside of South America. It acted on the central nervous system, blocking neurotransmission, impairing memory. The drug was composed primarily of benzodiazepine and scopolamine. Burundanga made victims completely suggestible, do whatever they were told, then selectively forget their actions. A victim could be ordered to surrender his life savings to a stranger—and never remember it. *Burundanga's a powder, administered orally. But it's odorless, tasteless, soluble in—water! I remember! A van. Men. Opened door.* He studied Blount. *And you. Squirting something in my mouth.* He turned to Tetlow. *And you. Pouring me a glass of water. Because of my size, they must've had problems titrating the dose.*

Blount rolled his eyes and spat at Tetlow, "And you were worried about overdosing." He grinned at Kevin. "You overheard us earlier, didn't you, Kincaid?"

"Heard what?"

"You've figured it out."

Kevin hesitated. "I don't know what you're talking about."

"Kincaid, even a skilled liar can't completely mask a moment of realization." Blount pulled out a gun and pointed it at Kevin's chest.

The limousine's brakes screeched as the vehicle slowed. "Why are we stopping?" he called up front.

Harris, the man in the shotgun seat, answered, "Southbound bridge is tied up. We can't get off and we've already passed the exit. We're locked up in the left lane, anyway."

"And the others?"

"The lead escort is six cars up front. The trailer's four behind. Both stuck, too."

"You're Collaborate," Kevin said.

"No, I'm a sole-source subcontractor." Blount waved his gun at Tetlow. "She's Collaborate."

Kevin threw Tetlow's hand off his. "Don't touch me, you bitch!"

"Kevin, you don't think—"

"You killed Helen!"

Blount laughed. "Perfect!"

"Blount, look what you've done!" Tetlow yelled.

"Irrelevant," Blount said. "We'll cure that with a higher dose."

"You bombed NIH!" Kevin yelled.

"It's all *your* fault. *You* consorted with terrorists. *You* assembled evidence against my client. And *you* planned to denounce the Collaborate."

"You murdered—"

"*You* forced us to dispose of AntiGen. And since we didn't know precisely who at the conference you'd informed, *you* left no choice but to kill them all. It was a perfect opportunity to eliminate both problems with one solution. It was so easy re-editing your conversations with Helen. Or should I say Tracy? The FBI was quite convinced by her phoned-in bomb threat."

"You framed her!"

"We immortalized her, like her now infamous colleagues."

Kevin hung his head. "So many people! You didn't have to—"

"You have to admit the beauty of it. We frame AntiGen. Let the FBI take them out. Stir up additional support for 601. Eliminate the leaks. Destroy the evidence. And, best of all, Dr. Kincaid, we have you all to ourselves, because the rest of this planet thinks you're dead."

The car began inching forward.

"I'll find a way out and—"

"In that very unlikely scenario, we have evidence linking *you* to AntiGen. You'd have a tough time explaining how the keynote speaker survived the blast at ground zero. Besides, your body is going to be identified in the rubble tomorrow." He smirked. "Of course, we can arrange for it just to be a mistaken identity. The Collaborate only wants what you've been paid to deliver: V_7."

"And if not?"

Blount turned and gazed out the window at the bridge railing. "Burundanga is cheap."

For the first time, Kevin had a clear view of the L-shaped scar on Blount's temple. His mind enlarged the scar. Froze the image. The parade of faces, profiles that had been racing through his consciousness, now accelerated, split screen. His photographic mind mapped that face to another. On the way to Belvedere. A BMW convertible he'd passed after leaving Helen and the children at Uncle Dermot's. A man, sitting in the front seat, waiting. The same one sitting here now. Kevin's mind replayed, in rapid succession:

Blount: I'm a sole-source subcontractor.

McGovern: Loring had your uncle killed. . . . They must've thought you'd come to his house alone. Wife and children in the back of the van, the tinted glass—I guess the hit team didn't see them enter the kill zone.

Blount, laughing: Perfect!

Kevin's body quivered. Chest, hands, face burning, he saw the man through white-hot rage. He lunged. Thrusting out his arm, he delivered a vicious palm strike with the heel of his hand to Blount's chin.

Blount's head snapped back. The gun dropped to the floor. Tetlow reached for the weapon. Kevin leaned back and snap-kicked. His foot struck her face. She wailed as blood poured from her nose. Harris in the front seat yelled. The car swerved as it crawled across the bridge.

Kevin reached for the gun, but Blount quickly recovered and punched Kevin's spine with a pointed knuckle. Searing pain shot down his legs, but he countered with a blind backhand fist. Blount caught it, twisted Kevin's arm back, and hit his spine again. Arm pinned, Kevin swiveled around, dug his feet into the opposite seat, and straightened his legs to crunch Blount. But the man ducked left, punched Kevin's hip, pivoted the legs away from the seat, and struck his neck.

Reeling, Kevin thrust out his legs, full force. His heels crashed against the window, shattering it. Glass spewed onto Tetlow's whimpering form. Blount struck Kevin's spine again.

Kevin jerked his head back and banged into Blount's eye. The strangling grip released. He glanced down. Didn't see the gun. Realized that it must be behind him—that Blount was going to recover it first. He had no choice.

He rocked forward, crouched, and launched himself at the shattered window. He tumbled through the aperture, out of the car, landed shoulder first on an adjacent car, rolled over the hood onto freezing asphalt on the opposite side, and scrambled to his feet.

I'm on the twin bridges!

Delphi

The little girl's muscles bulged as her chest contracted. Her back arched, stretching the bed's restraints to their limits.

"Fight it, Meredith!" Marguerite coaxed, her face pressed against the observation window.

The convulsion eased. Meredith's body slowly fell back on the mattress. Spent, the tiny figure crumbled into the bed. The attacks, first striking in midafternoon, had intensified during the evening. Marguerite quietly prayed for Meredith to at least be given some rest.

"Cascading generalized tonic-clonic seizures," came a deep, baritone voice from behind her. "The beginning of the end."

Marguerite prayed louder.

A thick hand touched her shoulder. "This time, I hope He listens."

She looked back. A husky man with broad, swooping shoulders and bushy, tilted eyebrows grimaced: Dr. Roderick Stevenson, Delphi's chief pathologist. "Is there not *something* you can do?" she asked. "Maybe more vector K_4 with—"

He squeezed her shoulders. Glanced back at the surveillance camera behind him.

"You're hurting me!"

Stevenson pulled her close to him. "Don't expose your face directly to the camera when speaking," he whispered in her ear. "This area's not bugged, but they can read lips. Now, what do you know about K_4?"

Marguerite squirmed, then noticed the camera pointed in her direction. Slowly, she turned away from it. "Only that it was used to add extra genes to the children's brain cells. And that it might save her."

"K_4 *made* her. K_4 *killed* her." he said. "You stole my username and password."

"I didn't—"

"What else did you access?"

Marguerite gazed at him. Was there a flicker of concern in his light blue eyes? "An autopsy report. And some papers on genes and vectors. That was all."

"Good. Come to my office tomorrow."

Marguerite quivered. "Or else?"

"I don't have an 'or else.' "

"Then why should I?"

"So few Newtons and Einsteins and Hawkings pass through this world." He sighed. "I can't bear cutting open another."

U.S. Route 1, Southbound Bridge

Kevin stood in the middle of three lanes of crawling traffic 170 feet above the Schuylkill River's cold, murky waters. To his left: cyclone fencing atop a guardrail. Thirty feet beyond and slightly below: the northbound bridge, its three lanes of traffic speeding at sixty miles an hour. Four cars behind him, a car door opened. Two men got out.

Kevin dashed between the slowly moving cars. The limousine doors opened. Blount and Harris jumped out, both brandishing automatics. Ahead, the lead sedan stopped. Its doors opened. The enforcers would have him trapped in seconds.

Pop! A bullet whizzed by his ear from behind.

There was nowhere to run. Unless—the cyclone fencing ended ten yards ahead, leaving only guardrail. He started running.

"Stop! We won't hurt you!" Blount shouted behind him.

He pumped harder, harder. Neared the end of the fence.

In the lead car, directly in his path, a man stepped out. Trained his automatic on Kevin.

In full stride, Kevin leaped onto the guardrail, propelled himself into midair. "Oh my God, oh my God, oh my God, oh . . ."

He sailed toward the other bridge's guardrail, below and ahead of him. He began sinking, terrified as gravity yanked him, the approaching guardrail rapidly rising. Rising. At the level of his feet. His knees. His hips. Like a trapeze artist, he stretched out his hands and braced himself for the catch. If it didn't come, there'd be a loping moment of expectation unfulfilled, then the long, long fall.

The guardrail was chest high. Chin high.

Kevin turned his head. Closed his eyes.

His groping hands banged into the cold, slippery guardrail. An instant later, his chest slammed into concrete facing, driving air from his lungs. His head spun from the impact, but his fingers locked tight. He hung, half-conscious, suspended 140 feet above the river.

Blount, Harris, and two others stood on the southbound bridge and stared across the gulf at Kevin dangling from the northbound bridge.

"I say he drops in thirty seconds," the first said.

The second aimed his automatic at Kevin, but felt Blount's muzzle in his gut.

Blount asked Harris, "Can we get to him?"

Harris looked behind him at rubbernecking traffic crawling around them. "Can't U-turn here. We'd have to get off at the nearest exit and double back. Three, four miles all total."

"Miles? He could drop in seconds!"

Harris shrugged. Blount looked at the second man, Gilman.

"Oh no! I'm not fuckin' goin'!" Gilman protested.

Blount shoved Gilman's head over the guardrail. "Kincaid jumped because you shot at him. If he drops, so do you."

Gilman nodded submissively.

To the other enforcer, "In the meantime, you go down to the end of the bridge, on the embankment, where the road splits, climb over the median, and circle back."

The man nodded and broke into a run, following traffic. Gilman reluctantly trotted a few yards away. He turned around, preparing for the leap.

Harris glanced at the cars slowly swerving around them, watching them. "Cops'll be here soon."

Blount angrily waved them on. "Harris, if Gilman—"

"I understand."

Gilman sprinted toward them, his arms pumping. Twenty yards. Ten. Five. He launched himself up, onto the guardrail. Catapulted himself into space.

Blount watched his man hurtle toward the other bridge—then drop below the guardrail, below the concrete facing. The man's head slammed into the steel underpinning. The body tumbled silently toward the river.

Arms stretched above him as if being torn from his torso on a rack, Kevin opened his eyes. His head was turned to the side. He could barely breathe: concrete was inches from his face. He glanced up at bluing fingers locked around the guardrail and pulled. His upper-arm muscles would not respond. He dangled, knowing he'd used all of the strength in his arms just to hang on. But his legs still had some small reserve. Struggling, he swung his hips side to side. Gently at first, then building momentum. His legs began swinging across the concrete face, like those of a gymnast performing scissor splits on a horse. Higher, higher his legs swung. His right ankle, reaching at the zenith of each swing, nudged the railing, banged it, then hooked on. Straining, his muscles in agony, slowly he reached the top. With one last burst, he cried out, and hoisted himself up and over. He rolled onto the bridge's asphalt surface.

A pair of headlights, horn blaring, bore down on him. He dropped.

The speeding car passed over him. Kevin lay frozen as the vehicle's undercarriage brushed within an inch of his face.

He leaped up the instant it passed. He was in the bridge's speed lane. Headlights and horns swerved past him.

"Kincaid!"

Kevin looked to the voice on the other bridge: there stood Blount, his automatic pointed at Kevin's head. Kevin turned to run. A bullet ricocheted off the asphalt beside him. He stopped. "Without me, there's no V$_7$!"

"You can talk as easily from a wheelchair!"

Kevin dropped to his knees, using the bridge bulwark for cover, and crawled. A shot struck the outside of the concrete. Another shot.

A pair of giant hands appeared on the railing beside him. They gripped and pulled muscular forearms over the edge. Harris tumbled next to him—and kidney-punched him. Kevin tumbled forward, wincing.

"You got real guts, doc," Harris chided. He stood and signaled Blount.

"Hey, Harris!" a voice called from behind him.

Harris turned as a muscular blond man came running, with traffic, onto the bridge. "Hey, Hood," Harris called. "He's over—"

Kevin shot his right heel back into Harris's thigh.

Harris yelped. Staggered back into the adjoining lane. A pickup truck struck him, threw him in the air, smashed his body again against the windshield. The pickup skidded and crashed into the guardrail. Behind it, a station wagon swerved, lost control, and plowed into the truck, blockading the bridge. An oil tanker, barreling down, slammed on the brakes. It jackknifed, crushing the other man before sweeping him out of existence.

The tanker exploded in a blaze of light, like a newborn sun. Booming air pounded Kevin's ears. The bridge rattled, knocking him down. Searing heat and instant fire.

Kevin ran as a swift wave of flame shot toward him. It singed his skin, sucked the air from his lungs. He glanced over his shoulder at the flame wall roaring behind him and consuming smashed vehicles, rapidly gaining. The end of the bridge was still thirty yards away. The back of his jacket burst into flame. In midstride, Kevin leaped up onto the guardrail. Jumped over the edge just as the flame wall roared down the bridge.

For an instant, he felt suspended in midair. Then, falling. Falling. His body felt electrically charged as dark, rushing air howled around him. His feet desperately reached for the solid ground his mind falsely promised he'd reach the next instant. Then the next.

Just like the railroad trestle he'd jumped from as a boy. That trestle had only been half as high, but he'd survived. He shot his arms straight up over his head, locked his hands, clamped his legs, and pointed his feet down to expose just a sliver of his body to the surface of the onrushing river. He tilted his torso back, hoping for a free return trajectory that would send him back from the depths of the river. If, somehow, he survived the—

Frigid water burst around him.

Blount screamed and kicked the tire of a slowly passing BMW. The driver lowered his window and yelled, "Hey, you! Get out of the road!"

Blount stepped up to the passenger door, stuck his gun into the surprised man's mouth, and fired. Blood, bone, brain splattered against the glass. He steered the dead man's car into the far lane. Quickly, he climbed back into his vehicle and turned the receiver on to Kevin's subdermal transmitter frequency, hoping for a voice, a background sound, any clue to his quarry's location. A crackling hiss greeted him. "Shit! It's either smashed or gone." He picked up his wireless phone and dialed his man in the trailing sedan. "Dostayev, get the rest of the group. Start searching along both riverbanks."

"Now? In the dark?"

"You fucking heard me! Now!" he yelled, slamming down the phone.

Tetlow cradled her nose with her bloodstained scarf. "You think he's alive?"

"Don't be an ass! If they find the body in the river tomorrow, there'll be a lot of upsetting questions. Like how Kincaid wound up dead in Philly when he's supposedly buried under a thousand tons of rubble in Bethesda." He pounded the car door in rapid succession. "We have *got* to get that body before morning!"

7

FRIDAY, JANUARY 24
Schuylkill River, Philadelphia

Kevin lay floating, facedown, in the river.

Impact had lasted an eternity. His body being driven into the river like a nail into brick. The burning iciness enveloping him as he plunged deep into the water. The angle of his fall looping his body in a great arc, propelling him feet-first back toward the surface, but not far enough. The freezing water robbing his breath. His desperate struggle up through icy murkiness. He never remembered reaching the surface.

He lifted his head and tried to wipe away freezing water from his eyes.

A frigid wave slapped his face. He swallowed a mouthful of river. It tasted rancid, like dirty water spun from a washing machine filled with muddy clothes. The foul smell was overpowering. He coughed and tried to clear his lungs. The choppy water slapped him again. He found himself being carried by the river swiftly downstream. To his right, he could see pale street lamps illuminating the West River Drive, the runners' path, and the underpass where he'd first lost Helen a few days ago. Now she was dead. He wanted to sob, but his chest felt frozen.

The river quickly carried him away. He tried to kick his legs, but they were heavy, unresponsive. Helpless, his body rotated in the rushing water. On the other bank, he could see the East River Drive and its row of boathouses outlined in bright white lights, like a neighborhood of Christmas gingerbread houses. Center City was less than a mile away. "Oh, shit!"

Kevin paddled wildly toward the lights, but the current drove him on. His back slammed into netting strung across the river. Behind him, water gurgled, hissed, and crashed. He grabbed one of the net's vertical support strands, but the current lapping against his fingers numbed them, then relentlessly forced him through an opening in the net.

The river thrust him forward. Burning-cold water filled his nose. His shoulder struck a cement dam. He spun, fell back-first over a twenty-five-foot waterfall. Torrents of river pinned him beneath the surface like a giant foot on his chest. Struggling on the river bottom, he gasped for air, dug his fingers into muck, and pulled. He felt his pinned body inch forward, then dug the fingernails of his other hand into muck. He pulled, inching forward. Again.

The crushing weight disappeared. He shot up—and wheezed just as he broke the surface. Thrashing and panting, slowly, slowly he regained his breath. He rotated over onto his back and floated down the now-tranquil river. Brightly lit buildings towered above him.

His head banged against a retaining wall. He turned around, dug his fingers into its worn, slippery surface, and, using his half-frozen forearms to drag his body up the wall, clambered over the edge. He rolled onto old train tracks along the waterfront, and stared up at the bright lights of Center City as he rubbed his frozen, burning thighs. Struggling to his feet, he swung his hips to propel numb legs. He drove himself to the next step. His rage swelling, he mumbled heatedly with each staggering step.

East River Drive

Blount hung up the phone.

"How'd Mr. Loring react?" Tetlow asked, her voice nasal from her packed, swollen nose.

"Pray that I find Kincaid's body. And you his notes," Blount answered. The phone trilled again. He hesitated before picking it up. "Yes?"

"Boyle here," a subordinate's voice responded. "I'm on the east bank, beneath the Market and Walnut street bridges."

"Find him?"

"No, but there's a homeless guy here who says he saw someone matching Kincaid's description."

"Was Elvis with him?"

"He says some guy climbed out of the river and headed east into town. Says the man was mumbling something about a V_7."

"We got him!" Blount slammed his fist into his palm. "His house is less than a mile from the river. Get the others, converge there, and wait for me!"

BFMC, Research (North) Wing

Kevin looked back at the north wing's emergency exit as the door slowly closed. After waiting to make certain that the fire alarm he'd just disabled would not sound, he sneaked up the stairwell to his fourth-floor office. The corridor was deserted. They hadn't come, yet. Warily, he punched in his code on the security pad outside his door, walked through his outer office, and entered his inner sanctum. He searched through his closet and found a set of underwear and a turtleneck shirt with a pair of slacks hanging next to his leather jacket. After changing clothes, he sat at his great oak desk, turned on his computer, and systematically began isolating every file on V_7. Rather than storing them on the personal or shared network system drives available through the hospital server, Kevin had deliberately kept all V_7 files on his personal computer's hard drive to prevent premature disclosure, like with K_4. That meant that the computer tower sitting on his desk was the sole repository of all V_7 files. He overwrote each file with gibberish, saved them, then deleted them. When he finished, he smashed the tower. All that remained were the archives kept in the vault, one floor down, and any papers remaining in Nguyen's office.

He headed to the lab. The LCD display indicated that no one was there. After entering, he moved swiftly through the computer stations, ultra-low-temperature freezers, and laminar airflow cleanbenches. Nearly at the rear elevator, he glanced at a lit glass-faced refrigerator and noticed a plate with ninety-six tiny wells and a set of ampules sitting alone on the top shelf. It seemed out of place. He stopped, peered in, and read the label: HACV.V_7.

"Oh, no! Peter must've been assembling V_7 *samples* as well as files for Tetlow!"

Was this the only sample of the vector? Nguyen had said that he didn't have time to finish; there was no way to ask him now. Even if every electronic and hard copy piece of V_7 was destroyed, just one drop of vector would be all the Collaborate needed to synthesize more. He surveyed the lab. Equipment spread to a cluttered horizon. It would take days to search it all. "You know there's more, someplace," he said to himself, staring at the ampules.

This is a hospital! You're a doctor, a surgeon for God's sake! You can't! an alternate version of his voice screamed in his head.

"But I can't let the knowledge spread, either. I have no choice."

He stepped to a computer terminal across the aisle and used his administrative clearance to access the lab's environmental systems. The lab had been designed with self-contained power and ventilation systems. He entered the code and cut those connections to the hospital, then isolated the lab's fire detection system, and disabled it.

Kincaid Residence

Alone in the limousine, Tetlow watched Kincaid's house: Blount and his men had slipped into the townhouse forty-five minutes ago—and were still waiting. "This is ridiculous," she mumbled. "They don't know him like I do!" She got out of the car, walked up the stoop to the townhouse, and opened the great front door. Three guns appeared in her face.

"False alarm," one of the men cried.

She walked into the living room. The curios lay toppled, the glass smashed. Painted Navajo pots and glazed Oriental vases were now colored shards splattered across the white carpet. "Searching? Or just frustrated?"

Blount started, "I told you to wait—"

"He's not coming here."

"You crazy? He could be here any—"

"He is not coming."

"And just what makes you so goddamn sure?"

"Because he doesn't consider this place home."

Kincaid's Lab

Bypassing the animal lab and computer archive room, Kevin opened the chemical storage closet filled with big brown jugs, powders, a circulation hood, and an industrial-sized refrigerator. He assembled some large beakers, mixing rods, a deep tray with ice water, and an eyedropper on a cart, then took a large bottle of carbon tetrachloride and mixed it with aluminum powder. A pungent odor burned his sinuses as he stirred. The mixture congealed into a thick syrup. He spooned some into a second beaker and capped both containers. Then he mixed peroxide with acetone, and immersed the mixture in an ice-water bath, slowly adding noxious sulfuric acid from an eyedropper as he stirred. He poured the concoction into three separate containers. The process required twelve hours for the solution to crystallize. How effective would it be after only a few minutes?

He left one of the acetone-peroxide mixtures on the central corridor floor and wheeled the remaining chemicals on the cart to the elevator. When the elevator opened, he wheeled the chemicals aboard, and locked it. He took one of the syrupy beakers and examined it. The formulation had called for a blasting cap, but what about matches?

He needed more power. He went back to the storeroom and placed four bottles of picric acid in solution beside the acetone-peroxide mixture. Picric acid was a powerful booster in crystalline form, but in solution? Backing into the elevator, carefully, he lit the syrup, slid the beaker down the floor. And waited.

It sputtered, fizzled—then sat there.

He had no time to reformulate. The elevator doors began closing.

A spark. A wall of fire hurtled toward him.

He pressed back against the rear wall. Trapped.

The doors closed. A concussion wave knocked him down. The floor burned.

The elevator doors opened onto the upper level. Alarms did not sound. Sprinklers did not activate. He dashed through the lab, burst out through its main entrance, and sealed the door behind him. *The alarm'll go off before it reaches the hospital,* he repeated into the night.

Tetlow hung up the limousine phone. "I've informed hospital security that there's an imposter trying to get into Kincaid's lab. So far, nothing. Two men I trust will meet us at the lab."

As the limousine pulled up to the north wing emergency exit, Blount deployed three men in sight of the key access points. He began checking his gun.

"Put that away!" she snapped. "This is a hospital for God's sake!"

Blount rolled his eyes. He and his driver followed Tetlow out of the limousine to a recessed entrance in the complex, and up two flights in a fireproof stairwell. Two towering hospital security guards waited in front of the lab. The lead guard stepped aside, exposing the biometric security device on the wall. The LCD that normally displayed the number of admitted personnel in the lab was flashing a flat, red line. "Busted, ma'am. Don't know if anybody's in there."

Blount shoved Tetlow aside. He ran his fingers over the door. His fingertips tingled.

Tetlow signaled one of the guards to push Blount out of the way. "This is *my* hospital," she said, handing the other guard her security card. "Open that door!"

The guard complied. The door immediately buzzed rejection.

Blount shifted onto the balls of his feet as she took the card from the guard and swiped it herself, this time with her thumb pressed on the security screen. The lab door began sliding open. Blount leaped back.

A fireball burst through the door.

Both security guards erupted in flames. One staggered toward Blount and fell, face-forward.

Tetlow shrieked: her scarf was on fire.

Outside Luray, Virginia   *2:07 A.M.*

The Chevy's high beams, swinging wildly with every rut, lit fragments of dark dirt road that wound through the leafless forest. Helen had chosen that car because the owner had carelessly left the keys in the ignition and the doors unlocked. Now, she knew why. "Next one I steal will have shocks," she muttered.

These same, dark ogre-trees had seen her as a little girl playing beneath their canopy. This was the last happy summer place of her childhood in Virginia. Lance had secretly reacquired the property two years ago. Could he have made it back here?

Her headlights touched a pile of diamond-shaped rocks abutting a tree. She slowed, pulled the car onto a hidden gravel parking niche, and turned off the lights. Overpowering darkness enveloped her. She flicked on her flashlight and got out of the car. The silence of the woods assaulted her. She stood shivering in the darkness, then started up an unsteady incline.

The rocky ground grinding into her feet became forgiving, familiar. She could feel Lance's warmth beside her. "*Race you back to the house*," he'd say, always winning. His presence, interminably mixed with her last happy memories, drenched these woods.

A twig snapped behind her.

She whirled around, fists clenched, and swiveled her flashlight like a beacon. Nothing moved in the darkness.

The wind picked up. In a clearing, nestled against the edge of the leafless wood, stood a three-room cabin. Helen saw it first through memory: its A-shaped roof and magnificent view of the valley, a quiltwork of farmland carved out of the forest and dotted by ponds. Then, her flashlight beam outlined the cabin's reality: its sagging roof, shuttered windows, and overgrown vines curled into the old log walls. She hurried to the thick wooden door, knocked, and squinted against the whipping cold, hoping that Lance would fling open the door.

Silence answered her. She turned her flashlight away from her house, and followed the beam to an old stone well to her right. She knelt, clawed into the semifrozen dirt beneath the handle, and found a key.

It still worked. The door creaked open. She flashed her beam around the cabin. Stillness stared back: a couch, a desk, a barren fireplace. She crept across somber floorboards to the back of the house. Clang!

Something flat, metallic smashed against her foot. She screamed as she swung her flashlight down: it was just a skillet. Overhead, her flashlight glimpsed a squirrel's tail skittering across a shelf.

She went through the back door to the generator, started the engine, then came back and switched on the lights. The cabin was stark: an old flannel-covered bed, a couch with worn cushions, a laptop and mini-screen TV sitting atop an old folding table. No filth, no clutter, no signs of struggle. He hadn't been here in weeks. "Lance, where are you?"

In the valley, the man lowered high-powered night-vision binoculars.

Loring Estate

Alone in the center of his grand ballroom, Loring listened by headset to Blount's explanation. The old Loring would have yelled and smashed everything in sight, like the outburst eleven years ago after

Bergmann had destroyed the SUE prototype at ReGenerix. But Bergmann had only destroyed the device and the lab—the data itself had been backed up. This time, the resident genius had not only taken out prototype and lab, but the data as well. Losing V_7 meant delaying the timetable a decade, probably longer. But losing Kincaid and having him resurface from the dead? That threatened the Collaborate's very survival.

When Blount finished, Loring asked, "Your plan?"

The mercenary's answer was unimaginative and likely unproductive: search patterns; interrogations of friends, associates, and acquaintances; monitoring bank accounts and credit cards; watching, waiting, hoping.

Loring strolled across the dance floor. "You overlook the obvious."

Penn View Motel, Philadelphia

". . . and two security workers confirmed dead in the five-alarm fire that engulfed a research wing of the Benjamin Franklin Medical Center tonight. Also, the hospital's senior administrator, Joan Tetlow, was seriously injured, suffering second- and third-degree burns about her neck. None of the reported dead or injured are patients. Hospital staff are being praised by firefighters and city officials for safely evacuating the facility, in what sources tell us is almost certainly arson . . ."

"So now I'm an arsonist," Kevin rasped as he watched the TV's snowy, greenish screen. The room pitched gently.

". . . began suspiciously in a hospital lab involved in gene therapy . . ."

A bright light appeared with a siren's scream outside his window.

". . . lab was under the direction of Dr. Kevin Kincaid, a leading . . ."

The siren passed, seeking some other emergency in the night.

". . . was one of two hundred sixty-three scientists killed in the terrorist bombing . . ."

The Penn View Motel: forty rooms of pressed-wood furniture separated by thin walls servicing one-night stands. It was a place to disappear, to end. Kevin had bought a bottle of cheap vodka for $30 off the desk clerk long after the state store had closed. And had gulped down the entire bottle in less than five minutes.

The ceiling violently spun. He knew it wouldn't be long before the Collaborate lost its last link to V_7. The whirling room blurred.

He blacked out.

You forgot me, a young girl's voice reverberated around him.

"Jessica?" he called out. "Kathy?"

Am I that easy to forget? the child-voice asked.

It wasn't familiar. "I don't know you."

You don't want to remember.

The darkness slowly dissolved, revealing Loring's great dance floor below him. Hundreds in tuxedos and evening gowns danced beneath spinning lasers. Spotlights, accompanied by thundering applause, turned on Kevin. He felt himself glide down the grand staircase. Adoring, beautiful people extended congratulations, offered rewards.

"Easy to forget, isn't it?" a voice announced from his left.

Kevin turned. There stood McGovern, arms crossed, leaning haughtily against one of Loring's bars. "Forget what?" Kevin asked.

"Only thinking of what *you* have lost," McGovern said. "What *you* have sacrificed."

The beautiful people stiffened, and stepped aside, like water parting before a ship's bow. A force propelled Kevin forward like a parental hand in his back.

"My people died fighting those you gratefully served!" McGovern declared.

The last of the guests parted. Two men in white coats, their backs to him, knelt, working. One, noticing Kevin, nudged the other. They stepped aside.

A dark-skinned little girl in chains gazed at him. The left side of her face was distorted, gnarled. Her shoulder was bloated, covered with bursting yellow pustules. Half of her body bulged with muscles beneath skin turned inside out. Part of her face was congealed like jelly, with lips on one side distorted, looking like wild fungus. "Remember me now?"

One of the unnamed, unknown child-victims of Collaborate experimentation.

"Video is so two-dimensional," McGovern said. "It takes three to make her real."

The child stepped forward. "It's easier to face the loss of everyone you've ever loved than accept that your work made children," her tiny voice squeaked, "like me."

"It was my fault," Kevin rasped.

"Guilt accomplishes nothing."

"It doesn't matter. I've nowhere to go."

"Yes, you do," a familiar voice called from the mezzanine.

He looked up. Helen Morgan stood at the top of the grand staircase. "Fight them, Kevin!"

"I destroyed the lab. Destroyed V_7."

"Go on fighting them!"

"Don't listen to her, Kincaid!" McGovern called from the bar. "V_7 exists now only in your mind. You've fixed the harpoon problem. Your newly modified V_7 will work, won't it?"

"It should."

"Then you can't risk letting them get it!"

"Kevin, without you, without V_7, how many more millions of unborn children will be condemned to suffer from genetic diseases?" Helen countered from the mezzanine. "Diseases you could have prevented."

"Kincaid, if the Collaborate gets control of a fully functional V_7, you know what they will do. Break humanity into subspe—"

"You don't know that!" Helen Morgan shouted at McGovern.

"The inevitable consequence of changing ourselves," McGovern countered.

"You're just a cynic!" Helen Morgan retorted.

"The difference between cynicism and realism is experience. I'd have thought you'd have learned that by now, Morgan."

Helen turned to Kincaid. "Kevin, think of those you'll save!"

"Kincaid, think of the unending hell you'll unleash!"

Helen reached out for him. "You've got to make things right."

"You do that by stopping the Collaborate. Here!" McGovern held up a bottle of vodka.

"Kevin, dear," a compelling voice called. Beside Helen Morgan stood a burned Helen Kincaid. She had little Kathy wrapped in her arms, Jessica gently rocking in a stroller by her side. "Strike back," his wife whispered.

"Strike back by denying the Collaborate its prize," McGovern said.

"Help us rest easier," she begged.

"You can't help them," McGovern said, suddenly appearing beside Kevin. "But you can *be* with them." Handing Kevin the vodka, "You've already taken the first step. You've drunk a lot, but you can't be sure. All you need to do is remember not to turn your head. Let yourself choke."

"I—I don't want to."

"Why else would you be here? You have to die. You want to die,"

McGovern said. "People can will themselves to die. Ask someone who knows."

A woman stepped out of the shadows.

"Mom?"

Bergmann Cabin, Outside Luray, Virginia

Helen stared at Lance's laptop screen. Cracking his password, *AlwaysLance,* had been simple. As skilled as she was at research, making sense of hundreds of saved files could take days. E-mails, newsnets, downloaded journal articles, abstracts, maps, website addresses—Lance was a master of investigative cyber-searching. Once he'd boasted that if God physically was on earth, then proof resided somewhere on the Net. He'd managed to ferret out the Collaborate's facility in Mexico and was convinced that somewhere lay another, far more extensive complex. Most of his queries had dealt with orphanages, charter schools, and private institutions centered around New York State's western lower tier and Pennsylvania's central-northern region. She surmised that he'd planned to identify the Collaborate's other center after returning from Tiburon. The trick in learning to understand Lance was to become reckless. Her eyelids drooped. "But not tonight."

She shut off the laptop and, before starting for bed, glanced at the TV. They hadn't found Kevin's body. Maybe, for once in her life, there was good news. She reached out, hesitated, then turned it on. The screen filled with a videotape replay of Trent in manacles. She turned up the volume: *". . . FBI and federal law enforcement officials have been stung by the escape from custody of Trent McGovern, alleged mastermind of the bombing at . . ."*

Pennsylvania Route 100, Chester County   4:23 A.M.

As Blount's sedan's headlights probed the dark road, Blount recalled how Loring's orders had been delivered with Grayson's calm, chilling exactness—orders that had to be scrupulously obeyed. The car slowed as it approached a three-way intersection. Headlights of the vehicle behind him shone in the rearview mirror. Blount pointed to the old stone bridge on the left. "Turn there," he told the driver.

The others in the second vehicle followed them over the creek and up the hill.

Fire: an imprecise weapon. Though Kincaid deserved ten times over the pain he was going to receive, the target itself—Blount found this task particularly distasteful: what kind of hunter shoots a lamb in a petting zoo?

Bergmann Cabin, Outside Luray, Virginia   *8:09 A.M.*

Helen lifted her head off the pillow of paper printouts. She squinted against the weak light of the blurred laptop screen. Strong footsteps vibrated the cabin's porch floor. Slowly, they approached the front door. Her blood chilled. The front lock clicked.

"Who—who is it?"

The bolt snapped.

She grabbed a knife beside the plate of corned beef hash she'd eaten. "Stay where you are!"

The door creaked as it slowly swung open. A tall, lean man with stringy blond hair and tattered jeans stood stiffly in the doorway. Helen dropped the knife. She started to cry. Unsmiling, gait stilted, he approached. She buried her head in his cold chest. "Lance! Thank God you're here!"

Unperturbed, he dragged her with him to the table.

"Don't you know how I've missed you?"

With Helen still clinging to his chest, he sat and began typing on the laptop keyboard. The screen fluttered. Search engines engaged.

"For God's sake, Lance, talk to me!"

He pointed at the screen displaying a list of orphanages, with their addresses, licensures, enrollments, charges, and facilities.

"What is it, Lance? Talk to me!"

She laid her cheek against the back of his neck. The side of her face quickly froze, as if pressed against pond ice. Her arms wrapped around his cold chest. He had not drawn one breath since she'd embraced him.

Lance turned back to her with eyeless, bloody sockets. She screamed.

She lifted her head from the pillow of paper printouts. Panting, she scanned the room: the knife still lay beside the empty plate; the door behind her remained securely locked. There was no Lance.

The laptop screen in front of her seemed to be fixed on the list of orphanages that her dreamed brother had conjured. *Was I was working on* that *when I fell asleep?*

Teeth chattering in the freezing room, she printed out the list, then returned to the primary search engine's home page to query each orphanage listed. On-screen appeared a jumbled array of search pattern options, pulsating advertisement boxes, marquee promotions, and news blurbs. She noticed a story about a tragic fire and clicked on it. Details of the fast-breaking story filled the screen. Her heart fluttered as she read. *Oh, poor—*

"The Collaborate! It has to be! That's why they—Kevin's alive!"

The man in the valley watched Helen bolt from the cabin and hurry down the wooded trail to her stolen car. He lowered his binoculars and picked up his wireless. "Subject's on the move." He listened for a moment, then answered, "I think she knows."

Delphi

In all her time at Delphi, Marguerite had never before descended to Level Two. She expected scores of bustling scientists, but the elevator doors opened onto an empty, drab-yellow corridor. After a biometric reader scanned her matching, color-coded badge and dinged its approval, she proceeded past several dozen offices on her right. The corridor gently curved around, like the outer rim of a great wheel. On her left she paused beside a sealed entrance marked "Access to Level Two Labs," then headed to Room 237, the office of Roderick Stevenson, MD, PhD. She entered a clerical anteroom. Its front desk was littered with unbound papers.

"Come in," a voice sounded overhead as a door slid open.

Stevenson sat behind an unpretentious desk in an office decorated with anatomical diagrams, and linkage and physical genome maps. He offered her a seat. "Meredith's condition has stabilized. Sadly, it's only a short-term remission."

"What do you want, Doctor?"

He quickly scanned her. "I need a research assistant."

"I'm fine where I am."

Stevenson clicked the mouse to his right, and swiveled the monitor toward his guest. It showed a frail, brilliant child resting quietly in a hospital bed. "In three days, she'll be dead." He added, "In four, so will you, unless you take what I'm offering."

"You don't know that for sure."

"If you don't see it, you're a fool," he said softly. "If you do, if you're in denial, snap out of it!"

She closed her eyes to hide forming tears. "You don't care about the children or me. Why should—"

"I was a county coroner for eighteen years. And in all that time, whenever I removed the sheet from a body lying on the table, beyond the childbirth stretch marks, the arthritic joints, the thousand little scars life inflicts, I'd first see a person. And for a moment, I'd feel a life lived. For so long, it was a mother beaten by an abusive husband. Or an abandoned homeless woman. Or a tattooed man whose throat had been slit, just like he'd done to the dealer on the table beside him. I came here to get away from all that." He cleared his throat. "Instead, I've cut open children with minds that could cure cancer, build fusion engines, become new Shakespeares. How do you make amends for devouring the seeds of your next harvest?"

"It's a little late, isn't it?"

"The position calls for a life sciences specialist. You're not fully qualified, but I can bend the rules a bit." He swallowed as he glanced away. "Marguerite, together, we might make a difference."

"What difference? Soon, all my children will be dead."

He looked around the room. "What about the next generation?"

Penn View Motel, Philadelphia

Kevin lifted his head off the worn carpeting. Bright light filtered through broken blind slats. The room smelled putrid and spun to a soap opera score blaring from the TV. He glanced at his damp shirt. Though he'd quickly drunk a toxic quantity of alcohol, he was twice lucky: one to have vomited during his sleep, and two, to have avoided choking. Fragments of last night's dream replayed at quarter-speed as he stumbled into the bathroom. Stiff-armed, he leaned over the sink and stared at water dripping out the faucet and disappearing down the rusting drain.

Fools. They don't understand, the McGovern-voice echoed. *You do.*

"Shut up!" he yelled, swinging his arm wildly. His hand struck an empty glass. It hit the wall and shattered. Glass fragments showered the basin. He picked up a two-inch shard shaped like a scimitar, held it to his face, and watched light refract off its facets.

Look at this place, Kevin! There's nowhere to go.

"I can't!"

Fill a tub with warm water. Sit inside, the melodic McGovern-voice droned. *You know how to make the cuts over the radial arteries. In a few minutes, you'll sleep.*

Kevin looked in the mirror. Beside the reflection of the TV, glazed eyes set in a pale, haggard face drenched in saliva, sweat, and vomit looked back.

Everyone, everything you've ever loved is dead. Why should you live?

Bright orange streaks appeared in the TV reflection: film footage of the fire.

Go on. Take a good look at what you've done!

Kevin glanced back over his shoulder. The building in flames was not Benjamin Franklin Medical Center. It was older, grander, with white colonnades and a porch. He whirled around. Raced toward the TV.

". . . night's fire at Halloran House has been ruled an arson." The fire footage ended. A blond TV reporter appeared in daylight against the smoldering remains of the structure. *"With more than a hundred challenged and special-needs residents dead, this loss of life has set off a series of investigations. Police are asking . . ."*

A hotline phone number for family and friends of clients at Halloran House appeared superimposed over the reporter's image. Kevin seized the phone.

Mobile Communications Van
Chester County, Pennsylvania

A man with a headset swiveled in his chair and gave the thumbs-up sign.

Blount nodded to the technician and permitted himself a feeble smile.

The Burn Center at Keystate Hospital
Chester County, Pennsylvania   *1:32 P.M.*

Kevin hurried past the elderly volunteer smiling at the information desk of Keystate Hospital's east entrance. He kept turning his head systematically to minimize the chance that someone might recognize him: the Association's spots were still blitzing national TV. Roving eyes met lingering glances as he strode down the corridor: a gray-haired man sitting on a bench reading a Ludlum paperback; a woman in blues and stethoscope drinking coffee; a mother and toddler eyeing a vintage Beanie Baby in the gift shop. He stepped onto the elevator and shut the doors before anyone else could board, and pressed number seven.

The woman on the hotline had confirmed that Donny was, indeed, alive, but critical. They'd only been able to identify him by a few personal possessions: he'd been burned beyond recognition. Kevin swatted away a tear before it formed. The Collaborate had maimed his brother to punish him.

The doors parted. He stepped out into a quiet, pale-green corridor and followed a sign pointing left. Through the double doors was the ICU-burn center: a circular nurses' station hub ringed by single-patient isolation rooms. A dozen blue-clad nurses scurried between offset rooms or manned cardiopulmonary monitors at the circular desk. He spied the carousel containing patient charts, strolled to it, and picked up the chart of Donnelly Kincaid. A desk nurse looked at him disapprovingly, but through harried years on the surgical floor, Kevin had developed an effective, commanding expression that enabled him to bend rules. The nurse returned to her work.

He flipped through his brother's chart, scanning the admission paperwork, progress notes, lab results, physician orders. Donny had fifty-four percent of his body covered by full-thickness burns and thirty-six percent by partial-thickness burns, plus smoke inhalation injury. According to the "burn rule-of-nines," which assesses the extent of body surface burned by nine percent increments, Donny was terminal. Kevin forced himself on toward Room 8. He stopped in the isolation-control anteroom and began vigorously scrubbing his hands with antiseptic, wishing he could wash away the past week. After drying them, he self-gowned and gloved, and slipped through the plastic isolation barrier.

Donny's face and upper torso were wrapped in bandages covering a thick coat of silver-nitrate ointment. There was an NG-tube and an intravenous drip running Ringer's solution and a synthetic, morphine-like opioid for pain. In the background, the cardiopulmonary monitor beeped steadily.

"Donny, can you hear me?" he whispered. "Are you in pain?"

He did not stir.

This is my fault. I didn't think they'd do something like this. I—forgot about you. He placed a gloved hand on the railing. Something seemed wrong.

Helen swerved the stolen maroon Mazda into the short-term parking lot in front of the hospital's main entrance. Brakes screeching, she slung the vehicle into the last legal space.

On the long drive up, she'd mulled over what she was risking. With the Collaborate thinking her dead, and with Trent running for his life, for the first time in eleven years, she had the chance to live like a human being. If Kevin was alive. If he was here. If he would have her.

Kevin studied his brother from the foot of the bed. The perspective was wrong. The legs appeared to extend all the way to the end of the bed. The patient lying before him had to be tall, but Donny was almost a foot shorter than Kevin. He bent down. The bed had no patient ID nameplate. He picked up the daily sheet of BPs and I&Os on a clipboard hanging on the end of the bed. The patient name listed was Brian Duling.

He stormed out of the isolation room.

"What have you done with my brother?" he demanded of the nurse sitting at the station.

"Excuse me?"

"Donnelly Kincaid. A Halloran House resident. Where is he?"

"Oh, him. Transferred to Room 203, west wing, an hour ago."

"You moved a critical burn patient from ICU within twenty-four hours of admission?"

The nurse scanned the screen. "His condition was upgraded."

Based on his chart, that's hard to believe. And why didn't his chart go down to the room with him?

"Take the elevator at the far end of the corridor," she said.

Kevin headed through the double doors and down the long hallway, past several sets of alcoves with vending machines, nurses' stations, patient rooms, and a lounge. An elevator opened at his approach. He pressed number "2". The expected mechanical whir of the car in its tracks vibrated through his feet, but he felt no sensation of descent. "What now?" He noticed the sign on the control panel:

CERTIFICATE OF OPERATION FOR THIS ELEVATOR KEPT
ON FILE IN THE CHIEF ENGINEER'S OFFICE
—KEYSTATE HOSPITAL
A PROUD NEW MEMBER OF THE
BENJAMIN FRANKLIN HEALTHCARE NETWORK

Slowly, he looked up. Behind a plastic shield in the upper far corner, an unobtrusive security camera watched, its red light glaring. He glanced back at the LCD. The elevator still hadn't reached the second floor.

The elevator slam-halted.

Kevin banged his fist against the red emergency button but the alarm did not sound. He slid his fingers along the edge of the emergency call box and tore off the gray steel: bare wires hung limply. Metal clanged overhead. The elevator rocked.

A hissing: loud, angry. The air tasted bitter, thick, choking. A burning odor seeped into his nostrils, smothering his chest. The room spun.

The elevator ceiling collapsed. Dark, masked figures crashed on top of him.

Wearing a black hat with the brim turned down, Helen strolled casually through the hospital's west-wing lobby, though she felt as if she were walking across an unsteady rope bridge above a pit of snakes. An army of security cameras silently watched. Her hat hid the left side and upper third of her face, but if the Collaborate was expecting her—*I must be crazy. If he's here, how do I get us out?*

She scanned the cafeteria and main gift shop as she headed to the elevators. Forty grumbling people milled around them. One elevator was marked "Out of Service"; two of the other three appeared to be stuck on the upper floors. When the lone operating elevator finally opened, less than a quarter of the crowd squeezed on. She turned around and gazed out a picture window as two EMTs loaded a patient strapped to a gurney into a white-and-red ambulance. One technician hurried around to the front of the vehicle, out of view, while the other secured the rear door. She moved closer to the window. The technician's pockmarked profile seemed familiar as he slapped the ambulance's rear door twice. Briefly, he turned toward the window.

Georgetown Mall! The fake FBI agent leaning over the mezzanine! "Kevin!"

Helen shoved her way along the edge of the elevator crowd. She broke clear, bolted across the lobby, and slammed into a woman carrying a tray of Danishes. In eight awkward strides, she regained her balance, then leaped over an empty wheelchair by the information desk. Pivoting sideways, she slipped through the glass sliding doors before they automatically closed.

She stopped and looked out at the drive from the main entrance. The ambulance was at the stoplight on the main street, less than a half-mile from the on-ramp to the interstate.

The stoplight changed. She dashed into her stolen Chevy, started it, and threw it into reverse. The sedan jerked back and banged into a parked hatchback. She put the car in *drive* and floored it, shooting the sedan forward. She swerved around the oval parking median. A silver Cadillac backed into her path. She slammed into its trunk and careered toward the parking lot exit: a narrow, two-lane path between stone-fenced walkways. A blue Toyota minivan appeared, blocking both exit lanes.

Helen swerved left. Her Chevy struck the curb, tipped up on its side, glanced off the top of the stone fence, and spun upside down.

The roof crashed beneath her. Screeching, tearing metal surrounded her. The car slid toward an upside-down concrete pillar supporting the parking garage.

Sparks ignited around her. The pillar grew close.

She shielded her face with her hands as the pillar filled the windshield.

Loring Estate   *8:05 P.M.*

" quite a week, old friend." Loring lifted a cup of Darjeeling, sipped, and returned it to its saucer, the delicate *ping* drifting away into his grand ballroom. Alone, cross-legged in the center of the floor, he drank in the paste-thick darkness and pointed to the cup. "You probably think there's liquor in here. Now would I? This is, after all, your memorial service."

A creak answered him from the mezzanine.

"Turnout is light, but then, you were never one for crowds." He reached for the cup and accidentally tipped it over. Diluted tea spilled onto the floor. "All right, I lied! It's full of gin!"

A gust of wind swept through the adjoining garden and struck the ballroom's south face, lightly rattling the great windows.

"Merlin, it's a shame you didn't live to see this. I've destroyed every threat to our future, and, except for one minor glitch, solved every problem. I'll have Kincaid's vector by tomorrow. Then finally, finally, we can start Implementation!"

A distant hum from the mezzanine. Was someone using the private elevator?

He stood without using his hands. "Old friend, I need your advice this one last time." He shuffled to the staircase. "The organization is under my stewardship. Bertram is on the sidelines." He moistened his lips. "Do I risk it now—or hope for a better opportunity later?"

A low-pitched whine wafted from the rear of the mezzanine. Elevator doors opened. A silhouette appeared against the elevator's lights, then disappeared into the darkness. The doors closed. Loring trembled as he followed the sound of the figure's footsteps across the mezzanine, along the railing, and slowly down the grand staircase. The man stopped two steps above the dance floor. Breaths staggered, Loring stared at the dark figure—wishing it was *him*; wishing it wasn't.

"Shall we stand here in the dark, Mr. Loring?" the man asked.

Loring touched an auxiliary panel behind the railing. Spotlights illuminated the foot of the staircase.

The man was bronze, sandy-haired, and neckless: a sanctioned courier. The man handed him a red-sealed envelope. Loring tore it open, scanned the single-sentence message, and strained to maintain his composure.

"Your response, sir?" the man asked.

How did he know? Loring's mind screamed. For appearances, he smiled, clasped his hands, and slightly bowed. "Tell Mr. Bertram I look forward to meeting him there tomorrow."

Site 341

Helen opened her eyes. She found herself lying in a padded chaise longue beside a matching chair. The room was a featureless white wall that curved into the floor. Harsh, overhead spotlights warmed her skin that the hospital gown did not cover. Her shoulders, her ribs ached. Bandages covered cuts on her forehead and cheeks. The nape of her neck bristled as she felt Collaborate eyes watching. Slowly, she rolled off the chair and staggered to the wall. Her fingertips, searching for the door, glided along the seamless surface.

A low-rolling hum echoed from behind her. She pivoted around. A door slid closed behind a woman with short-cropped wheat-blond hair and an ashen complexion. "We have matters to discuss," the woman said in a husky voice.

Helen lunged at her. The woman's left arm whipped around and deflected Helen's right forearm. Effortlessly, she dropped her left knee and flung Helen to the floor. Sprawled helplessly on her side, Helen winced. A hand agonizingly bent back her wrist.

"I'm not Collaborate," the woman said.

"The hell you're not!"

The locks on her arm and wrist grew tighter. "I'm your guardian angel."

Helen forced a laugh. "This is heaven. And I'm dead, right?"

"To the Collaborate, yes."

Helen lifted her right leg and swung it wildly back at the woman. A strong parry knocked it away before she twisted it into submission.

"You *and* your brother," the woman said. "I've watched over you for years."

Helen heard the low-rolling hum of the door. Long, loping footsteps approached. A pair of scrupulously polished black men's shoes stopped near her face. Helen tried to lift her head, but the woman had locked the bandaged parts of her face flush with the floor. A strong, minty odor assailed her.

"We went to great lengths to keep you both alive," the man said.

"Trent?"

Delphi, Stevenson's Office

The tedious hours Marguerite had spent trying to organize Dr. Stevenson's mounds of autopsy and cytology reports had helped keep her from fixating on Meredith. She also began to sense in Stevenson something she thought she'd never have: an ally.

The doctor emerged from the inner office. "I'll be out the rest of the day." He headed for the door, but stopped. "Marguerite, there are rumors that members of the elite are going to visit. I don't know who, but it's been years since anyone other than Loring has come."

"What does that mean for us?"

He looked over his shoulder. "Opportunity."

Site 341

The short-haired blond woman released her grip. Helen slowly stood. Eyes never wavering from Trent's, she punched him in the jaw. The big man flew backward and slammed onto the floor. Her arms shook, her belly hungry for more.

The woman's fingers pinched Helen's neck, sending electric shocks down her spine. "You only get one."

Trent scrambled to his feet. "Helen, let me explain."

"What happened to your organization is on national news. What happened to your people is body bags. What happened to your principles is obvious!"

His spent eyes focused on the woman in control. "There was nothing more I could do."

"Underestimation is a corollary to the sin of pride," the woman said. To Helen, "You—sit and learn." She released her grip. "Don't make me force-feed you."

Echoes of pain faded down Helen's back. She stretched her neck, then sat on the edge of the chaise longue. The woman glided into the chair beside her, propped her chin on a firm second finger, and stared with narrow eyes at Helen. Trent stood at attention behind the woman.

"This place is Site 341," the woman said.

Helen crossed her arms. "You need a decorator."

"We reserve our funds for guns, not butter." The woman smiled.

"The Collaborate strapped for cash?"

The woman looked up and behind her at Trent. "From your reports, I had surmised that she'd virtually cracked your cover."

"Both her and her brother were on the verge," he said. "I thought—"

"You know where Lance is. Tell me!" Helen demanded.

The woman nodded to Trent.

"Dead. I'm sorry," he said.

Helen clamped her knees. "Are you sure?"

"You got his package, didn't you?"

"What pack—"

"The one with your brother's videotape of the Tiburon installa tion. His log. And, naturally, the specimens," the woman said.

"*You?* You sent me Lance's package?"

"We took it from the people who killed him—Collaborate operatives in Tiburon. It's a decision on which I've deliberated long and hard. The jury's still out."

Cold swept over Helen's hands, arms, chest. "How?"

"We intercepted the helicopter carrying your brother's killers back to Tiburon. We retrieved the package, crashed the copter in the ocean, and made it seem like an accident. The Collaborate suspected we were involved, but wasn't certain. Ultimately, they decided to shut down the facility."

"How—did Lance die?"

"Unpleasantly." The woman repropped her chin on her finger. "Do you really want to hear specifics?"

Helen released a lung-draining sigh. She'd been preparing for this news for days, having confined the heart-ripping wails to a place well hidden from her consciousness. Swaying back in the chair, "Just who in the hell are you?"

"Kristin Brocks. Security and Intelligence Director, Defense Advanced Research Projects Agency."

She craned up at Trent. "You sold AntiGen out to—"

"You have it all wrong." Brocks smiled. "You see, *I* am AntiGen."

She looked from Brocks's stark smugness to the raised eyebrows on Trent's bobbing head.

"It's nice to finally meet one of my most imaginative employees," Brocks quipped.

"Anna, Straub, Cameron, they were—"

"Unaware. Like you."

Helen glared, then burst out laughing. "The creators of the Internet, synthetic blood, and of who-the-hell-knows what kind of electronic and biological weaponry—spending its time on misfit terrorist wannabes? How stupid do you think I am?"

Brocks forced a stunted chuckle. "You've long wondered where McGovern got three million dollars a year for his hole-in-the-wall operation that never got its name or message on local, much less national news? I've been signing your checks for years." The creases along her lower lip grew rigid. "And those 'additional personnel' that showed up from time to time at McGovern's call. Did you think they just dropped in out of the sky? And such reliable intelligence. Like the patent attorney who had Protein X-ACT."

"Which Trent denied us—"

"Because it risked exposing *us*. Besides, without me, you'd have been caught."

"Yeah, right!"

"Remember when Anna tried to disable the building's alarm, but couldn't? And the alarm didn't sound until *after* you left? Who do you think locked you out, then saved your hide? You were under surveillance the whole time."

"I don't believe you."

"I have video, right down to pictures of the corned beef hash you ate at your brother's cabin. Choose the date, the time, the place."

"Assuming I believed that, they nearly killed me in Georgetown. Where were you then?"

"There was nothing we could do."

"They killed Anna!"

Brocks did not blink. "Regrettable."

"Why didn't you do something?"

"That," pointing a finger, "was your job."

Helen launched herself out of the chair. "I was trying to rescue Kevin before your 'observers' cut me off. It was your people, wasn't it?"

"If you'd taken on Collaborate operatives at that time you would have been killed."

"And the car crash?"

"There were fourteen cars you could have stolen. Only one had the keys still in it, in plain view. This wasn't by accident—excuse the pun. The car you stole had additional safety features. But still, you were lucky."

"It was my life to risk."

"But you risked exposing *us*."

Helen leaned into Brocks. "What are you so afraid of?"

Brocks crossed her arms. "The facility in Tiburon was the Collaborate's initial, but antiquated, research site for germline genetic manipulation of the human musculoskeletal system. The intent was to design genes encoding proteins that would improve muscle function and bone-loading capacity. Because the facility was located on foreign soil we could not ensure that sales of such genetic advances would be limited to or controlled by the United States government. If Kincaid's K_4 vector had succeeded, the Collaborate would have established a financial and global political base that would threaten national security."

"But that's only the tip of the iceberg," Trent said.

"The Collaborate has Protein X-ACT," Brocks continued. "They can design any protein they can conceive and back it out into the genes coding for those proteins. They already have a vast library of genes and proteins. With Kincaid's new vector, they'll have the means for efficiently delivering their patented genes into living human cells. Many of these genes are designed to improve intelligence. With the expected approval of HR 601, the Collaborate will be free to sell its wares. Parents willing to pay any price to genetically improve their unborn child, or order up designer in vitro fertilization children, will scamper to Collaborate clinics around the nation. In reality, however, the Collaborate is setting up a de facto aristocracy. Their activities are not in the national best interest."

"We can only speculate on their long-term plans," Trent added.

"I met personally with Loring this week," Brocks said. "He offered me tea and laughed in my face."

"I've accessed databases from the patent office, the National Library of Medicine, NCBI, and BLAST. The Collaborate couldn't have built their genetic library or hidden their patents unless *you*, at DARPA, helped them!" Helen spat. "What frightens you most is what the Collaborate can do to *your agency*!"

Brocks spread her fingertips. "We create systems that control all information. Think we're afraid of a few wealthy industrialists?"

"Then why haven't you 'neutralized' them?"

Brocks chuckled and shook her head. "These aren't street schlubs. They're billionaires. We have economic and political ramifications to consider."

"You could expose them."

"With disastrous results."

"That's only half the story," Helen said.

Trent whispered to Brocks.

Brocks glanced back at him. "The more she unravels, the more she commits herself."

Helen spoke slowly. "DARPA is known, in its own language, for 'Technology Push'—identifying technologies that could make a difference, working those technologies to their limits and capabilities, and then translating those capabilities into military applications. Vectors, Protein X-ACT, the project my father was working on, they're all dual-use biotechnologies—commercial and military applications.

DARPA has the freedom to go into innovative agreements and trans-actions that bypass Federal Acquisition Regulations. So, are you and the Collaborate still partners?"

"Told you, she's bright," Trent said.

"And volatile," Brocks added.

Helen stood. "What *exactly* was my father's work?"

"Classified," Brocks declared.

"What hold does the Collaborate have on you?"

"You've blossomed in the last two years." Brocks folded her hands. "Years ago when Ian Wilmut cloned sheep, the public and the politi-cians were terrified that we were going to clone people. If the little secret we share with the Collaborate goes public, it would damage this country's psyche."

"Balance of terror," Trent said. "If we try to neutralize them, they go public. And both sides are destroyed."

"It's made them arrogant, uncontrollable," Brocks said. "The Col-laborate has penetrated traditional intelligence and counterintelli-gence channels. I can't use the resources at my disposal without them knowing first!"

Helen approached the pair. "So, you created AntiGen as your sur-rogate in the battle."

"Plausible deniability," Trent said. "AntiGen certainly appeared to be no friend of the government. Only Security Director Brocks and I knew otherwise."

"Actually, I created a number of independent cells, like AntiGen, across the country," Brocks said. "Yours was the most effective, as well as being in the right place at the right time."

"Do you know what you've done?" Helen stuck her face in Brocks's. "You've used up human beings of good conscience—and thrown them away."

"Quite the contrary. I gave them the opportunity to apply their lofty principles, to wage real war against a real enemy. And in your case, Tracy Bergmann, I gave you refuge. More, I gave you the chance to spearhead the battle against the man directly responsible for your father's death. Who else in this world could have saved your life *and* provided a platform for revenge?"

Helen felt as if she'd been slit down the middle, her innards exposed, raw.

"I gave you a new identity. I gave you a new face. I gave you a great purpose. I gave you all the tools you needed to turn the only man in the world who could complete the Collaborate's research plan. All proceeding beautifully—until your little ad lib outburst at the press conference ruined everything!"

"Your plan was simplistic. Kevin wouldn't have turned V_7 over to me because he thought I was his wife reincarnated. He's not stupid!"

"If you'd followed orders, not only would you have stopped the Collaborate, but Kincaid would have loved you as his wife."

"A man numbed, scarred, immersed in his work doesn't just give away that work to a pretty face. He needed companionship, trust. He needed someone to share his pain. Your plan never considered that."

Brocks sighed through taut lips. "We'll never know now, will we?"

"In all fairness, Director, her fallback plan was well-considered. Kincaid himself would have exposed the Collaborate on a global platform and turned over V_7 to AntiGen. Neither he nor any Collaborate remnant would have known that *we* arranged it."

"Except that Loring learned that Kincaid was going to expose them at NIH."

"How?" Helen asked.

"We don't know." Brocks admitted. "Fortunately, the Collaborate didn't make the link between AntiGen and DARPA, so they took out AntiGen in, quite honestly, an elegant plan."

"Elegant?" Helen barked. "They murdered hundreds of people! Scientists, our fut—"

"Scientists, from a societal perspective, are a cheap commodity. Good science, however, is priceless. The key is that Kincaid survived. In the greater scheme, he's far more important than the dead in Natcher Center, AntiGen HQ, or Georgetown."

"Then why did you let the Collaborate capture him at the hospital?"

"*Recapture.*"

Helen stared quizzically.

Trent answered, "Just after the bombing, they took him to an interrogation center. They had him there several hours before transporting him—"

"And you didn't break him loose?"

"That would have exposed us." Brocks sighed. "The only reason McGovern is here with us now is because I'll spend the rest of my life paying off the favors I used to break him out of maximum security."

"As I was saying about Kincaid," Trent said, "a Collaborate operations team transported him to Philadelphia, probably to access data from his lab."

"Then they already have V_7," Helen said.

Brocks shook her head. "Probably not yet. He escaped, and set fire to his lab. We sifted through the wreckage ourselves. We found nothing. After that, Kincaid dropped off the face of the planet. We didn't know where he was. Neither did the Collaborate. We had a six-hour window in which we could have taken Kincaid, with the Collaborate none the wiser. A real opportunity missed. My mistake—I allowed them to be more ruthless than me."

"Then why did you stop me at the hospital?"

"You'd have been killed. I wanted you to stay put in the cabin. McGovern would have appeared at your doorstep by noon. But no, you had to come gallivanting to Kincaid's rescue and, as usual, complicate matters."

Helen walked away, shaking her head. "Why should you care whether I live?"

"I have a mission for you." Brocks crossed her legs. "You and McGovern are to rescue Kincaid."

Helen whirled around. "Where's Kevin now?"

"McGovern was special forces. An expert in demolitions, weaponry, hand-to-hand, electronic countermeasures. He can get you in."

"Where is Kevin now?"

Trent said, "Kincaid will be alone, confused, probably drugged, tortured. It'll increase our chances if there's someone there he can trust."

"What makes you think he trusts me? I've betrayed him—twice."

"*Remotely* trusts, then," Brocks said. "It's a certainty that he trusts you more than McGovern. And the simple truth is that you're the only one."

"Where is he?"

"Are you in?"

"All right, I'm in! Now, where is he?"

Delphi: Level Two—Central Op Theater

Stevenson saw that Lewis Spann, Delphi's Executive Administrator, was perturbed: the man's great hands were on his hips, and he was glaring at him for entering the Central Op Theater so late. Usually, the operating suite was limited to a small surgical team performing exploratory procedures on one of the children, with a few spectators overhead watching via closed-circuit cameras. Instead, around a gurney, stood the executive administrator, three nurses, Director of Molecular Research Dr. Culver Ambrose, and an unidentified man wearing a violet badge—clearance for Level Five. Stevenson looked down at the man unconscious on the gurney. "Is that him?"

Lewis Spann nodded. "The one and only Kevin Kincaid."

Stevenson examined Kevin. The long, muscular frame was riddled with minor cuts and bruises, but the face—the face was strong, decisive. *Here I am, on the ground, watching the skydiver with a failed chute,* Stevenson thought. *I can't help. And I can't look away.*

"Come on, Doctor!" barked a pudgy man.

He looked back at the man's violet badge. *Level Five. They're anxious to begin.*

"Dr. Stevenson, please check Dr. Ambrose's suggested dose," Spann said, handing him a clipboard.

"Dr. Ambrose is certainly capable of calculating the correct dosage."

"I want a second opinion, Stevenson. We can't afford another mistake."

Stevenson flashed Ambrose a "what-can-I-do?" shrug, then took the clipboard. He scanned it. "Seems fine."

Spann looked up and called, "Begin recording. Tie everything into the mainframe." He turned to his Director of Molecular Research. "Dr. Ambrose, we should be able to extract the information from Kincaid shortly. So, when do you expect to have V_7 synthesized?"

Ambrose frowned. "Without knowing the formula or process, it's impossible to predict how long it'll take to synthesize the vector."

"I understand. Science takes time," he said.

"Exactly."

"Why don't you try that approach with the Chairman? You can tell him in person."

"Mr. Bertram is coming *here?*"

"Tomorrow evening. Any chance you'll be ready?"

Stevenson covered a smile. *Maybe the skydiver just opened an emergency chute.*

10:10 P.M.

Kevin stared at the multicolored drawing on the whiteboard.

"So that's what V_7 looks like," the familiar voice said.

Kevin whirled around. There, at the conference table, in his lab, sat Peter Nguyen.

"Amazing!" Nguyen declared. "It looks like, like—"

"Like a burrito with a pointed tail and an oversized pea in its belly," Kevin finished. Obviously, it was Peter—but his voice? It seemed much deeper than usual. "You got a cold there, kid?"

In the background, high-pitched whispers—the words lost in some lofty mist.

Nguyen's voice cleared. "No, I'm fine, Doctor. You were explaining?"

"Think of V_7 as being like one of NASA's old Saturn rockets. It has a three-stage delivery system, but its payload is a pair of chromosomes, not astronauts. The first stage is a viral-like harpoon, the second is a capsule, and the third, nucleosomes." *Have I been here before?*

"Could you tell me a little more about the harpoon?" Nguyen asked.

Kevin felt dizzy. "It—it resembles tightly coiled proteins in HIV and influenza viruses, and, uh, has a barbed end that attaches into the cell membrane. It's attached to a cyclic peptide nanotube which—is attached to a cochlear cylinder—which is a sheet of lipid rolled up like a crepe." He sat down beside the board.

"You promised to share. Can you please explain to us how to synthesize all that?"

Kevin turned around. Gensini, Pratt, DeVries, Horowitz, and the rest of his V_7 team leaders were sitting around the table with Nguyen.

"You must get this off your chest, Doctor. What if something should happen to you? Who would save the sick children of this world?"

Uneasily, Kevin nodded. Painstakingly, he described the multi-staged synthesis.

After he finished, Nguyen asked, "One last thing—you're certain that is the polypeptide sequence for V_7's harpoon?"

Kevin laid his painful head on the conference table. "That's what I used."

He began to hear those ethereal whispers, again. Fighting his spinning head, he tried to concentrate, picking up only a fragment: ". . . begin synthesis at . . ."

Kevin remembered a dream: his father, fishing, something about being a sloppy fisherman—and the vector?

He felt himself slip off the table. Roll onto the floor. *Yes, Peter,* he thought as he spun. *But don't you remember? Everything worked.* He slurred, "Except that the mice died."

Site 341

"... and Delphi's subterranean outer ring primarily has offices, sleeping quarters, and recreational facilities," Brocks said. Above the conference table rotated a holographic projection of Delphi: a pair of color-coded, compartmentalized, concentric structures four levels deep. "The inner ring consists of laboratories and secured conference centers."

"These schematics are accurate?" Helen asked, staring at the holograph from the far end of the table.

"We designed Delphi," Trent said.

Above the rotating, four-layer concentric holographic structure, a two-story stone baroque building appeared. "There's no direct access from the surface structure to the inner ring," Brocks said. Holographic arrows pointed to four cross-hatches connecting the rings on the upper, white level, on the second, yellow level, and on the third, orange level. "Bridges link the rings at ninety-degree intervals on the top three levels." Two additional holographic arrows appeared on the fourth, red level. "And at one-hundred-eighty-degree intervals on the bottom. All continuously monitored, of course."

"Where will Kevin be?"

"That will be determined when you arrive."

"Just me and Trent are supposed to pull this off?"

"It's strictly an 'AntiGen' operation," Trent said. "We're it."

"McGovern will be equipped with several innovations that should offset the manpower shortage," Brocks said. "You go tomorrow night."

Helen jumped up. "By that time, they could—"

"You'll need the cover of darkness. Plus it's too late to begin the operation tonight."

"We can't wait!"

"Thank you, Ms. Bergmann. That will be all for this evening. McGovern will brief you at the appropriate time. For now, get some sleep. Tomorrow will be—intense."

"Brocks, I swear, if Kevin's dead because we delayed, I'll get you myself!" The door slid closed behind her.

She thinks she loves him, Brocks thought. *Love.* She snorted. *It won't last. It never lasts.*

"The briefing?" Trent asked.

Brocks slid a disk down the table to him. "That's the profile. Study it. Your primary goal is to extract Kincaid. But your mission has additional objectives." At the bottom of the rotating holographic rings appeared a violet disk. "Level Five. We need to know what's there." She told him everything.

"Proactive option?" he asked after she finished.

"No. If it's what we think, it can be replaced. We just need confirmation. Also," she smiled, "we have an uncorroborated report that Eric Bertram himself will visit Delphi tomorrow. This may be the only chance we'll ever get."

Trent whistled. "Alive?"

"If at all possible." She turned off the projection. "You know the scope of this mission. The likelihood of failure." She leaned forward and clasped her hands. "You're authorized to employ an NNEMP with a ten-mile radius."

"Won't the Collaborate realize that we're behind it?"

"Eventually. But Delphi will be effectively isolated from the outside world."

"Not for long."

"We've considered that, too. We can't permit them to begin to implement."

"By that, I take it that the contingency plan has been approved?"

She nodded.

He hesitated. "That would be a mistake."

"The order comes from the Agency director, himself. The ramp-up for Operation WorldSweep is already under way. So if you want to stop our Final Solution—"

"I know. It's up to me."

8

SATURDAY, JANUARY 25
Potter County (North-Central Pennsylvania)   *3:18 P.M.*

Helen watched the helicopter disappear beneath the forest horizon. Sun filtered through barren white pines. A chilling gust surged
through the snow-covered clearing. Granular flakes began drifting,
hiding traces of where she and Trent had been dropped into the
wilderness. Her white thermal suit blended into the snowy terrain.
Pop!
She dropped to the snow.
At the edge of the clearing, Trent knelt, rifle at his shoulder. A cord
shot high into the air and entwined within the branches of a towering
pine tree. He tugged firmly on the cable dangling from the tree,
attached a pulley system, hooked on a camouflaged bag, and, hand
over hand, hoisted it into the air. In moments, the bag was invisibly
nestled sixty feet overhead. Trent melded the bottom of the dangling
cord into the lowest branches. From a pocket in his thermal suit, he
removed a palm-sized electronic notebook and touched a keypad.
Overhead, the canvas bag beeped.
"What is that!"
"RFW, specifically a tactical NNEMP," Trent said, straightening
his backpack.
"Huh?"
"Radiofrequency high-powered microwave weapon. Nonnuclear
explosives wrapped in special antennae. When detonated, it generates

a dense, broadband, high-intensity, short-duration electromagnetic pulse that induces a voltage surge in any electrical device, from can opener to mainframe. That one," pointing overhead, "will fry every piece of electronics within ten miles that hasn't been sufficiently hardened," pointing to his control pad, "like this gizmo here."

"Hardened?"

"Having specially designed electrical components resistant to an EM burst." Handing her a fully loaded nine-millimeter with silencer, "Use this with restraint."

She clicked off the safety.

"They're forecasting snow. It might cover our tracks." At his side, he secured an ominous-looking weapon that resembled an Uzi with an elongated silencer. "It'll be dark soon. Better get moving."

"How far is it?"

He checked the display on his control pad. "Exactly 6.32 miles. North-northwest."

"Miles? In snow?"

"This was the closest safe insertion point." He moved his hand to his weapon. "Keep up."

She stood, gloved hands on hips, "Or else I wind up like the others?"

He glared at her, his breath condensing like Satanic smoke. "You and I have a lot of ground to cover."

Executive Quarters, Level One (Southeast Quadrant), Delphi

". . . then, add Streptavidin to the cochleate cylinder to activate . . ."

Loring fast-forwarded through twenty minutes of Kincaid's interrogation. On the monitor, white-coated figures zipped around Kincaid, lying on a gurney. At the bottom of the screen, an imprinted time clock whizzed by. He clicked as the clock approached 22:53:30—

"You're certain that's the polypeptide sequence for V_7's harpoon?" Dr. Ambrose asked Kincaid. Ambrose's hairy neck obscured Kincaid's face from the camera.

"That's what I used," the bedridden Kincaid droned.

Ambrose turned to Delphi Director Spann. "We have it, sir."

"Upload that to the mainframe," he said. Ambrose shifted to his left. "Begin synthesis at once, Doctor."

Loring replayed the video's final thirty seconds while focusing on the gurney. For an instant, he glimpsed Kincaid's face. He reran it, zoomed in on his face the half-second it was exposed, played it again, and freeze-framed: Kincaid's lips were definitely moving. Loring buzzed a technician standing by in Central Security. "Enhance the audio at 22:53:58."

"Enhance for what, sir?" the man asked by intercom.

"Kincaid's voice. He's saying something I can't hear."

A series of weak, rumbling sounds emanated from the speakers. Cycle after cycle, the garbled sounds grew stronger.

". . . zepdhmiid . . ."
". . . sepdhmiizd . . ."
". . . sept dh miise d . . ."
". . . cept th mise d . . ."

"Is that the best you can do?" Loring asked.

"Yessir. The subject wasn't completely vocalizing. We can't pick up what wasn't there."

"What about lipreading?"

"Kincaid was obscured from the camera during most of that interval, sir."

Loring replayed the jumbled words in his mind. It sounded like— *mice?* He pressed a touch key on his remote. Lab Director Ambrose's low-ridged face appeared on-screen. "Status?"

"Proceeding well, sir," Ambrose answered. "I believe we'll have the vector synthesized within thirty-six hours."

"Encountering any unforeseen problems?"

"None so far, sir. Kincaid's dictum appears flawless. In fact, in chelating with EDTA—"

"Have you downloaded the information?" Loring asked.

"Yes, sir. To GenPerfekt in Boise and PolyPepGen in Frisco."

"Good. Now, I've been reviewing Kincaid's interrogation. You were the last one to question him. At the end, did he whisper anything? Something about mice, perhaps?"

"No, sir."

Loring switched off the monitor. *Bertram's due within hours. It's probably nothing, but now's not the time for surprises.* He clicked on the intercom. "Rouse our guest!"

Stevenson's Office, Delphi

Marguerite hadn't seen Roderick Stevenson since he'd been called away yesterday. He wasn't in his quarters, Medlab, or Pathlab. And except for a brief visit with Meredith, she'd been waiting for him in his office since 7 A.M. When she asked a few technicians passing by the office as to where he was, they shook their heads and scurried away.

The outer door opened. In crumpled surgical greens, Stevenson, face drooping, eyes dark, shuffled into the room and stumbled past her into the inner office. She followed him in and found him seated, facing the rear wall, his back to her.

"Dr. Kevin Kincaid, the man who created K_4, is here," he began.

She sucked in her cheeks. "Is he, now!"

"We're the ones that abused it, Marguerite, not him." He rocked in his swivel chair. "We've been interrogating him. He's developed a new vector, V_7. Supposedly, it works. Ambrose is synthesizing it on the lower levels."

"Opportunity," he had said before. "Could it save Meredith's life?"

"Possibly, but consensus is that Meredith is too far gone. They'd rather start fresh, in a controlled trial."

"They have the medicine to save her, but won't?"

"The final decision rests with a super-VIP expected to arrive shortly. I'm not optimistic."

"Do something!"

"If I did, would you be willing to risk your life, too?"

Was he asking for help or trying to entrap her?

"I understand your indecision," he said. "But—if I was going to turn you in, I'd have done it by now. And the plain fact is that we're running out of time."

She stared at the back of his chair. "How can I help?"

Marguerite sat listening quietly to each desperate step of Stevenson's plan. She felt as if she were trapped on the balcony of a building ablaze, flames at her back, bone-smashing concrete awaiting far below.

"When you return, there will be a CD in your upper left desk drawer. Take it," he said. "It'll contain the synthesis protocol for Kincaid's vector. If you and Meredith make it out of the complex, it might save her life."

She nodded. "And how do you get out?"

He hesitated. "One of us must hold the hammer."

Recreation Facility, Level One, Outer Ring, Delphi

Armed guards shadowed Kevin as he stumbled along curved, windowless walls that disappeared around the bend and formed the main promenade. As he walked along the deserted concourse, he noticed signs for various recreational facilities, including arcades, VR booths, golf simulation rooms, pool and Ping-Pong tables, a gymnasium, and a mini-theater. The arteries in his temples pounded. *They drugged me,* he thought. *Again.*

A figure emerged from an alcove ahead and motioned him to follow. "This way, Dr. Kincaid."

"Loring! You bastard!"

Kevin dashed toward the man. A heel caught him from behind and sent him reeling onto the floor. The guards grabbed him, carried him into a library off the main corridor, and slung him onto a black Naugahyde couch. Loring sat cross-legged in a recliner across from a butler table. Two guards stood at attention beside him, two more behind him.

"Dr. Kincaid, you are fired," Loring declared. "The lab you destroyed cost forty million dollars. I accept Mastercard, Visa, American Express, even a personal check."

"Too bad you weren't in it."

Loring chuckled, then pointed to an 18th-century sterling silver tea service. He poured himself and Kevin rich, aromatic cups. "Darjeeling, one of life's true delicacies. Frederick Grayson opened my eyes to it."

Kevin glanced around the room. "Where is the bastard? I figured he'd be at your side."

The smile dissipated from Loring's face. "Dead, I'm sorry to say."

Kevin smirked. As he picked up his cup of tea, a cold gun barrel touched his neck: a warning not to throw the hot liquid in his host's face. "Did you have him killed, too?"

After sipping, "I know you won't believe this, but once we've finished our chat, you're going to *want* to work with us." He took a small remote from his pocket and clicked. A screen lowered behind him. The picture snapped on: a man lying in a hospital bed in isolation, his arms heavily bandaged.

"Where is Donny?"

"Where he's always been—safe in Keystate Hospital. We just switched rooms." The video zoomed in on the foot of the bed, on the input-output sheet. "You'll notice continuous entries for today's date. And the time. The last entry was made an hour ago."

Kevin threw his teacup over the couch's arm. "You won't get V_7. Not for Donny's life! Not for mine!"

Loring placed the cup and saucer on the butler table. "I already have it."

Kevin's body chilled.

"We extracted the vector formulation from you hours ago. It's being synthesized two levels below us as we speak."

Including the modification? Kevin's mind screamed. *But if he has the V_7 modification, why is he talking to me?*

"For you and I to build a working relationship, we must clear up some misconceptions."

No, he can't have it! Does he suspect there's more? Is that what this is all about?

"To begin with, I did *not* order your wife and children killed."

"You're lying!"

"The rather grim-looking man you keep running into, the man you know as Briggs—his actual name is Blount—was overenthusiastic in executing—poor choice of words—his orders. For that, I am profoundly sorry. Blount was instructed to break into your uncle's residence and retrieve Protein X-ACT, which was legally and morally *my* property. Blount chose to char his tracks. I tried to save your life, and your family's."

"The hell you did!"

Loring snapped his fingers. Kevin heard the following piped around him:

> "Dr. Kincaid speaking," Kevin's voice began.
>
> "Doctor, I'm the head nurse on the neural wing. Your patient Mrs. Fitzroy's spinal cord implant may have dislodged," a low, muffled, gravelly voice said. "There's evidence of cerebrospinal fluid leakage. Possibly a broken lead wire on the implant."
>
> "I understand," Kevin's voice responded. "Right."
>
> "Her temp's way up, too—103.5. We're concerned she has a systemic infection."
>
> "Uh-huh. I'll be there ASAP."

The words, the conversation carried him back to the emergency call at Dermot's house.

"Is that authentic?" Loring asked.

Kevin nodded.

"You never did learn who that husky-voiced nurse was who called you back to the hospital on a false emergency, did you?" Loring asked. As Kevin shook his head, Loring said, "In retrospect, one might argue that that phone conversation saved your life. Had you not been called away, you might have died along with the rest of your family."

"You killed them!"

The on-screen picture of Donny disappeared, replaced by grid lines. Loring replayed a piece of the conversation spoken by the unidentified voice:

". . . she has a systemic infection."

An intricately folded jagged line appeared on the grid line.

"The nurse's voiceprint," Loring said.

"So?"

"She has a systemic infection," Loring said.

His voiceprint of those words appeared below the other pattern. The two patterns slowly moved toward each other, superimposed, merged. They were identical.

"You!"

"Yes, Doctor, *I* placed the call. Blount didn't see anyone else in the van with you. I never intended for your wife or children to be hurt. I am profoundly sorry."

Kevin was again in the worn minivan, driving along the marina. After a moment, he focused on Loring. "And what's your excuse for Helen?"

"I just—oh, you mean Helen Morgan as in Tracy Bergmann! You can't honestly believe she loved you? She was a terrorist, consumed with avenging her father. Nothing more."

"How do you justify Natcher Center?"

"The future is more beautiful than you can imagine. But for it to unfold, humanity must not see it coming. Your speech would have changed all that." He poured another cup of tea. "Besides, what are a few hundred compared to unborn billions?"

"If you already have V_7, what do you want from me?"

"I want you to help guide the future. Not be a relic in it."

"*Your* future."

"We'll have our first batch of V_7 tomorrow. We'll be assaying tissue culture transfection rates within a week. If those tests are successful, technically, there will be no reason to keep you."

"Don't expect me to cheerfully put my head on your chopping block."

"There's no one out there for you, Kevin. Where would you go? The world believes you dead. And if you did suddenly appear, there's sufficient evidence to implicate you in the bombing." Loring waved his arms. "Delphi is truly a wondrous place! Come to know it! Here, we all work for the betterment of man."

"Kill me and get it over with."

"Keep an open mind, Doctor. Besides your brother, I can offer you something no one else in this world can."

"Blount's head on a stick?"

"That, too."

Kevin released a furious laugh. "What else could *you* ever offer that would interest me?"

Loring abruptly stood. The guards came to attention. "You'll understand, once you've seen Delphi."

"Another shop of horrors like Tiburon?"

Guards hoisted Kevin to his feet. "Tiburon was a shoddy experimental station in the third world. Delphi is state-of-the-art." He started toward the exit.

As the guards dragged Kevin, he yelled, "There's no difference! Here you just brew your horrors in nicer cells!"

Loring whipped around. "Yes! And I'm brewing two especially for you!"

Central Security, Level Two, Delphi

The guard pressed his hand against the palm pad. "You can go in now."

Marguerite hesitated before entering Central Security. *I can do this!* she thought.

Occupying the entire northeast quadrant of inner Level Two, Central Security resembled a miniature mission control room of the old Johnson Space Center: rows of computer consoles with a giant screen across a hemispheric wall, and a raised glass box with stadium seating in the rear. Surrounding the main screen, monitors viewed the entire campus from swiveling infrared scans of the grounds to corridors, labs, and selected private offices. Down front, a platform led to a biometric-secured elevator. She checked for security personnel: one, two—

"What're you doin' here?" a third demanded, stepping in front of her.

She looked up at a burly, bull-necked security officer. "Uh, I'm Marguerite Moraes. Dr. Stevenson sent me here to get clearance for the lower levels. See, I'm only cleared up to this level," pointing at her yellow badge, then handing him a folded request form. As he examined the document, she glanced at his nameplate: Deputy Security Chief Ross.

The guard leered. "I'll have to confirm this. Wait here." He went to a console and navigated through personnel screens. "Come here. Gimme your badge. I'll key in a new one." He turned to the console behind him and began entering security codes.

She closed in from behind. "You can monitor the entire complex from here, can't you?"

He turned on her. "Get back. You're not supposed to see this."

"I'm so sorry," she said, pressing a tiny transmitter hidden in her lab coat.

Ross finished keying in the information. He turned and handed her a powder-blue badge.

A blaring siren sounded.

He whipped around toward the console.

"What is it?" Marguerite cried out.

"Fire! In pathology lab!"

Other guards quickly joined him. They all looked up. Overhead monitors snapped on, each carrying the image of Stevenson, partially shrouded by CO_2 gas spewing from a fire extinguisher that he directed at a benchtop.

Marguerite approached the console. She glanced down. There were the access codes! She quickly memorized them.

"Little accident down here," Stevenson called, his face prominently displayed on a dozen plasma screens, each presenting a different angle. "I left some formaldehyde too close to a heat source. Don't worry. Everything's under control."

Level Three, Delphi

Delphi personnel respectfully nodded as the electric cart puttered through Level Three's outer-ring corridor. Kevin glanced back at the armed guards riding in back, jogging warily behind and ahead on foot, and riding shotgun. Loring, the cart's driver, hit the accelerator. The cart lurched forward. Kevin braced himself in the backseat.

There's nothing he could show me to make me want to stay, Kevin thought. But Loring's last words on the Level One promenade haunted him. What could the man be "brewing"?

Doors parted ahead and to the left. Loring swerved the cart. They shot through a long, seamless tube thirty feet in diameter. Kevin scanned sleek walls whizzing by while looking for some forgotten opening that might lead to the surface. His rapid tour of Level Two's Medlab, Pathlab, the OR theaters, and Central Security had exposed no weaknesses. And even if he somehow reached the surface, Delphi was many miles from the nearest village, or so Loring had warned him. The cart stopped at the end of the tube. The lead guard entered a coded sequence on a touchpad, then placed his hand on a scanner.

They entered an expanse with a high-domed atrium. Laminar air-flow clean-benches, glassware, orbital shakers, centrifuges, PCR tubes, high-density lane sequencing systems with software interface analyzers, robotic arms swinging well plates for large-scale screenings, gas chromatographs, and ultra-low-temperature freezers spread to the horizon. Two dozen white-coated technicians turned toward the electric cart.

One man in a white coat rushed up to Kevin and shook his right hand vigorously. "Dr. Kincaid, it's a real honor!"

Loring pointed at the man. "Dr. Culver Ambrose, our director of research."

"Dr. Kincaid, your expression vector's delivery system is *brilliant*," Ambrose exclaimed. He turned around and gestured to the technicians who politely applauded. "We're synthesizing V_7 now. Would you care to help us, Dr. Kincaid?"

"Not a chance in hell!"

"Return to work, Ambrose." Loring floored the cart, spinning Ambrose onto the floor.

As they paraded down the path, Kevin watched lab techs gawk at him as if he were a holy incarnation. *Do any of you have any idea what you're doing?* he thought as he scanned their faces. Then he remembered: only a week ago, he'd been one of them.

"This lab's five times larger than BFMC's." Loring said. "Delphi is the most productive lab of its kind in the world. We've synthesized cloning vectors that don't express the inserted DNA like V_7, but just propagate it. We've synthesized insertion vectors that target specific positions in a host-DNA sequence and insert the vector and the foreign DNA, genes and all. We've synthesized replacement vectors that target positions in a host-DNA sequence and knock out specific genes. And last but not least, we've synthesized expression vectors like yours that insert foreign DNA into host cells and lead to synthesis of foreign polypeptide products—proteins. But of course, none of our expression vectors begins to match the scope and complexity of V_7." The cart scooted around a corner. "People used to think that sequencing genes was what really mattered. NIH's Human Genome Project and J. Craig Venter with The Institute for Genomic Research, all knocking themselves out to completely sequence human DNA—that genius went a long way. But not far enough. Identifying gene sequences isn't the key. Here, at Delphi, through intensive cloning of human genes, by homologous gene matching among human individuals, by paralogous gene matching among other members of the same human gene family, and by orthologous gene matching among other mammalian species, we've identified the subtleties of more human genes than any other place on the planet. But far more important than sequencing genes, we've learned to understand the language of *proteins*."

"Enter my uncle's program," Kincaid said.

"Yes, of course! Once you know a gene's function and the protein that's ultimately transcribed from it, through RNA intermediaries, you can work backward to figure out the gene's exact DNA sequence. Dermot Kincaid's Protein X-ACT software made it possible to elegantly predict how subtle changes in a protein's sequence of amino acids could alter its shape, its function, its utility. That surreptitious 'library' of proteins from the patent office you stumbled into? Most were designed and synthesized right here in Delphi."

"Like U.S. patent number 15,428,609. NMDA-Receptor, One and Two, Enhancer Seven is designed to facilitate NMDA receptor subunits at post-synaptic neurotransmitter receptor sites to allow overall faster transmission of glutamate neurotransmitters!" Kevin recited verbatim, seeing the words from days ago in his home.

"And others for altering muscle structure," Loring said. "It was straightforward sequencing the DNA and synthesizing the genes that would code for the new proteins." He pointed to both sides of the speeding cart. "In fact, we're now passing where most of that work was done."

Kevin glanced at the sequence analyzers and robotic arms on the bench tops. "Isolated genes are meaningless. They need to be strung on chromosomes. And you needed some mechanism on the chromosomes to control those genes—a way to turn them on and off. Otherwise, you get overproduction or underproduction of proteins coded by those genes."

Loring perfunctorily waved at the technicians. "We've taken regulatory genes from human systems: promoters that turn on protein production from RNA coded by DNA genes; enhancers that increase protein production from genes even more when needed; silencers that shut down protein production. And in just the proper balance to make our designer genes work."

"And you stuck your biologically regulated, functional designer genes—"

"On *'designer chromosomes.'* Yes, I've always liked that term. They've been making human artificial chromosomes since 1997. We, however, have refined them to near perfection."

"The 24th chromosome pair."

"Yes. That specimen from Tiburon contained one of our designer chromosomes. So, here we'd developed this marvelous new chromosome chockfull of our synthetic designer genes, and no vector to get it into the cell nucleus where it would work." He shrugged. "So, we had to make do with what was available. Which led to that primitive, ugly little facility. In retrospect, I'm glad we discontinued it."

"So you moved your Island of Dr. Moreau east."

Loring slowed the cart, his speech. "Tiburon was an outpost. This was, and is, the pinnacle of genetic science research. You'll appreciate that, once you're in charge."

"That will never happen."

The cart stopped. Loring switched positions with the guard. "Take us to Level Four." As the cart shot forward, Loring gazed back at Kevin. "In Tiburon, we experimented with physical improvements, transfecting subjects with a designer chromosome to enhance the musculoskeletal system. To improve physical prowess and manual dexterity." He leaned into Kevin's face. "But in Delphi, we moved beyond, to what life is all about."

Overlooking Delphi

"Tired?" Trent asked.

Six miles of cross-country hiking through snow-covered white pines had left Helen panting in the granular powder, her night-vision goggles eerily transforming the impenetrable dark woods into shades of olive green. In a glen half a mile beyond the woods stood a dual-winged stone building. High windows offset large wooden doors recessed beneath Doric columns and pediment. She found it a cross between a rotunda-less U.S. Capitol and an austere middle school.

"Delphi," Trent said.

She scanned the building, the grounds. "No guards?"

"To your left. At the circular drive."

She noticed six dark shapes emerge from the main entrance. "They've spotted us!"

"They have not. Now, sit tight," Trent ordered. "Perfect. That's probably their entire aboveground security force."

"Just six guards to patrol all this ground?"

"Too many guards draw attention. They tend to make locals think you're hiding something. The Collaborate greased a lot of state and yokel palms to have this place conveniently forgotten."

"And who greased the federal palms?" she asked.

He ignored her.

The guards formed two rows flanking the driveway. "What are they doing?"

"Lining up for parade."

"For Loring?"

"Loring's already here. I don't— Remove your goggles."

She obeyed. The green pseudo-lit forest disappeared, turning black, like the bowels of an isolation tank. Trent opened his palm pad and touched a corner. A tiny holographic projection appeared six inches above the ground. Helen immediately recognized the concentric, cylinder-shaped schematic of Delphi.

"They're probably holding Kincaid on Level One." The upper-most portion of the dual cylinders expanded, revealing an inner core divided into quadrants by four tubes, each adjacent to an elevator, and connecting to smaller compartments lining the outer ring. "If so, he's either off the promenade," pointing to a compartment due north on the outer ring, "near administration," pointing to the northern two quadrants of the central core, "or in the executive quarters here," pointing to the southern two quadrants of the central core.

"If not?"

"Then Level Two." The second slice of the dual cylinders expanded, revealing a similar structure. Pointing at the upper-right quadrant of the central core, "Central Security or," pointing to the other three core quadrants, "possibly Medlab, Pathlab, or an OR theater."

Helen noticed a small rectangular outline within the Main Security quadrant drawn like—elevators? "What about the two lower levels?"

The third and fourth levels expanded. Both appeared structurally similar to Level Two. "Those contain the main labs."

Helen scrutinized Levels Three and Four. She saw no schematic of the elevator that had appeared in Central Security. If the elevator on Level Two didn't access the lower levels, or Level One, where did it lead? "Basically, you're saying that Kevin could be anywhere in the complex."

"With this," tapping on the computer notepad, "I can directly access Delphi's internal surveillance system and locate him. In fact, I could disable the whole security system."

"But you won't, will you?"

Weak holographic light distorted Trent's face, creating false ridges over his eyes. He looked ghoulish. "The higher the tech, the stronger the finger points to DARPA."

"And you can't risk that, of course," she said sarcastically. She leaned into the holograph. "Then maybe you can tell me where that extra elevator in the security office leads."

Trent dissolved the holograph, leaving them in darkness.

"There's another level, isn't there? Something you haven't shown me."

"There's always another level," he said. "None of us knows them all."

"What's the rest of *your* mission?"

No answer.

"Tell me, or—"

"The gun's pointed at your heart. Please don't make me kill you."

Helen stared straight into the darkness. She realized that her automatic was out of position, at her side. But he was in the dark, too, and wouldn't know that. "And mine's pointed at yours."

"No, it's not," he said. "I'm wearing the goggles again."

Helen clenched her jaw. Checkmate. "This must be familiar for you. Always seeing the light while those around you are left blind in the dark."

Silence.

She hadn't expected that reaction from him. The Trent she knew would have reacted to her insult by launching into one of his famous tirades. She replayed her time with Trent at Site 341 and on the mission: the man had shown no signs of his familiar cheerful, bipolar self. No charming, familial appeal to their common cause followed by a sudden, unprovoked verbal or physical thrashing. In fact, Trent had shown no signs of any emotion at all. "So how was it, watching the rest of the group being slaughtered?"

"You think you know. Why don't you tell me?"

"Smugness, superiority, with some amusement thrown in. Am I close?"

"I warned them, repeatedly," he said. "They wouldn't listen."

"They always did before. Why not this time? Could it be because they no longer served your purpose?"

"I thought you hated AntiGen."

"Anna and Straub died for me." She sighed. "Yes, I wanted out, but I believed in what we were doing. And I didn't want our people to die. Can you say the same?"

"Paint me the monster. It's easier that way."

"Trent, you always called us *family*. Did any part of you ever mean that, even in the loosest sense of the word?"

"Families don't last. You know that. So does Kincaid."

"My family and Kevin's were real. Yours was—I don't know what to call it."

He hesitated. "I'm more like you than you think."

"I doubt it."

"You don't know the first thing about me," he said. "Not even my real name."

"So what is your real name?"

"Like yours, it no longer has any meaning."

"And what great tragedy makes you so much like Kevin and me?"

"You forget I'm still holding the gun."

"Your facade may have changed, but you're the same liar as always."

He took a series of long, forceful breaths. "Maybe my family was killed in a car accident. Or a plane crash. Or a bombing. Or maybe my wife just got up early one morning, took the kids, and disappeared. It's not important what tragedy we experience. What matters is how we deal with it. You didn't find me pining for my family for ten years like Kincaid. Or spending my life trying to get revenge like you. The point is, I dedicated myself to my missions, and served with honor. Not with whimpering or rage."

What happened to him? Helen wondered, but said, "Did I say I believed you? You're a user, Trent. That's all you know."

Something plopped beside her. She glanced down. Felt it: his gun. "Go ahead," he said. "Use it."

She picked up the gun, pointed it at him, and put on her goggles. Hands clasped around his knees, goggleless, he stared impassively in her direction. It would be so easy. "I need you to get Kevin out."

"Doesn't that make you a user, too?"

"We may not be on the same side, but we shouldn't be working against each other, either." She handed him back his weapon. "Trent, considering all we've been through, and what we still have to face, wouldn't mutual trust increase our chances?"

He chuckled. "Meaning that you want me to be honest with you."

"Damn you, Trent. For once, can't—"

"I'll tell you whatever you want to know—as long as it doesn't compromise the mission or the Agency. *And* isn't personal."

"Okay. Great." She watched him put on his goggles. "Before we get started, there's something that's been bothering me since I met Brocks. Something maybe you can answer."

"Ask."

"Brocks strikes me as an extremely bright woman. She conceived AntiGen, which was brilliant. She also planned for me to seduce Kevin by becoming his wife and stealing his vector. Yet even a basic psych profile would have made it clear that he'd never have given up his life's work for a pretty face—even his wife's. Tell me, Trent, how could such an extremely capable woman have concocted such an inherently flawed, inane plan?"

He sighed. "The intelligence director had—emotional components driving her plan."

"What do you mean?"

"If you repeat a word of what I'm going to tell, I will kill you," he stated.

There was no doubt in that voice.

"A little over two years ago, as Brocks was preparing to become director, she was in the throes of a deeply painful divorce." With a slight quiver in his voice, "Perhaps this contributed to her skewed perception of marriage and intimacy, something she thought she could use to manipulate Kincaid." Trent checked his weapon. "And that's all I'll say."

"All right, then. What about that extra elevator in the security office?"

"It leads to Level Five. And before you ask, I don't know what's there."

Helen noticed that the guards had lined up by the circular drive. "What are the cadets doing down there? Why are we waiting?"

"Eric Bertram," he whispered. "The Chairman himself is due to arrive."

"I thought you said—"

"No one inside or outside of the Collaborate has seen him in years."

"Brocks wants you to terminate him?" Answering her own question, "No, she wants him alive." Helen turned back to the guards lining Delphi's entrance. "So we're supposed to get Kevin *and* Bertram? What if you can't rescue them both?"

"Technically, we only need the formulation for V_7."

Helen dug her hands into the snow and threw an iceball at Trent's face. He effortlessly ducked. "You're asking me to betray him! Again!"

"He's liable to be confused, drugged. He may not even know the truth about his brother. He'll need someone to trust, to focus on: *you*. We need to know exactly, precisely what he's told them about the vector. He might not tell me the truth, but he will tell you."

"What if he's already given them V_7?"

Trent checked his watch. "If he has, in roughly three hours and forty-five minutes, the EMP will detonate. The entire complex will be hit by a massive EM pulse. Ground and air transportation systems will be downed. Communications will be knocked out. And Delphi's computer system will be a scrap heap."

"Won't they suspect DARPA?"

"EMPs are potential terrorist weapons. Which is why a cover story has already been released that I've been sighted in this area. They might buy that I'm the one who stuck it to them."

Helen thought about the plan. It had one significant weakness. "You're banking that none of Kevin's data were downloaded to any other Collaborate site."

"If there's evidence proving the contrary, the Agency is prepared to eradicate Delphi—and commence simultaneous global-coordinated assassinations of Collaborate members. It's desperate and ill-conceived, but—get down!"

A staccato *thwump-thwump* sound approached overhead. The treetops swayed to the beat of mini–air bursts. Muffled engine noises grew in pitch. Snowflakes swirled from trees as they were kicked up from above.

A helicopter! Helen thought, burying herself in the snow. "They've found us!"

A ground-cloud of snow danced around them. The copter rotor slammed gusts down against her back. Whining engine sounds peaked. Then dropped in pitch—fading, fading. The snow cloud settled around them. She lifted her head. Delphi's grounds erupted in bright white light, like a football coliseum for a night game. She tore off her goggles.

Delphi shined, a bright, lonely outpost in a sea of dark trees as the helicopter honed in on the circular landing site near the main entrance.

Level Four, Delphi

Kevin sat back in the cart. They entered a laboratory, a quarter the size of the main lab, one level above. More intimate, the place felt like a traditional physiology-general biology laboratory: black slate-top benches, cell culture incubators, brown-tinted bottles, pipettes, and microscopes. At the back of the lab, in the far corner to his left, was a sealed door marked "Electron Microscopy." Lab workers tended cages with white mice and rats stacked behind a plastic window.

Loring said, "This is Neurolab. We also have an extensive mathematical-modeling lab on the far side." The cart crawled on. "You know, Doctor, human beings today are no smarter than they were a hundred millennia ago. Oh, today we use telecommunication satellites instead of smoke signals, supersonic transports instead of hollowed-out logs. But Man himself remains essentially unchanged." He smiled. "We're changing all that—"

"With neurotransmitter receptors," Kevin finished.

"As you very well know, neurons in the brain and central spinal cord communicate with each other at synaptic junctions. Connections are made from the transmitting nerve's presynaptic edge to the receiving nerve's postsynaptic cleft by neurotransmitting chemicals that traverse the gap between them. Vesicles in the transmitting nerve excrete neurotransmitters that bind to specific receptor sites on the receiving nerve. Once a neurotransmitter has bound to the receiving nerve, it changes the nerve's permeability to ions like sodium and potassium—which, in turn, changes its electrical potential. With assistance from Protein X-ACT, we've figured out how to change those neurotransmitter receptors. We can make them bind more quickly to the neurotransmitters. We can speed up neuron transmissions. We can make the brain work faster."

"You're using glutamate, aren't you?"

"Glutamate is a prime neurotransmission of cognitive processes. We've been concentrating on the glutamate APMA-kinate receptors, because they evoke fast, voltage-independent synaptic responses, voltage-dependent NMDA-receptors, and metabotropic-subtype receptors, because they exert long-lasting neural signals. We back-coded for the genes that would produce these neural enhancers, placed them with gene regulators on the q arm of our designer chromosome, position 23q11 through 23q14, I believe, and used your vector K_4 to transfect experimental subjects."

"What kind of experimental subjects?" Kevin asked between clenched teeth.

"Developing human fetuses, of course."

Kevin lunged at Loring. Guards pulled his arms tight up his back. "Loring, the brain's a vast web of intricate neural networks—constantly sifting and analyzing information. It's a delicate balance of stimulating and inhibiting nerves, switching 'on' and 'off.' You just can't turn nerves on constantly! You short-circuit the brain!"

"Yin and yang, Doctor," Loring said evenly. "Light and dark. We observed the balance between inhibition and excitation of nerve cells and accounted for it through other designer genes on the chromosome."

"Glutamate induces long-term potentiation in the hippocampus and long-term depression in the cerebellum. With excessive glutamate neurotransmission, nerve cells degenerate. You get grand mal. Even status epilepticus. Massively stimulate glutamate receptors, and you destroy the brain!"

"On the contrary. We've produced spectacular increases in the children's working memory, like RAM, as well as permanent synaptic plasticity that's led to tremendous long-term recall. MRI and PET scans of the CA1 region of the hippocampus demonstrate significant increases in activity and physical development."

"*Children?*" Kevin whispered.

"You should've seen them. Toddlers, geniuses all. Each more bril-liant than any human being beyond the confines of this complex."

"What happened to them?"

"K_4. Incomplete transfection. Some brain cells incorporated the new chromosome. Others didn't. The result was unbalanced neural transmissions, leading to profound epilepsy, status epilepticus, and eventual neural deterioration. In any case, V_7 will solve the problem."

"The hell it will."

"Really?" Loring stopped the cart. "And just why not?"

Kevin realized his impulsive outburst had been a mistake—a big one.

Loring leaned close to him. "Is there a problem with V_7?"

"Not that I'm aware of." He hesitated. "I simply meant that K_4 didn't kill those children—your goddamn chromosome did! So you won't fare any better with V_7!"

Loring's eyes narrowed. He stared at Kevin a full fifteen seconds. Then said, "The autopsies indicate otherwise." To the driver, "The ele-vator in Central Security." Back to Kevin, "You'll soon have the opportunity to build on our work."

"Never!"

"You'll change your mind on Level Five."

Delphi's Landing Pad   *6:35 P.M.*

Lewis Spann squinted against snow spray kicked up by the heli-copter's rotor. Delphi's security guards stiffened as the copter's struts touched the snowy pad. The sounds of its engine abated. The rotors spun slowly from residual momentum.

Spann could not stop wondering whether the man on that heli-copter was, indeed, the Chairman. No one had seen the man in twenty-five years. But the visitor had correctly responded to the Chairman's private codes and had answered detailed queries that only the Chair-man himself could know. However, assuming the man on board was Eric Bertram led to a more provocative question: why was he here *now*?

The copter door opened. Four heavily armed bodyguards emerged and quickly checked the pad and building exterior. Spann smoothed a crease in his overcoat, then strode toward the copter. A figure in a long, dark wool coat with a matching, wide-brimmed hat stepped out, glanced at his guards, then trekked across the snow to the build-ing portico.

"Mr. Chairman, sir, I'm Lewis Spann, Executive Administrator."

The hat's brim, tipped forward, hid all but the Chairman's mouth. "Where is Mr. Loring?" Bertram asked, passing him without breaking stride.

"Interrogating Kincaid, sir."

"I thought we already had the information."

"Mr. Loring has a few additional questions. I'd be happy to debrief you, sir."

The hat nodded. "See that I meet with him privately when I'm finished."

Spann caught a glimpse of the face beneath the hat. "Uh—Mr. Loring will certainly be surprised."

"It won't be the last time."

Stevenson's Office, Delphi

Marguerite had been in the bathroom for some time, safe from the potentially prying view of the office surveillance camera. After the incident in Central Security, chances were that they were being watched. Stevenson slipped in and shut the bathroom door. Both hoped that anyone watching would forget that she was already in there, waiting.

She handed Stevenson a scrap of paper with the codes. "You timed it close."

"I started the fire the instant I got your signal." He committed the password and codes to memory. "Who was the guard?"

"Ross."

"I thought it would be him." Stevenson sighed. "Marguerite, I have to leave now. You're clear on what you need to do and where you need to be?"

She nodded.

"The CD containing the vector synthesis protocol is in your desk." He reached for the doorknob. "I—probably won't see you again."

She took his trailing hand and placed his gently between hers. He tried to smile.

Central Security, Level Two, Delphi

I thought he said 'Level Five'. What are we doing on Level Two? Kevin wondered.

"Level Five is only accessible through Central Security," Loring said. Seeing Kevin's raised eyebrows, "No, I didn't read your mind. But I've watched you more than ten years. I know you, which is why I'm so certain that in the end, you'll share our dream."

The guard touched the palm pad. Doors opened. Four giant security personnel quickly surrounded their honored visitors. The security chief personally greeted them.

"Level Five," Loring commanded.

The chief snapped his fingers. Like a Formula One pit crew, several guards swiftly removed the badges on Loring's entourage, replaced them with violet ones, and accompanied them across a platform beneath the giant main screen on the hemispheric wall. The cart puttered into a guarded freight elevator capable of swallowing a tractor trailer and pivoted around. The elevator door slid closed with an iron jolt and began a slow, whining descent.

As they descended, the hairs on Kevin's forearms stood erect. His skin, chilled at first, grew increasingly warm. He felt as though he were descending into hell. "I remember, when I was very young, going to church with my mother."

"That would be between your fourth and seventh birthdays, when your mother was looking to religion to solve her problems." Loring chuckled. "Old St. Gregory's Cathedral, on Fifth and Mason streets, I believe."

Kevin shook his head. The man seemed to know everything. "I remember the old priest becoming apoplectic when he talked about Satan, about hell. Air choked with fire and smoke. Screaming souls forever condemned to agony from pitchforks and molten rock."

"Fear is an effective tool. Instill it in a child till he's six, you've got him for life." Loring smirked. "So, what brought that to the surface? Imagining me with horns and tail?" A wide smile spread across his face. "You're saying that I've lost my soul—that's it, isn't it? Or maybe I never had one?" Putting his hands on his hips, "My soul is the sum of my intellect, my drive, and the cohesive chemistry that forms me. The first is superior. The second, unparalleled. And the third comes more under the umbrella of the science I control every day. Don't wave religion in my face, Dr. Kincaid. It debases life's true miracles—the kind we make ourselves. The kind I'm about to show you!"

"You can't understand."

"Understand what? 'That I'm violating the laws of Man and God?' Damn it, Doctor, haven't you realized by now? God takes His cues from men."

Loring's last words echoed from Kevin's deep past. Kevin could see those words, hear them reverberating in his mind. It was as if he were in a great library with stacks whizzing by him, the books on those shelves becoming less and less technical. He was moving backward in time, his own time: before Loring, before BFMC, before the tragedy, before he met Helen, before med school, before college. There! It was a paraphrase, but it was close enough. He was sitting in tenth-grade English, reading aloud the words of World Controller Mustapha Mond's revelation to the Savage. And he could hear Helen's voice from just several nights back, describing her father's work in tissue engineering: *"Daddy mentioned in passing that he'd created some sort of bottle. It had a Russian name. Polish, maybe? Began with a B, I think."* It had to be: *Brave New World.* The elevator stopped. "You've built Bokanovsky bottles!"

"Huxley's term is unscientific, but, yes, Doctor, we've built freestanding artificial wombs."

Overlooking Delphi

The stadium lights that had illuminated Delphi's grounds winked out. Only spotlights remained on the copter resting near the front portico.

"Damn, I couldn't see him!" Trent lowered his binoculars and opened a palm pad. He whispered, "Deactivate TDTTS. Enable."

Its tiny screen flashed: Voice Command Acknowledged—Negotiating with Host.

"What are you doing?" Helen asked.

"At night the grounds are monitored by an automated thermal detection tracking and targeting system. It works on body heat. Anything larger than a rabbit comes under fire."

The screen flashed: Sham Mode Enabled—0:59:59

"I've tapped into their security system. Disabled IR perimeter surveillance. Their readings will appear normal for an hour before the system comes back online," he said. As Helen started to stand, he yanked her down by her shoulder. "I lead. When we're within two hundred yards, we crawl."

"But you said—"

"We're not invisible. We don't want to be detected too soon."

Level Five, Delphi

The cart rolled into a twilight-illuminated chamber the size of a football field. Gleaming, black, titanium-vanadium, four-foot horizontal cylinders, supported on freestanding poles, lined up in rows of fifty to the far wall. Kevin felt deep, pumping sounds churn around him—sounds primal, warm, comforting. Loring and guards put on earplugs as the cart proceeded down the main aisle bisecting the field of black cylinders.

"Sorry, Doctor. You don't get a pair," Loring said.

Their cart met up with two others in the center of the room. Earplugged, white-coated technicians respectfully nodded as Loring, with entourage in tow, got out and approached the near cylinder on his right. Kevin found the background sounds soothing, calming.

"Touch this, Doctor," Loring ordered.

Kevin glanced at the impassive guards, and complied. The cylinder felt pleasurably smooth, surprisingly supple and warm, like a baby's tush.

"Bokanovsky bottle," Loring said, slightly loud because of the earplugs. "Interesting that both you and Bergmann share a penchant for that term. A bottle is sterile, inorganic. The inside of this," patting the cylinder, "is very human."

"An artificial womb."

"A *tissue-engineered* womb. We call them SUEs, Synthetic Uterine Environments. Most are dormant, for now."

"Bergmann's design?" Kevin asked.

"Like you, a visionary. Oh, he started off like his colleagues. We provided him with an unused embryo cell from a cryogenic container from which he derived his own line of stem cells. But Bergmann went far beyond Petri dishes. While his tissue-engineering colleagues busied themselves with trying to develop stem cells to regenerate cartilage, spinal nerves, or hair, Bergmann moved directly to the essence of life, the womb."

Kevin looked down at the cylinder. "What exactly is in there?"

"Cultured, living, vibrant, human uterine tissue grown and fixed onto an inert polylactic acid polymer scaffolding. Place an embryo or young fetus inside, add in appropriate nutrients and hormones, remove the waste, and voilà: Mom-in-a-can." Loring pointed to four ports along each side of the cylinder. "Fiberoptic access for easy viewing and/or intervention." Pointing to a monitor integrated on the lower near side, "Sonographic monitor and touch screen." He pointed to a series of green- and red-marked insertions along the sides and flattened ends. "Nutrient- and hormonal-infusion pumps. Evacuation and excretion tubules. Intake and output, carefully monitored, controlled directly at the unit site here, or through a network of integrated substations throughout this level. You could grow anyone in here. It's a shame Bergmann isn't with us to see his work come to fruition. His genius made him difficult." Winking at Kevin, "A trait common to his ilk."

"I doubt your goals were his."

"His were extremely limited. He envisioned SUEs as a way for infertile couples to have children ex vivo, a step up from in vitro fertilization, to be sure, but just another way for women to carry to term." Loring held up his arms. "Here, instead, we grow the future of Mankind."

Kevin leaned into Loring. A gun touched his back. "Christ! You're cloning people!"

Loring snorted. "Cloning is such a simplistic application of genetic engineering, one that perpetuates bundles of genetic mistakes. We've no use for it. As you certainly know, Doctor, a clone is a copy of an individual's genetic makeup. If that individual's genome contains deficiencies, say an allergy, a genetic disease, a mental illness, then all clones of that individual will have that same vulnerability. And of course clones don't pop out fully grown. They take as long as the original to develop. No, cloning invites susceptibility whereas genetically different individuals with inserted gene enhancements are not only an advantage, but more socially acceptable. You said it yourself at the press conference: 'Germline therapy embraces individualism. Cloning destroys it'"

Kevin scanned the room of black cylinders. The subliminal soothing sounds of heartbeats gnawed at him. "Where's the Collaborate going with all this?"

Loring signaled the technicians to disperse. All but the oldest piled into the carts, and disappeared into the thumping twilight. "Look about you, Dr. Kincaid. What do you see?"

"A nightmare."

"Machines submitting to Man's harmony. Components of a greater whole. With the right components, one can assemble a machine to challenge the heavens. That machine is Man." Stealing behind Kevin, "You've glimpsed only shadows of our work. The Library is but the tip, and the patent office just the safety deposit box. We'll breed humanity's future with the SUE. We'll design it with Protein X-ACT. We'll create it with V_7. Your vector is perfect for our needs. Single cells that have had designer chromosomes inserted don't seem to develop properly in SUEs. Our techs theorize that such engineered cells are somehow weakened, making Bergmann's synthetic environment too traumatic for them. Technically, altering a single cell by germline gene therapy might work well on the drawing board, but it's quite different in the field. The results are unpredictable. Germline therapy appears to be far more reliable after embryonic blastula development. Your V_7 makes that possible. With it, we can safely insert designer chromosomes at a much later stage, long after the fetus has initially begun to take shape." Loring glided to Kevin's front. "We've passed the age of silicon, chips, and hardware. Now it's carbon and biologics. We've come full circle, back to Nature. The silicon we use is but a tool to enhance the carbon we are."

"Bottom line, Loring. The Collaborate's going to use its genetic library with my vector to monopolize the ultimate operating system: human beings."

"*Guide* would be more accurate," Loring corrected.

"*Dictate* better still. The Collaborate is nothing but a bunch of maniacal, egocen—"

"We see on a grander scale."

"I know what makes a human being. Do you?"

"A week ago, you knew only your vector, your lab, and your guilt."

"I was your puppet!"

"Our voice. Look Kevin, I didn't bring you here to berate you. I want you to understand what a profoundly positive impact you've had on humanity, and how you can continue to contribute through HR 601."

"I wish I could renounce the damn thing!"

"James Watson, co-discoverer of the DNA structure, believed that the potential for curing human disease through germline gene therapy was so great that it should be implemented—regardless of the possible consequences of eugenics. You are in good company."

"What you're planning to do with it is unspeakable!"

"Nonsense. The legislation, as written, will allow children 'below the norm' to be treated so as to bring them up 'at least to the norm.' As more children are elevated to 'normality,' *or above* as the legislation allows, the average intelligence will increase. You, Kevin, will be personally responsible for raising humanity's average IQ perhaps a hundred points."

"What about Tiburon? Were you raising IQs there, too?"

Loring ambled among the black cylinders and ran a hand across each smooth surface he passed. "We live in a world of diversity. Diversity of goals, of standards, of morals. Not every culture prizes intelligence. Poorer economies need strong backs more than strong minds. Tiburon was to meet those needs. To enhance manual dexterity, physical prowess, muscular specialization in countries that need laborers for agriculture, manufacturing, mining. To raise the lesser world's standard of living. When we deactivated Tiburon, we transferred those operations here, to Delphi."

"Then why Tiburon in the first place?"

"It was easier to conduct those sorts of clinical studies in less-developed regions."

Kevin waved at the room. "Your designer chromosomes didn't work in Tiburon. And, from what you tell me, they didn't work here, either."

"The chromosomes worked; the vector didn't. With V_7, we solve that problem, thank you. And begin Implementation."

"Selling germline eugenics to the public?"

"To start."

"Loring, the Food and Drug Administration isn't going to grant you approval to hawk your germline designer chromosomes to the public based only on a few preclinical studies of tissue cultures and lab animals. You'll need years of testing. Clinical trials. INDs. NDAs."

"We'll offer germline products to people starved for greatness, even if vicarious. What would a couple pay to give their child the genes of a brilliant doctor? Or a financial wizard? Or a leading statesman? Time is our ally. It will inevitably pressure the reluctant into purchasing our designer chromosomes, or risk having their children, their *germlines*, rendered inferior."

"What about your 'service to poorer economies'?"

"We'll price that to go. Labor's cheap. Leadership expensive." Loring grinned. "And as for the FDA, we'll make trillions from the black market *before* the pretty paperwork ever arrives on bureaucracy desks. By that time, we'll be a global economy unto ourselves. The

FDA will cower before us. And if not," he shrugged, "we'll simply replace their personnel."

"Do you have any idea what V_7 and your smorgasbord of genes will do to humanity? Different individuals will carry a mix-and-match variety of your designer chromosomes into the next generation. That means that different people will have not only different *chromosomes*, but *different numbers of chromosomes*! You'll create different subspecies of man! Now, maybe these human subspecies will be able to crossbreed like different pedigreed dogs—and maybe they won't. They'll become entirely different species. What we know as human beings will become extinct! Even the blueprint for making Homo sapiens will be lost, blurred in time through different artificial chromosomes, transfected by V_7 into germline cells, and carried from generation to generation."

"Exhilarating, isn't it? And as a side benefit, fundamentalist and extremist religious groups, because of their ignorant beliefs, will exclude themselves from the process. They'll be left behind. For that alone, society should be in our debt!"

"You'll shatter humanity beyond repair!"

Loring sauntered toward Kevin. "We're counting on it."

"What?"

"It will ease humanity's transition to the next phase."

"The children—you grew them in this room, didn't you?"

"We have an extensive supply of donor sperm and eggs. And Bergmann's device is 99.9 percent efficient."

Kevin surveyed the thousands of synthetic wombs. "There's too many of these for just experimenting."

Loring beamed. "Do you know what distinguishes us from the rest of the world?"

"A conscience?"

"We think in terms of decades and generations instead of crises *dujour*. This is Year 17 of our first 30-Year Plan. We're running ahead of schedule, ready to begin Implementation."

"Bergmann saw your treatise. He chose to destroy his lab and himself."

Loring snapped his fingers. "I'd forgotten that Bergmann's daughter told you."

"How did you know that?"

"If only Wyndom had come to me after breaking into secured files and reading the Reconstruction Treatise, I'd've been able to show him the beautiful truth behind it." Loring shook his head. "Wyndom would never have bombed ReGenerix. Never sent Tracy away. Never set her on a course to turn you against me. And you and I would be standing here not as adversaries, but as colleagues."

Kevin stiffened as did the guards behind him. "The hell we would!"

"Wyndom had the same look after reading the Treatise." Then, in a rich voice, "Open your mind. I have so much more to offer."

Kevin waved at the room. "I've seen what you're offering."

"You've seen nothing."

"Selling designer chromosomes is the preamble. I know what you'll do with the trillions that will flow into your coffers." He moved close enough to taste Loring's breath. "Bergmann had good reason to call his device a Bokanovsky bottle. He must have known, deep down, you were funding far more than synthetic wombs. That you were funding the social template for an entirely new society. One resembling *Brave New World*!"

Loring applauded, the sounds of his cupped hands echoing across the great room. "Brilliant, Kevin! Here, with Bergmann's wombs, Dermot's software, and your vector, we'll begin genetically engineering the workers, warriors, and intelligentsia of Mankind's future!"

"A caste system! No, worse—castes are social. This is genetic! Species, subspecies, superspecies. People will be condemned to an inalterable station in life from birth. So will their children. And the germlines that follow—forever separated!"

"Like Huxley said, everyone ever born will know their place in life. And be happy with it. Oil driller, pastry chef, decision maker, all born and bred to their respective tasks. For the first time, the world will run like clockwork."

Kevin slammed a fist down on the cart. "Controlled by an elite beyond reproach. Huxley himself correctly pointed out that genetic breeding wasn't enough to keep a world in harmony. You need improved techniques of suggestion, beginning with infant conditioning. Managers who know the social and economic hierarchy inside out. Drugs like his *soma* to channel away unwanted aggression. And generations of totalitarian control. Without those mechanisms in place, you'll create the hell you claim to be supplanting!"

"We have plans."

"And how long will it take before you know you've failed? A century? A millennium? By then, it'll be too late to reverse the—"

"We're truly working for the betterment of Man," Loring stated. "Can the same be said of this world's governments?"

"What you're doing is morally abhorrent!"

"So society should be left to its own, without eugenics?"

"Absolutely!"

"You mean with the Chinese eugenics law recommending couples postpone marriage if one partner has a serious contagious or mental disease? Or sterilizing couples? Or destroying female babies because the parents want a male child?"

"That's just China. You can't—"

"Tribal massacres occur every decade on the African continent. Think those are about politics? No, they're about eugenics. Germlines. Genes."

"You can't equate—"

"And a little closer to home, ignoring racial issues, what about fat people? Ugly people? Deformed people? Think their genes are being passed on at the same rate as everyone else's? It's Nature. It's selection. It's eugenics. It's practiced every day, everywhere, by everyone." Loring paused. "Somebody has to make a decision about humanity's future. Should we trust our destiny to short-sighted politicians who can't see beyond their self-interests or narrow beliefs? Kevin, *we* offer a clear vision of a bountiful future."

"Who in their right mind would want to live in a 'Brave New World'?"

"Who wouldn't? Above all, people want happiness, if there is such a thing. Whether it's naturally generated or genetically engineered is, essentially, irrelevant."

"And what will your society accomplish? The purpose of civilization is to improve conditions for generations to follow. Your world will be regimented, soulless, existing only for the now. Look at the ants. They've been here a hundred million years, without change. What have they accomplished?" Kevin asked.

"They've found a system that works. And as to being soulless, even Pat Robertson, an icon of conservatism, once said that genetically engineered human beings have souls."

"People won't accept—"

"People *always* accept. Max Planck once said that an important scientific innovation rarely proceeds by converting opponents. Instead, in time the opponents die out and the succeeding generation adopts the new ideas as an assumption. We've known about the possibility of altering the human species for decades. Now, it's upon us. New technologies like HACV.V$_7$ can't be uninvented. Suppressed temporarily, yes, but eventually, inevitably, they resurface. By the time humanity realizes what has happened, the transition will be a fait accompli." Loring benevolently smiled. "We will fulfill your dream, Kevin. No one need ever again be born deformed."

Kevin took an outraged step toward his host. Guards restrained him. "And what do you *personally* get out of all this, Loring?"

"The satisfaction of knowing that I am saving humanity. With rampant overpopulation, the world running out of resources, and policy being driven by social and religious mores that are centuries obsolete, somebody needs to take the reins."

"Cut the altruistic crap. For people like you, power's all that really matters."

Loring clucked, "An artist wants his work hanging in the Louvre. The writer wants his novel declared a classic. The industrialist wants his name carved on buildings. The politician wants monuments in his honor. Even siring a child is just an inner drive to leave a legacy, and some small measure of immortality. In the generations to come, every child born into the new society will be raised knowing that their tranquil world was founded by *us*. They will venerate us."

"You mean *worship*."

Loring shrugged. "A small compensation in the scheme of things."

"It's wrong! We're a nation of laws. We have a government that—"

"Who do you think our silent partner was? We shared information, resources, funding, even the plans for this place, years before parting company."

"Why would the government be involved? What do they have to gain?"

"Somewhere, in a secret base hidden in the desert, is a room the size of a city, filled with Bokanovsky bottles." Slowly approaching Kevin, "Imagine a nation whose citizens need never go to war because it has an ever-ready-made class of nameless warriors. An unlimited supply of soldiers, without family, without ties to the citizenry, without sympathies that could weigh down long campaigns. A clandestine warrior caste with designed human chromosomes packed with superior genes enhancing physical and mental characteristics, enabling them to infiltrate and destroy terrorist groups and nations the world over—all created in SUEs like these. All made possible by your V$_7$."

Kevin closed his eyes against the thought. "No! I don't believe you!"

"I can give you the exact coordinates of that secret military base. Maybe one day, I'll show you." He leaned closer. "Then you might understand who the *real* enemy is."

"Even if it's true I won't work for you."

A smile broke across Loring's face. "I've spared Donny's life. I now offer you the life of the assassin who murdered your family. You can't tell me you don't crave revenge."

Kevin's hands ached for Blount's head, to crush it like a tomato. "It may have been his hand, but it came from your mouth!"

"Not true, but I can make it right." Loring drew closer. "Pull out the fiberoptic port on the unit to your left, then look at the monitor." Seeing Kevin's hesitation, "Go ahead. It won't bite."

On the screen adjacent to the SUE, Kevin watched a solid sphere of cells as it slowly aligned and realigned into a hollow ball.

"Recognize it?" Loring asked.

"A blastula, forming a blastocyst. The earliest stages of embryo development."

"No, no. I meant on a more personal level."

"Loring, what the hell are you talking about?"

"Don't you recognize her?"

"*Her?*"

Loring nestled beside him. "It's your daughter, Jessica." The lone technician whispered in Loring's ear. "I stand corrected. That's Kathy. Jessica's in the unit to your right."

The Grounds, Delphi

After crawling two hundred yards, Helen tasted ice chips and top-soil, her knees and elbows throbbed, but most of all, Trent's last enigmatic comment looped endlessly in her head: "*We don't want to be detected too soon.*"

They reached the west wing's back wall. Trent propped himself against a shadowed alcove twenty yards from the back entrance, opened his palm pad, and whispered, "Sequence two. West wing rear." He waited for a confirmation before unpacking his backpack. "Take off your suit." He tossed her a crumpled, flimsy garment and sneakers. "Put them on."

Helen unraveled an ankle-length white lab coat and attached color-coded badge with her picture. "We're just going to walk in?"

He stuffed his snowsuit into the backpack. "I put the surveillance system in this area in sham mode and uploaded false identities for us, but these badges only clear us through Level Four."

"Why not knock out the whole security sys—"

"We're supposed to be terrorists with hacking skills. If we bring down the whole system at once, there's no plausible deniability."

"What about the EMP?"

"They'll find it eventually. With carefully planted evidence, they'll conclude that I assembled it on my own." He started digging in the snow. "Come on, get changed. We've got to bury this stuff."

"No disguises? They'll recognize us!" She stopped. "You *want* them to recognize us!"

"We have to protect the Agency, no matter what."

She leaned into his face. "Trent, just how horrible is DARPA's secret?"

He glanced at the back entrance. "If we don't make it through that door in the next three minutes, we never will."

Level Five, Delphi

"No!" Kevin yelled.

"But they are, right down to their DNA microsatellite finger-prints," Loring said.

"You're lying! You said you couldn't clone—"

"No, we said we *wouldn't* clone. We're willing to make an enor-mous exception for you." Loring leaned against the cart. "When I real-ized that Blount had exceeded his orders, that he'd killed your wife and children, I had him go back to obtain tissue samples from every-one in the house and place them in storage. Over the last decade, we've developed very sophisticated nuclear transfer techniques. Transferring your children's nuclear material from their differenti-ated cells into an enucleated recipient egg cell was simple."

"Just because you have the technology doesn't prove—"

"Blount had to get cell samples from tissue not damaged by the fire," Loring softly said. "Your children died of smoke inhalation, so it was relatively easy to obtain undamaged tissue. Your wife, unfortunately, was charred. There was nothing to salvage—not that it would be the same to have a clone of your wife young enough to be your daughter."

"Liar! Helen's body was never found!"

Loring clasped his hands. "In trying to obtain a viable sample, sadly, Blount mutilated her body. The medical examiner would have seen it and raised too many questions. We couldn't allow that—which is why her body was never found. We cremated her and, of course, gave her a proper burial."

Kevin fought back tears. Both Loring's matter-of-fact delivery and his relaxed, open body language spoke the same, undeniable truth: Helen was gone, forever.

"It's so unfortunate that by trying to preserve her, we caused you ten years anguish by denying you closure." Loring whispered, "For that, I am truly sorry."

"Where are her ashes?"

"I'll show you sometime—after you begin work here."

"You expect me to work for you after what you've done?"

"We couldn't save her, Kevin." Loring walked over to one of the cylinders and caressed it with the back of his hand. "But what's growing in these SUEs are, indeed, *your children.*" As Kevin ran his hands over the monitor, Loring added, "They went so young. They never really had a chance. Only you can bring them back."

Kevin felt as if a hand was reaching up from his stomach and was squeezing his chest.

"Think of it! In two years, you can have your daughters back, exactly the way they were! We can even delay restarting Kathy so the age difference is identical."

He vehemently shook his head. "My girls are gone."

"They've already died once, in part because of you. Can you bear letting that happen again?"

Kevin's knees buckled. The guards steadied him. "What do you want?"

Loring leaned against the SUE containing Kathy. "Your interrogation had a gap."

"I thought you already had V_7."

"We do. But under sedation, you whispered something rather puzzling. You said 'except the mice.' What does that mean?"

Except the mice died, Kevin thought. *They don't know. I didn't give them the modification. Their V_7 formula won't work!* He shrugged.

"If there's a flaw with V_7 we have the people here to fix it." Loring knelt beneath the Jessica SUE and grabbed hold of a thick power cord connecting the tube to the floor. "But your unborn children will pay the price."

"No. Please!"

"Convince me."

A baritone voice echoed overhead: "Mr. Loring. Attention, Mr. Loring."

"Yes, what is it, Spann?" Loring shouted at the loudspeakers.

"Sir, the Chairman requires your presence in the boardroom," Spann's voice answered.

Loring took a deep breath, then shouted, "On my way." He climbed into one of the carts. To Kevin, "The guards will accompany you to your quarters. For your sake, for your children's sake, I'd suggest you start worrying a little more about *your* germline and a little less about everyone else's!"

Level One, Delphi

Loring reflected on Kincaid as the cart rolled through the Level One northeastern tube connecting to Administration. Yes, the man was probably telling the truth, but nonetheless, it was pleasurable manipulating him. Kincaid, like everyone, it seemed, was anchor-weighted by bonds of love, or family, or friendship. How much farther one's ship could go without such an onerous drag!

At the end of the tube a detail escorted his cart as it wound through the maze of offices comprising Main Administration.

It had been decades since anyone had seen Chairman Bertram. There were rumors: that Bertram was continually altering his appearance; that he was a deranged shell of a man; that he was long dead, his empire controlled by financial puppeteers; that he did not exist, but was simply an alter ego of some other Collaborate member. Why had he chosen to appear now?

The cart passed through the last checkpoint. Executive Administrator Spann and two of Bertram's personal guards stood outside the boardroom. The cart stopped.

Spann rasped, "The Chairman's waiting inside, sir."

Loring gazed into his eyes and noted his dry mouth. "What's the matter? You look like you've seen a ghost."

7:46 P.M.

Kevin stood alone on Level Five. Primal, throbbing sounds surrounded him. Rows of black cylinders stretched to an indigo horizon. He shouted, "You can't bring them back!"

"Oh, but I can," Loring's voice echoed. "Listen."

Kevin heard a muffled wail pierce the dark far behind him. He whirled around and weaved through rows of SUEs toward the sound. The crying grew stronger, insistent, familiar. He started to run, honing in on the source—a cylinder twenty rows down, four columns to the left. A second cry, weaker, arose near the first. He cut too sharply through a column and banged into a cylinder. The unit tipped over and smashed on the floor. Yellow fluid, like a broken egg yolk, oozed onto the floor. Five rows to go. Three.

He reached the source: adjacent SUEs. Shaking, he activated a fiberoptic portal. The monitor displayed a round, swimming fertilized egg. It quickly divided into a tight ball of cells. One end distended, creating a hollow ball that rapidly elongated into the primitive, gigantic head, body, and tail of a fetus. Tiny gill arches developed beneath the great head. Dark spots appeared and grew into eyes. Paddle-shaped limb buds appeared and grew arms, fingers. The head rounded, the shape becoming more human. "Jessica!"

The fiberoptic port on the adjacent cylinder activated. Its monitor snapped on. Another embryo began. He glanced back. In the first cylinder, infant Jessica had transformed into a toddler with frizzled blond locks of hair. On the other monitor, a second new embryo began taking human shape.

"Daddy!" came the cry from the first.

Toddler Jessica morphed into a young woman, the incarnation of Helen Kincaid. Screaming, she pounded frantically on the inside of her cylinder casket. Kevin beat on the cylinder from the outside, but it stood immutable. Young woman Jessica gasped for air. She violently convulsed.

Kevin tore at the cylinder's seamless surface. Jessica fell back into the synthetic tissue, dead. Her open eyes stared lifelessly at Kevin. Her flesh dissolved. Her skeleton collapsed.

"Daddy!" In the other monitor, a new toddler, Kathy, had formed, and began morphing into a young woman. Around him, in a spreading, crescendolike shock wave, were wails: strong, familiar, desperately needy. He lunged at Kathy's cylinder. It fell on top of his arm. He tried to get out from underneath the cylinder, but couldn't. It pinned his arm and shook as he struggled.

"C'mon. Get up," a deep voice bellowed.

Where did that voice come from?

"C'mon, Doctor. Get up!" it repeated.

Level Five melted away. Slowly, Kevin opened his eyes.

A guard peered over him. The man was shaking his arm. "Get yourself straightened up, *sir*. The Big Man wants to see you."

"Tell Loring—"

"Not Mr. Loring, sir. Chairman Bertram."

Treatment Room #3, MedLab, Level Two

Two guards slung Kevin into a chair, strapped his head, arms, and legs, then shined bright lights into his eyes. The outline of a third man appeared in the shadows. "Please forgive them," the man said. "They tend to be overprotective." The voice sounded vaguely familiar, but very deep.

"What's *your* approach—tea or torture?"

"Tea is an acquired taste. Torture, often counterproductive. Shall we try the third *t*—truth?"

"You have V_7."

"Loring has lingering doubts. I respect his judgment." The man drew tantalizingly close to the light. "He's offered you your brother's life, the head of your family's murderer, the resurrection of your children, and a chance to shape humanity's destiny. Truly the gods favor you."

"I didn't refuse his offer."

"Neither did you embrace it. Shall we return to the third *t*?"

"Truth? While hiding in shadows."

The man waved his right hand. The guards hesitated, then retreated. The man stepped forward and turned off the bright light. The after-retinal burn in Kevin's eyes persisted a few seconds as flashes of the face peering over him grew maddeningly familiar. It was a banker's face, seventyish but vigorous, vibrant. "Nice to see you again, Dr. Kincaid." Gone were the round, black-rimmed glasses, the frail demeanor. Frederick Grayson smiled.

"I thought you were dead!"

"As did Loring," Grayson said. "While in India I picked up more than a love for Darjeeling tea. Yoga was invented to enable the body to adapt to long periods of meditation. Masters have learned how to take it to the extreme, to slow one's heart. Simulate death."

"Grayson? *You* run the Collaborate?"

"Actually, it's Bertram. Eric Bertram. The Grayson identity enabled me to manipulate Loring's day-to-day operations. I have similar trusted roles with others in our group. It's made me seem omnipotent."

"Then why—"

"Did I relinquish it? Good Senator Jordan DeRay began to recognize me. We'd had dealings thirty years ago." Bertram shuddered. "Bigoted, disgusting man. I couldn't chance him putting disparate elements together. So, I died."

"So will I. And before long, I'll bet."

"I sincerely hope not, Doctor. Besides, wouldn't you like to hear the truth?"

"I heard it, in graphic detail, from Loring's mouth."

"That was Loring's truth." Bertram pointed at Kevin's bonds. The guards stood, quizzical. Bertram snapped his fingers. His men quickly released Kevin and sat him upright.

Kevin watched Bertram take three powerful strides toward the door: gone were Grayson's shuffling gait, the hump in his back, and that distinctive cane. "Naturally, that was an act, too."

Bertram turned back and smiled. "So shameful of people to pigeonhole others by their deformities. And shameful for me to use it to my advantage—though I will miss that wonderful cane." Looking beyond Kevin, "I wonder if the ones who come after will view us that way."

Kevin took a quick step toward Bertram. The guards seized him.

"Never try to touch me. My guards might kill you before I can stop them. Now let's take a little walk down the hall, shall we?"

"Do I have a choice?"

". . . ever heard the word *Qutub*?" Bertram asked.

Kevin checked the guards behind him as he proceeded down Medlab's main corridor. "No."

"Persian word. Means 'center of everything.' A cornerstone," Bertram said. "Most cultures have legends of rare individuals who operate on higher energy planes, who command great powers—a Qutub. It is said that no more than four of them walk the earth at any one time. They could be anyone—a poor rice farmer, a factory worker, a head of state. Anyone."

"Don't tell me. You're a Qutub."

Bertram smiled. "One finds a Qutub through meditation, or by attuning oneself to detect their higher resonant energy levels."

"How spiritual of you."

"After I'd made my fortune, when I had time to travel, I went on a personal quest to find one. I was walking a narrow, ancient street in Jerusalem with three others, all of us seeking that higher spirituality. Suddenly, our bodies froze in midstride. We could see and hear, but every voluntary muscle in our bodies became rigid. Around the corner came a man with a long, flowing beard, and dressed like a Greek Orthodox priest. He smiled knowingly at us as he passed. I could feel his energy radiate against my skin like the sun's rays. When the priest turned the corner, our muscular control returned. We ran to catch him, but he was gone. No one on that street had seen him pass. He must have been a Qutub." Bertram placed his hand on Kevin's shoulder. "I want to create one. And you, Dr. Kincaid, should assist me in fulfilling this noble endeavor."

Kevin looked into the elder man's eyes. This was not Loring. Though both men were asking for his help, the similarity abruptly ended there. Loring projected pomposity, condescension, intimidation. On the other hand, despite the obvious power the Collaborate Chairman possessed, Bertram projected the ability to pacify with a deep reverence for the unknowable—the culmination of varied experience. Kevin had felt Loring force him to kneel before the Collaborate's sword, but with Bertram, he felt as if the Chairman was sitting down with him and trying to enlighten him to some wondrous, though misguided, truth.

"I recognize the discontinuity between the genetic 'inside-self' and the physical/spiritual 'outside-self,'" Bertram continued. "That what one sees at a microscopic level of life may not correlate with what one sees at the macroscopic level. I recognize the *possibility* that one cannot examine the inside-self because it is not possible to simultaneously be on the outside, macroscopic and the inside, microscopic world—like the Pauli exclusion principle stating that two electrons cannot occupy the same position in space at the same time. But I believe that you and I can create the process which will make it possible."

"Grayson, Bertram, whatever you call yourself, if you truly believe in some spiritual Qutub, how can you permit your own organization to create such a soulless society?"

"Who said it was?"

"Loring. His Reconstruction Treatise—"

"Is a sham," Bertram finished.

"He doesn't think so."

"Nor does anyone beyond this room." Bertram started slowly down the hall with Kevin. "The Collaborate believes it's building an orderly, stable society that will last hundreds of millennia—a monument to their colossal egos. Let them continue to believe that. What I've set in motion far transcends that petty goal." Placing his hands behind his back, "Dr. Kincaid, where are we going? As a race, I mean."

I don't know. I've just been trying to survive.

"When I was a child, I remember watching reruns of an old, original, black-and-white TV show, *The Outer Limits.* There was one episode, 'The Sixth Finger,' about a man who walked into a booth and had his 'dominant genes accelerated to speed up the maddeningly slow inborn process of evolution.' Before long, the man had evolved six million years into our future."

"Ridiculous!"

"Maybe so. But while this country was enamored with bringing back extinct dinosaurs, *I* was building the future of life itself! Preparing to cross the next stage of evolution in a few generations instead of hundreds of millennia." He faintly smiled. "The process through which we will achieve this perfection—Accelolution—has already begun. And in the very room I'm about to show you."

"You're not accelerating evolution—just creating your own."

"Medicine and modern civilization have ended natural selection, evolution. Individuals with subnormal mental and physical capabilities survive and reproduce."

"Like my brother."

"A consequence of society. The genetic playing field has been leveled. Almost anyone can pass on their genes."

"And you plan to change all that with genetic engineering."

"I believe the current terminology is human inheritable genetic modification—HIGM. Isn't it ironic that at the precise moment in history when we've stopped evolution, we gain the power to create our own?"

"Sounds more like Excelolution—making people 'better.' "

Bertram stopped outside a door marked "OR Theater #2" and signaled his guards to wait. "With V_7, Accelolution becomes reality. We have an opportunity here to bypass evolution, to leap forward millions of years. That Qutub may have just been a peek around the next bend in our evolutionary road."

"A road leading where?"

"Neither of us can see, but succeeding HIGM generations will discover new insights and improve upon those generations to follow. In time a germline will be created that transcends the flesh, reaches out to the edge of the Universe, touches the face of God. And in so doing becomes God."

"Don't you see what you're doing? Your Accelolution won't create life in the image of God! It'll create it in the image of Man!"

Bertram put a finger to his lips. "Have you ever wondered why the night skies aren't filled with visitors from other worlds? Or the heavens buzzing with their chatter? There are probably a billion planets with life in this galaxy alone. And billions of galaxies beyond that. Statistically, we should have more tourists than a Caribbean resort at the height of season. But we don't. Perhaps because as life naturally evolves into intelligent beings that erect civilizations, it develops technologies to accelerate its own evolution, bypassing the need for space travel, or even the corporeal universe. A kind of ultimate technological inevitability." Bertram cleared his throat as Kevin stared. "Enough speculation. To the matter at hand. I require an answer from you. Now."

Kevin closed his eyes, his mind a whirling collage of priestly orations, family, work, and running—running. "I don't want your future."

"It's *your* future as much as mine. Come, see your handiwork."

The guards grabbed him from behind and shoved him through a doorway.

"Open your eyes!"

He found himself in a great operating theater. Beside him, in the center of the room, on a gurney, lay a delicate little girl with matted blond locks. Over the child's labored breaths, a monitor beeped her heartbeat. An i.v. infused a powerful anti-epileptic.

"Her name is Meredith. Beautiful, isn't she?" Bertram whispered. "One of the neurotransmitter-enhanced children."

Again his mind replayed the Tiburon horror in exquisite detail. "I thought they'd all died."

"She is the last. She probably has only a few days. Such genius. I could show you equations for a revolutionary theory involving gravitation and the cosmological constant that are thirty years ahead of their time."

Kevin reached out. Meredith rustled, then softly moaned.

"We have the designer chromosome that originally transfected her. And downstairs they're busy synthesizing your V$_7$. When they're finished we'll load the chromosome onto V$_7$, and treat the affected areas of her cerebral cortex with it. *If* V$_7$ works, it will probably save her life."

Kevin knelt beside her, and placed her free hand in his.

"She is the shining future. She owes her existence as much to you as to me. Ironic how you said you didn't want to be part of my future, yet now, in the flesh, you embrace her."

Kevin blinked rapidly over burning eyes.

"Spend a few moments alone with the child. Perhaps it will clarify your decision," Bertram said. Then, to the guards, "Two of you remain here. Allow him ten minutes then escort him back to his quarters. If he mentions anything sensitive to anyone, kill them. In the interim, I'll be on Level Five." Back to Kevin, "Doctor, if by some chance V$_7$ does have a flaw, here's a chance to put your noble principles to the test."

Outside MedLab, Level Two

Just before Marguerite left the Level Two tube outside MedLab, she reached into her coat pocket and ran her fingers along the flat plastic case. Yes, Stevenson's CD was still there.

Kevin emerged from the MedLab entrance with two forbidding guards behind him.

That must be him! Marguerite thought. She asked, "You are Kevin Kincaid?" He stopped and nodded. She continued, "You've seen Meredith?"

He glanced at the guards behind him.

"There are rumors that you can save her life."

"It's not safe to talk to me." He turned his back and started away.

"Please, if there's anything you can do—please don't let her die like the others."

The guards shoved Kevin into an empty cart. They disappeared down the tube.

Had he heard her? Did he care? Would it matter? Marguerite glanced at her watch. She was late. If she wasn't at Meredith's bedside when Stevenson—

Approaching Level One

Trent and Helen had penetrated the underground complex's main elevator. Trent glanced at the surveillance camera overhead, then returned to his palm pad. The elevator plunged deep beneath the surface.

"Was that really a school up there?" Helen asked. "There were classrooms, a gym, a cafeteria, everything."

"It was," Trent muttered, tapping furiously on the notepad keys, as he probed through Delphi's security programs.

"Where are all the children now?"

Trent checked the schematic on his notepad screen. Kincaid was locked in a room on Level One, outer ring, northeast sector, with two armed guards patrolling the exterior corridor. "Sequence three. Implement at CCTV sites on screen," he whispered into the pad. To Helen, "Kincaid's under guard. I've tricked the surveillance system into running a videotape loop of his last five minutes. It may fool Delphi's security for a while." He closed the notepad. "When the doors open follow my lead."

She brandished her gun.

He shoved it beneath her lab coat. "When *I* say!"

The elevator doors parted. The corridor beyond was empty.

"No one here, either?" she whispered.

"Probably keeping the area clear. We're going to stand out. Come on."

They headed to the right down the corridor, passing a slew of private quarters, a loping archway marked "Promenade", and a sealed tube gateway marked "For Authorized Personnel Only: Administration and Boardroom". Trent sensed fear in Helen's forced steps beside him. The others had died because they'd acted impulsively. This would not happen to her.

A sign indicated that Suites 101 through 120 lay beyond the bend in the corridor. Trent picked up sounds from that direction. He held out his arm and stopped Helen. "Shhh." Then he took out his notepad, rapidly entered a series of commands, and finished by whispering, "Manual enable."

The notepad's tiny screen flashed: Voice Command Acknowledged.

He handed it to Helen. "Keep it hidden. When I stop, you count to four, touch the icon in the lower left-hand corner, then drop to the floor."

"Why?"

"Just do what I've said, before they hear us!"

Helen hesitated, then placed her hand and the palm pad in her coat pocket.

Trent nudged her to his left. They turned the corner. A holstered guard appeared, then another farther down. The pair, flanking a suite entrance, snapped to attention.

"Please stop, sir," the near guard said.

Trent winked at the man and walked on nonchalantly.

"Please stop!"

Trent obeyed. "Just going to my quarters," he said as he put his arm around Helen's shoulders. "Be out of your way in a minute."

"This corridor is restricted!"

The near guard placed his hand on his weapon. The far guard blocked their path.

Helen dropped and touched the corner of the notepad. The corridor turned pitch black.

Remembering both guards' positions, Trent's right hand slipped behind his back and pulled out an automatic with silencer. He shot the rear guard while simultaneously pulling out a gun with his left hand. A quick *pfft* sound. Trent shot in the other direction with his left hand. Another *pfft* sound. Then two dull thuds.

The lights came on. Both guards were dead on the floor—one shot in the bridge of the nose, the other over the right eyebrow.

Helen slowly stood. "How'd you do that without the goggles?"

"Kincaid's alone in there," Trent said, pointing to the door beside them. "You should be the first one he sees. Press '8114' on the panel. I'll follow you in."

Trent heard the door open and quickly shut. He gathered the guards and dragged them by their arms. The door reopened. He dumped them in a corner behind a modular chest of drawers, then turned around. Helen and Kevin were tightly embraced. "Not now!"

Helen gently disengaged.

Kevin's eyes remained locked on her. "I thought you were—"

"I was. Without you," she answered. Before he could ask, "We came to rescue you."

"We?" Kevin's eyes met Trent's. His face cringed. "You!"

Helen grabbed his shoulder. "Trent got me here, inside."

"He wants me dead!"

"Were that true, you'd already be," Trent replied.

"Kevin, he's with the government."

"What depraved plan do *you* have for V_7, McGovern?"

"Something better than a perpetual dictatorship."

"Don't be too sure," Kevin said. "I have seen a possibility of walking in Eden, as equals, with God."

"Kevin, what have they done to you?" Helen exclaimed, holding him.

"I've done a lot of thinking. I know what the Collaborate wants, Helen. Accelolution. The Qutub—"

"Qutub!" Trent burst. "You've been with Bertram!"

Kevin nodded.

Bertram! Maybe I can take him alive! Trent thought. "Don't believe a word he says. He's the world's biggest liar. Bigger than Loring."

"I'm not so sure. Things aren't so—defined anymore."

Helen looked up at him. "Kevin, you act as if you're not coming."

He stroked her hair. "I love you and I want to be with you, but a little girl is going to die without my help."

"Have you forgotten that they killed *your* little girls?" Helen blurted.

"I have a chance to bring them back!"

Trent glanced at Kincaid's badge. *He's been on Level Five!* "Go on, Kincaid."

Kevin held her hands. "I know what your father was working on. His 'Russian bottle' was a functional artificial womb. They're growing two fetuses now, clones of Jessica and Kathy." His lower lip quivered. "Helen, I can have my girls back!"

"Kevin, that's not possible."

Lifting his head, "Ask McGovern. If he really works for the government, he'll know."

Trent again looked at Kincaid's badge. "That doesn't prove that they're growing clones of *your* children."

"They don't need to lie," Kevin said. "They have Donny hostage. They can kill him whenever they want."

Helen looked to Trent, who raised his eyebrows. She turned back to Kevin. "Donny is dead. He died in the fire."

"No, he isn't." Kevin pulled back. "I saw him!"

"On video, I'll bet," Trent said.

"A computer-generated image," Helen added. "I'm sorry, Kevin. Donny's gone."

Kevin brought his hands over his forehead. "And my girls?"

"What do you think?" Trent asked.

Kevin sank back into a couch behind him, Helen clinging to his shoulder.

"Grieve later, Kincaid. What exactly did you tell them?"

Through clenched teeth, "They have V_7—and all of my files."

"Shit!" Trent took two quick paces up and back. "Did they download the formula?"

"I don't know. Loring said they were synthesizing it here. They probably haven't yet."

Trent stormed across the room. "Where's Bertram?"

"Trent, let's just all get out of here," Helen said.

"Not without Bertram!" To Kevin, "Now where is he?"

Kevin turned to Helen. "Since you showed me the video, I've seen the torture of that poor little girl over and over and over." He choked. "You blamed me. Made me blame myself."

"Only to shock you into seeing the truth," she said softly.

"There was nothing I could do for her. For any of them." Exhaling, looking deep into her eyes, "The same went on here. More blood on my hands."

Helen clasped his arms. "It wasn't your fault at Tiburon. It wasn't your fault here. These are the Collaborate's crimes, not yours."

"This time, Helen, this time I can save at least one little girl." To Trent, "I know where Bertram is. *Who* he is. You want him? Then we take that little girl with us."

"Did you lose your fucking mind? I haven't even figured out how to get *us* out!"

"Take it or leave it."

"You're in no position to bargain."

Kevin lightly touched Helen's cheek. "I can't turn my back this time."

"Kincaid, be reasonable!"

"Here's your rational answer, McGovern. That girl is living proof of Collaborate experimentation. If you really want to crush them," pointing to the door, "your evidence is down the hall."

"Damn you, Kincaid!"

"Already done."

Trent glanced at the dead guards in the corner. "Put on one of those uniforms," he said. "Be sure to keep the blood off of you!"

Central Security, Level Two

Outside Central Security, Stevenson glanced up at the surveillance camera he'd just deactivated. That downed camera would be a dangerous blind spot later but for now it couldn't be helped. Stevenson gazed down at the man motionless on the floor beside the ether-soaked rag he'd used to knock him out: that guard was one of the lucky ones—he'd probably survive. Stevenson knew that if he succeeded, many of the man's coworkers would not. He lifted the unconscious guard's arm and touched the hand to the security pad. Just before the doors parted he slid the body out of sight.

Central Security was more crowded than Marguerite had described: five guards plus two of Bertram's entourage patrolling the secured elevator. Which meant that Bertram was on Level Five.

"What're you doing here, Doctor?" demanded a bull-necked guard beside him.

"I'm supposed to independently review Kincaid's interrogation." Stevenson motioned toward the glass-enclosed observation area in the rear. "I'll need the auxiliary booth."

"The Chairman's here. It'll have to wait," the guard said.

"This concerns Mr. Loring's interrogation of Kincaid."

"The Chairman takes priority."

"Get Ross. Now!"

The guard sneered, but complied.

Ross stormed up to Stevenson. "Ah, here's our little firebug." His colleague explained Stevenson's request. Ross said, "Sorry, doc. Probably in an hour or so."

Stevenson leaned forward. "The results of my research will be handed directly to Mr. Loring, who will hand it directly to Chairman Bertram. Perhaps we should call them *both* to verify—"

"No need," Ross pulled back. "Let him pass."

Stevenson felt Ross's glare all the way up the stairs. He closed the auxiliary control booth door, sealed it behind him, turned down the lights, strode to the console behind the seats, and entered the code. The system recognized him as Deputy Security Chief Ross. After months of gathering snippets of Delphi's security system, he now had to use that knowledge flawlessly. After identifying the physical systems and relays supporting Central Security proper, he manoeuvred through a maze of icons, then simultaneously transferred total control to his terminal in the booth while locking out overrides from the floor below. Systematically, he sealed the exits, disengaged the general alarm, cut off communications not routed through the booth, and shut down the ventilation system servicing the main room. With luck, it would be twenty minutes before he was discovered. When security personnel in the main security room realized what was happening, he'd cut off the lights. It would add to their confusion. But, more important, he wouldn't have to watch them asphyxiate.

Level Five

Which of these will generate the Qutub? Bertram wondered as he walked between rows of dark cylinders, his fingers dancing over the black sheen of their surfaces. *The real question is: Will I live to see it? Immortality is usually gained posthumously.*

An oscillating siren blared. Flashing red lights colored the expanse. Heavy titanium doors slammed closed. Bertram's guards jumped into battle-ready stance. The loudspeaker snapped on. An automated voice announced that Level Five had been sealed. The very human voice that followed announced why.

MedLab (Outside of OR Theater #2), Level Two

Kevin gazed warily at Trent leaning against the MedLab corridor while fully engaged with his notepad. Though the former AntiGen leader had successfully led them to within a few feet of OR Theater #2, Kevin fully expected his rescuer to turn against him. "What are you doing?"

"Tapping into the security camera beyond that wall," Trent replied. He flashed Kevin a quick view of the notepad's screen: a young girl, lying comatose on a hospital bed, and a dark-haired woman beside her. "Who's that?" he asked, pointing to the woman.

Kevin said, "Someone I met on my way out. She convinced me to save the child."

"Reason enough to shoot her," Trent muttered.

"Go to hell!"

"Already there, Kincaid. Got too much company." Weapon drawn in one hand, Trent's other hand played the touchpad on the wall. The doors opened. He charged into the OR theater.

The woman at the child's bedside screamed.

"Shut up! Who the hell are you?" Trent barked.

"Marguerite Moraes. Dr. Stevenson's assistant."

"What are you doing here?"

"Visiting Meredith. I was her teacher."

Glaring at her, Trent relaxed his weapon.

Marguerite's eyes widened as she saw Kevin enter wearing a guard's uniform. "This changes everything," Marguerite whispered in Portuguese.

"All right, Kincaid. I've shown my good faith. You show yours."

Kevin hesitated. "Eric Bertram, Frederick Grayson. They're one and the same."

"Grayson is Bertram?" Helen exclaimed.

"Where is he?" Trent followed up.

"Level Five, last I heard."

"Christ, the only access is through Central Security!" He paced the floor. Stopped as he glanced at Kevin's violet badge. "Maybe—"

A screeching siren blared. Red lights flashed. A second, inner set of doors slammed shut across the entrance. Overhead, shutters sealed off the OR theater's observation windows.

Trent ripped into his notepad, entering command after command to the security system. Every response was the same: Access Denied.

The loudspeaker snapped on. An automated voice calmly uttered: *Biohazard Breach. Biohazard Breach. Biohazard . . .*

"Kincaid, could V$_7$—"

"No. V$_7$ isn't viral-based. It's not a biohazard."

"It's a trap!" Helen exclaimed. "They've got us!"

The automated warning voice from the loudspeaker stopped. A human voice replaced it: "Marguerite, are you okay?"

The Boardroom, Level One, Delphi

Loring stormed into the executive boardroom and stuck his face in Director Spann's. "The hell is going on here?" he screamed above the alarm din.

Spann backed off. "Biohazard breach, sir. Sections of the complex have automatically been sealed off."

"Ambrose must've screwed up. He probably set off the alarm while synthesizing V$_7$ in—"

"It wasn't Ambrose, sir. The system indicates that the breach originated on Level Five."

"How is that possible? What was going on down there?"

"Nothing, Mr. Loring, absolutely nothing. We haven't been working with any infectives or virals that could trip the system—and certainly not on Level Five."

"Turn off that blasted alarm!" he yelled, clamping his hands over his ears.

"For some reason we can't."

"But I can," a masculine voice crackled behind them.

The high-pitched din stopped. Loring and Spann turned to the giant wall screen at the far end of the room. A balding man with a haggard face appeared on-screen: Roderick Stevenson.

"He's in auxiliary control," Spann whispered to Loring.

"I'm in charge," Stevenson declared.

"*You* are responsible for this?"

"I've locked down Levels Three through Five, and access to Central Security on Level Two," Stevenson stated. "Loring, you, quite frankly, are at my mercy."

Loring glanced back at Spann, who acknowledged by lowered his eyes. "Stevenson, tell you what. I'll offer you amnesty if—"

"Amnesty is not an offer."

"You're in the middle of nowhere, surrounded by hostile forces. We can wait you out."

"That decision really rests with your boss, doesn't it?"

The left half of the screen dissolved into a great dark room filled with rows of black cylinders. The picture zoomed in on Bertram walking calmly among the units.

"Merlin, can you hear me?" Loring called.

The on-screen figure looked up. "Dixon? Dixon listen to me. You must not negotiate. No matter what the consequen—"

The video connection terminated. Stevenson again filled the screen. "In biohazard mode the security system can evacuate air from any contaminated compartment. I can turn Level Five into a vacuum in minutes. Ever seen someone die in a vacuum? The blood boils at room temperature. The internal organs burst from the pressure gradient."

Loring slowly asked, "What do you want?" Stevenson's image dissolved into OR Theater #2. Loring's jaw dropped. It wasn't possible. That woman Bergmann, alive? And with McGovern? Inside Delphi?

"Release them," Stevenson dictated. "And give them safe transport out of here."

"No deal."

"Then watch me kill Bertram. You've got three seconds. One, two—"

"No, wait. Wait! I agree."

"I'll get back to you with final arrangements. Oh, and Loring, you won't be able to override the security lock-outs. And don't try a direct assault either. My position's impregnable."

"Stevenson, why—"

"Am I doing this?" he snorted. "You'd need a soul to understand."

OR Theater #2, Level Two

Trent glanced back over his shoulder and shook his head. "Kincaid, Bergmann's daughter, a kid in a coma, and now a secretary," he muttered. "This isn't a rescue mission—it's a fucking parade."

"I didn't catch that," Stevenson called out from the loudspeaker in one corner of the operating room.

Trent shouted, "I had it all perfectly planned. Free up Kincaid, penetrate Level Five, abduct Bertram. It would have worked if you," pointing at Kevin, "hadn't been so damned obstinate. And if *you*," pointing at the loudspeaker, "had kept the fuck out of this!"

"The hell with you, toy soldier," Stevenson shot back. "From now on, I only deal with the doctor."

Trent put a hand on Kevin's shoulder. "Kincaid, listen to me and I get us out of here. Listen to him and we're all dead."

"Tell the grunt that if he hadn't dropped in from the outside, I'd've had Marguerite and the child on a helicopter by now," Stevenson said.

Trent said, "You screwed up my mission."

"Dr. Kincaid, even the grunt must concede that I know this place better than any of you."

Trent retorted, "Stevenson, you idiot, I got in here by bypassing the security system without setting off every fucking alarm in the complex!"

Kevin kicked over a medcart. Syringes and vials crashed onto the floor. "Shut up! The two of you! I'm the only one they want alive, so like it or not, that puts me in charge."

"Excellent, Doctor," Stevenson began. "So now you can—"

"Quiet! Just a few hours ago, you were ready to drug and dissect me, so keep out of this!" Kevin shouted.

Trent said, "Glad you came to your senses, Kincaid."

Kevin whirled on him. "And you! After what I've been through, if I had a gun in my hand right now, I'd blow your head off!"

"Then who are you going to trust?" Stevenson asked.

Kevin thought a moment. "I need to talk to McGovern, in private."

"Fine. You knock some sense into the grunt, and I'll check back with Loring. Don't take too long." The loudspeaker clicked off.

"We've got to get Bertram," Trent insisted.

"Stevenson says that he's sealed on Level Five. If that's true then he's the chip keeping us alive. Once Stevenson breaks those seals he loses control and they're in here in seconds."

"Look, Kincaid, if we get out without Bertram, the Collaborate remains intact and roars back stronger, wiser than ever. But if we get him, we end it once and for all."

"What do you have in mind?"

Trent ran quickly through four scenarios to capture Bertram. Kevin intently listened to and questioned each plan. At the end Trent admitted that the best scenario had only a one-in-four chance of success, far less than that if they included the child.

"Poor odds," Kevin said.

"You think Stevenson is offering better?"

"No, McGovern, I won't do it."

Trent stuck his face in Kevin's. "There's more at stake than your life and the kid dying in that bed over there. Our government itself is at risk. Key members of the EC, too. The political ramifications could plunge Western civilization into chaos. The Collaborate's accumulated a lot of dangerous secrets over the years. And in a few hours, a series of events will be set in motion that will escalate beyond undoing."

"Then I guess we'll just have to get out of here," Kevin said, "Without Bertram."

Trent started to reach for his weapon. A gun barrel suddenly pressed against the back of his neck.

"Kevin's in charge," Helen said, her finger on the trigger.

"Put the gun down, Helen," Trent ordered. "Without me, you can kiss good-bye any chance of getting out of here alive."

"Trent, I've been fighting the Collaborate a lot longer than you and I'm tired, more tired than you can imagine," she said. "Nothing would please me more than to destroy them here and now. But I'm telling you, no matter how much we want it, we can't win the war *today*. Today we have to survive the battle."

The loudspeaker clicked on. "Loring's agreed," Stevenson declared. "Dr. Kincaid, what have you decided?"

Kevin looked to Trent and the cocked gun to his head.

"Come on, Doctor! I'm holding off an army!"

Trent whispered, "Go."

Kevin said to Stevenson, "Make the arrangements with Loring."

Stevenson called out, "Marguerite, do you have the CD with you?"

She dug into her coat pocket. "Yes." She showed it to Kevin.

"The synthesis protocol for the vector," Stevenson said. "If anything happens to Kincaid—at least the Collaborate won't have absolute control."

The Boardroom, Level One

". . . and then they all board Bertram's helicopter," Stevenson said.

"And fly across the moon, I suppose?" Loring asked Stevenson's image on the wall.

"The helicopter will set them down at a site of their choosing. When I receive a coded e-mail from them, then and only then, will I release Bertram."

"And you martyr yourself. How noble."

The tired man reclined. "Make the arrangements."

Spann leaned forward and whispered to Loring, who relayed the message to Stevenson. "The helicopter needs an hour for refueling."

"Thirty minutes. No more."

Loring glanced back at Spann who nodded. "But I want privacy in the boardroom to talk to my staff. Cut your video and audio surveillance on this room. You'll still be able to monitor communications to and from—"

"No!"

"Then I execute everyone in MedLab prima facie, and cut my losses!"

Stevenson hissed. "Thirty minutes." The wall screen winked off.

Spann headed to the door. "I can have an assault team ready in ten."

"Storm Central Security? There's closed-circuit cameras covering every square foot of the corridor. He'll see your team coming a mile away."

"We're not going to use a corridor."

"Then how do you intend to get in?"

"Through the Level Two lab adjoining it."

"There's no direct connection between the two."

"We'll make one. Sir, he's operating out of the auxiliary control room. Which means that the main room has been incapacitated, especially since we haven't heard a peep from anyone inside. Auxiliary control doesn't have the big board—only three working monitors. My guess is he won't think of or be able to check on the adjoining lab with everything else he's taken on. We'll break into Central Security before he knows we're there. Take him down in seconds."

Loring turned on the wall-screen. He gazed at the image of Bertram strolling through the black cylinders. *I don't want to lose Merlin, again. But the man made a fool of me for seventeen years!* "It comes time," he whispered to himself. Then said to Spann, "Your men topside. Have them break out the new-generation Stingers."

OR Theater #2, Level Two

Trent handed Kevin an automatic with the safety on. "Know how to use one of these?"

Kevin grimaced. "No." With thumb and forefinger, he handed it back. "And I never will."

Trent released the safety on his weapon. "No matter how many rounds this gun fires, it can't shoot 360 degrees at once," he told the others. "So, stay close, and do nothing provocative."

"Ready," Stevenson's voice sounded over the loudspeaker.

The inner doors to the OR theater opened. Then the outer.

Weapon poised, Trent ventured first into the hallway. Ten guards, hands on their automatics, lined the corridor. Like Dobermans awaiting their master's command, their eager eyes followed. Trent whirled around. The guards did not flinch. Satisfied, he signaled the others. Helen followed, her weapon drawn. Kevin and Marguerite wheeled out Meredith on a gurney with an i.v. pole.

Helen whispered, "Trent, I thought you said there were only six guards."

The Boardroom, Level One

The guards snapped to attention as Loring stood.

"Leave us," he ordered, his eyes fixed on Bertram's image strutting among the SUEs.

One guard said, "We'll be right outside the door when you need us, sir."

After they left, Loring shifted his eyes toward the wall screen and activated the audio. "Can you hear me?"

Bertram's image looked up. "Dixon? What's happening?"

"I struck a deal. Your life for Kincaid's and the others."

"I told you *not* to negotiate!"

"Would you prefer that I let you die?"

"If Kincaid surfaces, it's a disaster. If the specimen surfaces, it's over!"

"Specimen?"

"The child, Dixon! You cannot explain away her genetic structure. Seventeen years of work will be destroyed!"

"Seventeen years—a long time to run a practical joke. Tell me, Bertram, how many of those years were you laughing your ass off at me?"

"I never laughed. Never." He paused. "At times I guided."

"*Manipulated* would be a better word."

"Webster's defines *manipulate* as 'the act of falsifying for one's own purpose, or profit,' " Bertram said softly. "I acted for the group's greater good, and most especially for yours."

"How many of the others—"

"Did I insinuate myself with?" Bertram finished. "Is the question tactical or personal?"

"Tactical. Now answer."

"Just as I thought—personal. If you'd wanted to know for tactical reasons, you'd have asked *who* I've been with. But you asked *how many*, as in wanting to know how many ways I violated your trust." Bertram stepped closer to the camera. "Dixon, I am your friend. In point of fact, I'm almost certainly your only friend."

"Was Merlin ever truly Arthur's friend? Does a child love a doll for itself, or because it can be controlled?"

"I took you by my side on the greatest quest in human history. I bolstered you, bent to your whims, guided you when you strayed. What more could one ask of a friend?"

"Honesty. Trust."

"Had not that ass, DeRay, forced my hand, you would have learned it all. And as for trust, in time, I'd have made you Chairman." Bertram rubbed his hands. "I still can."

"I no longer need your blessing for that!"

"Bravo, Dixon! The most overlooked step in utilizing power is knowing when you truly have it. Yes, you could justify sacrificing me to regain Kincaid and preserve Delphi. The others are so afraid of me that they wouldn't object. Yet, if that's what you genuinely want, why am I still alive? Could it be that you are not yet willing to take that last step?"

"I'm already heir apparent. What else could I want?"

Bertram smiled. "Your old vizier back."

Loring kicked the conference table leg. It snapped, nearly tipping over the entire table.

Bertram chuckled as he leaned on a black cylinder. "Now you understand the true loneliness of power. The price for preserving the empire is the life of your only friend."

Peptide Laboratory, Level Two

Spann panned his flashlight across the darkness. His beacon touched lab benches, distilling glassware, and spectrometers. The second-floor peptide lab was deserted, its personnel temporarily reassigned. He turned off the flashlight, activated his night-vision goggles, and pushed forward, assault rifle ready.

"Helicopter refueling team. Report," crackled Spann's senior surviving security officer over his headset.

"Refueling team leader here. Ready to commence," Spann responded, smirking. The madman Stevenson, bunkered next door, would never see through the deception.

Spann shined two quick flashlight pulses at the entrance. Three other beacons briefly appeared. In the olive-green light of his goggles he watched his squad approach.

"Lab secure, sir," one man announced. "May we turn on the lights?"

"Negative! Cameras in this lab aren't IR-equipped. Keep them off so the target won't know we're here. Surprise is our only advantage."

The Grounds

Kevin and Trent stepped out from the front portico. Whipping wind slammed ice particles against Kevin's face. The snow-covered field outside Delphi's main entrance reflected full-power stadium lights. Set on a circular landing pad 30 yards away, the helicopter's overhead rotor slowly spun, kicking up snowflake microbursts. With Trent, he scanned the grounds: there were two dozen guards with rifles, including six sharpshooters on the rooftops. And one with a long tube propped on his shoulder.

"Shit! A handheld missile launcher," Trent complained. "Even if we get off the ground they can shoot us down." He looked back at Helen,

Marguerite, and the child still waiting in the portico. "How the hell am I gonna get out of this one?" Slowly, he reached inside his pocket. The clicks of readying rifles echoed around him. Gently, he withdrew his electronic notepad, and gingerly opened it.

"Get moving, McGovern!" a voice shouted from the cold.

Trent whispered into the notepad, "Protocol Zero. Enable."

The tiny screen flashed:

Voice Command for Protocol Zero Acknowledged
State Time Delay

"Zero seconds," he answered.

Voice Command for Time Delay Accepted
Zero Second Delay
Awaiting Final Command

"It'll work. If it doesn't kill us first!" he mumbled.

Peptide Laboratory, Level Two

"C'mon! Move it! Move it!" Spann yelled to his men, placing plastique on the wall. They were taking too goddamn long.

One man said, "The elevator to Level Five runs right along this wall—and we won't do nobody any good charging blind into an empty elevator shaft."

A voice crackled over Spann's headset. "Refueling team. The escapees are on the surface. Repeat, on the surface. Disengage."

Spann countered, "We need two minutes."

"They're almost at the helicopter."

"Copy," he answered. To his men, "We've lost our safety margin! Go!"

Auxiliary Control, Level Two

Stevenson watched the three monitors over the auxiliary control panel. One showed Marguerite, Meredith, and company hurrying through the snowy field to the helicopter. The second showed the deserted corridor outside Central Security. The third randomly switched around the complex. All was quiet—too quiet. "Loring, what are you up to?" He switched the third monitor to an overhead view of Level Five: Bertram was strutting like a general among black cylinder troops lined up for inspection. Bertram was the cause of all this. No matter what, he could not, would not be allowed to go unpunished. Stevenson configured his control panel to evacuate Level Five's air supply with a single touch.

On the first monitor, Marguerite, fighting the wind, was practically beneath the slowly spinning helicopter rotor.

Thunder!

The ground shook violently. Knocked Stevenson off balance. Smoke, debris filled the darkened main room. Chunks of glass wall separating auxiliary control from the main room exploded, hurling unbelievably fast toward him.

Bullets ripped into his body. Threw him against the control panel. His hand struck a flashing red light.

The Boardroom, Level One

Spann's voice broke over an open channel in the boardroom. "Sir, we've retaken auxiliary control."

"Excellent," Loring said. "Now release Chairman Bertram."

"When we, uh, we—before he died, Stevenson initiated the emergency procedure. The air on Level Five is being evacuated."

"Stop it!"

Spann hesitated, "We can't."

"Cut the power!"

"The backups will automatically kick in. I'm sorry, sir. It's irreversible."

Loring kicked a chair beside him into the wall, then switched on the monitor. Bertram staggered between black cylinders, his hands clamped over his ears as if trying to keep them from exploding. The veins on his neck engorged. His hands suddenly clutched his chest. Feverishly, he gasped for more and more rarified air. He slumped to the floor, his back propped against a SUE's metal leg. His mouth O-shaped, his body, a fish dying on the deck of a boat.

Loring repeatedly slammed his fist on the table. "Merlin, it's me."

The Chairman looked up, eyes glazed. "Oh! It's *You!* So many names! What shall I call You?"

"It's me, Dixon."

"Dixon? Shall I not call you Host of Hosts? Brahma? Allah? Jehovah? *Adonai?*"

Hypoxia, oxygen deprivation, Loring thought. *His brain is starved for air. He's hallucinating.*

"Or shall I call You by Your true, forbidden name—Yahweh?"

"Merlin, we—we can't save you."

"You speak to me of being saved. Shall I not dwell with You in Your house—forever?" Bertram weakly waved his fingers at the black cylinders. "I have made Your—Qutub."

Loring watched him slip toward unconsciousness.

"To—walk on every level of—con-scious-ness. Walk with—You!"

"Merlin," the screen appearing watery, "don't die."

"To—touch—Your face." The Chairman slumped over. His body heaved, convulsed. Then settled.

Loring turned off the monitor. He took a series of long, passion-purging breaths, then reopened communications with his subordinate.

"Spann here, sir. I'm profoundly sor—"

"Spare Kincaid, if possible. Kill the rest."

The Grounds

The helicopter's rotor blades whizzed uncomfortably close to Kevin's head. He ducked as he pushed Meredith's gurney toward the chopper door. Trent, in the lead, had already boarded, with Helen close behind, brandishing her automatic. Marguerite stood beside the comatose child strapped to the gurney as they began loading her. Kevin kept his eyes forward, pretending not to see the many guns trained on them as he kept his mind tunneled forward, as well, trying to convince himself that Loring had lied, that the two embryos he'd abandoned were not Jessica and Kathy reborn.

Mini-geysers erupted in the snow around the group.

Screaming bangs from rooftops reached Kevin an instant later.

Four bullets ripped into Marguerite's chest. Blood spurted onto the child. A fifth struck her forehead. Marguerite's head jerked back. She collapsed in red-stained snow.

Using the side of the gurney as a shield, Trent tumbled into the snow, reached into Marguerite's pocket, grabbed the CD, and shoved Kevin forward. Three-quarters of the gurney slid into the chopper.

Kevin spotted a helmeted man, gun drawn, rushing from the cockpit. "McGovern!"

Trent whipped around. Shot twice.

The helmeted man slammed back against the cabin interior, his face awash in blood.

"Shit!" Trent cursed. "Now I've got to fly this thing myself!"

Sparks flew from bullets striking the hull. Trent shoved Kevin again, lurching him and Meredith into the chopper, then launched himself into a forward roll and bolted for the cockpit. Helen embraced Kevin as they dropped to the floor beside Meredith's gurney.

Trent reached the cockpit, slid the CD into his notepad and ordered it to begin uploading files. A deafening barrage of bullets sailed into the cabin. Two struck the gurney's legs. The engine whined. The cabin churned with vibrations from the rotor.

"We're taking off!" Helen exclaimed. Three more bullets struck the gurney's legs.

"They're zeroing in!" Kevin shouted. He glanced at the open cabin door. "I've got to shut that!" Six bullets struck around them.

"No! You'll be killed! I won't lose you again!"

The cabin floor moved. The snowy ground began falling away.

"I think we made it!" Kevin started to stand.

The cabin pitched forward as if a tentacle had reached up and latched on. The chopper climbed slowly, but it yawed twenty degrees toward the open cabin door. Treetops passed a few feet below them. The helicopter wasn't climbing.

"Something's clamped on!" Trent yelled from the cockpit.

Kevin moved cautiously to the open door, and looked down: a guard dangled below, one arm clamped over the port landing strut. The man swung his legs wildly back and forth in a scissors motion, trying to overcome the helicopter's motion and to pivot them up onto the strut.

"One of Loring's men," Kevin yelled. "Must've jumped on just before we took off. That's why they stopped shooting."

The guard's legs caught the strut. Locked on. The cabin jerked, tilted almost forty-five degrees toward the open door.

"Get him the fuck off now before he kills us all!" Trent screamed.

The guard reached up. One hand was nearly at the cabin floor.

"Helen! Your gun!"

She stepped forward and pointed her automatic. The guard reached back with his free hand, drew his weapon, and fired.

Helen's gun flew across the cabin. She recoiled, grasping her hand.

Kevin stepped back. Glanced at her.

"I'm fine!" she screamed, cradling her hand. "Get him! Get him!"

The guard's free hand grasped the cabin floor. Then came the gun hand. Kevin grabbed the gurney with Meredith and rammed it over the guard's gun hand. The man yelped. His weapon disappeared into the night. Kevin pulled the gurney back from the edge, but the man grabbed one of the wheels and starting hoisting himself into the cabin. Kevin felt the gurney yank. Instinctively, he grasped with both hands. The guard fell back.

The gurney, with the unconscious child strapped in, sailed out of the cabin.

Clinging ferociously, Kevin felt himself slide with it. His ankles slammed into, then latched on to a seat frame bolted into the floor.

With the guard clinging tenaciously to one of the wheels, the gurney with Meredith, buffeted by the copter's turbulence, swung wildly in the open air.

Rotor blades chopped overhead. Treetops, like a sea of pointed daggers, rushed below. Cold, driving air blasted Kevin's face. His arms, holding guard, gurney, and girl, strained. His ankles dug into the seat's metal support. The dangling guard swung back and forth, trying to latch on to the copter's landing strut. Hanging on to them all, Kevin felt his arms being ripped from their sockets.

The helicopter pitched. Helen reached down, wrapped her arms around Kevin's legs, locked her fingers, and pulled, trying to help reel in him and the gurney.

"I'm losing control!" Trent shouted from the cockpit.

Helen's fingers slipped. The helicopter jerked. She went crashing against the far cabin wall.

The guard began climbing up the straps holding Meredith to the dangling gurney.

Kevin's shoulders burned white hot. His locked fingers, icy numb.

"Make him let go or we'll all die!" Trent yelled.

"Let go, Kevin!" Helen echoed.

"Not—thissss—tiiiimmme!"

The guard was halfway up the gurney. Still climbing.

"Kevin, for God's sake, let go!"

"Nnnnnnnooo!"

The guard was within striking range. Kevin screamed in agony.

Meredith awoke. Turning back and up at Kevin, she gazed at him with wide, bright eyes. Her lips did not move, but he thought he heard a tiny voice in his head: *It's all right. It's all right.*

For an instant, the pain vanished.

The helicopter dropped.

A treetop struck the gurney. Swatted away Meredith, gurney, and guard into the dark forest below.

The helicopter immediately regained altitude.

Helen pulled Kevin back from the edge, the image of Meredith's face still burning in his eyes. "McGovern! You did that deliberately! You killed her!"

The Boardroom, Level One

What had Merlin meant by 'Qutub'? Loring wondered. Some sort of spiritual embodiment of the primitive notion of God? Ravings from his hypoxic delirium? Or something deeper, buried in the Plan? He'd spent a considerable time alone with Kincaid. What had they discussed?

"Sir, they're getting away!" Spann's voice shouted from the console.

Loring rolled his eyes. "Shoot them down, idiot!"

"But Kincaid's aboard!"

"Shoot 'em down, anyway," he said. Then added quietly, "Guess now I'll never know what Merlin meant."

Bertram's Helicopter

Trent saw a flash from Delphi's receding grounds. In the back of his neck, he felt the missile screaming toward him like an executioner's ax the instant before decapitation.

A small clearing appeared in the forest below. Probably too small. It would have to do.

He activated his palm. "Protocol Zero. Initiate!"

The tiny screen flashed: Acknowledged. Initiating Detonation.

Trent envisioned the EMP exploding in the tree miles away, followed by an intensely powerful blue electromagnetic pulse sweeping across the forest at light speed.

The chopper bucked wildly. Sparks erupted from circuitry on the panel, and overhead.

Something whizzed by the cockpit. Gyrated madly into the dark forest.

It missed!

Angry buzzing blue arcs burst from the cockpit circuitry. One arc struck his shoulder, burning it. He fought the stick, trying to set the copter down for a soft landing.

Eighty feet. Seventy feet. Below tree level. The chopper spun.

He heard Helen screaming in the cabin behind him.

The controls died.

The Boardroom, Delphi

From the day Delphi had gone online, all the designers and engineers had assured Loring that this was impossible. Yet here he sat, in the dark—his entire complex immobilized. Outside his sealed door he could hear shouts, scrambling feet, grunts. The red emergency lights kicked in. Slowly the boardroom door rolled back. Spann and the three guards who forced open the door entered.

"Sir, power is out throughout the complex. Emergency systems have been restored in Levels One and Two," Spann said. "We're hoping to restore the lower levels in an hour."

Those levels depend entirely on recirculated air. Without power, there will be casualties, he thought.

He looked at his stopped watch. "An EMP, wasn't it?"

"That would account for the widespread power and hardware failures."

McGovern, it had to be! How'd he get it? On his own? Or—

"We saw the Chairman's helicopter go down, sir. The crash was unsurvivable."

"I want that confirmed."

"The pulse knocked out key components of our ground and air transport. It'll be hours before we can get anything rolling. And the crash site is too far to send men out on foot in the dark. We'll get people there by morning."

"Communications?"

"We'll have something jury-rigged in two hours."

"And the mainframe?"

He swallowed awkwardly and shook his head.

"Fortunate that I had the good sense to download V_7 off-site."

"Sir, I, uh, I apologize for—"

"Shut up!" Loring jumped out of his chair and shoved Spann. "I don't want to hear you. I don't want to see you. I don't want you breathing the same air as me. In fact," his eyes widening, "I don't want you breathing air at all." He signaled the guards. Two seized Spann, kicked out his legs, and forced his head down. "See that he suffers the Chairman's fate."

The guards dragged Spann, screaming, toward the door.

"Oh, and gentlemen, be sure to let your supervisors know that I have a public function in New York tomorrow night," he whispered to the guards. "If I'm late, Mr. Spann is going to have a lot of company."

Potter County, Pennsylvania

Trent glanced first at the chopper's wreckage, its main rotor still lazily spinning from angular momentum, then at Kincaid, somber, shivering in the snow, with Helen hunched beside him. Neither was injured. He took out the EMP-resistant communicator.

"Mission status?" a male voice from the communicator asked.

Trent hesitated. He had Kincaid. He had the V_7 formulation. Almost certainly the EMP had wiped V_7's formula from Delphi's computer core, and there was no evidence that it had been downloaded off-site. Through Kincaid he'd learned of the contents of Level Five, plus Bertram's identity. "Success."

"Acknowledged." A pause. "ETA seven minutes."

He estimated that they'd crashed three-plus miles from Delphi. The complex's ground and air transport were likely knocked out. It would be hours before the Collaborate could launch an effective search party—still longer to locate the crash site in the dark. "We need a cleanup unit for crash site and three bodies."

The cleanup unit would sanitize the crash site and provide three bodies burned beyond identification. The Collaborate would never know that they had survived.

"And an urgent message for the Director," Trent added. "Tell her the data were burned. Strongly suggest canceling Operation WorldSweep. Repeat, cancel." He glanced back in the direction of Delphi. *We've beaten the Collaborate. For now.*

Private Quarters, Site 341   *11:45 P.M.*

Helen sat quietly on the futon while Kevin paced the spartan quarters Brocks had provided. Tomorrow would bring more long debriefings. He returned his gaze to the TV: a bus deposited Cary Grant along a long, open road in *North by Northwest.*

"You've been so distant since we escaped," Helen said.

"I've had to make choices no one ever should. I let my children die. Again."

"You weren't at fault ten years or ten hours ago. Loring wasn't going to resurrect them."

"I couldn't save even one little girl. I should've held on, no matter what."

"We'd've all died."

"McGovern deliberately knocked her loose."

"What matters, Kevin, is that we're alive."

"And together," he added without hesitation. *Is that what I really think? Really want?*

On TV, Cary Grant stood alone by the side of a dusty road stretching to the horizon. A car whizzed by, kicking dirt into his face, onto his worn suit. The man had nowhere to go, no way to get there, and no one with whom to go.

"What do you want to do now?" Helen asked.

"I don't know what we can do." He stopped pacing, sat beside her, touched her cheek, and gently lifted her chin. "But I know what I want."

She gazed into his eyes. "And what's that?"

Bringing her face close to his, "For us to be together."

She brushed his hand from her chin. "There's no room for three."

"Three?"

"You, me—and Helen Kincaid."

"My wife is gone. I just needed to know that she really was." He gently held her face in his hands. "All I can do is look to the future—and hope that you, Tracy, are in it."

"How can I ever be sure?"

He gathered her in his arms. Their lips ignited.

After a long, lingering kiss, she gently pushed him away. "But for how long?"

"You've studied me." Half smiling, "You know how seriously I take commitments."

"Is that what this is—a commitment?"

"I love you."

"I love you, too," she rasped. "In Georgetown, when I'd heard that you'd been killed, I almost passed out. At that moment, I was semiconscious on an island, somewhere, with a blue-green ocean lapping against pure white sands. In the distance, a warm, red sun was sinking below the horizon. And there was a boy, a beautiful little boy, in navy blue cutoffs, laughing, running, turning cartwheels across the sand. Our son, Kevin."

"And where were you and I?"

"I was sitting in a long, lazy, lounge chair, with my belly swollen with our next child. And you were there, beside me, holding my hand. Let's you and I make it happen."

Machine-gun fire from the TV caught Kevin's attention. He watched a biplane chase Cary Grant down the road and drive him into the dirt in a volley of bullets. "As things stand now, it never will."

She gently turned his head back toward her.

She buried her head in his chest. "I want to have a life with you."

"So do I. But the Collaborate is still out there."

"Let someone else take up the fight," she whispered. "It's our time, Kevin."

"We haven't stopped the Collaborate. Unless we do, our life together will be a string of rooms, like this." He leaned down to her. "I'm certain our hosts are listening. Cuddle close, and whisper so they can't hear."

"But we'll still be together."

"Until DARPA and the rest of the government decides that we're more trouble than we're worth and we wind up like that little girl. No, Tracy, if *we* are going to have a future, *you and I* must stop the Collaborate."

"How?"

"I don't know. We'll need something with shock value, like—like what they did to those kids in Tiburon. You don't still have a copy of that video, by some chance?"

Tracy smiled, remembering that she'd given it to Anna for safe-keeping before they went to Georgetown. Anna had never been a prime target of the Collaborate. With AntiGen implicated in the Bethesda bombing, and the FBI closing in, the Collaborate probably didn't have the time to search her apartment. And the feds. They probably hadn't yet screened every one of Anna's videos, particularly an innocuous one labeled "Family Picnic" in German? "No, but I know who might," she whispered. Then told him.

Kevin shrugged. "Even so, what would we do with it? Give it to the networks? Think they'd show it? The Collaborate's influence reaches everywhere. The minute we try to peddle it—" He mock-slit his throat.

"We could put it on the Net."

He shook his head. "No credibility."

"So where does that leave us?"

Kevin glanced at the TV. On-screen:

Dr. Kevin Kincaid was standing beside a woman in a wheelchair with a young girl sitting in front. His hand on the woman's shoulder, Dr. Kincaid said, "This is Anne Butler and her daughter, Claire. Anne suffers from Huntington's disease, a debilitating disorder that strikes people in the prime of life. Thirty years from now, Claire will be sitting in a wheelchair, too. It might have been prevented if she'd been able to undergo germline gene therapy before . . ."

Kevin turned away from the TV. Tracy gaped at it.

He said, "With all that's happened, how can you possibly look at—"

"Kevin, that's the next-to-last commercial. How many times will they run it?"

"I thought you knew everything about them."

"Just their contents, not their broadcast schedule. Answer my question."

"Counting prime time on all the networks, cable, and late-night, too," he shrugged, "who knows?"

"Tomorrow's the last commercial, right? How many times will they run that?"

"Just once, a two-minute spot during the Super Bowl. You couldn't ask for a bigger audience."

She stared at the TV a full minute. "That's the answer."

Meeting Room, Site 341

Kevin, with Tracy, smiled slyly at one end of the conference table.

"It's late. Or early, depending on your perspective," Brocks said, with Trent eyeing them from the other end. "What are you two up to?"

"Bugs in our room not working?" Tracy asked.

Brocks faintly smiled and placed her hands, palms down, on the table beside Trent's.

Kevin nodded. Tracy said, "We know how to stop the Collaborate."

Brocks half frowned. "It's too late. They downloaded V$_7$ *before* we knocked out Delphi."

"So what are you going to do?"

"That, Ms. Bergmann, no longer concerns you," Brocks said.

"They're going to bloody war," Kevin said.

"An interesting slant, Doctor. Care to elaborate?"

"I've spent time with the Collaborate. They're ready for you. You won't beat them."

"And the two of you can?"

Kevin deferred to Tracy. "Anna Steitz's possessions. Where are they?"

"Impounded by the FBI."

"Do you have access to them?"

Brocks leaned forward. "Possibly. Why?"

Kevin glanced at Tracy. "Your idea. Floor's yours."

Brocks listened attentively as Tracy explained. "Problem is, we only have eighteen hours," Tracy said when she finished. "Can you produce the spot in time?"

"Yes, but there are ramifications. First you, Dr. Kincaid. Although technically we could 'resurrect' you, you'll have to remain 'dead.' You cannot return to the life you once led—ever. Do you fully understand?"

"Yes."

"And you, Ms. Bergmann, we'll have to create another new identity for you, too."

Tracy reached out and took Kevin's hand. Their fingers intertwined. "As long as we're together." Kevin laid his other hand on top of hers.

"I'm so happy for you two," Brocks monotoned.

"Two conditions," Kevin declared. "First, Tracy and I stay together. Someplace private, comfortable, worry-free." Looking at Tracy, "A place where we can live our lives full measure. Raise a family. Run free with our kids on some secluded beach."

"Sounds delightful. And the other?"

"Release V_7—publicly. I don't want my work kept as a military secret."

"No problem," Brocks shot back.

Kevin leaned forward and planted his fists on the table. "Don't patronize me! I'm deadly serious. You *will not* take my discovery and turn it into a weapon. The Collaborate subverted my work once— hell if I'm going to let the government do it, too!"

"Doctor, we have no intention—"

"Loring told me about your own city-sized Level Five."

"And after all his other lies, this one you choose to believe?"

"Remember K_4? I won't permit a repeat performance. Not by the Collaborate. Not by you. Those are my terms."

Brocks grinned. "I don't need you. I could digitally synthesize you both."

"The media will analyze the tape after it's played. If it's a fake, you can kiss your life and your agency good-bye."

"Once I have you on tape, what's to stop me from making your deaths more *permanent?*"

"And throw away such a valuable resource? Even now the Collaborate would take me alive if they could." He pushed back from the table and appraised Brocks as she considered the offer. Her cold eyes brimmed with distrust. Was that coming from her or reflecting his own? "Your window of opportunity is closing."

She stared at Kevin, then at Tracy. Finally, she said, "Very well. But you two will have to do it yourselves."

"That was never part of the plan."

"It's the only way this Agency can maintain plausible deniability. And it's a deal-breaker."

9

SUPER BOWL SUNDAY, JANUARY 26
Network Headquarters
West Sixty-sixth Street and Central Park West
New York City   *6:35 P.M.*

Tracy gazed longingly out the taxi's window. To her left was the festively decorated Tavern on the Green and the darkened beauty of Central Park; to her right, the towering sandstone and marble-faced Network Headquarters. The cab whipped around the corner of Central Park West, weaving through double-parked trucks blocking narrow West Sixty-sixth Street. She felt Kevin's hand caress hers. She gazed at him. The face that smiled at her had been altered: eyes browned, hair darkened, jaw bearded—disguised, as was hers. She said, "If my life had turned out right, I might have been working in this building today, instead of—"

"We're here," the cabbie said, stopping in front of a set of wide glass doors set in rose-colored marble. "Make sure you have your IDs. And you, Bergmann, the tape. I'll pick you up here when you're done. But while you're in the building, you're on your own. So, get in, get it done, and get out."

Tracy stepped out of the cab first. A cold gust whipped against her, carrying with it the charged aroma of the place, of the life she'd always wanted. *This is as close as I'll ever come.*

Tavern on the Green, New York City

Proffering bits of conversation with endearing smiles to fellow guests, Loring worked the great mirror-and-glass room as if the party were his—but it was the Network that had procured Tavern on the Green that evening for its Super Bowl bash to thank sponsors unable to attend the game. Loring spent time building his personal network of contacts, appraising their strengths and weaknesses, and picking new, possibly useful strategies. After gracefully inveigling his way through a pair of surviving dot-com CEOs, he hit an unexpected pocket of empty floor space and used the moment to down the gin warming in his right hand. He glanced at the game on the huge plasma TV the Network had brought in to display the game. The first half nearly over, the Super Bowl had been a game of aerial attacks and resilient defenses. Like the Collaborate.

Trent and the others were dead, their bodies confirmed at the crash site. But Delphi had been damaged. Preliminary estimates: $200 to $250 million for hardware replacements; four months to bring it back online. But V_7 had been safely downloaded to Boise and San Francisco. The next Quorum Summit would be tumultuous; the organization had never before needed to choose a chairman. Possessing V_7 was powerful leverage, but some members would blame him for the damage. Blame had to be skillfully shifted.

". . . meaning to ask you, sir. How did you stop the SEC investigation?" Loring overheard a senior vice president from a utility software firm ask his CEO.

The CEO answered, ". . . Hired my own investigator to check on the SEC investigator's background. Got a few juicy details. Nothing solid, though."

"What did you do, sir?"

"I laid out the SEC investigator's skeletons in front of him," the CEO said.

"But if you didn't have anything solid—"

"Hopkins, just present the framework. Your adversary hastens his own downfall by filling in details. It works most of the time." The CEO laughed. "But don't try that on me."

Loring grinned. *Simple, yet effective.* He replayed last night again in his mind. *McGovern! Escaping FBI custody? Possessing an EMP? Knowing Delphi's location? Breaking through security lines?* He flashed to the image of Brocks, beside him, swinging on the chairlift. *Tomorrow, I'll have a little conversation with you, Director. Demand reparations. You'll hem and haw, but in the end, you'll agree. When the others see how I personally bent DARPA—oh yes!* He focused on the corner of the giant screen: 3:20 left in the first half.

He turned toward a glass wall in the back of the restaurant. Twinkling lights strewn across naked trees adorned the patio outside. Beyond was Central Park West with the dark expanse of the Sheep Meadow stretching off to the left. In front of the glass, tables sported imperial buffets: seafoods, lamb, breads, pastas, salads, desserts. And squeezing between guests, Blount picked delicacies from a table like a homeless man plucking scraps from a Dumpster. Loring strode up to him from behind. "What do you think you're doing?"

Blount swallowed a mouthful as he balanced plates piled with giant shrimp, crab claws, and rock lobster tails.

"You're supposed to guard my body, not fill yours! You're lucky I let you live after the way you handled Bergmann's daughter."

"But Mr. Loring, you told me to back off. Give you breathing room to work the par—"

"You're hired help, not a guest. Go out and wait by the limousine!"

Blount turned on his heels and stormed out of the restaurant.

Merlin you were right. "Loyalty too long is dangerous."

"Mr. Loring?" a strong voice boomed behind him.

Loring turned to a strapping man with a stout jaw, a thick shock of graying hair, and a disarming and deadly-if-crossed smile.

"Jack Derrick, Network president. Pleasure meeting you."

"Nice party, Derrick. You've done quite a job over the last eighteen months. Ratings in the eighteen to thirty-nine age groups are up twenty-three percent, I believe."

"Thank you, sir. Your spot will be coming on during the first half-time break. I—" Derrick's cell phone beeped. "Please excuse me a moment while I take this."

He nodded and started away.

"Who is this?" Loring heard Derrick scream into his wireless. "Who is this?" Loring whirled around and saw Derrick, ashen, cover his phone's mouthpiece and rush behind a divider in the corner of the room.

Network Headquarters

Tracy and Kevin stopped outside a door marked "Robovideo Operations." Tracy checked the hallway twice. They were alone. "Brocks's IDs have gotten us this far," she whispered.

Kevin stole a quick kiss. "I'll be out here if you need me."

She swiped her card through the slot. The door clicked open.

The room was narrow and lined by shelves filled with thousands of tapes, horizontally stacked, each labeled with a ten-digit bar code. Ingrained along the center of the long axis in the floor were yellow tracks on which awkward-looking robotic devices chugged: each periodically stopping, scanning tape bar codes, removing tapes with an extended mechanical arm, and shoving them into tape-player slots according to a preprogrammed selection. She skirted around the lumbering automatons and checked the stacks. Three shelving units down, she located tape number 1113207031, pulled it from the stack, and checked the label:

Client:	Association to Cure Genetic Disabilities
Agency:	Hedges, Coates, and Jones
Title:	Germline Gene Therapy: For the Sake of Our Children
Length:	2 minutes (120 seconds)
Production:	Ellison Michaels Productions, Inc.
Date:	December 2

Helen snapped the tape guard with her thumb, scrunched the tape itself with her fingers, and stuck it in her coat pocket. Then she placed an identically marked tape in the empty slot.

Tavern on the Green

". . . do you understand?" the voice from Jack Derrick's wireless phone dictated.

The Network president took a deep breath. "How do I—"

"Right now, you're standing behind a divider in the southwest corner of the restaurant with the phone in your left hand and a half-finished Gibson in your right."

He looked around. "I need some assurance that you won't—"

"No assurances, Derrick. You simply have no choice!" The caller hung up.

"If it's a hoax, we'll be a laughingstock," Derrick mumbled. He stared helplessly at the giant screen: it was already halftime. "Christ, I can't take that chance!" He punched in a preset number on his phone. "Derrick here. Who's producing in Miami?" He listened. "Patch me through to his mobile unit. Now!"

Network Headquarters

His arm draped around Tracy's waist, Kevin led her out the main entrance. A taxi pulled up. The driver rolled down the passenger window. "Done?"

They presented a thumbs up.

"Get in. Have you at the helipad in five."

Kevin opened the rear door for Tracy. As she climbed in he glanced down the street. He froze. The universe condensed to a black tunnel—a tunnel that led to a balding man with an L-shaped scar. Kevin's blood superheated. "It's *him*."

Tracy peered through the cab's rear window. "Who?"

"Don't you see him? Across the street?"

"Who?"

"That's right. You never met him. It's Blount!"

Tracy reached out and seized his hand. "Kevin, no."

"He killed everyone I ever loved!"

"Except me, Kevin! You still have me!"

"Get in, Kincaid," the driver ordered.

"Shut up!" Tracy snapped. To Kevin, "Walk away, my love! He's as good as dead."

"But he's not! And I—I can't face myself until he is."

"Think of the life we'll have together!"

"I am." Tearing, "If I let him go, it'll haunt me—haunt us the rest of our lives."

"Kevin, do as your heart tells you, and you risk destroying us *and humanity!*"

"I love you." He cradled her hand. "Have faith in me." He closed the door.

She stared at him, her lower lip quivering. "Driver, go."

"I can't leave without Kincaid!" the cabbie responded.

Tracy reached into her purse, withdrew an uncapped pen, and put the point to the base of the driver's neck. "Drive!"

Tavern on the Green Valet Lot

Blount took a last drag on his cigarette to ward off the cold then flicked the lit butt into the hedge. He hoped the goddamn place burned down. *Fifteen years of loyal service and he's got me fuckin' standing in the valet lot like some fuckin' kid!* He lit another smoke. *So Kincaid got away the first time. Big fucking deal! I got him back, didn't I? Loring, you fucked up.* "So don't blame me!" he blurted.

"You talkin' to me?" asked a car jockey standing by a Lincoln.

Blount released a wisp of smoke that the wind gnarled and whisked away. He ambled to the rear of the restaurant by the Dumpsters and high hedges. *Floyd Elliston made overtures last year. Bet I could work for him!* An icy gust chilled him. *But if Loring becomes Chairman, I'm screwed! Unless I—*

Something crashed against his back. Slammed him into the Dumpster.

He reached for his gun.

Another blow struck his back. The gun flew out of his hands and skittered across the asphalt. A fist struck his right shoulder. He crouched into a ball and blindly shot his left leg back. It struck soft flesh. He reeled and threw a side kick into his assailant's ribs. Panting, he turned. Sprawled on the asphalt, beside the high hedge, was Kevin, sporting a false beard and loosened moustache. "Thought you were dead!"

"I'm gonna kill you with my bare hands!" Kevin quickly righted himself. Searing pain shot across his back.

Blount laughed at the man, six inches taller than himself. "Don't think so, amateur! I felt a couple of your ribs snap."

Kevin winced. The pain spread across his rib cage, heightening with each breath.

Blount reached into his empty holster.

"Not such a big man without a gun, are you, Blount? I'm not a frail woman. Or a defenseless child. Or mentally impaired."

Blount spotted his gun six feet to his right. Kevin, twenty feet away, spotted it, too, and started toward it. Blount swooped down. Grabbed it. Pointed it at Kevin. "Don't worry. I want you alive. You're my ticket to greener pastures."

Kevin started toward him but stopped as Blount's hand stiffened.

"That doesn't mean I have to turn you in *whole*," Blount added.

Kevin smirked, ignoring the fiery pain radiating across his ribs. "It might be cold, but still, a nice night. Clean, crisp, and there's good paths."

"What're you jabbering a—"

"Perfect for running," he said. And lunged through the hedge.

Blount fired twice. But Kevin had already disappeared into the brush.

Tavern On The Green

Loring reached for a glass of Dom Perignon and caught the final few seconds of the software giant's commercial on-screen: a young girl and boy, hand in hand, running through a wheat field that transformed into towering spires beneath a green dome surrounded by a cratered landscape of jagged peaks. A blue-and-swirling-white Earth rose over the horizon. What do you want to create today? appeared in futuristic font across the bottom.

Think you create the future, do you? Loring thought. *Man has a spark of nobility that will always set him above machines. We will see that it is forever true! Watch!*

Across the screen, the somber image of Dr. Kevin Kincaid, hands clasped, appeared before a background of dreamy, rushing blue clouds.

Loring scrunched his eyebrows. *I don't remember the commercial starting that way.*

"If you are watching this," the Kincaid image on-screen said, "then I must be dead."

"What!" Loring exclaimed.

The Kincaid image said, "During the past week, I've come into your homes and asked you to call your local senator and express your support for House Bill 601, to lift the ban on germline gene therapy. *I was wrong!*" Kincaid's image faded, replaced by a high, barbed-wire fence surrounding a granite block building in marshland. Then, close-ups of children with misshapen limbs, some limping, some dragging themselves across the enclosed yard, some tumbling like unbalanced tops. The muscles in their necks, or upper arms, or thighs, grossly bloated. "This was an experimental facility on Isla de Tiburon, a secluded Mexican island," said Kincaid's voiceover. The images continued. "Every child you are seeing is dead."

Loring's glass slipped through his hand. Shattered the silence.

"Tiburon was destroyed days ago to keep this secret," Kincaid's voice continued. "These children, still in their mothers' wombs, were victims of germline gene therapy experiments. They were injected with genes designed to create stronger, more powerful muscles. See what happened instead?"

Gasps, like bubbling mud pots, erupted around the room.

"The evil that created this cloaks itself as a charity. It calls itself the Association to Cure Genetic Disabilities. In truth, it is an assembly of industrial and financial elitists who intend to dictate our future through genes *they* decree we will carry!" The Kincaid voice paused. "Look closer at their handiwork!" A toddler, shackled to a wall, filled the screen. One side of her face was bloated, with hideously distorted muscles. Ulcers oozed across her shoulders. Beside her, a man in a white coat with a scalpel—

In the dining room, a waiter dropped his tray. Two elderly women fainted.

On-screen the man with the scalpel ripped open the shackled girl's blouse. The left side of her body bulged with huge chest and abdominal muscles far thicker than a bodybuilder's; her right side was frail, withered, undeveloped.

"Genetic experimentation, manipulation, domination," came Kincaid's voiceover. "They call themselves the Collaborate. If . . ."

Central Park West

Weapon-ready, Blount poised beneath a lamppost on the paved path a hundred feet to Kevin's left. He turned slowly, scanning the park for his prey.

Kevin crouched silently in a patch of bushes. It wasn't supposed to be this way. Using surprise as an ally, he'd planned to hit Blount blind from behind with a flying side kick, disarm him, incapacitate him, and finish him with a choke hold. Instead, Kevin's rib cage felt as if it were being dissolved by acid. He tasted something warm, mildly bitter. *I'm bleeding internally.* Cut off from the nearest street traversing the green, Blount had forced him east, into the park, on foot. The gaily illuminated restaurant lay seventy-five yards to his left, past the waiting Blount. Behind him were a baseball diamond and stands; open field, well lit, a place Blount would easily cut him down. Ahead lay the dark expanse of Sheep Meadow. Cutting through that terrain would be risky. An asphalt path crossing in front of the bushes led deeper into the park, but lampposts illuminated it. He muffled a groan. Grabbed his side. And remembered his runs down West River Drive to deaden the pain, deaden himself.

"I should've finished the job in Frisco," Blount called out. "Killed you all then."

Kevin leaped out of the bushes and onto the runners' path. "Here's your chance, asshole!"

Startled, Blount fired.

Missed as Kevin burst down the path.

Tavern on the Green

On the giant screen, set against the frozen image of the agonized, screaming face of the little girl, appeared in block letters:

RESPONSIBLE MEMBERS OF THE COLLABORATE—

ERIC BERTRAM:	BERTRAM INDUSTRIES
EDWIN DIXON LORING:	BFHN SYSTEMS, REGENERIX, POLYPEPGEN
FLOYD ELLISTON:	LONE STAR EXPLORATION & ENTERPRISES
ANDREA BELLER:	SINO-AMERICAN UNION, INC
WOLFGANG VORPAHL:	BUNDEßTABEN FINANCIAL TRUST

The list continued as, in the background, Kevin's voiceover resumed: "The Collaborate, through its many companies, has patents on hundreds of proteins." The names slowly disappeared, replaced by a stream of U.S. patent numbers and titles.

Frenzied, Loring scanned the room. Didn't find him. He grabbed a stout tuxedoed man beside him. "Where's Derrick?"

The stunned guest gaped.

"The Network president! Where is he?"

". . . and with these patents, the Collaborate will synthesize genes to create proteins that supposedly will make us stronger and smarter," said Kevin's voiceover. "And through germline gene therapy, they'll create children to serve *their* dreams." The background turned black. The tormented girl's image faded. "If you are seeing this, it's too late for me. But it's probably not too late for humanity. *Stop* the Collaborate! Give our children a chance!"

Central Park West

A shadowy figure zipped across the path and headed into Sheep Meadow's dark expanse.

Blount emptied his automatic's entire clip at the shadow but it darted away. He dropped the useless clip, reached into his pocket for another, but found none.

Thirty yards away, in darkness, the figure stopped.

Blount fumbled through his coat, his pockets, desperately searching for another clip.

The figure seemed to grow taller, straighter. A strong voice cut through cold, dead air. "Face me, coward!"

Tavern on the Green, Men's Room

Loring swatted the Gibson from Jack Derrick's hand, smashed the man's wireless, grabbed him by the shoulders, and threw him down. The Network president crashed, face-first, against a urinal divider and tumbled onto the tiled floor.

"Why didn't you stop that propaganda?" Loring screamed. "You had plenty of time!"

"Couldn't!"

Stepping over the fallen divider, Loring put his foot directly on Derrick's throat. His Adam's apple crackled beneath Loring's shoe.

"Why?"

"Found—one—bomb. Maybe—others hidden. Threatened to blow up—Network."

Loring pressed in his heel, then released. "Who? Who threatened you?"

"Terrorists."

"Who?"

"Trent McGovern! AntiGen!"

Sheep Meadow

Hunched over, blood trickling from his mouth, Kevin protected his cracked ribs. "I only learned about you a couple days ago but I've thought a lifetime about what I'd do."

Blount grinned. Pulled out a six-inch serrated blade.

Kevin hesitated as his mind replayed parry-check-counter defenses against it.

"You look scared, Kincaid. Guess it runs in the family."

"What do you mean?"

Blount twirled his knife. "Before the fire, your wife got down on her hands and knees and begged me not to kill her precious kids. I mean, the old fart and his wife were already dead. I promised, if she agreed to do me." He winked, "Man, she was fucking good! No wonder you pined for her so long!"

Kevin shook, a waking volcano.

"After I was finished—I had to break my promise. She was a fucking mess. Which is why I couldn't let them find her body with the others."

Kevin's eyes were awash in heat.

"And your brother! Putting that simple puppy out of his misery was an act of charity."

"I'll kill you!"

"I won't kill you. Oh, I'll mess you up some. The girls will never flock to you. But," shrugging, "my new employers won't care."

"Don't count on it. The Collaborate's going to be downsizing." Kevin grinned as he told Blount about the commercial switch.

Blount cocked his head. He stared strangely. "You're a dead man!"

"Go ahead. Oh, I forgot. You can't. I'm not a defenseless child."

Knife in right hand, Blount lunged.

Kevin instantly pivoted left. The blade bypassed him. His right hand hooked around Blount's wrist and twisted it away as his left forearm smashed into Blount's upper arm. The elbow snapped. The blade dropped to the grass. Kevin's left arm continued forward, his palm bashing Blount's ear. The man staggered. Kevin's right arm swung around the back of Blount's neck, and under the throat. Locking his left hand onto his right wrist, he lifted the headlocked Blount up by the neck.

Cartilage crackled. Blount flailed wildly.

Arms still locked around Blount's throat, Kevin jumped up, then deliberately fell backward. Blount's head struck the frozen ground first, full force. Momentum rolled him onto his stomach. He lay still.

Kevin stared at the body lying beside him. Lower lip quivering, eyes burning, he shook with great sobs.

A strong gust came from nowhere. Kevin felt something move in the stunted grass swaying a few yards away. He looked out, half hoping to see a specter of Helen standing in the distance, baby Kathy in her arms, toddler Jessica at her side. Knowing that now they could finally, finally rest.

A whipping *thwump-thwump* sound approached from overhead.

He looked up. A searchlight shined in his face.

Tavern on the Green

Loring gazed through the glass wall in the back of the restaurant, beyond the twinkling lights strung across the patio, into the darkness of Sheep Meadow. Behind him the bar was busier than ever. He took a swig of bitter champagne, his mind desperately calculating a way to resurrect his world, now in shambles.

First, of course, the Network would issue public statements that it had been coerced by terrorists, that the commercial was a fake. It would give extensive coverage to its retraction: commercials, news stories, special segments on national news and cable for starters. That was easy. Answering unanswerable questions—that would take work. Why had the terrorists chosen those particular business leaders? Just what did happen on Isla de Tiburon? Where does the suddenly resurrected McGovern fit it? And what about those patents? The U.S. Patent Office would be forced to reexamine patents issued to Collaborate companies. *The members will be running around like chickens without heads. I'll call for a full assembly tonight. But I'll need a viable strategy.*

In the distance, a bright light hovered over Sheep Meadow, then descended: a helicopter.

A Collaborate member? Couldn't be. There's none within a thousand miles of New York.

Sheep Meadow, West Side, Central Park

Kevin shielded his eyes from whipping air and searchlight glare as the helicopter set down. He stood, fists clenched, prepared for whatever Loring might throw at him.

The helicopter door opened. Out stepped Tracy. She rushed into his arms, her lips uniting, igniting with his. A wave of purifying release swept through him, momentarily driving away the pain from his aching ribs.

"I hate to break up this tender moment, but we've got to go," Trent

McGovern called from behind them, his words distorted by spinning blades overhead. "You two are supposed to be dead, not making out in the middle of Central Park."

"The commercial?" Kevin asked.

"It played!" Helen squeezed him. "All of it!"

"How'd you find me?"

"Think we'd risk the whole operation without watching you two every second?" Trent said. "Besides, we expected something like this."

"Blount almost killed me."

Trent grinned. "But he didn't." He turned back to the helicopter.

"Are you free, my love?" Tracy asked.

He nodded. Smiled. Kissed her again.

Tracy caressed his cheek. "Let's begin our new life togeth—"

She screamed. Collapsed on the ground, clutching her leg.

Behind her Blount crawled on the ground. He lifted his blood-stained knife. Tracy's abdomen lay exposed.

Kevin snap kicked. His front leg struck Blount's arm. The knife flew into the lighted grass. He side kicked him in the ribs. The assassin curled up.

Blood dripped from a deep gash on the back of Tracy's leg. "I'm all right, Kev—"

Blount threw a backhand fist. Kevin stepped on it. Slammed his other foot against it. The wrist snapped. Blount cried out.

Kevin reached down, grabbed Blount's coat lapels, and lifted him up high over his head. He could taste the white-hot agony from his ribs. An instant longer and he'd buckle from the pain.

Blount glanced up at the helicopter rotor spinning dangerously close.

Kevin saw the fear in the assassin's eyes. Had Blount seen that same terror in Helen's eyes? In Jessica's eyes? In Kathy's? In Donny's? Dermot's? "No more! No more! No more! No more!" His arms cocked. His knees bent, coiled like a shot putter's. His pain would not stop him—could not stop him.

"No! Please!"

Kevin heaved Blount straight up.

The helicopter blade paused a barely perceptible instant.

Blood showered Kevin. Trails of it splattered over Tracy. The blades hurled Blount's partially decapitated body ten yards to their right. The top of the head rolled, like a quarter on its edge, beside the body.

Kevin quickly inspected Tracy's wound, then tore a piece of fabric from her dress and applied it to the gushing site. "Got to keep up—the pressure." He began to cry.

Tracy stroked his hair, covered in sticky blood, as he worked. She started crying, too.

Trent stood over them. He pointed at the helicopter, then at Blount's body. "Get rid of that!" he snapped to one of his men back in the copter. He gazed at the overhead rotor, partially stained, then back down at Kevin squatting beside Helen. "Amazing what rage can do." He knelt. " 'Something of vengeance I had tasted for the first time, as aromatic wine it seemed on swallowing, warm and racy; its after flavor, metallic and corroding, gave me a sensation as if I had been poisoned.' Charlotte Brontë." He helped Tracy to her feet, then turned to Kevin. "No matter how justified, you never forget the face of the first one you kill. Become inured to it—as I once told an old friend—and in the end, you become what you kill."

"Let's just get the hell out of here."

Trent silently led them to the helicopter and helped them board. His wireless rang. He answered it with a strong *yes,* then listened for thirty seconds. "Understood." He hung up. "Change of plan," he told the pair as they settled into their seats. "I'm not coming with you."

Tracy started, "But you agre—"

"This won't affect your end of the bargain." He headed out, alone, into the field.

The engine whined. With one hand clamped over Tracy's wound, another around her shoulder, Kevin peeked out the window as they lifted off. Trent strode to the edge of the helicopter's circle of light. And disappeared.

Tavern on the Green

As Loring watched the helicopter lift off and fade into the night, his solution was born—a solution that had the potential to turn this fiasco into a Collaborate victory and destroy DARPA's credibility. *You'd have approved, Merlin. I'll lay it before the entire membership.*

The phone in his breast pocket rang. Some members were probably panicking, but surely none would be so incredibly foolish as to try to contact him on an unsecured line. He turned away from the glass wall. "Loring here."

"Still partying?" the masculine voice asked. "Are you immune to humiliation? Or just too stupid to recognize it?"

Loring tried to match the voice to the membership list. "Who is this?" There was a very long pause. "Goddamn it. Who the hell is this?"

The voice whispered, "Look behind you."

Loring's limbs grew icy. Slowly he turned. On the patio, beyond the glass wall, stood a tall man, phone to his ear, face alit with a great smile: Trent McGovern.

Loring dashed across the room, knocking down a woman in a red-satin evening dress just before he blew by the maître d' and exited the restaurant.

"Blount! Blount!"

A cold gust slapped his face. No Blount, nor any sign of him.

He charged into the valet parking area, found his limousine, got in, and slammed the door behind him. "Get me to my jet! Hurry!"

The driver remained silent.

"Didn't you hear me, idiot? Get going! Now!"

"But we're still waiting for the last of our party," answered a feminine voice in the front seat.

Loring reached for the door. Someone punched his back. He froze as a gun barrel jabbed his neck. Another gun appeared in his face from an unfamiliar man in the driver's seat. He retreated into the leather upholstery. A woman's face emerged from the front-seat shadows.

"I knew you were behind this," Loring panted.

Brocks smiled. "You knew too late."

"Release me or we'll take DARPA down with us!"

"Your organization was just exposed in front of a billion people. I'd say that Collaborate members around the world are more concerned with their own survival than revenge. It will be over for them—soon. Besides, *you* are the only one who knows that *I* am responsible." She folded her hands. "Dixon, on the chairlift, do you remember saying that you'd like to meet my 'fool ex-husband who treated me so badly'?"

Loring nodded warily.

"Well, here he comes now."

The car door opposite Loring opened. A cold blast surged as a man plopped in, his right hand filled with party mints from the restaurant.

"McGovern? You're Brocks's ex?"

Trent grinned. "DARPA can still keep a secret or two."

Loring leaned back. "Well played." He crossed his arms and turned to Brocks. "Now, perhaps we can come to terms."

"What could you possibly offer that I cannot take by force?"

"The identity of and access to all Collaborate files incriminating DARPA."

Brocks put a finger over her lips and thoughtfully looked away. She nodded. "I can afford to be munificent."

"Great! Then we can—"

"But I choose not to." Her eyes met Loring's. "Before this is over you will tell me everything." She looked to Trent. *"Everything."*

Trent smiled at Brocks. "Thanks, Kristin." To Loring, "I have not forgotten Rockville. Be assured that from now on, neither will you."

Loring turned to Brocks. "You won't kill me. I have too many important friends—"

"Who are already distancing themselves from you," she finished. "Like many of your colleagues, you'll disappear. When you have wealth, they call it 'seclusion.' When you don't, they call it 'missing.'"

Eyes glazed, Loring shrank back into the cushions.

"But, Dixon, I am not uncivilized. Let me offer you the same kindness that you extended to me on the mountain." She handed a flask to Trent, who jammed it in Loring's chest.

"What's this?" he rasped.

"Darjeeling tea," she answered.

Loring unscrewed the lid. The contents generated no sweet aroma. The liquid itself was vapid. "It's cold."

"Yes." Brocks beamed. "The steam has gone out of it."

PART FOUR

IMPLEMENTATION—(7 MONTHS LATER)

10

AUGUST 31
Fort Powell, Central Nevada

Despite the cooling breeze from the speeding jeep, the hot August sun over Nevada's Great Basin still burned Brocks's pale skin. As her driver swerved around a dusty corner past a marine platoon drilling beneath the broiling sun, she cringed at the openness of distant craggy mountains set against the cloudless sky. Fort Powell itself was 140.7 square miles of bleached desert peppered with mock-up buildings for anti-terrorist maneuvers. Her driver swerved again and headed down a straight dirt trail that led to an adobelike structure.

"That's it ahead, ma'am," the corporal said. "Dead center of the base."

Brocks spent the rest of the ride spitting sand out of her mouth. The jeep left her in front of the small, windowless block building. The corporal jumped out and removed a key from a chain around his neck. "You have yours, ma'am?"

She again became aware of the chain with the piece of hot metal touching her chest. "Yes."

"Good, 'cause I'm not allowed inside. And it's a long walk back," the corporal warned as he inserted his key in the slot on the block wall. A thick metal door swung open.

Brocks stepped inside. The door slammed shut.

The room was empty, except for a plastic-sealed control panel and biometric devices on the wall beside three elevators, and so silent that she couldn't even hear the jeep outside rev up before shooting into the desert. She submitted to a standard palm print, voiceprint verification, and retinal scan, then inserted her key in a slot by the control panel and turned. The elevator door on the left swung open. A synthesized voice warned her that the elevator would descend at high velocity for two full minutes. The doors closed.

The bottom dropped beneath her feet. She clamped her hand over her pounding chest. "Someone'll have to send down my stomach," she muttered.

Her wireless rang. She answered, surprised that it could work so far underground.

"Finally, I reached you." Kevin's voice came through clearly. "You've supposedly been unavailable for months."

"How did you get through?"

"Never mind." He paused. "You know the question."

"The vector appears to be what you promised, but we still need more testing."

"How much more?"

"That's difficult to say."

"Brocks, you're stalling."

"We can't release V_7 to the public unless we prove it's safe. Perhaps you'd like it to go the conventional route—the seven to ten years for conducting preclinical and clinical studies, filling out the paperwork, and getting FDA approval." Before he could respond, "Be realistic, Doctor. You've seen the potential for catastrophic misuse. Are you personally willing to accept the consequences of releasing the genie from the bottle?"

"We had a deal!"

"But we didn't have a timetable."

"You're using V_7 now, aren't you?" he asked in a low voice. "Not testing—*using!*"

Silence.

"It's not ready. I won't stand for another concentration camp!"

Brocks wanted to hang up. There was no need to subject herself further to abuse, embarrassment, or worse—recrimination. Kincaid was powerless to stop what was occurring at the bottom of this elevator shaft. So was she. Idealism was infectious but it was also curable. "Doctor Kincaid, things are complicated. You're not seeing the big picture. And I will not compromise the safety of this nation on an agreement I made under duress."

"The Collaborate was working toward a totalitarian world." Kevin paused. "What kind of world are *you* working for?"

"After what terrorists did to us, you ask that? For the hostile forces that this nation still faces from without *and* within. For the mothers and fathers who don't want to have to worry that their children will be blown up in a building, bridge, or plane. Or gassed from a crop duster. Or poisoned from the water they drink. Or murdered by a disease resurrected from the Middle Ages. Or burned beyond recognition by a homemade nuclear bomb." She cleared her throat. "Don't you know by now? We're not just working for the betterment of Man. We're working for his survival." Brocks put away her phone. The elevator doors opened. An MP in a jeep met her, whisked her down a sterile white corridor, punched in a clearance code on the jeep's dashboard, and drove through a gaping entrance at the corridor's end.

The jeep burst into a spectacular grotto with a ceiling high enough to have its own weather. It dwarfed Delphi's Level Five. They sped by row after row after row of black cylinders. Dozens of technicians moved among the rows like bees pollinating a cornfield. The MP abruptly swerved the jeep to the right and slammed the brakes approximately sixty SUEs from the central corridor. Three men lifted their heads: Dr. Quentin Hicks, director of DARPA's Defense Sciences Office; a tall, robust man in uniform she assumed was the general; and a man she did not know with thick glasses and a white coat. She climbed out. The MP zipped away.

"Glad you could join us," Hicks said, a trace of sarcasm lacing his voice. To the military man, "General Warwick Gray, this is Kristin Brocks, the Security and Intelligence Director."

The man bedecked in metals and ribbons shook her hand.

"Dr. Ronald Moffat, Chief of Research and Development," followed the man in the white coat.

"Brocks, look around you," the general boomed as he gazed around. "Twenty years from now this will be ten full divisions of elite warriors. And that's just the beginning. One day we may never have to worry about the defense of this nation or its ideals."

"The General and Dr. Moffat were just remarking how much useful data they obtained from Delphi after we dismantled it," Hicks said.

"And we have you to thank for it," the general said to Brocks.

She nodded graciously. "But you didn't bring me 2,500 miles for the tour."

"Quite right. I wanted this kept confidential." The general cleared his throat. "We're facing losses."

Brocks glanced at their faces. "I'm afraid I don't understand."

The general deferred to Moffat. "Before we proceed with full-scale implementation, we're conducting a preliminary study on a thousand units. Most of the test fetuses we're running in these SUEs are in their sixth month of gestation. The current mortality rate is two percent, but it's increasing—exponentially. At current projections we're looking at a total loss of all the test fetuses before the end of the eighth month of gestation."

"Why not remove them from the units and put them in incubators like standard neonatal ICUs?" Brocks asked.

"Because in every case, the fetus's cells are lysing—literally bursting from within. It's as if their bodies were full of needles puncturing their cells. And it's nonviral." Moffat shook his head. "I've never seen anything like it."

Hammerhead Beach, United States Virgin Islands

Stretched out on his lounge chair, Kevin gazed at the red sun sinking into warm waters that lapped the unsullied beach. One hand crumpled a piece of paper; the other held a wireless to his ear.

"You can put down the phone, dear. You know she won't answer again." Tracy stretched out beside him, placed the financial page of *USA Today* in the sand, then shifted uncomfortably in her lounge chair, her hand cradling her beginning-to-show belly within her silver swimsuit. "What did she have to say?"

"Nothing unexpected."

She patted his hand. "Bill 601, as written, is dead, my love."

"But DeRay, that idiot bastard, wants to ban *all* gene therapy, including *somatic* which is perfectly acceptable and can't be subverted for eugenics. What a moron!"

"But if DeRay hadn't sponsored the ban on germline gene therapy in the first place, who knows how many more years the Collaborate could have continued before anyone realized what they were doing?"

"Doesn't matter anyway." He turned away. "I was so naive."

Tracy glanced at the headlines on the financial page in the sand. "Collaborate-controlled companies have taken a nosedive. We're in a bear market now."

"There will always be new companies and new investors to take their place." He clenched his teeth. "We have accomplished nothing."

"We've created a backlash against the misuse of germline gene therapy. More than sixty-five percent oppose—"

"That number's soft. The sixty-five percent is among *older* people who oppose *any* kind of gene therapy, including somatic." His mind replayed the encounter on Level Five, in perfect clarity, with Loring quoting Max Planck: "*Important scientific innovation rarely proceeds by converting opponents. Instead, in time, the opponents die out and the succeeding generation adopts the new ideas as an assumption.*"

Then he replayed his last conversation with DARPA's S&I Director.

Her hand reached out and gently touched his. "You knew Brocks was lying when we made the bargain, otherwise you'd have given her V_7's modification right then and there. And you and I wouldn't be the only ones in the world to know of its existence."

"I warned them not to use it."

"I am going to say this once. And you are going to repeat it after me and accept it. Ready?" She tightened her hand around his. "'I am not responsible.'"

He did, reluctantly.

"You, my brilliant husband, have important decisions to make."

Kevin uncrumpled the paper in his hand, gazed at the stereoscopic drawing of the harpoon-sequence modification that would make V_7 work. Would change humanity. "God, the more I think about it, the more I'm convinced that we're worse off than when we started. I can't sit by and let the military dictate humanity's future. Neither can I unleash V_7 on an unprepared world. The slope's too slippery. We're already tottering over the edge." He folded the paper into a glider and launched it at the horizon. The paper plane tipped up its underbelly as if saluting a fallen comrade then dove into the sea. A finger of water enveloped it, straightened its creases, and carried it away with the receding tide.

"Are you certain that was the right thing to do?" she asked.

"There's too great a potential for abuse."

"But you remember the formulation?"

He grimaced. "I remember everything."

"Then if you really believed that V_7 is too dangerous, that it must be destroyed at all cost, you still have one task to perform." Tracy turned to him. "Are you planning to kill yourself?"

He reached out and took her hand. "I'll never willingly leave you or the baby."

"In your heart, Kevin, you've always known what's right. It's how I knew I could trust you. It's why we beat the Collaborate."

He kissed her hand. "I love you."

She gazed at the sunset and released a long sigh. "Don't throw V_7 away."

"I don't understand you. After all we've been through, how can you say that?"

"When you carry a child, your perspective," she looked away, "changes."

He smiled at her.

"You think that's my hormones talking? Well, you're wrong." Gently holding his fingers, "Have you forgotten what you dedicated your life to?"

Donny—and curing genetic diseases, he thought. "That was before I understood the power in my hands. Power I never wanted, never asked for."

"Power belongs in the hands of those who don't want it," she said. "You've experienced the horror this technology can create. You've also envisioned its blessings. Who better than you to make the choice?"

"What about humanity's future?"

"What about *our* future, Kevin?" She placed his hand over her belly. "You're touching him now."

"You said 'him'!" He sat up.

"At the doctor's yesterday. It's confirmed." She smiled. "We're having a boy."

He tumbled out of his chair and hugged her.

"I'm so happy to have you as my husband." She started to cry. "And our child—he's the *luckiest* child in the world."

He knelt beside her, kissed her hand—and heard her words echo in his mind: *"Don't throw V_7 away."* Slowly, he brought his gaze up and into her eyes. "Why is our son so lucky?"

"Because you are his father." She whispered, "And because of what you can do for him."

He gazed at her belly. "What else did the doctor say?"

"Kevin, what would you do—if there was a problem with the baby?"

FOR MORE INFORMATION ON GENE THERAPY: WWW.GERMLINE.NET

If you are interested in learning more about gene therapy or issues surrounding germline (a.k.a. germ line and germ-line) gene therapy, I invite you to visit an independent web site that I created: www.germline.net.

Scheduled to launch in late December 2002, www.germline.net is an integrated gateway of web links to authoritative sites pertaining to gene therapy and genetics. Links will lead the visitor to web sites that provide free information on: gene therapy and genetics, key gene-therapy research centers, past and/or ongoing clinical trials, bioethics, professional (medical) journals, research societies, online libraries, disease support groups, key government resources, companies research-ing gene therapy products, developments in biotechnology, medical and genetic glossaries, and developments in gene therapy categorized by disease.

In addition, if you are interested in some of the scientific papers and documents that I used to construct *GermLine,* I invite you to visit the bibliography page and other interesting info at my (author's) web site, www.NelsonErlick.com.

—Nelson Erlick